DUE SOUTH

An Untidy Unraveling in the Carolina Lowcountry

B J Bartmann

PREFACE

Looking in from the outside naturally provides a perspective different than the view as a native Charlestonian, just as a gem may not seem as precious if one has always had it. I recognized the Lowcountry as hallowed ground when first I drove in with moonlight peeking through the sprawling branches of a liveoak canopy. I was spellbound.

Charleston is the backdrop for the story of every mother's epic relevance. The privilege of being a parent comes without a user guide. Nature chooses the genes, the cells, our innate tendences. From the first breath of air, nurture prevails. I hope that you will see some of yourself here, recognizing how every life choice ripples out in concentric circles, changing the flow altogether as circles meet and blend. No step is without consequences, whether by intention or by chance. This story follows a Washington lawyer who finds Charleston by intention, as I did, from the outside coming in, and about the possibilities waiting here for wanderers with an open heart.

Thanks to Riki, who first believed, to Peter who gave me the greatest gift, to Kim who has opened my mind, to Dee with whom I am safe, to Andra who hung on while we raised each other, and to you, the readers, who give me a chance.

betty.bartmann@gmail.com

For all who have experienced the inescapable

allure of the Lowcountry

And for Brandon, the light of my life

PROLOGUE

The window was open. A gauzy curtain billowed gently in the breeze as she pressed her back against one of the white pillars alongside the house, breathing suspended as she listened for sounds inside. She heard nothing but the rain, now merely a soft patter. Thunderstorms had cooled the night, and the South Carolina Lowcountry could enjoy a brief respite from summer's sultry heat.

Lights were out in the neighborhood. Here in old historic sections of town, inhabited mostly by the staid and steady upper class, bedtime came well before midnight. There was no one on the street, the only sound that of the receding rain, drops still falling at a gentle pace and streams rushing to the storm drain, providing welcome white sound, she thought, as a backdrop.

She removed her sandals soundlessly, striving to stir not even a grain of sand on the concrete, cool on the soles of her feet as she crept toward the open window. Her right shoulder steadied her against the gray stucco as she sorted the sounds, sifting out street static. A simple forward bend would allow her to look inside, inching from the right side of the window until she could see his bed. Her head moved cautiously toward the opening between the silky curtains.

He was on the bed. Resisting the urge to pull back quickly, she forced herself to remain still, allowing her eyes to focus on him in the dark. Lightning flashed dully as the storm moved offshore, and she could see in its pink glow that there was a striped sheet loosely draped over one leg and foot. He was lying on his back, his breathing regular and his eyes closed. One arm was thrown out with the hand hanging over the side of the bed, palm up, and the other was folded across his chest. He was wearing nothing at all, and his partial erection was apparent.

Moments passed while she stood stooped in position, observing silently. He snored intermittently, a gasping gobble of air, and the arm across his body twitched. Was he deeply asleep, she wondered, his senses saturated in alcohol? She straightened and rotated back to the left, pressing against the house. Five minutes passed. Nothing changed. She slowed her breath, willing regularity in its rhythm.

It was time. She noted the sandals, directly across the porch from the window. It would not do to forget them.

Knee deep in adrenalin, she stepped around once again to face the window, crouching to have another look. Yes, there he was, in the same position. Bending right, she placed both hands on the window ledge and gently lifted her left leg up and over the sill, feeling the bottom of the curtain brush her foot as it grazed the floor inside. There was carpet, plush and soft. Her foot was planted firmly now, and she had only to swing her head and body in a careful arc down and in.

Eyes trained on the bed, she lifted the trailing right leg, brought it across the sill and stood upright inside the window. The bed was across the room, and a piece or two of clothing lay crumpled at its foot. The ceiling fan hummed above him, and she recalled the wood grain blades trimmed in copper.

A dog barked somewhere outside, startling her. Still he slept. His chest rose and fell, and she could hear him breathing noisily through his mouth, his lips parted.

She was only eight feet from him, standing tense and rigid. Flexing her shoulders, she made a conscious effort to focus as she moved across the room, time suspended and intent congealed. Her bare feet made no sound as she crept to the side of the bed, glancing at the open window, orienting herself to flee.

She stood over him, drinking in the moment. The old straight razor came cleanly from her pocket, her fingers securely around the white pearl handle. Releasing the blade as she raised her right hand, she reached out with her left to form her fingers firmly around his erection, slicing cleanly until the blade made contact below her fingers.

It was done. Pulling back the blade and turning to the window were one motion. The background sound to her escape was a garbled shout, then a howl which expanded in her wake as she swung out the window and her feet hit the porch. Bending to grab the sandals with her left hand, she ran barefoot from the porch and onto the sidewalk. She left East Bay Street, turning the first corner, but the sound of his voice followed her onto Atlantic as she ran a block and turned again, up Church Street in the dark, now silent, toward Tradd Street.

SUNDAY

1

Charleston, South Carolina, is a world of its own, a separate culture shaped by a turbulent history and a stubborn refusal to let go a drop of its idiosyncratic essence. Julia had known since her first visit home with Celia from college that living was fuller here and breathing deeper and slower. There was no winter as she had known it up north, just a damp, drab couple of months when folks dug out their sweaters and raincoats and feigned a chill. Spring was coming. Renewal was always just around the corner. Both the natives and those blessed to adopt it as home knew the Lowcountry's appeal. This was the Promised Land, heaven as close as mortals can know it.

Green came early, new and tender shades of jade, lime and sage born of a deep decaying underbelly fed by the vibrant marsh, dotted with dogwood, redbud and azalea blossoms. The scent of spring could be better nowhere on earth, heavy with wisteria and honeysuckle. Above Sullivan's Island and the Isle of Palms, the moon rising over the Atlantic to grace them and the peninsula Charleston shone for them alone. The ocean breeze whispered lyrically, kissing the spire of Saint Michael's and dipping to drop a dew born in the sea upon the quaint, charming gardens beside graceful homes throughout the self-dubbed "Holy City".

The very ceiling changed as one approached Charleston. Southern sky was magnificent, its cloud formations towering and blossoming shades of white against a crystal blue. In the summer, it was always only a degree of humidity away from an afternoon or evening thunderstorm when the saturated atmosphere could hold no more.

It was just such an evening when lightning worked to discharge the heat of the day and thunder growled and rumbled around the city, hanging low over the harbor and the islands before finally giving way to heavy showers, rinsing further inland the saccharine sulfur scent of Westvaco's paper mill just across the river.

2

Julia flinched. The lightning was so intense against a black composite of sea and sky that each bolt startled her anew. Power had been out for half an hour as the storm neared the beach, making Julia feel one with the darkness, embracing its intensity, leaning into it with her mind. There was comfort here, as she knew there would be.

Mother Nature, she thought, the only reliable in life, the only constant. Nature could be trusted: its certain ebbs and flows, its unvarying volatility, its rainbows after rain. If only people were as worthy of trust, relationships as deserving of confidence.

Another thunderbolt followed a brilliant flash of lightning, arresting reverie. Julia raised the glass to her lips and rose from the rocking chair, stretching her hand out across the railing to see if rain was beginning. The first drops were always the best, coming from the light somewhere, cleansing, bringing purity.

"Julia?" came the familiar voice. "Jules, are you here?"

She had almost forgotten that she was waiting. "Out on the porch," Julia responded.

She turned. Finally, the comfort of a friend. Her tears were unexpected, and as the thunder rolled out to sea and the rain began in earnest, Julia thought that nothing could have felt as reassuring as the presence of the person longest in her life: Celia.

"I'll get the Kleenex," Celia grinned, kicking off her shoes and feeling her way toward the balcony. Julia giggled lamely through her tears, dropping back onto her seat like a rag doll. When Celia returned, carrying the box of tissues and a wine glass of her own, Julia mopped her face, streaking mascara, cleaning with tears, running her fingers back through her thick dark hair to get the damp tendrils off her face. Celia sat opposite, putting her feet on the ottoman with Julia's. They looked at each other and at the receding storm, sipping the wine, one friend waiting for the other to find words.

"Great storm, huh?" Julia finally managed.

"Yeah, just great. It's pitch black out there. Look how dark it is across the harbor with no electricity. It's eerie."

"Divorce," Julia said simply, more tears trying to build, "I really didn't expect to be impacted by this; it's just a piece of paper."

"So?"

"So it's like you predicted; it's hard. That Decree was sitting in my mailbox, I guess, since Friday. I hadn't checked since then."

"It's no more than a paper confirmation of something you already knew. It's black and white evidence that your new life has begun, Jules. Are you having regrets?"

"No regrets, exactly; it's just sad, disconnecting from a long part of my life. Jack's known me almost as long as you have, Cele. He knew me the way I was, a college kid, knew me then and now and in between, you know? I don't have that history with anyone else except you, so a big chunk is gone from my life. I don't want it back, but I don't want it lost either. I want the ache and the venom rinsed out of the memories so I can just keep the good parts. I thought I had dealt with all this last fall when I came here."

Julia sighed. "Maybe we could just drink about a dozen glasses of wine," she proposed, tipping her glass to her lips, "and wallow in our woes like in our college days."

Celia smiled, amused. "Can't. You're in front of Judge Engle first thing in the morning with that custody petition, and you'd never make it at our age with a hangover. We can't drink like that now. Too many calories and too much pain the morning after."

"Ah, yes, Judge Engle. At least I've prepared. Now that you mention it, I have a pleading on the computer waiting to be printed."

"Well, Julia, honey, you've got a reputation to build, and you know how hard we Charlestonians are on foreigners." Celie grinned.

"I'm not a foreigner."

"Were you born here?"

"No."

"Then there's work to do. I'll explain it again." Celia enjoyed this. "If your great-grandma wasn't born here, then you're just an interloper, a weed in a garden of roses. Every impression you make is important. Acceptance is not inevitable. Tomorrow is a new chance to display your brilliance and your southern charm. Just inch along waiting to be real."

"Like the Velveteen Rabbit?"

"Like the Lowcountry Velveteen Rabbit."

"Yes, so you've said." Julia sighed, almost smiling.

"Since Pete's in Savannah this week and the girls are at camp, how about if I just sleep here and make sure you have enough caffeine in the morning to keep making a name for your capable self down at the courthouse? I wasn't looking forward to driving back across the bridge in the dark anyway."

The tears almost came again, tears of gratitude for Celia's care, of sadness for the life she had ended, and of exhaustion just thinking of the new life she was starting: a new life in a new place just showing traces of feeling like home. A tiny office just off Broad Street with a shingle of her very own and a tinge of familiarity just beginning to grow as she made her way into town every morning and back across the

Cooper River every night to the house she had loved the moment she saw it. Home now. Here near the sea and Celia.

"I'll set up the pot for morning," Celia offered. "And I'll print out your file. If you want to talk some more, I'll be up. I'll probably wait for the power to come on so I can check Jimmy Kimmel."

"Thanks, Cele. I'll sleep better if you're down here. You're the rock, and everything else just keeps on flowing over me. What would I do without you?"

"What's flowing over you is the beginning of a wonderful life, so just resign yourself to it."

Julia almost smiled. "By the way, haven't we been hearing those sirens from town for quite a while now? There seem like so many, even for a stormy night with the power out and all."

"I'd have been here sooner, but the cops stopped me at the foot of the bridge coming over. They were stopping every car, just shining a flashlight in to look around and asking to see licenses. And even then, it seemed like there were sirens wailing everywhere down toward the Battery."

"I guess we'll have to hear about it in the morning on the news."

"Go on, Julia. Try to get some sleep. Don't forget I'm here."

"I won't forget. Not ever. Thanks, Cele."

3

Quinn Ravenel walked slowly up Tradd Street toward her very own newly found apartment, content to let the rain wash over her. As rivulets formed and ran off her face and clothes, she had the sense that maybe, finally, she was being rinsed clean, that the sole secret of her past was washing away right now, here on this sidewalk along Tradd Street and into the storm drain, leaving Quinn free. What a night it had been, its events both unexpected and long expected. She had taken her life back.

She smiled as her house came into view: the broad white-pillared entryway with steps leading to her tiny apartment on the upper level, its usually welcoming porch light now a casualty of the power outage. The wailing of sirens was just blocks away, but Quinn chose not to hear them. They had nothing to do with her.

Climbing the old wooden steps, Quinn slipped out of her sandals, now thoroughly soaked, and left them just outside her door. They were not special, she thought, and she might just throw them out. She could burn them and bask in the smoke. On second thought, further ceremony was not needed. It was over. She had done what she had to do. She had saved herself. It seemed both so real and surreal.

After climbing the creaky steps built by artisans long passed, Quinn padded to the kitchen, enjoying the squeak of damp bare feet on the knotty pine floor. She took a bottle of Evian from the refrigerator and drank it in one long series of swallows with her head tilted back and her hair and clothes forming puddles on the kitchen floor.

"I can sleep," Quinn smiled, shedding the wet clothes where she stood and using them to absorb the rain from her hair. Padding to the bedroom, she opened the window to allow the Lowcountry of Carolina inside, breathing deeply of its comfort. She walked with a sigh to her bed and dropped upon it, damp but warm, curling herself around the big, soft sea-colored throw Grandma Rose had knitted for her years ago. There would be time tomorrow or the next day to look for curtains. There would be time to build an appropriate wardrobe for her teaching job in the fall. There would be time to start lesson plans, spend time with Grandma Rose and make friends, a new time in Quinn's life. College finished, she was a kindergarten teacher, validated by her hiring at Charleston's best private school, a classroom of her own awaiting. The end of the storm rumbled away, the lightning tame now, flashing an occasional receding pink. Quinn sighed deeply, curled tight onto her side, facing the window, and slept.

4

The telephone ringing woke Sonny from a sound sleep and a dream he was enjoying. He rolled over, reluctantly reaching for the phone over the large lump that was his English sheepdog Tork. "My man, I'm sorry," came the voice when he mumbled 'hello'. "I think you should get over here."

"What is it?" Sonny queried sleepily, running his hand through his graying hair that needed a good cut. His left hand found the alarm clock and pulled it to him. One fifteen in the morning.

"Nasty knife assault. Gonna surprise even you. Colonel Howe's home on East Bay. An attack on his son. The ambulance is on its way to the hospital with the victim. Meet me at the Howes'. Fifteen minutes?"

"Yeah, okay, Chief. Make it ten." And Sonny hung up, swinging his feet onto the floor, grabbing boxers and a shirt from the drawers still open beside his bed. "Sorry, Tork, old boy. Now you can have both sides for a while." Seeming to understand perfectly, the big shaggy dog yawned, sighed and stretched his full length across the center of the bed. Sonny pulled on a clean pair of pants and a well-worn pair of sneakers with no socks, tying them with a swift flick of fingers. Grabbing his wallet, keys and police ID, he was out the door into the rain.

Sonny Legare had slept beside that pup since he found it wandering cold and hungry one night five years earlier near the yacht harbor over on the Ashley River. There were plenty of other dogs he could have picked up and taken in over his years of patrolling one beat or another with the Charleston P.D., but this one proved irresistible. He had obviously not been fed or cared for in a while, and he couldn't have been more than three or four months old, although even then he was a bulky, big-pawed animal.

When Sonny approached him, he was neither friendly nor afraid. He sat still while Sonny checked for a collar or tag. He didn't wag his tail or whine or even act particularly interested, like he'd already done this routine before and had low expectations he would benefit from it in any way. But those big brown eyes, still curious but guarded, were the ones Sonny had seen so often in boys on the streets who were headed in the wrong direction but still not hardened. One can rarely offer salvation, Sonny knew full well, but in this case, he was going to give it a shot.

After he coaxed the bedraggled pup into his car and took it home for a warm bath in his own tub and a good meal of real hamburger, with the bun, and half a can of peas on the side, they retired to bed where the sleeping arrangement began. Both snored. Neither minded. Sleeping to the soft roll of the boat Sonny called home suited the pup just fine.

Sonny had slept alone since his wife died in a car crash seven years earlier, struck by a drunk driver who ran a red light at seventy-four miles per hour on a sunny mid-afternoon just before Christmas. They had been married for four months. One of her gifts for him was on the seat beside her, wrapped at the department store. It was the only jewelry he wore: that gold watch on his wrist, and the wedding ring.

He was grief-stricken and lonely, clinging to his job as a lifeline for many months while returning to his old socially reclusive ways. Some of the guys started playing poker at his place every other Thursday night, and now and then a buddy or two from the department joined him to fish at either the Stono River or out on Sonny's boat. That was the current sum and total of Sonny's social life. A ruggedly attractive man by many accounts—fit, graying slightly—he had spent little time purposefully in the company of a woman in those last seven years. He and Tork jogged most mornings, and when he wasn't at his desk at the station, he and the dog could be found tinkering on the boat at the Ashley Marina.

Being awakened in the middle of the night twice a month was routine. He had the drill down pat: pull on the pants, shirt and shoes, grab the tie, carry breath mints in the cruiser, get coffee as soon as possible. He pointed his car in the direction of the peninsula, off the boat in fewer than five minutes, and started clearing his head. The Howes were high profile, their son fourth-generation military. The Chief wanted Sonny on the scene in a hurry. He was hearing sirens now as he crossed onto Lockwood Drive, emergency vehicles converging with his. His own was silent, but he was moving quickly, unimpeded at this hour by traffic, curling easily along Lockwood into South Battery, along the harbor and past the tip of the peninsula at White Point Gardens.

Rounding the point, he could see multiple reflections of the red and blue lights bounding off the clouds, the buildings, even the water, gyrating in syncopation to distort the landscape, lending an uncanny aura to the dark. Cars were parked zigzag and askew where officers answering the initial call had jumped out and run to respond. The ambulance was already gone, but its backup sat directly in front of the house.

Sonny spotted the Chief just preparing to leave with Colonel Howe and his wife. He sprinted to the car for a quick word before they left, tying his necktie on the run.

"I'm getting these folks on over to the hospital, Sonny. The scene is yours from here, but I'd appreciate your coming over to talk with General and Mrs. Howe as soon as you can. They're taking him to Roper. Bring somebody with you who was first on the scene, would you?"

5

Celia lay curled on the big, comfy sofa in Julia's den, listening to the rain and the mellow but melancholy strains of Ramblin' Rose coming softly from Julia's old but reliable audio system in the honeyed tones of Nat King Cole. She had tiptoed upstairs to make sure her friend was sleeping soundly. Julia appeared lightly asleep, but her breath was shallow and arrhythmic, her cheeks and forehead not yet relaxed.

It had been a hard day. Too bad, she thought, that the divorce decree had arrived, an unwelcome interruption in the flow of Julia's settling into her new life in Charleston, always home for Celia. The marriage was, after all, over months ago, maybe truly toxic for years.

But it had to be set in stone by some judge's signature on a piece of paper and sent to Julia on a mail truck, placed impersonally in her box and opened when Celia was not there with her.

Too bad that Julia had not seen years earlier what she was chasing and from what she was running. Too bad Celia did not know how to show her. Too bad, Celia smiled ruefully, she herself had not burned the church on that morning sixteen years ago instead of dutifully showing up as the maid of honor. But they were both young then, neither knowing what life held in store, both hopeful, idealistic, naïve.

That small ceremony had been beautiful, Julia radiant. It was for her both an end and a beginning—the end of wondering if the handsome, eligible Jack Bauer was really going to marry her, the beginning of what might against all odds have turned into a beautiful marriage but had almost inevitably spiraled ever so slowly down the never-ending slope of Julia's insecurities and Jack's insensitivity to them.

He was attracted to her acute and deep intelligence, her quick wit, her way of drawing people to her without even trying, just with a look, a smile, a few words that were always the right words at the right time. Something about her was magnetic, not only to Jack but to the friends she treasured and to acquaintances, colleagues, and to strangers she somehow touched in passing. Jack, even then toying with political ambition, saw in Julia a valuable asset as well as a life partner. When he initially paid her attention, Julia was stunned.

She dated, of course, mostly dividing the small pie of her social time between Josh Higgins, a fellow law student who sought her out for study partner as much as dinner date, and Ben Evans-Kahn, a resident in the emergency medicine unit at Georgetown University Hospital she had met when taken there by ambulance after eating what later proved to be tainted food at a diner near the campus. They marveled at the relationship that had begun while Julia vomited for hours in her cubicle in the ER and Ben stayed with her after his already-endless shift was over. The bleary-eyed Ben and the nauseous Julia, even then, made each other laugh.

Neither relationship was "serious", though both young men obviously adored Julia and valued time with her. She seemed to each more than a sister but not quite a lover, which suited the state of all their lives at the time quite well. Time was premium. Work and its study were consuming for them all, draining away life energy, leaving very little to pursue relationships of depth. So Julia was accustomed to a low-level flirting with these two proven friends, comfortable to curl up with and fall asleep over the books.

Josh was a classic bookworm, a borderline nerd, quite brilliant, and sparring with him was better than food and drink for Julia. Ben was cute, fun, and they were comfortable together. Jack Bauer was lightning and thunder, awakening in Julia a gut-level fascination she had forgotten since high school. She was somewhat in awe of him, his status as the sought-after, eligible Washington bachelor, his casual self-assurance. She needn't have been; she was his equal in every way but experience.

They met at a boring but mandatory fund-raising event for a new oncology wing at Ben's hospital. Even the residents were required to appear, dates on their arms, dressed appropriately. Mingling with doctors and their wives, Julia and Jack literally collided on the landing of the spiral staircase. Julia, half-running as usual, was going up the stairs on the right. Jack, gazing at the dancing couples below, was coming down, holding the handrail with one hand and his drink extended slightly left. The drink and Julia met coming around the corner at the landing, Julia's hasty movement just catching the Jack Daniels and sloshing it out of Jack's hand and upward onto her left ear and the side of her face. The glass dropped quietly to the carpeted stair, but the liquid splashed across Julia's cheek, onto her neck and down the left front of her dress, borrowed from her roommate. Julia gasped, her hand going to her cheek. Jack, regaining his composure immediately, removed the neatly folded handkerchief from his pocket and dabbed Julia's face, neck and, smiling all the while, followed the trail of fluid down past the shoulder, dabbing near the strap of her dress, pressing droplets from the velvety hollow between Julia's breasts. Taking her hand, he mopped the palm, holding it up slightly to go gently between the fingers. Their eyes were locked. Neither had spoken. If only he had just called Julia a clumsy oaf, Celia thought, and gone back to his date.

But he had told Julia his name and asked hers, and the course of Julia's life was changed by a long chapter whose impact Celia now intended to help her mute until tempered by time, the ripeness of reason, and a cumulative overlay of experiences to renew Julia's faith in life and in herself. The move here to Charleston was a big step. Setting up her law practice was keeping Julia occupied, as was the refurbishment of the old house on Sullivan's Island. She was going to be okay now; Celia would see to it.

6

Sirens seemed to be everywhere, blending, endless. Red and blue lights flashed from the top of police cruisers and ambulances, their light reflecting eerily from windowpanes and wet pavement, drowning the natural sounds of a southern summer night. Reg remembered vaguely hearing the deep, throaty voice of a tree frog very near just before this racket started. Now he tried hard to focus. When had the pleasant croaking turned to sirens and his damp but quiet seat in this unfamiliar garden terrace to a raucous, spinning scene from some bad rainy-night movie? Why had he even left the party, Reg wondered, vaguely recalling his sloppy, unsteady descent on the front steps. What a party it had been, good friends celebrating graduation, confirming a rite of passage into real life earned by long, hard hours of study, four years with minimal sleep, and late-night into early-morning hours of cramming, drinking, laughing and growing up. Reg had paid his dues, earned his admirable grade point average honestly, basked in the college atmosphere, and with his heart and soul, not to mention his enviable talent, helped his school win the NCAA national basketball title in his division this year. He was the star, the All-American, leading the team and the division in points scored and assists in a season. Old records had fallen at his quick and skillful hands. He was Reg. He was "the" Reg Fallon, the third pick overall in the NBA draft, a dream more than come true and yet newly, impossibly real. The brothers were proud, and Reg Fallon was launched into the real world unlike any of the others, some of whom would go to Wall Street, to inherit family businesses, to law and medical schools. Reg would be going next week to play big-time basketball in Dallas, Texas.

It doesn't get better, he thought fuzzily, groping for the rail he had held to lower himself down to this step. So much to celebrate, he thought, and so much to drink. Too much, enough to cause a morning of painful regret and a scolding from his embarrassingly proud but ever-watchful mother.

He was almost upright when hands, several hands, attached to arms both black and white and all ceremoniously rough, pulled him to his feet, a voice near his left ear calling, "Here, I've got him!"

Uniformed police officers were suddenly all around, crowding into the little garden, trampling carelessly the petunias and caladiums Reg remembered trying not to tread upon when he lowered himself to sit on that little street side step. His mother's voice--"Keep those big feet away from my geraniums" --came to his mind. Someone held him by his left elbow, and someone else pushed him toward the ground, hard. Stumbling, he once again regretted having so much to drink. Disoriented and struggling in vain for clarity, he heard himself protest weakly: "Hey, what's..."

"Look here. Look," an officer shouted very near Reg's pounding, swimming head. A flashlight on the veranda just above them illuminated the scene in the garden, seeming to Reg blindingly bright. A man and woman held the moving lamp, she clutching a yellow robe around her and he in a tattered pair of pajamas. The light shone on the dozen or so officers, some with guns drawn. It shone in their eyes and made them squint. And it shone on the pearl-handled straight razor on the ground just by Reg's foot, blade exposed, making the still-sticky blood glisten on the blade as rain eroded the edges of the stain and carried trickles of red into the flower bed.

"Bag it," someone roared. "Now. And get him in the car." Reg heard the woman on the veranda gasp. He was dragged to his feet, pushed, pulled, shoved into the back seat of the nearest cruiser. The siren sound was deafening, seeming to come from almost inside his head. He was dizzy, trying for a reason he couldn't understand to follow the movement of the blue lights. The world spun, and Reg knew he would vomit. He tried to tell someone to open the window, but the doors were locked and the two officers in the front seat sped off down East Bay Street toward Broad, lights spinning and sirens blaring. He vomited onto the floor as he heard the driver say into his radio speaker, "We've got him. We're comin' in."

MONDAY

7

Residents throughout the east side of the peninsula were awake and curious about the middle-of-the-night commotion. Word had spread, semi-accurately at best, that there had been a break-in at a residence on East Bay. Adeline Ravenel, seeing Rose on the veranda of the big house, had walked over seeking whatever rumors were buzzing about. Rose was sitting on her rattan rocker with a mulberry-citronella candle, visible only as the rotating lights from one of the squad cars circled regularly across her, illuminating her silver hair and her flowered silk robe.

Rose Beauregard Pinckney was eighty-three years old. Her mind, she liked to say, was almost as good as it had ever been: sometimes in and sometimes out. Factually, apart from the arthritis that she deemed a considerable nuisance, she was in excellent health both of mind and body. Having written during her adulthood four historical novels of the old South, she was revered and still regularly requested by the College of Charleston as a guest instructor and by every group in the City wishing to add wisdom and spice to an event. One of her favorite pastimes remained "hanging out", as she called it, in the college library with the young people. She maintained that this kept her from dwelling upon her surely imminent demise.

Rose's home on East Bay was a treasury of history, Southern and personal. It was not only that she loved the Old South, but that she understood it. Her great grandfather had fought in the Civil War beside Lee, had helped attack Fort Sumter, and had told and retold his many and colorful stories as often as Rose had wanted to listen. He had lived only until Rose was twelve, but she knew he had been her best resource and had inspired in her the love of things and times gone by, slipped sadly away as one generation passed subtly into the next, one memory at a time.

Rose Pinckney had locked onto little Quinn Ravenel the day she and her mother moved into Rose's carriage house. Quinn was only five then, but the attraction was mutual. Quinn gravitated to Grandma Rose from the first chocolate chip cookie in Rose's cozy kitchen. Once she began talking and Rose Pinckney began listening, as she did so remarkably well, Quinn never stopped. Her little life lay bare, all told, at Grandma Rose's kitchen table. And Grandma Rose intended full well to scoop up this little waif in her arms and give her more than enough of all that she was missing. She was a lovely child, afraid of nothing, eager to understand everything. Grandma Rose was drawn to her, as she was to every needy creature, captivated by the possibilities yet untapped in this sweet child. And then there was the mother.

Adeline Ravenel was the kind of woman you could picture in a corset ad in a mail-order catalog with the laces pulled so tight her lips were blue. Even when she smiled, which was rare, it was a pursed, stingy expression and one which did not look comfortable on her face. What temperament and intellect must the father have had, one wondered, to produce the child Quinn, so blond and pure, so delightfully warmhearted. So for having survived the tragic death of that father a year before and now the move from New York City under the tepid care of her widowed mother, life gave little Quinn a gift: Rose Beauregard Pinckney.

She and little Quinn got along famously, each recognizing the other from the beginning as filling a need, extending the love of a family. Rose reveled in the little girl's pleasure and curiosity, reading to her for hours on end and taking her to every Charleston establishment for afternoon tea. How her little face glowed when they were addressed as "ladies" by a waiter in one of the local cafes. She would let her learn first to be a little lady, Rose Pinckney decided, and then they would expand.

And expand they did, Rose and her young companion, at every possible opportunity. Quinn Ravenel learned of the South where her father was born. They walked often by the house on Huger Street where her grandparents had lived years before and where her father spent his childhood. They recreated him in loving conversation as Quinn was not allowed to do with her mother, and she recalled his love and good humor, the fairy tales he had read and re-read to her, the birds, butterflies and bugs they had watched together. He had been a good father, warm and watchful, gone too soon. They even mused about why Adeline had chosen to come back to Charleston, her husband's boyhood home. She had no connection to it other than that, and they concluded in the summary and adult fashion Rose and Quinn often adopted that Adeline simply had no other home.

Quinn was never critical of her mother. She simply spent as much time as possible out of her presence. And Adeline seemed quite satisfied that her daughter was happily occupied away from her. She had little tolerance for Quinn's curiosity and exuberance, let alone her developing penchant for giggling and hilarity. So Rose Pinckney befriended the woman the very best way she knew how in order to spend time with Adeline's daughter. It required a certain duplicity, but Rose decided it was well worth the trouble. She assured Adeline that it was good for an old woman to have a child so near for companionship, that it relieved her loneliness and eased her constant fear of dying all alone and not being discovered for days. Once, she heard Quinn snickering under the stairway at her morbid ramblings to Adeline, and she knew that the child, even at her tender age, was acutely aware of her small pretenses. Adeline, engrossed as she was in the distinctly futile struggle to insinuate herself into Charleston's society, either did not suspect or did not care.

As Rose peered up over her spectacles at Adeline now in the eerie moving light from the police cruisers, she wished mightily that it were little Quinn, now grown, who was there with her on this disquieting night. But at least Quinn was back in town and would be a regular part of Rose's days once again. She had tried to prevail upon her to live here in the big house after college, but Quinn insisted she needed her own place. If Adeline were not still entrenched in the carriage house so close behind, Rose suspected, Quinn might be here with her now. But it was almost morning, she thought, and she could call Quinn to come by for a nice, long catch-up visit.

8

The doors to the surgery annex flew open, banging against the walls in the early-morning quiet, and Dr. Grayson Hughes strode through, peeling the surgical gloves. They fell right into the waste container, his aim obviously not affected by the exhaustion of four grueling hours in the operating room. He was buoyed through these ordeals by his relative youth and by the ever-fresh challenges of his highly successful surgical practice.

"Doctor!" He was immediately assailed by the high-pitched overwrought voice of an anxious mother. She rushed toward him, followed closely by her husband of forty years, his expression taut, wary, prepared for the worst. They were Mutt and Jeff, the two of them--the proper little stick woman and the colonel. Her primness was shaken, threatening to dissolve in a flood of further tears if the news was bad. His voice was steadier but his tone equally uneasy as he caught up with his wife and braced her with a hand on one shoulder. "Doctor?"

"Please, let's sit down." Grayson motioned toward the sofas in the now-empty surgical waiting area. Scurrying to be seated, they both turned toward the doctor, their faces that hospital-induced mixture of expectation and dread.

"He came through the surgery just fine," Grayson reported. "Mac is young and in good physical shape. His military conditioning has served him well, and he's strong and healthy enough to bounce back from this. It will take a few days, and we'll have to keep an eye on him for a while after that. Barring complications, he'll be home recovering on your cooking, Mrs. Howe, in less than a week."

Relief crept across each of the features of their faces, the worry lines relaxing, lips trembling freely now, and tears trickling down both their cheeks.

"Oh... oh... oh," was all she could manage, her voice wispy, weak. Putting her face in her hands, she leaned gently forward, covering her eyes with the handkerchief she had been twisting between her fingers for most of the night.

"Thank you, Doctor Hughes," the colonel spoke sincerely, laying his arm comfortingly over his wife's shawl. "We're more grateful than we can possibly tell you. But what about..." He groped for the right words, but Grayson Hughes knew the question.

"Penile reattachment is not a routine procedure, Colonel. From a surgical perspective, the wound was clean, and he'll be getting a few days of antibiotics to prevent infection. We were somewhat concerned with the blood loss, but for now, we didn't feel the need to transfuse. Dr. Grant is the specialist, and he'll be right along to explain it to you. He did a beautiful job, and I wouldn't be surprised if all systems, so to speak, are 'go' before long."

With a faint grin and a hand on the shoulder of a concerned father, the doctor rose to leave. "I think a couple of hours of sleep are in order before my morning patients, and I would sure recommend the same for y'all. You've had a long, hard night, and Mac will be asleep for hours now."

He held out his hand, and George Howe grasped it firmly with both of his. "Thanks again, Doctor," he offered sincerely.

"We are so very grateful," Martha added, rising as well.

"We'll be talking," Hughes said, turning to go. "Y'all get some rest now."

The two policemen rose as soon as they saw the doctor turn. They had been waiting on that hard bench along the hall all night, one in plain clothes and one in uniform, taking turns refilling coffee cups. They had read all the available magazines, scouted the surgery wing for more, and had resorted to discussion and review of the various police cases of which they both had knowledge. The distraught parents had not been able to leave their watchful post for even a moment. No helpful information had been forthcoming from the mother and father, however, no matter the tactful and concerned nature of the questioning by these seasoned officers. The parents appeared genuinely bewildered about what had happened, their sensibilities reeling that any such savage deed could be part of their world. Colonel Howe had been to war, had seen barbarism and violence at its worst, had taught it at the Academy, steeled himself against it and developed, he thought, the required tolerance for bloodletting in its place.

Its place was not, he had reconfirmed on this night, in the ordered and obliging world of his everyday life, crashing insolently into his vanilla reality and exposing his wife to its horror, her illusions shattered. Although he had reconciled in his mind the inevitable connection between his male child and the knowledge of weapons, blood and honor, he was in no way prepared to acknowledge the kind of unspeakable act inflicted on his son tonight.

Someone had violated his son in sacred places, had come near him in his home, in his own bed in his sleep where one should be safe. Some fiend had held a knife deliberately above the sleeping body of his son, had looked at him vulnerable, and had mutilated him while his father slept nearby. This animal could have cut his throat as easily, and maybe the colonel would have thought it less offensive. With considered aim, this demon had sliced away MacArthur Howe's very maleness, cutting his organ almost off and slipping quietly away into the night leaving him screaming in pain and outrage. Who could fabricate such a distasteful and vicious act? He would be not only a criminal, but obviously deeply depraved as well, thought George Howe, comforting himself thinly with the thought. It was impossible to guard against the maniacal machinations of a madman.

The officers concentrated now upon Dr. Grayson Hughes, approaching as if to pass by them without a sideward glance. They rose in unison, positioning themselves well into the doctor's path.

"Could we have just a minute, Doc.?" Legare, the rugged plain-clothes officer spoke quickly before Grayson moved by. "You might be able to help us."

"What can I tell you, fellas? I'd be happy to help, but I'm the doctor, you know. I was just there for the surgery, not for the crime." He almost smiled.

"Funny, Doc," the detective himself cracked a smile. "Did he tell you anything before he was out for the surgery, anything at all that might help us?"

"By the time I saw him, he was prepped and already under anesthesia. The E.R. staff moved as fast as possible, and they had him ready for us."

"Those people down there didn't get anything either. We already talked to them. Between the pain he was in, and then the drugs you guys gave him to relieve it, he wasn't in any condition to say anything to anybody. So can we talk to him now?"

"You've got to be kidding," Hughes answered, shaking his head. "This guy won't be coming around for hours. We don't want him moving or feeling any pain. I'd say, per the instructions I've left at the nurses' station, he won't be awake any time before dinner. In fact, I can guarantee that. I just told his mom and dad to go on home, but I don't see them leaving. They're probably waiting to talk to Dr. Grant. And don't try to sneak in with the patient before you clear it with me later today. I want to be sure this poor guy is stable before you start grilling him. I know it would boil my blood pressure to wake up and have to start talking about my body parts, especially that one, being almost sliced off."

"Okay, Doc," agreed Legare. The officer in uniform hadn't spoken. "Will you be around here later, say six or so?"

"Probably will. I usually try to make my rounds about dinner time."

As Dr. Hughes left, movement in the waiting area once again caught the attention of the officers. Dr. Ed Grant was making his appearance to talk to the parents. Grant, the officers knew, was the city's preeminent urologist. He had done a vasectomy for the younger officer a couple of years before, and the man remembered him none too fondly, although the procedure had been routine according to the doctor.

"Not much need to wait around for him, I guess," Legare spoke resignedly. "What a waste of a night. We might as well go on back downtown and see what the evidence guys have come up with while we sat around here. Let's just speak to these folks before we go."

The officers walked quickly toward Colonel and Mrs. Howe, anxious to be on their way after a long and fruitless night. "Excuse us," Legare got in before the doctor had begun explaining his work to the two. "We just wanted to let you know that we'll be going now. Best of luck with your son, and we'll be in touch with y'all. Oh, by the way, if the boys left anything out of place at your house after you left, you just give us a call. I'm sure they went over that room with a fine-toothed comb, and let's just hope they got something that will help us get the bastard-- excuse the language, ma'am--that did this." Martha Howe smiled wanly, too tired to deal with the officers and too eager to talk with Dr. Grant. But her husband shook hands with Legare and Wilson, thanking them for their concern.

As the officers retreated, the full attention of the parents was on the specialist. "How is he?" asked the young man's mother. "Will he be all right? Will he ever be the same?"

"It's too soon to know for sure, Mrs. Howe. I'd like to reassure you more fully, but all I can offer right now is my initial sense that things went well. There are in this area of the body several critical systems with which to be concerned, and I have every reason to believe that we were successful in restoring each one of them. The reason for letting your son rest just below consciousness for the next few hours is to give these little repairs time to heal in place without stress of any kind. It is my hope that the urinary function, the sexual function and the blood flow will all be perfectly normal. If there is dysfunction of any kind that time reveals, another small procedure could perfect what we did tonight. Like I said, I can't make promises, and this is a procedure no one does often enough to know it routinely, but you should feel hopeful. I can offer you my own confidence. Do you have any specific concerns?"

"It seems... well, such a delicate spot to work in, Doctor," Martha Howe tried to choose her words. "I guess you've stitched it back together?"

"Yes, exactly," the doctor nodded. "There will be a startlingly minimal amount of scarring within a year or so if we did as good a job as I think. The wound was clean; we got to work on it relatively quickly; and transfusion has so far been unnecessary. He did have significant blood loss, but this rest and the fluids we'll be giving him will start the process of building that back up. He's in great shape. That helps."

"Can we see him now?" pleaded Martha, again near tears. "Just to look at him?"

Dr Grant hesitated, wavering between the rules and the distress before him. "I don't generally do even this," he offered, "but let me walk you over to Recovery and let you peek at him through the glass in the door. I'm going to keep him in there for the next several hours so that the staff can keep the closest possible eye on him. Would you like to do that? It's all I can offer. I'm sorry."

"Oh, yes. Yes, please." Martha Howe was on her feet, her bag already over her shoulder.

The doctor led the way down the hall, around the corner and through two sets of double doors to a final set with glass panes at eye level. The sign read "Medical Personnel Only Beyond This Point". The smell of the building had changed from standard hospital scent to distinct disinfectant. Everything here was white and chrome, exuding sterility.

"Look right through here," Grayson pointed into the area beyond the doors. Martha stood on tiptoe to peer through the small section of glass, and her husband positioned his head beside hers. There were three beds in the recovery area, all along the same wall and all surrounded by medical equipment: tubes, monitors, lights blinking rhythmically. None of the three patients in the beds was awake, and each looked pale and fragile in hospital white.

"He's alive," Martha sighed, and fainted. It was a sudden and momentary collapse, and as quickly as she became limp in the arms of her husband and the alarmed doctor, her color began to return, and she smiled the strongest smile of the night and the morning. "Please forgive me," she said, obviously embarrassed. "It's been a long few hours for a mother."

As no chairs were near, the doctor continued to support Martha on one side, and George on the other. "Maybe we should take a look at you, Mrs. Howe. Are you still feeling faint?"

"Absolutely not. I waited all night to see my son breathing, and now I think I can rest for a while. Straightening on her own, she smiled again. "Let's go home for a bit, George. I need to freshen up before my son needs me."

9

The morning that dawned over Charleston harbor showered sunshine across the shimmering sea and drizzled it onto the quilt over Celia, waking her gently, tickling the corner of her eye with a petal of light. Smelling the brewing coffee she had set up the night before, she stretched, wiggled her toes and sat up to look across the water. All is well, she thought. Celia was a morning person who had long ago categorized waking a huge daily pleasure, a return to consciousness to find that life had chosen to bestow upon her another sunrise. Even after a modicum of sleep, such as these past few hours, she welcomed each morning as one granted to her to savor. It was partly her education in psychology and partly just her nature.

Padding across the kitchen, Celia poured two cups of coffee, hers with cream and sugar, Julia's black. Humming as she climbed the stairs, she knew she would find Julia sound asleep, arms and legs flung across the whole bed, cover twisted here, there and around her. No, she smiled, pushing the door fully open with her foot, Julia was not a neat sleeper. What a shame to have to wake her, but a new day called, and a judge with a ticking clock and a full calendar would not take kindly to any delay caused by a late-sleeping counselor tardy to his courtroom.

"Jules," Celia spoke softly, sitting down on the side of the bed, "do you smell the coffee? Freshly brewed, freshly poured, made just to order for the one and only Julia Slaton McKenzie, Esquire, Counselor at Law, now of Charleston, South Carolina." A corner of Julia's lips turned up ever so slightly, but she did not move, and her eyes did not open. "Come on, sweetie. I'm here to help you start a dazzling new day, the first of the rest of your superb new life, as they say. And you've got exactly one hour to be in your car crossing the bridge so that Judge Engle does not ban you from his court, the practice of law and the State of South Carolina."

Julia opened one eye halfway, taking in a deep breath and holding it. She exhaled a multi-tiered yawn. Propping up on one elbow, she reached for the coffee, her first finger curled to fit the handle of the cup.

"Thanks for being here last night, Cele. Thanks for always being here for me."

"It's my pleasure and my plan, you know. You're a treasure and a jewel, Jules." Celia smiled, recalling how often she'd used that line when the friendship was new. "One day soon, you'll have to acknowledge it yourself." She raised one eyebrow slightly, casting upon Julia that familiar superior expression she had used since college, one that always made Julia laugh.

"Gotta go," Celia chirped, jumping up from the side of the bed. "My first appointment shows up at ten, and I guess I should sort of be there." Celia was one of three partners in a practice of clinical psychologists. "Since I'm without family this week, do you want to have dinner?"

"Absolutely. Call me."

"I printed out your file for this morning. It's on your briefcase," Celia called over her shoulder.

Julia was stretching herself slowly awake as Celia left the house.

10

When Officer Wilson and Detective Legare arrived back at the station after their all-night vigil at the hospital, they were greeted by a roomful of assorted officers not usually present at seven-thirty in the morning. Those who answered the initial call with the paramedics just after midnight were still there, along with Chief Gadsden, both assistant chiefs, several investigative officers and the entire staff of the evidence division. Strangely, however, there was no buzz and bustle, none of the usual stir associated with early-morning excitement. The policemen were draped everywhere, some in uniform, some not. The Chief was chewing his lip quietly, and one of the detectives had bitten the edges from his Styrofoam cup, something he did when agitated. The room was silent. Certainly, this was not the headquarters of a manhunt in progress, and it appeared that several the officers who would be involved in such a search were sitting around this very room looking either puzzled or exhausted.

Legare spoke first, stopping short as he entered the room. "What's this, boys? Did someone put decaf in the pot again?" He removed his tie, somewhat the worse for its night's wearing, and slung it across the back of his chair, the only empty seat in the room. Everyone knew that Sonny Legare was cantankerous about his space. No one sat in Legare's chair or moved anything on his desk. There had been scenes, and Sonny was admittedly territorial.

He ambled across to the coffee pot, filled his cup and struck a pose, leaning with one hand on the counter facing the room and sipping his coffee with the other. His eyes narrowed, and one eyebrow rose as though of its own volition. "Okay, let's have it. What's goin' on?"

There was an audible sigh from the Chief, and several of the men straightened. "Here's the thing," started the youngest man in the room, boyish-looking in his uniform. "After you and Wilson left the scene for the hospital last night, half of us in the division showed up at the Howes' to go over the place. The rest of us scoured the entire neighborhood and half of downtown Charleston talking to anyone who might have seen or heard anything. We thought someone crazy enough to do that might still be hanging around. It wasn't until an hour or so later, but it paid off."

"It's just too easy, and it just don't fit." The chief chimed in, shaking his craggy head and wiping one of his eyes with the back of his pudgy hand.

"What's too easy?" Legare barked, becoming impatient. "Am I getting out of here and getting some sleep, or have you got something? Just why are all of you sitting around here like old hangdogs, anyway? What the hell is going on?"

"Here." The Chief tossed a file onto Sonny's desk. "Look for yourself."

Sonny returned to his desk, opening the folder as he sat down. His brows came together, and he scrubbed at his forehead with the pads of his fingers as though trying to erase the oncoming headache. All eyes were on him. He flipped the several pages, laying them out across the desk, frown deepening. The folder lay empty. He took a long, slow breath.

Legare shook his head. "It just don't figure," he muttered. "Just when you think you've seen it all." He restacked the papers and placed them neatly in the folder. They were waiting, he knew, for his direction. The Chief, an import from Savannah a dozen years back, had been accepted and was generally well liked by his subordinates. Still, Sonny Legare was unofficially in charge, had been for years. If you didn't like him, you at least respected him. If he wasn't always congenial, he was at least always fair. He spun his chair around to look over the group again.

"You boys mean to tell me we're holding Reg Fallon for this? Reg Fallon?"

No one spoke. No one even moved.

Sonny rubbed his forehead again and momentarily closed his eyes. What a way to start a day, he thought, and what a way to begin a week. "What's his status?" he asked finally. "Is there a lawyer involved yet? Has he asked for one?"

"His mother says she'll get their lawyer this morning," one of the officers replied. "Do you want to talk to Reg before the lawyer shows up? We've got him in the big holding cell downstairs. He's pretty hung over and damned scared."

"Let's just play by the rules. Is everything you got down at the lab?"

"Yes, sir."

"Then I'm gonna catch a couple of hours sleep at the boat. I don't even want to think of that kid down in that cell. I've watched him play ball since high school. Hell, I've sat at a couple of games beside his mother, bless her soul. "If this don't just beat all," he murmured on the way out, shaking his head in disbelief. "Reg Fallon!"

11

Julia glanced down at her watch and cleared the counsel table of her files, putting everything in order before leaving the courtroom. Knowing they were close to a resolution, the judge had stayed on the bench later than his usual lunch recess. The mother who was her client in this custody case had already made her way out, shaking from the tension of the past few hours but pleased that her small son would remain in her care. She had hugged Julia at least three times in the last two minutes, offering lunch, but Julia knew that she would, at already after one o'clock, need to eat while working. This hearing had taken longer than she planned, and she had a two o'clock appointment with a new client. There might be no lunch at all.

At times like this, she thought longingly of the staff, including her own devoted assistant, upon whom she had relied in Washington, and of the multiple layers of electronic devices that had kept her always in touch. Today, the simple answering machine in her one-woman office was telling callers that she was in family court for the morning and would return calls this afternoon. And the afternoon was upon her. Julia sighed as she made her way to the exit door, leaving behind only the opposing counsel and his client conferring over events of the day.

Willa Fallon jumped from the hallway bench the moment she saw Julia, all but pouncing upon her. Her long morning's wait outside the courtroom had deepened and broadened her anxiety, and now she was beside herself with worry and fear.

"Oh, Miss McKenzie, thank the good Lord. I was wonderin' if you was ever comin' out, and they wouldn't let me in. Please, Miss McKenzie," her words tumbled out one upon another, "they've got Reggie; they've taken my boy to the jail. Please, please, help him. I don't know what to do or where to turn, and I thought how good you was to us, helpin' us with the basketball folk, and you bein' a lawyer and all, and I don't know no other lawyers. Please," and she laid her hand imploringly on Julia's arm, the tips of her pudgy fingers grasping tightly enough to make little indentations in Julia's flesh. New tears came streaking down her cheeks, making fresh tracks over those of the many others they followed. Willa looked as if she might have been crying for weeks.

Julia set her briefcase on the floor at the end of the bench and gently steered Willa Fallon back to the seat, sitting beside her and offering her full attention, accomplished only after she had recovered from the frantic mother's ambush.

"Mrs. Fallon, slow down and tell me what's happened. Here," she added, pulling a dry tissue from a pocket of her briefcase, "don't cry. Let's just talk, and you tell me about it. We'll work it out, I'm sure." She took both of Willa Fallon's hands in hers, holding them still in Willa's lap. "Okay?"

"Oh, Miss McKenzie, Reggie's a good boy; you know he is. You know that, don't you?"

"Yes, I know that." Passersby tried not to stare at the scene, obviously one of extreme distress, not unusual in the hallways of a family court.

"Well," Willa continued, her voice cracking, "they say he hurt the Howe boy—you know, the colonel's son. He was stabbed last night, and they say it was Reggie. But I know my boy would never do anything like that, not ever. You know that, don't you, Miss McKenzie? Don't you know? He's a good boy, Reggie is, a good boy."

Julia recalled, picturing him in her mind, the young man whose contract to play professional basketball she had negotiated with the Dallas Mavericks. He was, of course, tall and muscular, the look of an athlete. Julia had assessed him as a very decent young man not overly taken with himself and his talent and good fortune. He had treated Julia with the greatest respect and, more impressive to her, always showed openly and without hesitation a sincere devotion to the mother who had raised him alone on her income from two jobs, a grade school education and the intractable will to make a good life for her son. Willa Fallon, before today, always seemed to be smiling. Because she always did the best she could, she had confided to Julia, life had given her Reggie.

"Okay, Willa, let's get your pocketbook and walk over to my office. It's just a block, and we can sit down there and make some calls and work this out. I'll call out and get us some iced tea and sandwiches, and we'll find out about Reggie. You've got to calm down so we can deal with this. You know I'll help you, or I'll find out who can."

"Can we see him, Miss McKenzie? I need to see my boy."

"We'll call from my office and ask about that. Then you'll have time to explain it to me and to dry your tears so Reggie won't have to see you upset like this." With that, Julia took the distraught mother by the elbow, collecting her pocketbook on the arm with her own briefcase, and guided Willa down the hall toward the exit to Broad Street where they stepped through the door into the humidity-heavy heat of a late July Charleston midday.

12

George and Martha Howe sat together by their son's hospital bed, waiting for him to return to consciousness as the doctor had predicted.

"Some of his color is coming back, "Martha offered encouragingly, knowing full well that it was herself she was consoling. George was beside her, but his thoughts were elsewhere, as they had been since the doctors assured them that everything about their son's recovery was going well. George did not have, she knew, her sense of acceptance about life and its varied and unpredictable offerings. He did not deal well with any situation in which he did not feel fully in control. And he did not feel in control here. Doctors were in charge, and nurses, and even mysterious pieces of medical equipment that claimed for themselves conspicuous importance. His son's very life had depended, for the past many hours, upon these others. Things were out of the colonel's control.

He was struggling with the guilt caused by his failure to protect his son. He had been right there, after all, right in the house. "I don't see why I didn't hear something," he said for the hundredth time.

"George, dear, you must stop this," his wife repeated. She had been reassuring him all night and most of the day that it was not his fault, that some cunning culprit had hurt their son, someone who had not been seen or heard by anyone, in a capricious act of cruelty. There was simply nothing they could have done, no way they could have known. "It's going to be all right," she continued, patting the back of his hand with hers. "Just keep thinking about what the doctor said. He's going to be just fine. Everything is going to be just fine."

"I wish you had slept more at the house, Martha," the colonel turned his concern to his wife. "I know it's not comfortable trying to rest here. Are you feeling all right?"

"I'm feeling just fine, George. All I need now is to see my son open his eyes and know that we're here with him."

A nurse, young and blond, came into the room carrying a tray of tubes and syringes. "I need to draw some blood. Would you mind waiting just outside for a moment?" she asked kindly. "It won't take long."

"Do you know when Dr. Hughes will be here?" Martha asked the young nurse. "We were hoping he was going to see our son this afternoon."

"I'm sure he'll be along any time now," the nurse smiled. "He never misses coming by to see his patients."

The parents left the room, Martha glancing back at her son twice on her way to the door. "Let me run down to the cafeteria and get you something," George Howe pleaded with his wife. "We don't want you getting faint again. It's time for a really late lunch or an early dinner."

Sonny Legare was standing at the nurses' station, checking again to see if the doctor was available. He needed permission to talk to McArthur Howe. He had questions. In lieu of forensic results, he needed the Howe boy to identify Reg Fallon as his attacker. He wanted answers. And he wanted them soon.

13

Her day had not gone as planned, Julia reflected as she opened the door at home, still concerned about Willa Fallon. Her calls over sandwiches to the police department had not been reassuring. To the contrary, she had wished the distraught mother was not sitting across the desk when Julia learned that Willa Fallon's son was likely to be charged with the attempted murder of MacArthur Howe, IV before the day was over. Detective Legare seemed to believe, to his chagrin, that it looked very bad for Reg Fallon. The evidence was circumstantial, fingerprints and blood samples not yet matched, but being found with the razor all but in his hand in a state of utter drunkenness sitting in the dark in the Howes' neighborhood was plenty of reason to hold Reg as a suspect.

Julia had taken Willa home while her afternoon appointment waited. She could do nothing short of that. Reluctant to leave the distraught mother alone, she had convinced Willa to call a sister to stay with her until Julia could report back with more details. She could not, without further inconveniencing other clients, see Reg until early evening. Her area of expertise was not criminal law, but Willa would hear nothing of another attorney. She could press the issue at some later time, Julia decided, if this charge stood and criminal defense was truly necessary for a trial. It puzzled her. Reg Fallon had seemed to her a genuinely fine young man.

She would know more shortly, she sighed, dropping her mail and briefcase near the door as it closed and dialing Celia to cancel dinner together. This was supposed to be a quiet recovery evening, she thought, longing only for a hot bath, bubbles creeping over the edge of the tub, a pot of herbal tea beside her. She had discovered that nothing was more relaxing than bathing under the open window with the sound of the sea just outside, an ocean breeze tweaking the suds. What a discovery the sea had been, and some guardian angel or charming urchin had saved this house, this spot, for Julia. The guardian angel was in truth Celia's Grandma Rose who had not used the house in years. It had been rented for a time after the Beauregard Pinckneys all grew up, married and found their separate and newer spots on the Isle of Palms or at Hilton Head. Then Rose had closed the old house, shuttered against possible storms, and left it tended by a handyman and a gardener, used only for an occasional overnight with friends or family. When Celia's best friend came house hunting, she deeded it to Julia for a fraction of what it was worth, happy to have it once again inhabited and appreciated.

And appreciate it Julia did. She reveled in it, took comfort from it, savored her solitude for the first time since childhood. There was joy here; she could sense it from the moment she set foot inside. Some of it came with the house, and some came in with Julia herself, a whole slice of her person somehow previously untapped. It was a nest in which she would weave contentment, a place to heal, a home for just Julia.

It was an old beach Victorian, presenting both the accompanying charm and the hundred-year-old house maintenance challenges. Julia began the previous autumn making it her own. She put the handyman to work repainting and replacing the wood trim, which had weathered many a blistering, humid Atlantic summer. The house was set beachfront on the finger of Sullivan's Island that seemed to curl and point into the harbor toward Charleston proper. Not sporting naked stilts like many of the other beachfront homes, the ground level of this house was surrounded with white latticework upon which climbed a trailing fig peculiar to the sandy soil. The trim had always been white, and Julia chose for the exterior a marine blue-gray, which made her feel that she and the house blended with the sea and the sky. The handyman, now somewhat more than part-time with Julia, would apply three good coats before winter. She often joked that she must quickly increase her caseload so that she could support her dependence upon the handyman.

Julia had zealously worked on the interior with her own hands, lovingly painting walls room by room into the colors she had always wanted around her, for years deferred to conventional neutrals, the tastes of a conservative husband and a pretentious Washington decorator. Her spacious, high-ceilinged kitchen now glowed with shades of sunny, butter yellow trimmed in white and a deep-sea blue. All the appliances were new, gleaming white, except for the old, double porcelain sink with brass faceplates proudly dated when the house was new. It had to stay, reminding Julia of women before her who had looked out over the harbor thinking thoughts women all shared with their hands in the dishwater.

She held her cupped hands under that old brass faucet just now, rinsing them, then filling the kettle with water for tea. If not a bubble bath, then she would at least savor a cup of green tea on the porch in the waning dinner hour for a few precious minutes before freshening up to talk with Reginald Fallon. Only Willa's pleading had moved her to visit the jail. In Washington, she had rarely been near the bars that held society's captives. It was not on her wish list, but it seemed the sole decent recourse. She knew the drill, the routine first questions for a criminal defendant, had studied and evaluated hundreds of answers to those questions as she helped prepare civil cases. She could find appropriate criminal counsel for the young Fallon if it proved necessary.

The whistling of a steaming kettle interrupted her wandering thoughts, mingling images of today's startling events and yesterday's reckoning with a marriage long over and yet still capable of causing melancholy, longing for something or someone she had wished for but never really found. She poured the water into the little antique teapot rescued one day last week from a second-hand shop on King Street, letting it steep over the tea bags as she settled on the porch into her favorite cushioned wicker rocker.

Looking out over the harbor, Julia filled her cup and cradled it in two hands, enjoying its warmth even on a midsummer late afternoon. There was something comforting about a nice, hot cup of tea, its aroma, its soothing caress on a parched throat tight from a stressful day. Julia had grown to appreciate the small comforts, the little things that brought her joy. Or maybe, she thought, she had just come to understand that these pure little joys were always there if one was open to them. The tea, the sea, the moment gave her pleasure.

Sitting, sipping, Julia was acutely aware of her newfound capacity to enjoy. It was okay--suddenly, surprisingly okay--for a pleasure to be hers alone. She could share, had always been eager to share. She would share many times on this wonderful porch with Celia and, surely, with new friends she would make. But this moment in time, captured with intent, inserted purposefully between her day's work and her surprise evening assignment, belonged to Julia alone, and it was okay. It was scrumptious. Celia diagnosed Julia as just now learning to enjoy her own company, to trust her own instincts. Celia said the unsatisfied longing Julia felt was to know herself, to be kind to herself, to become content. Celia said she needed a cat.

After a time, Julia stretched her legs, wiggled her toes, and reluctantly postponed further indulgence. Grabbing a banana to eat on the way, she stepped back into her shoes and headed toward town.

14

Sonny Legare sat alone in the large poorly-lighted space when Julia entered, his feet on the desk, reading what was left of the morning newspaper. The few hours of sleep he'd managed midday had revived him somewhat, but he hadn't thought shaving important before he came by the station this evening. Seeing Julia McKenzie always made him uneasy in a way he hadn't bothered to analyze, like being a kid in one of those little shops full of porcelain and glass. She startled him now, opening the swinging door with her foot so that it swung back and forth after she entered.

"Oh, it's you," she said in that way of hers he couldn't decipher. He resisted the urge to pull his feet from the desktop. "I need some help."

"Yeah?" he drawled, "What can I do for you, McKenzie?" He finally dropped the newspaper, leaving the feet in place.

"Listen," Julia pressed on intently. I need to know what you have on Reg Fallon before I see him. Could I look over the paperwork?" She'd barely taken a breath. He had never seen her flushed or hurried, but then their meetings were not an everyday occurrence.

"What's your interest?" he asked first, finally sitting up straight and dropping the feet.

"I haven't decided," Julia replied, rushing her words. Her return to town had been accompanied with surges of angst and uncertainty. Criminal defense was serious business. People's lives often hung in the balance. "Willa Fallon came to me for help. She was sitting in my office when I called earlier."

Sonny leaned forward in his seat, his eyes narrowing. "You're not gonna get mixed up in that situation, are you, McKenzie?" He looked directly at her, as if willing her to say 'no'. "It's gonna be some messy business, this one, like we don't see around here. Hell, it's not even your kind of case, is it? Don't you have a nice, civilized practice?"

"Look," Julia pushed on, single-minded, "I don't know what I'm going to do. For now, I'm all he's got. I worked with him on the Mavericks contract, and I found him to be a bright, seemingly decent young man. Liked his attitude. Loved his mother. And now this. So will you please help me out here?"

Sonny offered the file. It was right in front of him, centered on his desk. "Take a seat and look it over," he said. "I don't like this any more than you do. Always thought the Fallon kid was okay. Hell, he had every damn thing going for him. It just makes you wonder."

Julia pulled a chair close to the front side of Sonny's desk and opened the file, softening slightly. This wasn't his fault, she reminded herself. He was just doing his job, and word had it that he did it extremely well. She had looked at the man before. He was attractive, but she sensed gruffness, had heard him called a recluse. If he was a good cop, then it couldn't hurt to have him on her side tonight. In fact, somewhat out of her element here in the criminal domain of legal practice, she mused that any ally would suffice.

She flashed him a sudden and sincere smile. "Thanks, Detective. You're right about my not doing much of this kind of work. But when a nice woman like Willa Fallon, comes asking for help for her son, I had to at least come and see Reg. Like I said, I got to know him a little and liked him, so I can't imagine this charge having any basis in fact. At least it happened too late to make the morning paper, so it's not quite the talk of the whole town yet. Any insights you want to share?"

"The unpredictability of humans just never ceases to surprise me," Sonny responded. "I took the kid his dinner tray myself. I wanted to make sure that he's doing okay. He's not. He seems stunned, and he insists to anyone who will listen that he doesn't know anything about this. I wish I could believe him, but it looks bad. He's anxious to see his mother. I guess for now he'll have to settle for you."

"Thanks, Detective. I do appreciate it. Can I check back with you after I see Reg? I might need copies of this stuff."

"I'll be here until I get a call from over at the hospital."

"Someone sick?" Julia asked.

"The Howe boy, McKenzie. I'm waiting for him to regain consciousness so I can talk to him. Did you forget there was a victim while you're gettin' involved with the Fallon kid?"

"Almost, but please update me on him as well, if you don't mind."

"I wish you'd think about what I said before you get in too deep, McKenzie. This Fallon boy--and don't get me wrong; I like the kid--is up the creek if there's enough to charge him. I don't know why he'd do such a thing, but no reason is gonna be good enough. You're just starting to make a name here, run with at least the medium-sized dogs; some people never do. This is a hard town on outsiders, so don't go down with Reg Fallon. Since the victim is the Howes' son--and thank god he's alive--even the Broad Street boys won't keep Fallon from doin' time. At least let one of them take the heat for defending him. You seem like a nice lady, Julia McKenzie. Seeing you come stalking through that door like you did tonight beats my usual shoulder-rubbing with the stuffed-shirt defense lawyers any day. You scare me a little, but I'd hate to see you run out of town on a rail."

Julia wasn't sure if those remarks were accompanied by a grimace or a half-smile, but she blushed at the unexpected words. "Thanks again, Detective," she managed, and headed out of the room and toward the holding cell.

Martha Howe noticed the first fluttering of her son's eyelids as he neared consciousness. She had been standing beside him for an hour, just looking down at his face, now and then stroking his cheek. She didn't notice that her feet ached; her entire being was willing her son's recovery, trying to transmit her life energies to him. She was thinking of the night she bore him. He'd been a beautiful baby, looking for all the world, even then, the perfect little boy. Having lived for her husband until that day, she had lived since for the two of them. MacArthur Howe IV was everything she had wanted. She had adamantly refused her husband's offer of a nanny, spending every possible moment with the baby--rocking, cuddling, seeing to his every wish. Martha was fulfilled. The baby thrived.

George Howe had indulged his wife's wish to spend so much time with little Mac. Though he didn't heartily approve and often accused her of coddling, his gratitude for the son she had given him after their years of trying allowed him to humor her. Martha glowed, and he supposed that made it worthwhile. He knew nothing about babies, after all. He simply wanted a son, and he bided his time until the child would be old enough to qualify, looking in on him every night in the nursery. It was a shame, he thought, that one had to suffer through all these years of babble and crawling to get a son of one's own. He held the child four times during his first year of life. Twice the baby wet through his diaper, and twice he cried ferociously.

The father and son bonding began when little Mac was about four, able to play rough to his father's satisfaction. Now they could wrestle and tumble, shoot from behind bushes in the back yard, and have real conversations. At five years of age, Mac knew the name of every NFL quarterback, felt at home in his father's office, and did a crisp salute. The colonel's old combat boots sat at the foot of his bed, and Mac's mission, as he understood it, was to grow into them.

How he had grown, his mother recalled as she looked at him in the hospital bed. He had become everything his father had wanted in a son, and more than a mother could hope for. How could this unbearable thing have happened to him, her baby, their perfect creation? Why would some stranger pick their house of all the houses in the world? Would her precious Mac ever be the same? Could he forget; could any of them forget? Could she ever go to sleep in the dark again? She stifled her horror. He was almost awake.

"George," she whispered toward the chair where Colonel Howe was absorbed in his reading. "George, I think he's waking up."

The Colonel came to stand on the bed's other side to wait as their son did indeed appear to be regaining consciousness. "Do you think we should call the nurse?" Martha asked anxiously.

"I'll get her," George replied, hurrying toward the door. It opened before him, and the doctor entered just in time to see his patient open his eyes, peering groggily around the unfamiliar room. He looked for a moment at Dr. Hughes, without recognition, and moved on to let his eyes come to rest on his mother's face. She held one of his hands in both of hers, and now she began to stroke the back of that hand reassuringly as she spoke softly, smiling.

"You're going to be all right now, my darling. Mother's here, and so is Daddy. Everything is just fine." She continued this reassuring monologue as Mac searched her face and then the room again, not yet trying to speak. His eyes paused on several objects in the room, studying, struggling to orient himself, not moving in any other way. Doctor Hughes stood at the foot of the bed, observing his patient's return to consciousness, resurfacing from a sea of sedation.

Mac's eyes seemed suddenly to focus, then opened wider as he appeared startled, drawing his hand quickly away from his mother and reaching down his body as recall overtook him. Dr. Hughes saw the onset of fear and moved quickly to the bedside, laying his hand firmly on the young man's shoulder. "You are all right, Mac. We stitched you right up, and you're good as new. Nothing to worry about. All you need is a little rest."

His hand still in place over the sheet and on top of the bandages, the fear in Mac's eyes abated only slightly. "It's okay?" he questioned, doubt heavy in his voice, his words soft and slurred from the medication.

"Yes, it's okay," Dr. Hughes repeated firmly. "You're going to be just fine. I want you to rest tonight so that we can get you up and around tomorrow." With that, he patted the patient once more on the shoulder and walked toward the door. "I'll be checking on you early in the morning."

George Howe followed the doctor into the hallway, while Martha continued to speak soothingly to her son.

"How is he doing, really?" the Colonel inquired as soon as the door closed behind them. "Do you think he's going to be all right?"

"It looks to me as though he's on the road to recovery," the doctor smiled, perusing the chart in his hands. "His vital signs have improved at each reading all day long, and he's perfectly stable now. I would say he's coming along very nicely and should be much more alert tomorrow."

"He's pretty groggy," his father worried. "Is that normal?"

Doctor Grayson closed the chart, checking his watch. "It's normal, and it's good. We don't want him to move around too much just yet. Tomorrow will be soon enough for that." He stuck out his hand to shake the Colonel's, saying goodnight. "You might want to see that your wife gets a good night's sleep, Colonel," he turned back to say. "I think this has taken a greater toll on her than she realizes. I'm going to tell them at the desk to drop a couple of sleeping capsules in an envelope for you to take with you. Maybe you could get her to take one. Reassure her that it's going very well, and y'all have a good night now."

The Colonel returned to the room. "Dad?" his son's voice entreated immediately.

"You can't tell through the bandage, Son, but you are all right. The doctor did a great job, and you know I wouldn't lie to you. He says you'll be walking around tomorrow and that the important thing for now is that you sleep through the night and get your strength back."

A measure of relief came slowly across the young face. "Dad?"

"Yes, Son."

"Will you stay?"

"We'll be right here, Son. Your mother and I will be right here." His voice grew husky.

Julia felt the fatigue creep over her as she waited in the County Jail anteroom. A fitful night's sleep and a long morning battling over child custody were catching up with her, she thought, not to mention the unexpected developments of the afternoon. Pushing her shoulders back over the top of the uncomfortable chair as far as possible, she rolled her head from one side to the other, listening to all the crackling sounds coming from her neck and trying to envision the knots reluctantly relenting. The banana had not been enough. She longed for a hamburger, aspirin and a tall glass of iced tea, straight, minus all that lemon and sugar these Southern folks seemed to enjoy. One could live on and die for this city's cuisine, she thought, but she would not develop a taste for sweet tea.

Reg Fallon entered the small room when a deputy opened the door. He looked drained, sick and lost. Julia motioned for him to take the seat across from her at the little table, hoping to make him comfortable enough to talk easily, wishing to discover quickly the truth of this situation. "Hey, Reg," she spoke warmly, holding out her hand for his. "Can I go out to the machine and get you something to drink while we talk—Coke, coffee?"

"No, thanks, ma'am," Reg answered. "I'm not sure I could keep it down. They brought me dinner, but I couldn't eat it. I just want to get out of here. How's my mom?"

"Well, she's upset, of course, but she's doing okay. She just wants you home."

"There's nowhere I'd rather be, Miss McKenzie. If I get out of this mess, I might not leave home again for the rest of my life." Reg's voice broke, and Julia saw his lips tremble.

"Okay, Reg, I'm here to help you. Your mother wanted to come, but for now they only allowed your lawyer. Let's start by assuming you and I can get to the bottom of this. Can you possibly just trust me here?"

"You helped me before, Miss McKenzie, but I just don't see how I got here or how to get out. One minute I'm celebrating with my friends, thinking my life is just the best, and the next I'm puking in a cop car on the way to jail. They think I did something to Mac Howe—tried to kill him?"

"Reg," Julia tried to speak soothingly while remaining matter-of-fact, "someone did attack the Howe boy. And the police found you awhile later somewhere near his house sitting on a step with a straight razor right beside you. It's natural they would suspect you, so it's up to us—you and me—to set things straight. You tell me everything you remember, starting with the party last night. Can you do that?"

"Sure," Reg replied, dropping his head forward and holding it between his hands. "Some of it isn't very clear because I really did have too much to drink. It was such a great time, one of the last times we'd be together before all of us go our separate ways, and we were just drinking and kidding around and telling stories about the last four years. It was great."

"And then..." Julia prompted.

"Well, I know some of the guys had left. I wasn't ready to leave. I'd drunk too much, and I think I was just going to walk outside a little and get some air. I remember almost falling down the wet steps when I came out of Kellers' house."

"Whose house is that?" Julia wanted to know, making notes now.

"Cat Keller. It's his folks' house over on Michaels Alley. They like us to come over there, even though we're kind of rowdy. They're cool parents, nice people."

"Okay, go on. You decided you needed some air."

"Yeah. I don't have any idea which way I went or even where I was when the cops came. I know I was sitting down. I remember some flowers. I think I had walked for a while, but I don't remember where. And I knew sitting there—it was a brick step--that my behind was getting soaked through, but I didn't care. I was feeling a little sick from all the beer, kind of dizzy, but kind of happy too. I didn't mind that it was raining on me or that I was drunk or that I was probably going to throw up and then have a raging hangover. I just sat there feeling happy. And then suddenly there were sirens and lights everywhere and the cops grabbing me." He shook his head, looking up at Julia now with eyes full of fear and confusion. "I swear I didn't do anything, Miss McKenzie. I swear on my mother's Bible."

Julia believed him and was relieved.

"Reg, what about the straight razor they found? Do you have any idea why it was there where you were sitting?"

"I don't own a straight razor, don't know anyone who does. Now I'll be having nightmares about them for the rest of my life."

"The lab results of the blood on the razor aren't back yet. Neither is the fingerprint analysis. We can hope it's not the weapon, but you see how it looks, Reg. There's an attack, a bloody razor, and you beside it sitting in the rain. Do you know Mac Howe?"

"Not very well. He graduated a couple of years ahead of me and went off to school and then the Army right away. I saw him around when we were in high school; he played ball for Bishop England. But we didn't run in the same circles."

"So there's no reason for any bad feelings between the two of you?" Julia probed.

"I sure can't think of anything. I can't say I liked him, but I haven't even seen him more than half a dozen times since high school. Except when we were on the basketball court, I didn't play in his league." After a pause, Julia saw the faintest hint of a smile. "You know, I sure would like to buy my mama a big house right in his block now that the playing field is leveled some."

Julia smiled back, encouraged at any sign of the old upbeat Reg Fallon. "Okay, look, Reg, I know this isn't a cool place to hang out for a night or two, but can you just be patient until tomorrow? No judge will want to come down tonight to talk about bail, and I need some more answers and some crime lab results before we decide what to do. I also think we should associate a real criminal lawyer if you're still in here by tomorrow night. I don't regularly practice this kind of law, and we want the best if we do need one."

"For the first time in my life, money is not a problem," Reg grinned wryly. "But I'd gladly give back all the money and the contract if this would go away, Miss McKenzie. So, I have to sleep in here tonight, huh?"

"I'm sorry, Reg. We don't want to alienate a judge as our first move. But I think I can get you a good pillow and blanket and some Alka Seltzer and toast. And I promise to be back here by noon tomorrow. Can you live with that?"

"Like I have a choice." Reg dropped his hands on the table, palms up, gesturing resignation to a situation over which he had little control. "I'm in your hands, Miss McKenzie. My whole life is in your hands." And then, one more glimpse of the lighted-hearted Reg Fallon whom Julia had come to know: "Don't blow it."

Julia gathered both his big hands, those of a signed and sealed professional basketball player, between her own small palms. "Try to get some sleep, Reg. I'll go over and reassure your mom, and maybe tomorrow we can get to the bottom of this. Hopefully, you can look back on this in a year and describe it to your pals as an 'experience'." With that, she gathered her things and rose, knocking on the door for the guard to let them out, she to her freedom and Reg Fallon back to a jail cell for the night.

It was another hot night in the Lowcountry, and the air conditioning at the city jail was mediocre at best. Julia decided she would try to impose upon Detective Legare to make Reg more comfortable for this night. It wasn't a lot to ask, and he was obviously no more convinced than she that Reg was guilty. Peeking into the big room where she had left the detective, Julia was disappointed to find him gone, his desk lamp off, the room empty save one lone deputy in a far corner hunched over a filing cabinet. "Excuse me," she called. "Is Detective Legare gone for the night?"

Startled, the young man turned and pulled himself upright. "I don't know, ma'am. I was told he went over to the hospital. Can I help you?"

"No, but thanks anyway. It wasn't important." She backed out of the room and headed toward the outdoors and her car, wishing there was another way to send Reg what she had offered. Lost in thought, she almost collided with Sonny as he returned to the building.

"Oh, Detective!"

"Oh, McKenzie!" he returned, copying her expression. "Hey, you must be finished with the Fallon boy. How did it go? Can you spare a couple of minutes to come back in? I've just been over to the hospital."

Julia turned around, and Sonny opened the door for her. "I'm glad you came back," she admitted. "I was going to ask you if Reg could have another pillow and a blanket and maybe some Alka Seltzer and toast. He's still feeling pretty bad, and being frightened half to death isn't helping. I'll go get the Alka Seltzer and some bread for toast if you could see that he gets it," she offered, using her best imploring expression.

"I swear you've got enough on your plate right now, McKenzie. I've got an Alka Seltzer and Tums stash in my desk, and I can make toast down in the kitchen. I'll take care of the kid myself if that's okay with you, Counselor."

"A cop with a heart, Detective? I'd really be grateful. I need to get over and see his mom before it gets any later. I know she's worried sick, and I don't know what I'm going to tell her."

"Well, you can tell her, for one thing, that the Howe boy can't identify his attacker. He'd had a few drinks himself earlier and was virtually passed out on his bed when this happened. He just saw a figure—one he describes as far smaller than Reg Fallon—run over and crawl right out his bedroom window. He was in pain and shock, bleeding quite a lot and in no position to pay attention to anything but his own suffering. Hell, McKenzie, I can't even imagine it. All he remembers is waking up screaming. They say he was still screaming when they got him in the ambulance."

"I sure can't imagine Reg Fallon doing this. Keep me posted on those lab results, will you? And thanks again for your help, Detective."

"You're welcome. You think you might start calling me Sonny, then, McKenzie?"

"Well, Detec—Sonny—," Julia grinned. "If you keep being this good to my client, I'll call you anything you want." And she left the building once again.

Dreading Willa Fallon's reaction, Julia slowed her pace. The newspaper would have this story in the morning, she was sure. It was a devastating turn of events for everyone: for the Howes, for the Fallons, and for Charleston, whose sons were making news for all the wrong reasons. Reg Fallon was recognized on the street, hounded by little boys looking for his autograph, a talented local kid turned sports hero. His promising basketball career had been touted in the region's news for a couple of years and was recently highlighted in Sports Illustrated. He didn't need this. Neither did Charleston. And neither did Julia.

17

Quinn Ravenel woke feeling, even before she opened her eyes, as though she had shed an old skin, free from the secret she had carried like a millstone for four years. Without the weight of it, she could breathe. There was no one she could tell, but her message had been delivered to the only other person who knew.

She let her eyes open, breathing deeply of the morning, the sun, the light creeping over her. Lying quietly, she thought of the day ahead and of the life stretching before her, both glorious now with possibility.

Quinn looked forward to her visit with Grandma Rose this very morning. If only she could tell her the whole story, sharing her years-old pain and newfound deliverance, but that was unthinkable. She would share her excitement about teaching, about having a post-college life of her own, about once again being near Rose herself, the dearest person in her young life.

Quinn did not want to see her mother when she visited Rose, so she always arrived after Adeline had left for work at the bank. She would choose not to see her mother again ever, but that would cause questions, ones to which she was not prepared to respond. Grandma Rose would likely understand if Quinn severed the mother/daughter relationship, such as it was, but Quinn sought to leave well enough alone and simply maintain the entrenched emotional distance between her mother and herself. She had considered geographic distance as well, but Charleston was her home. Rose was her family. Teaching at Porter Gaud was her new job. The four years away at school were enough. And Rose had mothered her so well as to make that other woman nonessential in Quinn's life.

After a long and satisfying shower, Quinn pulled on a sundress she was sure would please Grandma Rose and plopped herself into the driver's seat of her new yellow Volkswagen beetle. Rose had given it to her for graduation, together with its new license plates reading "BABYLUV", always her pet name for little Quinn.

The homecoming sensation always washed over her as she rounded the curve onto East Bay, but the attachment was to Rose Pinckney's home, not her mother's. Rose had effectively plucked Quinn from the psychological clutches of Adeline Ravenel. Damage had already been done, injury subtly inflicted, but Rose offered refuge and a constant healing by loving Quinn with her whole maternal heart. This was her own heart's home, Quinn thought as she parked on the side street off East Bay. It was where she had first felt safe after the death of her father. Bounding up the steps, she could smell the sweet bread Grandma Rose was baking. It was Quinn's favorite.

TUESDAY

18

Charleston, South Carolina, mid-morning on any day, is a lovely sight to behold. The old East Battery house of the Beauregard-Pinckneys was just far enough around the bend after leaving Broad Street at the Exchange Building to allow a stunning view across the harbor toward Fort Sumter and the tip of Sullivan's Island. On a clear day, one who knew the landmarks could identify the tidal flats separated from Old Mount Pleasant by the Hog Island Channel. Rose could pinpoint, looking past Castle Pinckney, just where the beach house was situated across the bay, still occupying its spot where she had enjoyed so many summers and where she now hoped Julia McKenzie was finding a measure of contentment. She had approved of Celia's friend since college and had grown fonder of her with each encounter. Having her in the old beach house, someone who would love it as Rose had, was a great relief and satisfaction.

The view this morning across the water invited photography, and much of that was in progress among the usual flock of tourists, mostly in groups of two and four, climbing the few steps to the walkway along the high battery. The waves in the harbor still shimmered in the slanting light from a morning sun, but the heat and brightness of midday were approaching, moisture already collecting on the brows of sightseers who would soon descend for lunch upon the bounty of eateries in this city of famously mouthwatering cuisine.

Julia, back in the office early, sustained herself with coffee until Celia, unannounced, brought fresh cornbread with sausage and warm red-eye gravy, cajoling her friend into a late breakfast on the cluttered desktop.

"You'll have to take a break and eat it," she smiled. "I made it myself. At least one of us can cook." Julia had long acknowledged no skill in the kitchen. "Any word on the situation with Reg Fallon?"

"I'm waiting for a call about blood and fingerprints. Maybe that will clear this up. Otherwise, we'll need a real lawyer."

The bond between the two women bore the depth of a sister relationship, and Celia was delighted to have her best friend now, against all odds, so near. She recalled holding her emotional breath until Julia's move from Washington to Charleston happened, afraid until the last moment that Julia would change her mind. But she had not. Julia had arrived. The truck with her belongings had arrived. Celia knew that it was both a bold and a tentative step, a wobbly but successful navigation through a large rapid in the fast-moving river of Julia's life for which she had braced and which she had weathered almost without flinching. Now she was on Celia's supportive shore, anchored in the gently flowing current of Celia's beloved Charleston.

She sensed a comfort level developing in Julia with her surroundings—the beach house now hers, her cozy little office space, even the growing security of being sought after to represent friends of friends of local clients. The life she was building was hers, and she was beginning to appreciate it, constructed on the foundation of her own work, her own reputation, her own fledgling faith in herself.

"You, of course, are a real lawyer. And you're here," Celia said simply. "It makes me happy. I'll check in after I get the girls from camp this afternoon."

Julia smiled, momentarily relaxed and entertained. "You know, Cele, sometimes I feel at home here. Remember when you'd tell me to just look due south, and that's where you were? Look at us now. People stop by to say hello. People wave from across the street. One of the basket ladies knows my name. And have you seen that picture I hung last week out in the waiting area?"

Laughing now, both women got up to look. It was the familiar but always compelling picture of a dark storm churning up Charleston's harbor.

"Just eat the food," Celia reminded as she closed the door.

19

"The prints don't match," were the first jubilant words out of Reg's mouth when Julia was permitted into his cell just after noon. "The fingerprints on that razor aren't mine. The blood is Mac's, but the prints aren't mine. Detective Legare came to tell me a while ago. Can you get them to let me out of here now? I'm hungry."

Julia smiled at the news. She was glad to see Reg looking more like his old self and pleased at the new development.

"Detective Legare wasn't at his desk when I came by, so I guess I'd better try to track him down. I'm glad to be able to say that you look much better today. I wouldn't have given a cent for a photo of the way you looked last night," Julia joked.

"The detective went by my house to get a set of clothes and let me shower and change this morning. He seems like a pretty good guy, and I think he believes me."

"Well, let me go find him, and I'll be back," Julia said. "Don't get your hopes up about breaking out of here right away, but it's looking better, isn't it? This should make it likely that a judge will set bail. Hang in there, Reg." Julia, her spirits raised, set out to find Sonny. It was easy. He was back at his desk, sipping Pepsi from a can.

"I thought you were going to keep me posted on lab results," Julia said, taking the chair beside Sonny's desk.

"And I thought, being a hot-shot lawyer and all, that you'd be easier to find so I could do just that," Sonny retorted. "I left a message on your machine a few minutes ago. Don't you have a cell phone?"

Julia laughed. "I'll give you the number. Giving everyone a cell number is so reminiscent of the rat race. Doesn't it almost run counter to the culture here?"

"They call it progress, McKenzie. Even I'm attached to mine."

Both smiled.

"So Reg tells me he's off the hook," Julia continued. "Are y'all ready to let him go home?"

"That's wishful thinking, and you know it. We can't match the prints on the knife to the Fallon boy, but I'm waiting for the ones from around the Howes' window and maybe by the bed where the victim was sleeping. I told Reg it was a hopeful development, but you and I know the prosecutor will say he wore gloves."

"Well, I guess I'd better make arrangements for a bond hearing then. And I wanted to thank you for taking care of Reg. He told me you got clothes from his house. Maybe you're not as bad as I've heard." Smiling widely, Julia got up. "See you later," she waved over her shoulder.

20

Rose Pinckney was warm to the center of her heart listening to Quinn's animated chatter. And the liveliness of Quinn herself--pouring the tea, slicing the bread, swiping at the counter with a dishcloth--delighted Rose. Flitting around the kitchen, then sitting balanced on two legs of her chair, she retold a memorable episode from her last days in the dorm at Smith College or a blunder she felt she had made in interviewing for a job, knowing that all her stories were received as gifts by Grandma Rose, that her company itself was precious to this woman. She would gladly have lived in this very house with Rose but for the nearness of her mother, still an overriding consideration.

"I'm going to rely on you, Grams," she carried on, "not to feed me this way often enough to get me fat. I could eat this sweet bread all day, you know, and then start over again tomorrow. I guess one of these days you'll have to teach me how to make it myself, or is it a secret?"

"I don't have any secrets from you, Babyluv, you know that. I'll share with you anything I happen to have stored in this old head of mine."

"Your mind is sharper today than mine will ever be, and you know it, Grams. I'm a college graduate now, with papers to prove it, and you can still talk circles around me on most any subject."

"I'm grateful my mind is better than my knees," Rose responded, tapping her cane on the wood floor.

"Because of you, I probably know more about the Civil War than any kid in the South. And because of the way you tell it, I'm as fascinated by it as by any current event. I'm going to model my style as a teacher after just the way you share knowledge, Grams. The kids I teach will be all the better because you've been in my life."

"It is I who am the better for having you in mine, little girl. And don't you forget it. Now don't make me weepy with all your flattering. Let's clean this up and go sit in the garden. I've got so much blooming right now that I can hardly keep up with it. I surely have missed having you to help me in the spring and the fall these past four years. Wait until you see what I planted in that bare spot where the old, gangly rhododendrons used to be." She rose gingerly, using the edge of the sturdy table for support, bending knees more carefully as time passed.

"Where's the morning paper, Grams?" Quinn asked, brushing crumbs from the table into her open hand. "Want to do the crossword with me out in the garden like we used to?"

"Yes, let's," Rose replied. "I think it's still on the little table by the front door. I'll get us a pencil."

"You can bring a pen, Grams. Now that I'm a college graduate, we won't make mistakes, will we?" She hooted with laughter, and Rose followed suit, shuffling her way to the half bath for a quick stop before going out to the garden.

"Shall I pour us some iced tea to take out?" Quinn called.

"That would be lovely, dear."

Quinn set two blue crystal glasses on the counter next to the refrigerator and went to get the newspaper. Picking it up, she glanced at the lead story, headlined in bold print, front and center. She froze for a moment by the front door, quickly scanning the page. And then the paper fell to the floor, its pages fanning across the hardwood entryway, and Quinn ran out the door, leaving it wide open behind her as she ran down the steps.

Heat and humidity in Charleston were the summer's norm. Julia's introduction to it had come in her college years during regular trips home with Celia, becoming acquainted with both her friend's family and her native Lowcountry. Bonding with the place had been gradual, although she felt immediately drawn to the aesthetic grace of the city and captivated by the pace of its comings and goings, so unlike her then-customary hectic days in Washington, D.C.

She initially judged Charleston insular and self-absorbed, an assessment she still found apt but now less a disparagement than a fond critique. Foreign policy meant the City's relationship with the South Carolina legislature in Columbia or discussion of repairing the highway to Savannah. Any concession to the world outside was probably made, Julia mused, by a cursory reading of world events on the front page of Sunday's *Post and Courier* with a once-weekly nod to its questionable import or its impact on life in Charleston. This city had collectively had its fill of wars and calamity, had them on its doorstep and in its parlor. Thus, days when the southern sun simply shone and news highlighted the current Dock Street Theatre performance suited Charlestonians just fine, thank you.

Theirs was life as in a time capsule. Horse-drawn carriages moved gaily and leisurely through the streets, some still cobblestone, tour guides gesturing and holding forth to their captive audiences, and life proceeding at a pace just as well suited to days when a horse was the standard mode of transport. On Church Street, Julia saw a district court judge riding his bicycle past her office window to and from the courthouse daily, rain or shine, never hurrying, always lifting a hand in friendly greeting to locals and tourists alike. Such eccentricities were doted upon here, quietly lauded and applauded. It seemed that to be a "character" in Charleston was the endearing norm rather than the exception.

The message on Julia's answering machine when she returned from the courthouse that afternoon was in Celia's familiar voice but without her usual accentuated drawl. Her tone was urgent and the message puzzling.

"Julia, you know I'm halfway down to Beaufort to get the girls from camp, but please do this for Grandma Rose and me. Quinn Ravenel is at the jail--yes, the jail--charged with something serious. Please, please go. I'll call you the moment I get back to town, probably around ten. Thanks, Jules. Love ya'."

Julia had met Quinn Ravenel a few times in passing. She knew her as a young friend of Rose Pinckney, but the girl had been away at college until this summer. In what serious trouble could she possibly be? Rose and Celia had always spoken of her as a bright young woman, an education major, but Julia knew little else. She would certainly prefer to get to know her under other circumstances. This, she thought, would make more visits for her to the Charleston jail in a week than she had made in the previous nine months.

22

"This is the damnedest thing I've ever seen, McKenzie," Sonny said, holding out a file as Julia perched once again in the chair across the desk. "Reg Fallon just may not need a lawyer after all."

"What?" Julia asked.

"Believe it or not, someone else confessed. This little blonde girl came running in here awhile earlier saying she's the one who assaulted Mac Howe. She insisted we had the wrong guy and wanted us to let him go right away."

"I don't understand," Julia responded, her brow furrowed.

"You may not have a client. He may just have been in the wrong place at the wrong time, which would take you out of the catbird seat." Sonny looked pleased.

"Is this a credible confession?"

"I find it hard to believe, but she was spilling the whole story when I told her to stop talking. We called the public defender's office. She offered her fingerprints. They match the ones on the razor. She's back there in a cell."

"I'm more than surprised, but isn't it wonderful that our instincts about Reg were correct?"

"We can't hold him now. I'll have one of the boys take him on home if that's okay with you, Counsel."

"Yes, please. I'd like to see his mother's face. Bless her heart."

"Would you rather I let you take him on home yourself?" Sonny offered. "You could be there for that reunion."

"Well, strangely, I'm here about something else entirely. I got a message from Celia that her friend Quinn Ravenel was being held here. Can you find out for me?"

Sonny sat still, his eyes narrowing slightly as he looked at Julia. He just looked. "Surely not," he said finally.

"Excuse me?"

"Your friend sent you here looking for her friend, whose name is Quinn Ravenel?"

"Yes."

"It's not possible." Sonny shook his head, chewing his lower lip.

"What's not possible? What?" Julia didn't know whether to be amused or annoyed.

"McKenzie, the young woman who came in here confessing to the attack on Mac Howe is Quinn Ravenel."

Now it was Julia's turn to sit quietly, trying to unravel her thoughts. She'd considered a pile of unpaid parking tickets, a DUI maybe, even reckless driving. But this?

"You can't possibly mean..." Julia's thought trailed off mid-sentence as she tried to process. She held Sonny's gaze, absorbing the implications of his newest revelation.

"Tell you what, McKenzie," Sonny said. "Why don't you just run along home, and we'll pretend this never happened. Hell, I'm not convinced it's possible. What are the odds? For you, I mean."

"Well, if I were a drinker, I'd be getting one now. I must either need new karma or new friends. The ones I have are keeping me too near the fire. But I have to go see this girl."

Sonny nodded. "I suspect you do. It's beginning to be *déjà vu*. I'll have her brought to the room, same one you used with Reg. And I'll be here when you're through. We might both need a drink after this day."

The matron opened the door, and Julia tried to clear her mind, standing to greet the girl who entered and stood across the small table. Even after hours in a cell, Quinn appeared fresh, her denim blue sundress barely wrinkled. She smiled directly at Julia, a warm, open smile, and held out her hand. "Hello, Miss McKenzie." She was surprised. "Did Rose send you here? I'm so sorry I ran out this morning without saying anything to her."

"It's okay. She must have called Celia. She's the one who asked me to come. I'm sure she'd be here with me, but she's just now on the road driving the girls back from camp."

Quinn was beautiful by almost any standard, her long blond hair crimped to her shoulders, perfect cheekbones accenting clear, blue eyes, her youth becoming, her gaze guileless and straightforward. This was surely not the wielder of a razor or a crazed criminal. Celia had been right. A mistake had been made. Again.

"Can you tell me how in the name of heaven you could be involved in this?" Julia asked without preamble, abandoning her plan to first make Quinn comfortable with her.

"I did it," Quinn said simply.

"You did it?" Julie repeated, stunned. "What do you mean, you did it?"

"I just did it, Miss McKenzie. I've known I was going to do it for a long time. I just didn't know when. I had to wait for everything to be right. It was almost right a week ago, but there was a fan in the window, so I waited. Last night everything was perfect. So I finally did it." Quinn laid her palms open on the table in front of her as she finished, as though she were explaining something that was out of her hands.

Julia was openly astonished now, her lips apart, disbelief showing. She waited, thinking Quinn would say more, possibly laugh aloud at her own absurd assertion. Quinn waited as well, quietly letting Julia absorb what she had said as though her explanation was clear and sufficient, as though that was just the way things were. Julia could not even formulate a question. Had she heard wrong, misunderstood? Surely this girl was not in a position to be kidding around with her. Was she possibly dealing with a person who appeared normal but who was patently unbalanced?

"I think there's coffee outside, and I've been needing a couple of aspirin. Can I bring you a cup?"

"Sure, I'd love one," Quinn responded, settling back in her seat and folding her hands in her lap. "Does that mean we're going to be talking for a while?"

"Do you want to keep talking?" Julie asked.

"Well, I'd really like to get out of here. Is that going to happen if we talk?"

"I'll do my best, Quinn, but you've got me a little puzzled now. Let's get the coffee and start over, okay?" Julia pushed her briefcase onto the center of the table between them, fishing for her notepad and pencils and laying them on the table. She replaced the briefcase on the floor, pushed her chair back and left the room, closing the door behind her.

The matron waited in the hall just outside the door. "Are you finished?" she asked.

"I think we may just be getting started," Julia replied, wondering to herself what was to come. She glanced at her left wrist while her right hand filled the cups. Six o'clock. She didn't feel tired any more. The aspirin and the coffee would renew her enough for several more hours. And she was somehow certain that the conversation that lay ahead would keep her undivided attention.

23

We've got to stop meeting like this," Sonny drawled when he looked up to see Julia. "Have you come to see if I'm free for dinner?"

"I stepped out to get some coffee, and I need copies of Quinn's file, a judge and a bondsman. I hope I can get Judge Stoney to come down. What do you think?"

"Hey, he's definitely the softie in the bunch. If anyone can do it, it would be you. It's dinnertime, so that's not in your favor. Who's gonna post the bond even if Stoney allows it?"

I don't know. Her family, I suppose. I know this is an imposition, Detective, but if I can pull this together, would you consider looking them up? I'd owe you a dinner for this if you'd get them over here."

Sonny was feeding the papers from the Ravenel file through the copier. He looked up at Julia, contemplating his response. "Yes to the dinner. And I think it's just her mother."

"You know her?" Julia asked absently, pawing in her briefcase. "Do you have bail bond paperwork?"

"Yeah, it's over here." He opened the largest cabinet and pulled out several folders, handing them to Julia with the copies. "Take what you need."

Silent, Julia removed pages from the folders, studying each one carefully. Though not her usual kind of work, this was basic. She picked what she needed and held out the folders. "Thanks again, Detective. I'll let you know when I get this set up. Please don't forget Mrs. Ravenel."

"Are you sure you don't know her? I'm putting pieces together now. I think she lives in Rose Pinckney's carriage house, has for years."

Julia looked up, recalling. "No, I can't place her. But you'll go and get her if I need that?"

"I won't forget. Just don't you forget about the dinner."

Julia smiled, lifted a hand in parting, and had already forgotten.

24

Julia set two cups gently on the small table between her and Quinn, careful not to slosh the coffee from the Styrofoam cups. "There's no sign of cream or sugar out there," she explained. "We'll have to make do with black."

"That's okay," Quinn responded genially, "I don't drink coffee because I like the taste anyway. Sometimes it just feels like the thing to do. Like now." She smiled that open smile again, challenging Julia to believe that there was something real about this unlikely situation. "Thank you for coming," she continued. "I didn't know what to do after I was put in the cell. I hadn't thought that far ahead."

"Well," Julia spoke now, "why don't you just tell me about yourself apart from this. And if we're going to work together, would you mind if I record what we say?"

Quinn shrugged, unconcerned about the recording, and Julia pulled a small device from her briefcase and punched a button. "Okay. Just tell me a little about you, Quinn."

The girl took a minute to consider her response, resting her chin on steepled fingers. "I'm almost twenty-three, just back from school. I graduated in May from Smith College, degree in early childhood education, and Porter Gaud has hired me to teach their progressive kindergarten class this fall. I'm excited about it. I love little kids. I was born in New York City, and I moved here with my mother when I was five. That's when I met Grandma Rose, and she and Celia have pretty much been my family ever since. There's not much else to tell. I think I'm pretty ordinary."

This girl, Julia thought, was certainly not ordinary, nor was this whole implausible episode. "Ordinary people generally are not arrested for slicing off someone's body parts," she asserted warily. Maybe it was time to get down to business here. "How are you involved in this?"

"MacArthur Howe raped me when I was seventeen, Miss McKenzie. I was a virgin. I had not encouraged him in any way. I have not had sex with a man before or since. I waited a long time for my revenge, and last night was my time. It's as simple as that." First ordinary, now simple, Julia thought. And this girl was decidedly sincere. What was the next question?

The obvious question: "What did you tell the police, Quinn. What have you already said, and to whom?"

"When I came here to tell them Reg didn't do it, they wanted to know how I knew he didn't. I told them I did it, and that's how I knew, because that was the truth. That's about all I said. The detective suggested I should have an attorney before we talked any more. He took my fingerprints and gave me one call, so I called Grandma Rose, and the detective called the Public Defender."

"Did you tell the Public Defender what you just told me, Quinn?"

"No, he just stopped by to say that he would work me into his schedule tomorrow, and he told me not to talk to anyone until then.

"So he doesn't know about the rape?"

"No."

What about the police, Quinn? Didn't you report the rape when it happened? Is there a police report? Was he charged?"

"Mama wouldn't let me. She said I should be ashamed, which I already was. She said nice girls don't talk about such things, and we would pretend it never happened. To this day, she has never discussed it with me."

"You must have told someone. You were so close to Rose. Didn't you talk to her?"

"I couldn't bear to risk that she'd see me differently as well, Miss McKenzie. I didn't want anyone else to think I wasn't a nice girl."

"So you told no one? Not in all the time since it happened? No one?"

"Only at school after hours of classes and thousands of pages of reading about children and what they deserve did I slowly realize the harm done to me on that night. I came to realize it objectively, separate from the low-grade grief I carried over a loss I still can't say I fully understand. And I can't say when I decided what I was going to do. At some point, I just knew."

Julia felt a tightness in the center of her chest. She wouldn't know why until she analyzed it later, but Quinn now did seem closer to normal, and the whole story was, if not simple, at least clearer. Julia wanted to help, wanted to take this child home and comfort her. She saw her now as the victim extracting her measure of retribution. She stopped the tape and pushed back the straight, uncomfortable chair.

"I'm afraid the law may not see it that way," she had to say, recalling why she was there. "I don't practice criminal law, Quinn, but I think you're going to need someone who does. You don't want the Public Defender, although he's a competent enough guy. I'll help you get someone. And you can call me Julia." She smiled now, wanting Quinn to know that she was a friend, someone who could be trusted.

"I'm not exactly sure why I need an attorney at all. No one can change what's happened. But if I do need someone, then I'd like it to be you."

Julia quelled the lump in her throat. She would not want to fail this girl. Enough of that had been done already. "May I think about it overnight? And in the meantime, I'll see about getting you out of here." She smiled again, reassuringly, her training taking over as she snapped shut her briefcase, wondering as she spoke if Quinn would be spending this night, and many more, in jail.

Gathering her things, Julia thought ahead. She would have to find a judge, get a bondsman, rush an immediate hearing. "Don't worry. I won't leave you here all night wondering what's happened, okay? If you can be patient for a couple of hours, I'll be back for you. And I've asked one of the detectives to bring down your mother."

"Mama won't be coming," Quinn stated simply. "I'm sure she'll be horrified."

Julia stood still, absorbing.

Quinn continued: "My whole life was sidetracked by what happened that night. Looking back, I don't know who was the accomplice: him or her. I thought of it, to survive, like closing off a room of a house where you don't want to go because something awful happened there. I closed an area in my mind, in my life, just blocked it off by sheer will to save the rest of me. And I never opened that door until the other night. Now it's okay. I've fixed it, and I can live in my whole self again." Justice, Julia mused. If only the recorder had been running. It might not work for a jury, but it certainly worked for her. "I'll be back," she said, and hurried out of the room.

Having received assurance from Judge Stoney that he would take the bench promptly and briefly to hear her at 9:30 p.m., Julia now searched the phone book at her desk for a number for Quinn's mother. "Ravenel," she murmured, her finger skimming the column of names.

There it was, she assumed: A. Ravenel on East Bay Street. Would A. Ravenel have the means to get her daughter out of jail, especially if the judge did not see fit to set a reasonable bail? Checking her watch, Julia dialed, tangling her fingers, dialed again more carefully. She had not rehearsed what she would say. The telephone on East Bay Street rang, rang again, and was answered on the third ring.

"Mrs. Ravenel?" Julia asked.

"This is Mrs. Ravenel."

"Mrs. Ravenel, I'm an attorney and a friend of Celia Rutledge. I've been talking with your daughter and have agreed to represent her, at least for now. There's a judge on his way to the courthouse to set bail for Quinn, so I'd like to send a deputy sheriff to get you so you can be there for her. We can discuss the bond amount and how to post it after the judge has ruled. I know this must be very upsetting for you. I'll be there to do whatever I can to help you both. Could you possibly be ready in about fifteen minutes?"

"Mrs. Ravenel?...............Hello?" The line was dead. Had she disconnected? Julia had not noted the number; she had to look it up again, chiding herself for her carelessness. She dialed this time with care and sat back in her chair, telling herself to slow down and breathe deeply. This is not Washington, D.C., she reminded herself; it's Charleston where even haste is slower. The telephone was not answered this time until the seventh ring.

"Mrs. Ravenel, I apologize. We were disconnected. As I was saying..."

"Stop," came firmly from the other end of the line. "Please do not call me again." And once again the connection was broken, but this time not quietly. Julia heard the receiver click. She held hers out from her ear, looking at it as though it had itself offended. Then, replacing the receiver in its cradle, Julia let her jaw drop, as if for an audience.

What?!

The Judge was not happy. His demeanor as he swished in from the anteroom and took the bench evidenced his displeasure at being here instead of at home in his comfortable recliner in front of the Braves game. If this matter was dispensed expeditiously, as he intended, he would be in place for the seventh inning.

Julia observed the judge's expression, not unexpected, and calculated quickly how to best placate him so that her plea would not fall on deaf ears. She must convince him quickly that the urgency was real and that she was not wasting his time. The door opened on the courtroom's side, and a deputy guided Quinn across the front of the room to sit beside Julia. Silence prevailed as Judge Stoney opened the file before him, squinting at its contents, peering occasionally over the rim of his glasses. How does he see her, Julia wondered anxiously. How will he reconcile the facts on paper with this young woman sitting beside me?

He finally spoke. "Okay, Counsel, it appears that you've brought me down here to set bail at this hour for a defendant who either attempted murder or succeeded at highly aggravated assault, informally admitted to the attack, and whose prints are all over the weapon. Am I missing something?"

"Yes, your Honor. My client has not confessed, nor will she do so. Her brief conversation with the arresting officers is not on record and does not constitute a confession. My client will plead not guilty. She has ties to this community and is no danger to herself or anyone else. She has no previous record of any kind, not even a parking ticket. She has just graduated from Smith College with a 4.0 grade average, majoring in early childhood education and has been hired by Porter Gaud to teach kindergarten there in the fall. She has no reason to flee this Court's jurisdiction. We would respectfully ask the Court to remand her to the care of her family on her own recognizance until the preliminary hearing on this charge, Judge."

Turning to the prosecutor's table, where Allen Cantrell was already on his feet and wagging his head, the Judge intoned his usual: "And what is the State's position, Mr. Cantrell?"

"The State is frankly dumbfounded that counsel would even suggest release for this defendant, Your Honor. We needn't have wasted the Court's time. Not a danger? She just sliced off someone's penis, your Honor. Not during an argument. Not in the heat of passion. She did, according to the preliminary police report, climb calmly through the victim's bedroom window and attack him asleep in his own bed. Maybe she is deranged, maybe psychotic. Whatever the case, even I would not feel safe tonight knowing she was back on the street. The State strongly urges that no bail opportunity be afforded this defendant and that she remain in custody until trial, at which time we are confident she will be convicted."

"Ms. McKenzie?"

"This defendant, I repeat, poses no threat to anyone. She will enter a "not guilty" plea. There is nothing clear-cut about this case, your Honor, except the unequivocal right of the accused to fair treatment pending trial. We ask again that the Court allow Miss Ravenel's release. No insurance is necessary that she will remain here during this investigation. This is her home."

"I've heard enough to rule," the Judge growled. "There's enough in this folder alone for me to hold this girl without bond until trial or until hell freezes over. It may not have been a confession, but this police report stands on its own for the little she did say before she was advised to get counsel. She wasn't even reluctant to admit she assaulted the victim. The weapon is here. Her prints are all over it. I want to be exceedingly certain that, if she is on the street pending trial, someone has a large vested interest in her staying on the straight and narrow and in her remaining in Charleston. I'm inclined to deny the motion for bail altogether, but given that there are no priors and that baseball is playing on my television at home in front of my favorite chair, I'll set bail at one million dollars." The gavel rapped hard; his Honor rose immediately, and his back was already turned when the first words of objection poured forth from the prosecutor. Those words fell on deaf ears; the hearing for bail was adjourned.

Julia sat, laying her hand over Quinn's on the edge of the defendant's table. Whose fingers were trembling, she wondered, hers or Quinn's or both? Quinn was pale, silent, her eyes searching Julia's face for explanation. "You'll have to go back with the deputy until I get the details worked out," she said quietly, squeezing the hand inside hers reassuringly. "I'll be down in just a few minutes to let you know what's going to happen. Can you bear with me here?" As though there were an option, she thought. As though she had a clue what she was going to do next. As though a million-dollar bail was a blow she could be dealt and keep putting one foot in front of the other until she reached the door. Julia was stunned.

When Quinn had gone, Julia gathered her papers and turned, hoping to see Ms. Ravenel or a bail bondsman or both. There was only Detective Sonny Legare, sitting at the back of the courtroom leaning on the bench in front of him with his chin in his hands.

27

Quinn leaned back on the concrete wall, her knees pulled to her chest, eyes closed against the reality of her confinement. The matron had been kind enough, allowing her to use the real restroom on her way back to the holding cell, then offering a blanket Quinn hoped she wouldn't need for this night. What, she wondered, could Julia McKenzie hope to do for her? There had been no sign that bail would be forthcoming; no one was in the courtroom for her hearing but the lawyers and one policeman sitting in the back. He had been the one she talked with earlier in the day. His questions had been spare and straightforward, as had her answers. She'd simply told him what she had done.

What an interesting turn of events, Quinn mused, for her to be sitting in a cell waiting for someone out there in the world to decide her fate, just when she thought she had taken her destiny back. Of course, what she had done was wrong in the eyes of the law of the state, but it had been so right, so necessary. She could not take it back, just as MacArthur Howe could not ever give back what he had taken from her. Nor did she wish to take it back. She did, however, wish not to spend the night in this damp cubicle with the ugly, stained sink and the rat sounds in the wall.

28

"I see you got your hearing," Sonny offered as Julia approached the courtroom exit beside him. "I thought I most likely shouldn't miss your performance tonight because it may be one of your last ones before they run you out of town on a rail."

"That's just the kind of help I need right now," Julia retorted, grimacing. "What in the name of heaven am I going to do for that child now? I called the mother. You might have given me a hint before I did that, Detective. I take it you knew?" Julia dropped onto the bench seat beside Sonny Legare, temporarily lacking direction. The folder containing Quinn's paperwork was clenched tightly in her fingers, and she closed her eyes, suddenly realizing the nearness of tears. "I've gotta think."

"I didn't know what to expect from that little girl's mother. But I was hoping for the best. Come on outside with me. I'll help you clear your head. How about some coffee?"

"I think I already had too much a little earlier. My insides are shaking. It could be the coffee. It could also be that I've bitten off more than I can chew. I'm waiting for the 'I told you so', Detective."

"That won't be coming right now, Missy," Legare assured her lightly, placing his hand under her elbow. "Come on. Let's go."

All the daylight was gone now, but warmth enveloped them as soon as Sonny opened the door to outside. "What can I do to help?" he asked. "I'd offer the cool million if I could, but that's pretty much out of the question. You know, don't you, that I'll see that no one in there bothers that young lady?" Trying to breathe deeply, Julia accepted Sonny Legare an unlikely ally. "If we can't spring her, I can at least promise to keep her safe from harm."

They had walked half of the block toward Julia's office when she stopped suddenly, nearly dropping the file. "I have to call Celie. It's just after ten, so she may be back now. Hurry." Julia walked quickly now, again purposeful, regaining her composure. Sonny kept pace, acting the companion role she had unconsciously assigned him. They entered Julia's office together, and she flicked switches for light. She paced as she held the phone to her ear. Sonny took the chair in front of the desk, waiting for whatever unfolded.

"Celie," she gasped finally, "thank goodness you're there."

29

Julia's anger built rather than dwindled as she drove back to the jail. It was late. She had, as Celia instructed, picked up Quinn's bond from Rose Pinckney, who was still wide awake and dressed to appear in person to bring Quinn home. Julia assured her she need not come, but she was certain that Rose would wait by her front window, her hands clasped in prayer, until she could touch Quinn.

It was clearer to Julia now why she had connected as she had to Quinn Ravenel. It was the mother Julia knew so well because it was her own. They came from the same mold. Julia's life was steeped in it, her every relationship tainted, her sense of self only now developing, thanks to extensive loving guidance from her best friend who just happened to be a clinical psychologist.

Celia had changed Julia, coaxing her out from under the spell of her childhood and toward an emotional health heretofore foreign to Julia. Her mother had not struck her, had not neglected her in the classic legal sense. She had always been fed and clothed and taken to see the doctor if she was sick. But she was unseen by and unknown to the person most important in her young life except on the most superficial of levels. Julia always knew that she was not quite acceptable, something of a disappointment. Whatever her accomplishments, they were never good enough; her mother's expectations for Julia were forever unmet. Julia tried. Her lifetime of trying and coming up just short was the salvage from which she had to build a life.

It was what had left her vulnerable to Jack Bauer. She saw that now, as Celia had told her often enough. Her subconscious had sensed in Jack the same apartness, the unreachability, of her mother. But Jack sought her company, listened when she spoke, saw her face instead of something on its far side. He had her mother's power, which she later saw she gave him, to judge her inadequate. But Jack did not do so, at least not in the early months of their relationship. Jack, she was convinced, loved the real Julia McKenzie. So, raised and trained in the way of remaining in that line of fire, Julia became Mrs. Jack Bauer.

There was, Celia assured her repeatedly, no substitute for a good mother. The footprints left by a bad one are indelible, the damage lifelong and life altering. But we are each given the tools with which to rebuild, she insisted. Charleston had rebuilt, better and stronger, after Hugo; Julia could and would recover from Mama.

Quinn's mother had laid quite a trap, Julia thought darkly. The rape was bad enough, but the negation by the mother of Quinn's pain and innocence was an outrage, a final sabotage of a little girl's attempt to become a whole sound woman. Julia wanted to cry for them both, for Quinn and for herself.

She leapt from the car, slamming the door behind her hard enough to rock the little black Honda. The mother wouldn't come, she kept thinking. The mother hung up on me. Storming across the gravel parking area, she lost a shoe on the pebbles and stopped to remove the other, realizing as she did so that her hands were trembling. It was nearly midnight. Her feet hurt, as did her head, neck and shoulders. Sonny was talking with the bondsman in front of the glass partition as Julia opened the door.

"The woman is a moron," Julia growled through gritted teeth. Startled, the two men stopped mid-sentence and looked her way. "That poor kid would have been better off in an orphanage." Realizing her demeanor, Julia quieted and blushed slightly. Not very professional, she thought. "Sorry," she murmured. "It's been a really long day."

Sonny, recognizing that he should not show amusement at Julia's behavior, simply brushed it off. "The judge obviously didn't expect this bail to be posted, especially not tonight," he said. "They don't even have the paperwork ready for posting and release. Someone had to go over to the judge's chambers to get the file, but they're on it now. Have a seat; you've gotta be bushed. Here," he took Julia's shoes from her hand and offered one of the chairs in the drab waiting area. She sat gratefully, leaning the chair back slightly and resting her feet on another.

Julia fished a check from her briefcase and handed it to the bondsman. "Thanks for coming down. I guess you're accustomed to these odd hours and sticky situations."

"John Curtis," the bondsman introduced himself, holding out his hand. "Yeah, I'm taking over this business from my dad, so I'm learning the ropes and trying to get my sleep when I can. Sonny tells me you're new here, so thanks for using us. I hope this works out for you."

I hope it works out too, thought Julia, trying to gather strength to be positive for Quinn. "It's good of you to take a check at this time of night."

John Curtis grinned. "My daddy told me there are some people you can take a check from and some you can't. It's up to me to know the difference. Ms. Pinckney? Good as gold."

Just then the door buzzed and opened between the outer and inner areas, and Quinn Ravenel emerged, looking only slightly the worse for her day in a jail cell. Thanks to Rose Pinckney, she would be spending the night in a real bed.

30

Night. Charleston. Its sounds—the frogs and crickets and a night bird or two—could have belonged to any time in the world, any place. It was a primeval song, low and deep. In the dark, below the stars, tides caressed the city's fringes and marshes pulsed, warm and wakeful, weaving their way throughout. Sonny absorbed it from the deck of the boat, listening as waves lapped gently. He was finishing a beer, looking across the slow-moving Ashley River toward Albemarle Point. This river, this town, was comfortable to him, familiar and constant. He could sit here—right here—and almost feel Annie beside him. If he just closed his eyes and let his hand drop down to scratch Tork's ears, he could feel her breath, hear her laugh. These were his momentary hedges against the accustomed loneliness, these and the job.

The job had certainly had his whole attention the last few days, he thought. What an unexpected turn of events, and then another and another. This would be a different story entirely from the one of Reg

Fallon and MacArthur Howe. When this one found its way to print, it would be a scandal. General Howe's son a rapist? How would that sit with the South of Broad folks? And yet, his accuser was all but the granddaughter of Rose Pinckney whose blood was as Lowcountry as one could get. His next task, he decided, was to extricate Julia McKenzie from this situation. She was in way over her head.

Julia saw the night from atop the island-bound span of the new Arthur Ravenel Bridge over the Cooper River. She smiled now, remembering how the old bridges had terrified her in the beginning, the one into town especially narrow. This new arching testament to modern construction technology, named for one of Charleston's elder statesmen, was a pleasure to cross. Lights twinkled along the shore, and those aboard the USS Yorktown shone brightly to her right, lighting Patriot's Point. Julia had her car windows down, enjoying the moist breeze off the harbor and the smell of swamp and sea. The place had a hold on her now, and she had no desire to break its spell. God lived here Himself at some point, she had decided, maybe lived here still, so she was content to do the same.

Another day. Another surprise. Celia was probably tucking in her precious daughters after the scramble to help Julia get the bail money and a couple of reassurance calls to Grandma Rose. Julia was almost home. And for tonight--just for tonight--Quinn was safe; Julia had delivered her to sleep at Rose's house.

Quinn lay flat on her back in the dark, eyes closed, listening to the hum of the ceiling fan. This night was unforeseen. Now it would all come back to haunt her, her newfound deliverance diluted. Grandma Rose had tucked her in just like she was a little girl, asking no questions. But the questions would come, ones she had never intended to answer. The box in which she had so carefully guarded the nightmare had been opened, and now she could see the scenes as clearly as she had on that night, July 21, four years earlier.

The Howes lived just a couple of blocks away when Quinn and her mother moved to the carriage house on East Bay Street. Quinn was five years old, and Mac was about seven. They had never been friends or playmates. Mac was several grades ahead in school, and Quinn had never sought his company. In high school, he had flirted mildly with her a few times, generally calling her "scrawny kid". Plenty of girls liked him; he was "South of Broad" with parents of both money and influence.

Quinn dated, but her concentration was on getting into college and running on the high school track team.

Quinn was slender and her motion fluid. The coach had encouraged a daily routine, so even during summers, her practice course throughout high school had been around the seawall from her house, passing the now-familiar antebellum homes, across Beaufain and down Rutledge circling Colonial Lake, and then Queen Street back across the peninsula to East Bay and home. On a good day, she ran it twice.

It was such a day when, just starting her second circuit as the sun went down, she passed the Howe's gray stucco home as usual.

"Hey, scrawny kid," Mac called out to her as she passed. Quinn raised her hand without slowing. "Hey," he called out again, sprinting down his driveway after her. "You're just the one who could help me if you'd slow down."

"Help?" she had responded, slowing.

"I'm locked out of my house, and my parents are out of town. I broke the window, but I can't fit through. I'm betting you can. How about it? Will you crawl in there and unlock the door for me?"

"So there's some advantage to being a scrawny kid?" Quinn asked, grinning.

"Okay, if I call you a gorgeous babe, will you do it?"

Quinn turned, still jogging in place, hesitant.

"I'm late and hot and desperate. Take pity?" he crooned, bestowing on Quinn one of his best boyish grins. Passing under the white-painted circular arch onto the piazza along the driveway, she saw that he had indeed cleanly broken out one pane of a side window, clearing it of protruding glass. It was an opening too small for him but probably not for her.

"Your parents are going to love this, huh?"

"It's the only thing I could think of. Do you think you could get through?"

"Let me try it." Quinn oozed her lean body through the window, thinking the hips might be just too much, but then she had her hands on the floor inside and knew her legs and feet would slither through behind her.

"Okay, so it's dark in here. Which way to open the door?"

"Just go out into the hall and take a right. Through the kitchen, you'll be able to see your way to the front door. I'll meet you there."

Quinn could see her way to the door of the room. It was apparently Mac's own room, the bed unmade, the décor strictly Army. The hallway was darker, but she felt her way along it to the right, seeing an opening she assumed was the kitchen. She was feeling just a little smug that this big military guy had needed little athletic her to get into his own house.

Mac's bulk came hard against her in the little hallway, his arms going around her shoulders and his chest pressing her face. Stunned, she opened her mouth to release the automatic scream, but his hand was quick to cover her face, turning it up toward his, meeting her eyes in the semi-dark. "Surprise, baby," he said.

31

Willa Fallon needed no introduction to heartache. She had known it her whole life, losing her father at age seven, growing up dirt poor. She dropped out of school quietly after the sixth grade to help her mother with four siblings, two younger brothers and two younger sisters, each of whom graduated high school and fanned out to raise families around the country.

Reg was born when Willa was nineteen years old, still helping to raise her brothers and sisters. She had loved Reg's father, but he left town when Willa told him about the pregnancy. He never called, never knew he had a son. The pregnancy went well, and Willa adored Reg from the moment she laid eyes on him. He breathed at birth without prompting, a portent of what their lives would be. Reg brought pure joy to Willa's somber existence.

Always an excellent southern cook, Willa began to cater a few of her special dishes to small events. Word had spread, and Willa's little catering business now served Charleston's elite. Meals at many a gathering south of Broad Street started with Willa's she crab soup and ended with her Southern pecan chess pie.

Sitting by the empty hospital bed, Willa marveled at the havoc that had engulfed them in the blink of an eye. Two days earlier, she was content to a degree she never expected. Her son was going to play professional basketball; then he was in a jail cell; now he was in surgery. His bones were broken, his kidney bruised and his brain swollen.

The room door opened, and Willa jumped to her feet, but it was not a doctor or nurse bringing her son; it was the police detective who had come to get her in the early morning hours. Reggie had called to tell her he was coming; the detective had come instead.

"How are you doing?" Sonny asked as Willa sank back into her seat. "I stopped at the nurses' station, so I know he's still in surgery."

"They workin' on his head," Willa replied. "They say they can't fix the rest of him until they fix his head." Her chin dropped to her chest.

"Ms. Fallon, I don't know what to say. I wish I could change this, go back in time. Is there anything I can do for you?"

"Jes' let me be wakin' up an' all this be a dream," Willa said. "An' I guess you can pray for my baby."

"I've been doing that all night and morning," Sonny assured her. "I wish I had taken him home myself."

"The policeman who was drivin', is he...?"

"He didn't make it. He was on the side of the car that took the hit directly."

"They was almost home." Willa's hands covered her face, and her shoulders shook with fresh sobs. "Almost home."

WEDNESDAY

32

Every single time she rounded the corner from Broad onto Church Street, Julia had to smile at her shingle, brass with engraved lettering, over her very own office door: Julia Slaton McKenzie, Counselor at Law. The name still looked a little lonely there with no partners, no long list of associates. Jack had been a partner in the old D.C. firm, and Julia would have become one. She had paid her dues, done her time in the law library, held enough hands of the lower-fee clients. And she had proven herself. Just when they were ready to move her up, she had moved on. Anyone who came to her office now did not come to a multi-layered firm with its own billing department on the fifth floor; Julia was on her own.

On my own. The realization was becoming somewhat less daunting as the months passed. Julia had replaced the old weatherworn black entry door with one of elegant and solid oak, her first concession to appearing the part she meant to play in her new surroundings. The doorway was recessed a foot or so and one step up from the sidewalk, somewhat protected from direct weather. Still, she had coated the new door with several coats of marine varnish for good measure. It gleamed in dappled morning sun as Julia turned the key.

Her office spaces were small, just a tiny waiting area opening to the right into a larger room she had shelved from floor to ceiling for her books. Her own office, to the left of the waiting area, had a Dutch door, split in the middle so that one could open the top, the bottom, or both. She had considered replacing it but was growing rather fond of its versatility, allowing her as much privacy in her office as she wished in any given situation. It also seemed just quaint and quirky enough to suit her in her new life.

She had brought her desk with her from the firm in Washington, one she had chosen with care to accommodate her penchant for spreading out paperwork. Its surface took half the space in her small office, leaving room for the two comfortable chairs she found at an estate sale the week after she arrived. She had painted the office herself to match the soft aqua stripes in the chair cushions.

The window behind her desk chair, as well as one in the shelved library, opened onto Church Street where the horse-drawn carriages passed regularly giving tourists the flavor of the City of Charleston.

Julia was reminded this morning of why she had chosen her library table, snugly centered between the four walls of books. Its surface was a thick, beveled oval piece of slightly smoked glass with flattened ends. Julia had discovered at a deposition several years earlier the value of seeing the hands and feet of those sitting around such a table. She could assess her clients and colleagues as they worked and talked, feet tapping, hands clutching the sides of the chair or worrying handkerchiefs or pockets.

Julia placed her briefcase on the corner of her desk, stood her umbrella in the corner behind the door, and started the coffee. At the old firm, coffee had been brought to her desk upon her arrival, along with several newspapers and her schedule for the day. Each situation had its rewards. Here, she would make the coffee in her own little Keurig on the antique table against the wall, ready for those who came in to wait or visit. Many of her first days in this office, she had drunk the whole pot herself during a day of organizing, learning local customs and willing a client to appear. Due in large part to Celia and Rose Pinckney's extensive circle of acquaintances, clients had come, most with small problems and sufficient money to pay Julia to solve them, a few with large, ongoing situations and the money to afford Julia's services well into the next decade. Just the previous month, after shepherding a million-dollar home sale to settlement, she had felt comfortable buying furniture for her living room at the beach house. For months, boxes had decorated that space while Julia settled in and vacillated day to day about what she could do, be and afford.

Looking around her now, she was pleased with the surroundings she had created. After their very late night, Quinn, Celia and Grandma Rose were not due until ten-thirty. There was time for Julia to get her thoughts in order. She would be among friends, but Quinn's dilemma was no laughing matter. Their discussion around the table this morning would be profoundly serious.

33

"Oh, my darling, you're up." Martha Howe was surprised and delighted to see her son seated upright in the chair beside his hospital bed. "Did we miss the doctor this morning?"

"No, Mother, but he's coming soon. The nurse said he wanted me to get out of the bed this morning." MacArthur Howe IV was looking more like himself. His eyes were clearer, and his color was returning to normal. "Hey, Dad."

The colonel shook his head approvingly. "They can't keep a good man down, can they, son. You're looking more like yourself this morning."

"Thanks, Dad. I'm not very steady on my feet, but the nurse said that's from blood loss and I'll get my strength back pretty quick.

"Your mother has to get over here the minute she's dressed. You know how she is. It's all I can do to get her out of this hospital for just a few hours of sleep. Now that she's seen for herself that you're doing well, maybe we can get a little breakfast downstairs."

You go on, George," Martha waved her hand, dismissing her husband. "All the nourishment I need is seeing my son looking well."

Just then the doctor appeared for his morning rounds, smiling when he opened the door to see his patient sitting up.

"Well, well," he said, opening the chart. "I see it's going quite nicely in here. Any nausea this morning, Mac?"

"No, sir. I'm kind of hungry. How about some bacon and eggs with a side of cheese grits and some biscuits?" Mac grinned.

"How about some Jell-O and a piece of dry toast?" The doctor grinned back. "Now tell me how you're really feeling. I see the nurses got you moving this morning. That's good. And I'm glad to see you're not running any fever to speak of. How about pain or dizziness?"

"I'm a little dizzy, mostly when I move, and I have quite a bit of pain, you know, where I was cut." His face reddened slightly as he answered the doctor, taking care not to look at his mother.

"Perfectly normal. We'll take a look at how it's healing when I come by this afternoon. Dr. Grant should be available then. And you can move around here in the room and even down the hall a little if you feel up to it. I can see you have plenty of company today, so I'll see you again later. Good to see you folks," the doctor nodded to the parents as he left the room.

The colonel followed him into the hall. "Might I have just a minute, doctor? I was wondering about something."

"Sure. What can I tell you?"

"Well, I don't know exactly how to ask this or who to contact, but is it possible that the nature of this attack on my son not be publicly known? I mean, is any of this medical information available to the public or to reporters?" The father was obviously ill at ease but compelled, nonetheless, to have answers.

"We here at the hospital don't talk to anyone without the permission of the patient, Colonel Howe. No one will hear it from us. You'd have to talk to law enforcement about what's public in their reports, but what's known in here stays in here." He put his hand on George's shoulder. "He's doing well; I'm very pleased."

The colonel, thankful for that reassurance, stepped back into his son's room. Mac's mother was behind the chair rubbing his neck and shoulders.

"I'm going to run down the street to the bakery and get some coffee for me and some tea and a bagel for your mother, son," he said. "And I don't see how a couple of fresh-baked pastries could do you any harm, do you?" He winked at his son. "Anything else you want me to bring back?"

"Thanks, Dad. A few doughnuts would be great."

"You're such a rascal, George," Martha chimed in. "And your son takes right after you. In a day or two, we'll be having those eggs and bacon at home in our own kitchen. You just go on, now, and hurry back.

And, George," she added before the door was closed, "that morning sun will be right in your eyes, so fasten your seat belt."

34

Morning light streamed through Rose's kitchen window, creating patterns on the old oak table top, shafts of sunlight exposing tiny particles in the wisps of steam from Rose's hot cup of tea. Celia had arrived a few minutes earlier, carrying a lidded paper cup full of Starbuck's double caramel latte and dressed in her usual stonewashed blue jeans. Looking every bit the Charleston lady in her lace-collared navy linen dress, Rose was ready for the trip to Julia's office to talk about little Quinn. She'd been up since just after dawn, pondering.

"Grandma, you're dressed to kill, and we're only going over to see Julia. We could have asked her to come here. Would you like me to do that?" But her words fell on ears tuned to another wavelength, one in which Rose heard the high-pitched, always grating voice of Adeline Ravenel: Adeline, who had become so tediously familiar over the past eighteen years, who had witlessly for all that time relinquished to Rose the great pleasure of her daughter's loving companionship, and who had the previous evening left her only child in a Charleston jail cell without apparent qualm.

"I've said for years one ought to have to qualify to be a mother," Grandma Rose snapped. "Do you suppose that woman is going about her business as usual this morning? Do you suppose she even wonders what happened to her daughter? Can she really be that, that..." Lost for a word that suited her, Rose paused, throwing her hands in the air, a blood vessel pulsing on the left side of her throat.

Celia reached across the table and placed her palm atop Rose's hand, thoroughly wrinkled and covered with gray and brown age spots. "Look, Grams, it's okay now, thanks to you. She's not sitting in jail; she's right upstairs here with us.

"Look what those two mothers—Mac's and Quinn's—have done," Rose mused, shaking her head, "each a prisoner of her own warped raising, I suppose. There is no greater power on earth than that of a mother over her child. I pray every day that I was just a good enough mother, just good enough."

"There will never be on this earth a better mother than you, Grandma. My mama and her brother were, oh, so fortunate to have you. So are we, and so is Quinn. Don't go getting all worked up over

68

something that wasn't your doing. Besides, we don't want Quinn hearing you talk like that, do we? It's about time to wake her."

Rose was not quite finished. "I've known these women for years, watched those babies grow up. Martha Howe made her son accountable for nothing, allowed him to believe he had some particular entitlement in life. I call it 'spoiling'. Adeline Ravenel made her daughter accountable for everything yet gave her none of the knowledge or skills to be so. She simply looked past that lovely child, worrying about how Quinn reflected on her.

"Look at the carnage each of these women left in her wake. Look at the damage done to this precious young woman due almost solely to the misguided mothering of those two women. I do declare that in my next life I shall oversee choosing who may have children. I do declare. And now I'm finished," Rose sighed heavily, glancing toward the staircase to assure herself that Quinn was not within earshot.

"Please don't fret," Celia pleaded, though she agreed thoroughly. "Let's go and talk with Julia. She's smart, and she's ours. She will help us work this out so Quinn can get on with her life. She's going to be a great teacher. She'll be a good mother someday too."

Rose wished she could somehow let it rest. "How did I see her the very next day and not know?" she sighed wearily, invoking new waves of review and remorse. "I saw her every day back then. I've been over and over it in my mind. How could I not have known? Something was amiss before she went away to school, but I let it go. Quinn went off to college alone with her burden when she needed me most. How can I criticize her own mother when I let her down so?"

"Okay, Grams, enough talk of water that's way under the bridge. You finish your tea, and I'm going to get Quinn. I heard the shower, so she's up. When she's ready, we'll go." Celia bounded up the stairs just like she did when she was a little girl, Rose thought.

"Hey, kiddo, are you decent?" Celia asked through the door. "We heard the shower. Can I come in?"

"Sure," came Quinn's reply. "I'm still in my undies. Do you mind?"

"Nothing I haven't seen before. If I just sit on your bed, maybe we could talk while you get ready?"

"You're not fixing to do a shrink routine on me, are you?" Quinn asked, poking her head out the bathroom door. "Just because you do that for a living doesn't mean you can play around in my head. No offense, of course! If I needed a shrink, you'd be the one I'd call."

"Gee, thanks."

"Just let me finish drying my hair. I could have used you yesterday while I was spending my day in a cell."

The hair dryer recommenced its hollow song, and Celia used the time to consider how to approach Quinn, a girl she had known most of Quinn's life. Julia's recounting of the story had caught Celia completely by surprise. Understanding what goes on in people's minds was indeed her daily work; she felt, like Grandma Rose, that she had failed. This story would certainly explain why Quinn had talked little of boys through her college years. It would explain the distance from her mother that she had not tried to bridge. But the capacity to hurt someone, to plan it and carry through and walk away, fit no part of her character Celia had ever seen. To see it and understand would be as important to her as any patient she had counseled.

The hair dryer stopped. Time was up.

Sitting down on the bed across from Celia, Quinn pulled on cotton shorts and a conservative white button shirt. Celia found herself analyzing everything. She took a deep breath and plunged in.

"Help me out here. I don't even know what to ask you. Julia told me you did this to MacArthur Howe, and she told me why. This is not shrink to patient; this is girlfriend to girlfriend. Since I taught you how to dress your dolls and play jacks, could you please explain it to me yourself?" She had spoken softly.

Quinn was quiet for a few moments. "Celie, I don't know how to explain this. I never expected to have to, don't you see? He did something to me, and I did something back. It's between him and me. Do you see that, Celie? He would not have understood crying and whining or public accusation. He understands what I did. He would have understood nothing less. I could have lived with nothing less. I never intended to speak of it again. I certainly never wanted Grandma Rose to know about it. How much does she know?"

"Honey, she's waiting downstairs now to go with us to see Julia. She knows the bare bones story, which is all any of us know, just what you told Julia last night. You know she would do anything for you. She will accept whatever you tell her, and so will I, so please tell us both the whole truth. Grandma is stronger than you and me together, and twice as smart. She loves you as though you were her own. You know that."

"Yes, I do know. That's why it's so hard. I don't want to let her down." Quinn's lips trembled, and she reached for a tissue.

"Just a few minutes ago, that's what she said about you," Julia confided. "She can't imagine why you didn't tell her what happened four years ago. Honestly, I can't either. You must know that if you had told her she would have ripped MacArthur Howe limb from limb, and probably his parents too."

"Well," Quinn smiled slightly, "I kind of already did that." Her eyes met Celia's, and they laughed, once again mischievous little girls sharing secrets.

"Look, Celie, I took a few psychology courses myself in the last couple of years, and I see what happened back then, although I'm still not very objective about it. I went home and told Mama. She acted like it was my fault. Somewhere in me, I must have known better, even then, but after she made me feel so ashamed, I never told anyone else. I could not have endured it if you and Grandma Rose were ashamed of me too. I showered until all the hot water was gone, but I don't think I started to feel clean again for about two years."

Celia slid across the bed and put her arms around Quinn. "Oh, Honey, I could have helped you. I would have killed him for you." Both were crying now.

Quinn pulled her face back for a minute from Celia's shoulder, meeting her eyes. "I thought about that too," she said.

35

The pace of Julia's last couple of days was reminiscent of life in Washington. Wishing she was walking in the surf, she was daydreaming when her office door opened, jingling the bell she'd attached to its handle. Expecting Celia and Quinn, she was surprised to see Detective Legare.

"I hope you don't mind my just coming by," he spoke tentatively. "I wanted to tell you myself about Reg Fallon, unless you've already heard."

"You said last night you were letting him go. Did you need an excuse to come by and see me?" she teased. But the detective did not seem in a good humor.

"Can I sit down?" he asked.

"Of course. Do you want some coffee?"

"Thanks. I could use some invigoration." He let Julia go to the outer room to get it. "I think it'll take more than caffeine to perk me up this morning, though."

"Okay, what's up?" She set the cup in front of Sonny. "I've got Quinn Ravenel coming by shortly. Her bad fortune is good news for Reg, though, right? Talk about being in the wrong place at the wrong time!"

"Well, McKenzie, Reg Fallon seems to have hit the jackpot in that department." He paused and rubbed the new growth of stubble on his chin. Julia waited, puzzled at Sonny's mood. He looked up, meeting her gaze. "There was an accident last night. The car I sent to take Reg home was hit head-on by a pickup truck crossing the median. The other driver was drunk. The officer's dead. And Reg is in surgery. I just saw his mom at the hospital."

Julia was stunned. "Is he going to be okay?"

"I don't know. He has multiple injuries. I'll keep checking on him every couple of hours." Sonny got up from the chair. "I just thought I should tell you before you heard it on the news."

Julia got up too, coming around the desk to put her hand on his arm. "I'm sorry, Sonny. Did you know the officer well?"

"He's only been here a couple of months. I had to call his parents in Wisconsin. They're on their way. I should have driven the Fallon boy myself. It was after midnight when they left the station."

"This is horrible, Sonny, but it isn't your fault. You can't take responsibility for every cop out in a car doing his job."

"Reg Fallon shouldn't have been in that car at all. He shouldn't have been in jail. I should have put it all together quicker. Anyway..."

The door opened again, and this time it was Celia, Rose and Quinn. They were ready to plan a strategy to extricate Quinn from a quagmire that had just deepened. The ripples were ever growing, if not in a legal sense, then as consequences of one's decision affecting another, and another, and then another. Julia had never given much thought to life's chains of events and the shadows they cast. She would do so soon, she thought, very soon.

36

The day had not yet heated fully. Out on the sidewalk at the corner of Broad and Church Streets, Sonny opted for a walk down Broad.

A little time feeding the pigeons, he thought, might help his perspective. It sure beat going back to the hospital to see if the Fallon boy was still alive. He stopped at a Broad Street deli for bread, and seated himself on a bench in Washington Park facing the side of City Hall, wishing himself temporarily invisible. The pigeons came immediately to see if he had food, bobbing themselves closer with each pass, very little apprehension remaining for people. They were too well fed to maintain a healthy wariness.

Sonny had always enjoyed the quiet of this spot. On the sidewalk, just yards away, busy people and inquisitive tourists bustled about, but here behind the tall wrought-iron fence, birds and squirrels seemed to sense what Sonny did: peace. From this bench, he could see the ladies weaving and selling sweetgrass baskets by the Post Office steps, somehow a comforting sight. The tourists were as likely to buy from them here as at their stalls in the open-air market. This was, it was said, the Four Corners of Law: the Post office on one corner, the Courthouse, City Hall and St. Michael's Church occupying the other three. But here in this small park around City Hall, where thick, gnarled branches of liveoaks wound their way among the leaves of three-story-tall palmetto fronds, nature prevailed.

Not a cloud sailed the sky above St. Michael's, it's weathervane indicating a breeze from the ocean. How many times had that vane been replaced, Sonny wondered, since George Washington attended services on this corner in that very sanctuary. There had been fires and hurricanes and war. Confederate loyalists had painted the steeple black in an effort to obscure it in the night sky and protect it from shelling by the Union Army. Sherman's troops had stolen the bells right out of the steeple near the war's end. But here it stood, having withstood, its white spire looking sound and stately against the sapphire sky of a Southern midsummer.

Two of the pigeons had taken a perch on the iron arm at the other end of the bench, and another was nearly on Sonny's foot, waiting none too patiently. Their beady little eyes were all fixed expectantly on him. If the mayor came out and caught him there feeding these birds, he would be toast; the whole squad room would know by tomorrow. But what the hell, he decided. He was seeking a little solace, and he found it here. It had been a somber morning, an unsettling few days, and he deserved some momentary foolishness. Life is short, he had discovered, and it would never be long enough for him to part with it willingly.

After a few slices were broken to bite-size and tossed, Sonny got up and passed on the remainder of the bread to a blonde-haired little girl who had been watching with her mother from a bench across the park. Mother prompted a "thank you", but the excitement in the child's eyes was enough. She took over the pigeons, and Sonny turned down Meeting Street toward Queen, going nowhere in particular.

Passing the Mills House, he waved to the doorman who had stood there as long as Sonny could remember, still straight-backed and enjoying his job. Trying to picture himself at that age, Sonny thought lovingly of his own parents. He would have to visit them soon, though he still did not understand their retirement to Florida. He would get a new deep sea fishing rod and reel and retire, if at all, to his boat right where it was on the Ashley River.

The spire of St. Philip's now loomed directly overhead, darker and taller than St. Michael's. In this churchyard and the section across the street lay the remains of signers of the Declaration of Independence and the Constitution. There was the tomb of Vice-President John C. Calhoun and, further back, that of DuBose Heyward who authored "Porgy". Crossing the street, he entered the annex to the old cemetery. Souls rested here, he mused, right in the center of things just as they had lived, enjoying the ambience of the city and the passing of tourists and horse-drawn carriages. On the stones were the Old Southern names of Moultrie, Pinckney, Rutledge, Guerry, Rhett, Gadsden. But the one that drew him, now as always, was just off the street, the resting place of one Edward Kriegsmann Pritchard. It was a large stone cross, gray and unembellished save the engraving: "Every day, take time to think of the many blessings for which we should be humbly grateful."

Sonny had always been impressed that Mr. Pritchard, rest his soul, had left for the living not some trite comment upon his own life but a reminder to grasp and savor the moments we are granted. However troubled he was on this morning, he mused, Sonny had the good fortune to live here and the good sense to appreciate it.

Taking his cue, he looked again at the steeple. A few puffy white clouds now drifted above it, typical of an August midday. His stomach growled, complaining that the morning's coffee was not enough. He would count his blessings, he thought, on his short walk back to the unmarked cruiser.

37

Willa had spent a few minutes in the hospital chapel, pleading with God, making offers she hoped He could not refuse.

"I guess this is my reminder that things can always get worse," she said to her son, unconscious and heavily bandaged in the bed. "If I'd known this was ahead for us, I'd most sure have told you to stay right in that jail. And if we gets outa here alive, there ain't nothin' goin' ever get me down again, Reggie. Nothin' ever, you hear? Dear Lord, please save my baby. He's a good boy."

Willa kept both her hands wrapped around Reg's left hand when she wasn't wiping away her own tears. His other hand held the needle conducting a life-sustaining intravenous drip. Lights on a bank of machines monitored his breathing and heart rate, and the nurse came by every fifteen minutes since they brought Reg from the surgery to check the draining of fluid from around his brain. Willa was most frightened by the tube emerging from the massive white head bandage, fearing in some irrational way that his life was seeping away into the stainless-steel receptacle.

She was just getting accustomed to the steady, rhythmic sound of the machines when one of them emitted an alarming beep, setting free in her the unremitting panic she had barely managed to control for hours. It brought a nurse immediately, who assured Willa that the sound was a malfunction of the machine, not of Reg's body. Once again, the nurse offered a pill to calm the mother's anxiety, but she declined. The nurse made a note to take it up with the doctor; Willa was too near the edge, poor thing, and there were already too many patients to care for. It was not unheard of for the attending loved one to be survived by the original patient.

Out at the nurses' station, Sonny was asking about the patient as well, bracing himself for the answer. The nurse assured him that young Mr. Fallon was doing as well as could be expected, but that Sonny could not go into the room. Sonny was doubly relieved. He wanted Reg to be well; he did not want to see him.

On the other hand, he could check on the Howe boy while he was here. It would be worth a trip to see if Mac had recalled anything helpful since they last talked. He took the stairs.

As Sonny opened the door from the stairwell, George Howe was coming from the elevator. "Good afternoon, Detective," the colonel greeted him. "I was going to call you, so I'm glad you stopped by. Any progress toward unraveling this mess?"

"I wanted to see if Mac remembered anything since we last talked. And I can share a couple of things with y'all, but let's talk in the room, shall we?"

The two men opened the door to find Martha and Mac playing a game of rummy. Mac was back in the bed, but he looked well enough, and his mother was positively beaming over his recovery.

"Well, Son, you are looking better by the hour," George said. "I assume you're beating your mother at cards again?"

"I thought I'd let her win this one, Dad. She's had a hard day keeping me company. How was the smoke?"

George nodded.

"You're a smoker, colonel?" Sonny asked. "I'm surprised."

"Yes, I can't give them up," George replied. "Martha's been after me for years, but we all have our little vices, don't we? I had to go outside the building to have one. The whole world frowns on us smokers these days."

"Well, I'm glad my addiction is fishing," Sonny smiled. "I wanted to come by and check on you, Mac, and see if you remembered any little thing at all that might be helpful to us. Sometimes just one detail can be the key."

"I thought you'd made an arrest, Detective," the colonel said. "You said you were holding that Fallon boy. What more do you need?"

"Fallon?" Mac questioned. "You don't mean Reg Fallon?"

"Yes, we did question him," Sonny said, "but we've got another lead we're following pretty closely. That's why I wanted to talk with you again, Mac, in case you'd thought of anything at all."

"Dad, why didn't you tell me that?" Mac asked his father. "I don't get it. Why would Reg Fallon..."

"Sometimes it's just bad genes, son," the father interrupted. "The boy could play ball, but he obviously lacked character. You can look at a boy's raising and tell about these things."

"Actually, Mr. Howe, we've let the Fallon boy go. We arrested another suspect last night, and I wanted to ask your son about her."

"Her?" both Mac and his father asked in unison?

"Do you have any acquaintance with Quinn Ravenel?" Sonny asked, watching the young man's face.

"What?"

"Quinn Ravenel. Apparently, you went to the same high school."

"You're not saying you suspect a young woman of this, are you, Detective?" Martha injected. "That's absurd. There isn't a young lady in this town who would do such a thing."

"I remember her," Mac said slowly, revealing little in his facial expression or his eyes. "She lived just down the street from us since we were little. She was a quiet little kid, had no father. I think Ms. Pinckney might have adopted her or taken her in or something. But she was just a scrawny kid."

"You've got to do better than that, Detective," the colonel interjected, "or I'll have to go by and talk to the Chief myself. I could accept that the Fallon boy had just reverted to the behavior of his roots, but this is preposterous. No girl could sneak up and..." He didn't know how to finish. The unthinkable had just become more so. This was not acceptable. "My boy is an officer in the United States Army."

Sonny remained still for a few moments, letting the information settle upon everyone in the room, watching. No one spoke. He looked at MacArthur Howe. Mac looked at him. If Sonny was expecting signs, they were not forthcoming.

"I hope none of this nonsense is leaking to the press, Detective." The colonel finally found his voice again. "I was meaning to ask you what those vultures could find out from you. We certainly don't want anything like this printed in the local papers. I'm going to go right down and talk to the Chief about the problem of the media. Do you understand me, Detective?"

Sonny understood. "If there's nothing else you want to talk about, Mac, then I'll be going on back to the station myself. You know where to find me." And he left.

38

Julia hugged all three women, recalling the last embrace she shared right here. She and Celia had laughed together then, not realizing what a lightness there was in the moment. When we are least aware, Julia thought, moments when we take for granted the bliss of our own ignorance, counting it security, fortune is at work deciding our destiny. Each of us, some of the time, is at the center when that die is cast. Others are on the fringes, affected largely or slightly. Sometimes, it is hard to tell the difference.

Julia noted how pretty her friend still was, her complexion glowing. Celia always covered her face in the sun, and her hat collection was extensive. Removing today's choice, straw with a flowered ribbon, she shook out her hair, a cross between red and blonde, depositing the hat on Julia's coat rack and both her sandals on the floor at its base. Celia wore shoes only when necessary and was well on her way to convincing Julia to do the same. Julia kept on her shoes this morning, as did Rose and Quinn, as they took seats at Julia's table. A pitcher of lemonade with four glasses sat at the table's center, along with a box of fresh Krispy Kreme. Her legal pad, favorite pen and a few file folders were piled by her chair.

"Julia, you're looking wonderful, as usual," Rose began, reaching out to Julia across the table. "I'm looking forward to seeing you tomorrow evening."

Julia tried to switch to her brain's scheduling track.

"Oh, I do hope you're coming," Rose went on. "You remember, we're getting a few friends together to discuss the plans for next year's Spoleto Festival. It's nothing formal, dear, and I would love for you to meet some of the people who will be there. You just never know when some young man might catch your eye," she added, with a twinkle in her own.

The three other women smiled and shook their heads. Rose was infamous for, among other things, her incorrigible matchmaking. More than a few young Charleston couples had toasted her at their wedding receptions.

"Okay, on that note, let's get down to the situation at hand," Julia suggested, uncapping her pen. "Even though it was an exorbitant amount, I think we're extremely fortunate to have gotten Quinn released on bond. I was somewhat concerned that the judge would refuse to release her at all pending at least a preliminary hearing. So, we must be very careful to do nothing to cause that bond to be revoked."

"What does that mean?" Quinn asked.

"Well, we just want to be very cooperative at every turn, comply with the district attorney's requests for information when possible, not leave town, not rock the boat."

"Should we be very worried?" Rose asked. "I don't wish to say it aloud, but could Quinn go to prison?" She looked at the girl beside her. "I'm sorry, dear. I don't mean to frighten you, but let's be realistic at the start. How serious is this, Julia?"

"I don't like to advise people to 'worry'," Julia responded. "We should be appropriately concerned. What's happened is very serious in the eyes of the law. I think one of the first things we should do is consider bringing in an attorney who specializes in criminal defense. I will do everything I can, but this is not my area of expertise, as I told you, Quinn. It's your life we're talking about, and we should use the best resources we can find. I have a couple of people in mind, but I thought maybe one of you would have a suggestion. I know you're acquainted with everyone, Miss Rose. Is there someone you'd recommend?"

"Oh, my, let me think." Rose pursed her lips and closed her eyes.

"But wait," Quinn chimed in. "I don't want someone else, Miss McKenzie. I told you what happened. I don't want to go over and over it, especially with a male person. Most of the lawyers are men, you know, especially the ones who defend criminals."

As serious as the circumstance was, Celia had to laugh. "Sweetie, I swear you were born with attitude, and I just love it. But you do see what Jules is saying, don't you? It's not about what we think. We love you. It's about making a judge—right, Jules? —understand it."

"I think maybe we could call Jordan Guerry," Grandma Rose offered. "He's a good, gentle man, but I know he does criminal work on a regular basis. What do you think, Celia? You know Jordan?"

"I think we should let Julia meet with him and explain the situation," Celia agreed. "If Julia needs him, then you'll give him a chance, won't you?" she looked at Quinn.

"I suppose."

39

Julia knew Jordan Guerry. He had a reputation as a stickler for detail and for winning his cases. She thought him mild-mannered and unassuming, unlike some of the others who had none too subtly tried to intimidate her away from what was clearly a boys' club. She found it amusing and somewhat of a challenge, a game she could win simply by hanging around and carefully claiming her measure of success. Celia was delighted to explore with her friend the old closed circle, seeing it from a local perspective. Her perceptions of her town, her little southern society, were stretched and reshaped by seeing it through Julia's eyes.

Jordan Guerry was born here, as were his parents and his grandparents; he was automatically 'in'. When Julia left word that she wished to talk with him, he called back almost immediately. She offered to come to his office; he was available around five o'clock.

She arrived promptly at five, just as the receptionist for the firm was leaving for the day. She showed Julia to Jordan Guerry's office, a large, masculine room with lots of mahogany and leather. He came around the desk to extend his hand, and Julia shook it. "Sit down, please," he said. "Can I get you anything—coffee or a soda?"

"No, thanks," Julia answered. "I won't take a lot of your time. Have you heard about the attack on MacArthur Howe a couple of days ago? I know there was a small article in the paper, but not many details were released."

"Yes, I did hear talk of that at the courthouse this morning. It piqued my curiosity."

"Well, that's good, because I was hoping you might be interested in being associated to represent the attacker. Her family called me, but I don't do enough criminal work to feel comfortable handling this alone."

"Who are the family? Are you at liberty to tell me?"

"Oh, of course. Rose Pinckney and her granddaughter Celia Rutledge are, for all practical purposes, her family. I tend to forget that they are, in fact, not related. But that is another story, and the one at hand is complicated enough."

"Did you say 'her'?" Jordan asked.

"Yes. Quinn Ravenel is her name. She admits to the attack, but has not made a formal confession. I told the judge at the bond hearing that it is our intention to plead 'not guilty'. That's where you come in, if you will. It is Quinn's contention that MacArthur Howe raped her and that she was meting out her measure of justice."

Jordan Guerry's eyes widened slightly. "Was there a charge of rape?"

"She never reported it."

"Because?"

"You know the standard reasons. She was ashamed and blamed herself, although I have no reason to think it wasn't rape in the purest sense without any provocation on her part whatsoever."

"Is it too late to get any kind of physical or forensic evidence to support her rape claim?"

"It happened four years ago."

"Four years?"

Julia smiled because his surprise was so genuine. It was an improbable scenario, she knew. She had tried to put it in perspective since first hearing it herself, but it was difficult. "I know you'll want to hear the story from her, Jordan. Shall I tell her that we can meet, the three of us, at your convenience? Then you can decide about associating on the case."

"Of course, of course." He flipped the page of his appointment calendar to the following day, running his finger quickly down the page. "I'm free tomorrow between noon and three. Could we get together then?"

"I'll make that work," Julia answered, getting up to go. "Thanks again for your time, and I hope we can work together on this. I'll call your office in the morning about the time. Shall we come here, or would you rather come to my office?"

"I'll be waiting for a jury to come in, so if you don't mind, let's meet here."

Jordan walked Julia to the outer door of the offices. She thanked him again, wondering if this was the man who could help her weave a defense, wondering, more to the point, if there was any defense to make.

40

Julia answered her phone on the first ring. "Hey, Jules," Celia said. "I just wanted to see if you're okay after all that heavy stuff today."

"I was going to call you shortly," Julia responded, plopping into her softest chair, removing her shoes. "I just got home, and I'm beat."

"If you'd answered your phone, I would have invited you to come to the house for dinner. The girls are dying to see you and tell you all their camp stories. You can't be a favorite aunt and not be hanging around here, you know."

"What was for dinner?"

"Hamburgers on the grill, but that's not the point. It wasn't about the food. It was about the company."

Julia was smiling. "Could I be invited for tomorrow night?" she asked.

"You're not only invited, but I think it's a command performance for both of us at Gram's, remember? It's her Spoleto thing with Joe Riley and company. She really wants you to come. So how about pizza with us and then we can dress together here. Just bring something in with you in the morning, like that little yellow dress with the strap on one shoulder and the little white flowers."

"I'm too tired to think about it right now, but after a good night's sleep, maybe. I saw Jordan Guerry this afternoon."

81

"And?"

"He wants to meet with Quinn tomorrow afternoon. I haven't called her yet, but I'll do it next."

"What do you think of him? I didn't want to ask in front of Quinn and Grams."

"He's a nice enough guy, impeccable reputation, ugly brown socks with his black shoes."

"Jules, you're becoming quite bad, and I love it. Last year, you wouldn't have noticed if he was barefoot. You're coming along nicely." Both women laughed. "So is he acceptable for what we need? Could you work with him?"

"Sure. It will be interesting to see how he approaches Quinn's defense. I'll let you know tomorrow after he talks with her. How was Quinn after y'all left my office? And how is Grandma Rose? Is she getting through this okay?"

"I'll tell you later about my conversation with Quinn, and we'll just keep an eye on Grams. She can't understand why Quinn didn't tell her way back then."

"There's so much I don't understand that it makes me tired, Cele. But tomorrow is another day."

"I love you, Jules. Good thing you're brilliant and talented and that you went to law school."

"Yeah, yeah, so I'll call you tomorrow after the meeting "

"Don't forget the dress."

"Bye, Cele."

THURSDAY

41

Julia expected the meeting between Quinn and Jordan Guerry to go well. It would quell her uneasiness about this case to have onboard a practitioner whose every day was filled with the nuts and bolts of criminal defense. It would be one thing to practice her skills on a petty thief or a traffic law violator. It was quite another to have the life of this young woman in her hands.

Having used the morning to return calls and rearrange her schedule, she picked up Quinn at Rose's house just before one o'clock. Rose waved from her front window as they drove away. She had asked Quinn to remind Julia of the get-together that evening.

"Are you going to be there?" Julia asked Quinn.

"Spoleto is great fun," she said, "but I just want to enjoy it, not plan it. I'm not ready for politics and city business. I'd rather iron or clean toilets." She wrinkled her nose and smiled. "What I'll probably really do is read in my room in Gram's upstairs and then help her clean up when everyone is gone. She insists I stay with her for the moment, at least at night. I don't mind."

"It must be nice to have someone like Rose in your life, kind of like having a fairy godmother."

"I've thought of her that way myself. I wish she were my real grandmother or, better yet, my real mom. Can you imagine having a mother like Grandma Rose?"

"I've tried," Julia answered, "but that's another story. You and I will have a conversation about mothers one day soon, Quinn. I think it would be good for both of us."

They parked in the small lot behind the offices of Comings and Guerry and got out onto the sweltering pavement. "Why don't you come out to the beach house this weekend?" Julia suggested. "You and I could get to know each other. Celie tells me you're a beach person."

"I love it. That's partly why I wanted to live back here again. Grams used to take me all the time when I was little. She would sit under a big umbrella, and I would lay right in the surf and let it wash over me. Celia likes her sunscreen, and I like my tan. I'd love to come out."

"Good, it's settled then. You can decide if you want to invite Celie and the girls or if it should just be you and me. If you don't mind being the guinea pig, I'll try to cook us something."

Cool air washed over them when they opened the door to the Guerry offices. Jordan was talking with the receptionist. "Good afternoon, ladies," he smiled. "Come on back. I was just asking Connie not to bother us unless my jury comes back."

"Jordan, this is Quinn Ravenel," Julia introduced her young client, watching the other lawyer assess her in light of what he knew of the case.

"Of course," he said, extending his hand warmly. "Can I have Connie bring us something to drink?"

"I could use one more cup of coffee," Julia answered, looking at Quinn.

"Nothing for me, thanks. I'm fine," she said.

They took seats, and Connie brought the coffee for Julia and Jordan. He prepared a pad and pen, and Julia noted that his socks today were black.

"Okay, Miss Ravenel, why don't you just tell me what happened. Julia gave me the basic facts, so you tell me the story as you see it, if you don't mind."

Quinn did not look ready. She glanced at Julia, as if for support, taking a deep breath. "Before I went away to college four years ago, Mac Howe raped me, Mr. Guerry. So the other night I crawled in his bedroom window and cut off his penis. Well, I guess I didn't cut it completely off. Julia tells me they've sewn him back together at the hospital. If he had shot me, I would have taken the gun and shot him back. But he didn't. He raped me. I considered for a long time how to repay him in kind, and this is as close as I could come. There doesn't seem any way exactly for a woman to repay a rape. I did the best I could."

Julia noticed as Quinn talked that Guerry's hand had left the desktop and crept to his lap. He was not taking notes. He remained silent for a minute, but Quinn did not continue. That, it seemed, was her story.

"Yes, well," he cleared his throat, "it's quite a stretch to connect your recent action to a four-year-old unreported crime. You never reported the alleged rape to the police?"

"No, sir."

"Did you talk about it to any of your friends or a teacher or family member?"

"I told only my mother, and she wasn't helpful. I told no one else, and I never intended to."

"I don't suppose you kept anything that would evidence a sexual assault, something like a piece of soiled clothing?"

"No, sir. I threw everything away the next day."

"Did you ever date Mac Howe or have contact with him socially?"

"We never dated. He didn't live far from me, and we went to the same high school. Lots of girls liked him. I never particularly did."

"Would you have suspected him of that sort of behavior?"

"Absolutely not."

"When you thought about wanting justice, why didn't you go to the police? There is no statute of limitations on rape as a crime, you know. You could have filed a charge against him last week instead of taking matters into your own hands."

"Matters were always in my own hands. After my mother told me not to mention it again, it was my problem. I knew I was alone with it, and I isolated myself from it until I grew up enough and gained the strength to deal with it. And now I've done that."

"Miss Ravenel, in the eyes of the law, what you're saying isn't reasonable. You're telling me that you thought about this for four years?"

"Yes, sir."

"And you gave considerable thought to the ways in which you might take your revenge?"

"Yes, sir. Considerable."

"You were away at college during this time. How did you do in school?"

"My grade point average is a straight 4.0. I studied."

Julia could not tell where Jordan was going with this line of questions, but he was not making her more comfortable that a case could be made in Quinn's defense. Quinn had not wanted to come here. Though obviously tense, she seemed fairly at ease with her answers, straightforward with Guerry as she had been with Julia. With no hesitation, she acknowledged her act without translating it to misconduct of any nature. Normally, this mindset would be interpreted as sociopathic. Julia watched Jordan Guerry's face carefully.

"Fortunately for you, Miss Ravenel, intellectual capacity is not an indicator of mental stability. That has been demonstrated in any number of cases, some of them my own. I assume, Julia, that you are proposing an insanity defense here, and I would certainly concur. I see no other way to go. Is that your thinking?"

Startled that they had progressed to this point so quickly, Julia did not immediately respond. Quinn did.

"Are you saying that you think I'm nuts, Mr. Guerry?" she asked, having quickly processed his question to Julia.

"Don't take offense, Miss Ravenel. I'm talking of a defense under the law that I think might be our best option. It's the defense that claims you did not understand the rightness or wrongness of your actions at the time you did them, that under the pressure—in this case, long-term, bottled-up distress—of dealing with the rape, your emotional stability was compromised."

"I'm not going to say I'm crazy." Quinn's voice rose just slightly. She looked to Julia for confirmation. "There's no way I'm going to say I'm crazy."

Julia knew she had to intervene. "I really wanted to hear your opinion before we made any decisions, Jordan," she said. "Frankly, I was not rushing to construct a defense until we talked with you. I've explained to Quinn that criminal defense is not my specialty." She turned to Quinn. "Do you understand what Mr. Guerry is saying? He's not saying you're crazy; he's just saying we should consider claiming that the rape pushed you over the edge so that in the moment—just that one moment—you were disconnected from the rational part of your mind which would have stopped you. Is that substantially correct, Jordan?"

"Yes. The prosecutor will take issue, of course, with the fact that you had those four intervening years. It's a legal defense, not a personal criticism, Miss Ravenel."

"So after we say in court that I'm legally insane, then I can walk out and teach kindergarten?"

Guerry was somewhat taken aback. "I'm not sure you'll be teaching kindergarten under any circumstance. The charge itself may prevent that. If you were the parent of a five-year-old child, wouldn't this give you pause?"

It was Julia's sense that this meeting was going nowhere good. She couldn't read the expression on Quinn's face. It could be anger, or she might burst into tears. Neither reaction would help her with Jordan Guerry. Julia was trying to conceal her own unexpected anger at Guerry's categorical approach to Quinn's dilemma when the buzzer on his intercom reprieved her. He pushed the button. "Yes, Connie?"

"I'm sorry to interrupt, Mr. Guerry, but the jury is in. Shall I tell the judge you'll be right over?"

"Yes, thank you, Connie."

He looked across the desk at Julia and Quinn as though he too was relieved. "I apologize, but I do have to get right over to the courthouse. Why don't you discuss my recommendation with your client, Julia, and get back to me at your convenience? I'm at your disposal if you'd like to talk again." He turned to Quinn. "It was a pleasure to meet you, Miss Ravenel. Whether or not we talk again, I wish you the best of luck with your defense."

Quinn said nothing at all.

42

Celia's house smelled wonderful when Julia opened the door. They no longer knocked at each other's homes. Julia was family here. "I thought you said we were having pizza," she called out. "This doesn't smell like pizza."

Two girls were upon her as she crossed toward the kitchen. "Aunt Julia," they squealed.

"Baby girls," she squealed in return, though neither of the girls was a baby. They had grown up, each a young beauty in her own way.

"Hey, ladies, be careful of Auntie Julia's pretty dress," Celia cautioned as she poked her head around the corner. The yellow dress was hanging across Julia's shoulder, in danger of being crumpled. "Here," Celia said, wiping her hands on a dishcloth, "let me take it." She ran up the stairs, hanging the dress across the banister at the top while the girls settled around Julia on the sofa.

"Okay, girls, you tell Julia all your stories and show her your pictures from camp. I know I said pizza, Jules, but my last patient cancelled, so I came home and made crab cakes. How does that sound, maybe with a little cole slaw?"

"It sounds divine," Julia replied. I haven't eaten since my banana and yogurt this morning. I'm famished. Where's Pete?"

"He's on his way."

The girls piled onto the sofa on either side of Julia, both talking at once. One of the distinct pleasures of living here was the frequent company of these adolescent women. Tyrney was eleven and Katey thirteen, both blue-eyed with their mother's strawberry blonde hair. Julia had relished her front-row seat in their childhood, so unlike her own. It was a carefree existence, packed with play and pretend and trips to the beach. How did one call ahead from pre-life and order someone like Celia for a mother, she wondered.

Julia always felt at home in Celia's house. She and Pete had bought this one just last year about the time Julia moved to Charleston. It was a traditional brick two-level on a corner lot surrounded by liveoaks and mature shrubs, and Celia's way with gardening was the envy of her new neighbors. She had pruned and clipped and transplanted, and her little corner lawn was now a beautiful display of purples and lavenders mixed with yellow and white. Even her simple foliage plants were a lovely combination of greens and textures. People and plants, Julia mused, were both coaxed to their best by Celia Rutledge.

Cooking, of course, had become one of Celia's passions as well, evidenced by the tempting aroma emanating from her kitchen on most days. Her cookbooks now had a bookshelf of their own. It was such homey pleasure to be in this house, so full of love and warmth.

"Hi, honeys, I'm home." Pete was announcing his arrival to all his girls. "You too, Jules," he added. "Smells good."

Celia and Pete were high school sweethearts, one of those happy-ending stories still unfolding according to script. Celia had known throughout her college years that Pete was the one, and he had apparently been as certain. They were married a year after Celia's graduation, by which time Pete was like a brother to Julia. Tyrney had not been born until several years later. They had begun to worry that children were not in their future, but after Celia called to tell Julia she had made an appointment with a fertility specialist, her lingering case of flu was diagnosed as morning sickness.

Since then, and especially after Katey's birth two years later, Celia had struggled with added pounds that did not suit her. Her love of cooking did not help. But she was in fact just softly round and had grown into an earthy girlishness that suited her perfectly. Her thick, strawberry-blond hair, cut just below her earlobes, added to that youthful glow she still maintained, not to mention the year-round sprinkling of freckles.

"Y'all come, now," Celia called to them from the kitchen. "The biscuits are just coming out of the oven. Please wash your hands, girls."

The two trailed into the main floor half-bath to get ready for dinner. Julia washed her own hands in the kitchen, letting the sounds and smells of this house wash over her. Celia was humming along with a Floyd Cramer sound track as she put the biscuits on the table.

"Those girls are just between being children and being way smarter than you and me," Julia marveled. "They got to ride horses at camp and swim in a real lake, I'm told. They made it seem infinitely more exciting than any old ocean."

"They'll be right out to your house to swim in that boring old ocean at the next opportunity, honey. But it is nice to break up their summers with a change of scenery. This is the second summer they seem to be chatting about the boys who are there. I'm very confident about the supervision there, but it's making me a little crazy."

Julia smiled. "Knowing all the answers because you're an expert in shrinking heads doesn't help a bit when it's your own kids, does it? You're going to turn that hair gray between now and when those girls get married and settle down."

"Don't I know it, Jules. I see now how easy it was when they were three and five and were awed by Barbies and a playhouse. I have so many pictures all disorganized and saved on different devices. I need to organize them so the girls can have them for posterity, but who has time for that?"

"I'll help you," Julia offered. "We can do that during one of those long, cold nights when there's a foot of snow on the ground."

"Snow?" Pete queried as he came into the kitchen. "You girls cooking up plans for a winter holiday to a place I can't afford?"

Both women laughed. Pete, an architect whose work was in demand throughout the South, could afford most anything Celia wanted. His success allowed her to curtail her work hours to concentrate on patients of her choosing and spend more time with the girls.

Dinner was a casual affair, interrupted once by the telephone—a boy for Katey—and again by one of the door-to-door salesmen who so annoyed Celia. Nevertheless, everyone finished the meal too full for dessert, and Pete volunteered to clean up the kitchen so that Julia and Celia could have the time to get ready for Grandma Rose's party. He avoided these events when possible and enjoyed using the girls as his excuse, choosing to spend his social time on the golf course.

"Okay," Julia said, toweling off after a quick but refreshing shower, "now tell me about your talk with Quinn."

Celia had showered first and was half dressed and looking for the right shoes for her blue linen dress. Since her shoe collection almost matched that of her hats, this could be quite a search. "If the girls would stop playing dress-up in my closet, it would be a lot easier to find two of my own shoes that match," she called out from behind the closet door.

"If you only had a few pairs," Julia retorted, "it would be a lot easier to find two shoes that match. For a person who's barefoot whenever possible, your closet is especially puzzling."

"If you were fat like me, you'd understand why I prefer calling the attention down to my feet. They're the only things that aren't chubby, so I have to enjoy them."

"Wouldn't a good therapist tell you that those few pounds you've kept don't make you 'fat'?" Julia called back.

"Very funny. Here, I found it. I did have a good talk with Quinn. It was hard at first, but then she opened up and I think we both felt better."

"What's your take on all of this? Jordan Guerry made it very clear that he thinks an insanity defense is the only way to go, and so did someone I called at my old firm in D.C. this afternoon. Quinn says she won't do it."

"There's nothing crazy about Quinn Ravenel. She was always the most grounded little child I knew, much more so at that age than either of my own, bless their hearts. She never expected things, you know, always seemed so happy just to be treated well. I wish you knew her better, but I guess I've been selfish hogging your time for my own girls. I've loved her like a little baby sister for years, so I feel as bad as Grams not to have known about this."

"Can you help her sort it out now?" Julia appealed to her friend. "Can you help me, if I take this on, to be sure she comes across as just what you said: normal and grounded?"

"Absolutely. I intend to spend enough time with her to get to the very bottom of her little heart. I can't let this haunt her the rest of her life. Will you hand me that hairspray?"

Celia was nearly ready now, and Julia was fully dressed and combing her hair. "I want to help her," Julia continued. "I feel a closeness to her because of her mother. It's my mother too, you know? We both have that hollow space that affects our lives. When I called her mother about the bond hearing, even I was shocked."

"I hadn't recognized that connection you two have," Celia admitted, surprised. "You're good, kiddo."

"Yeah, maybe, but I don't know that I'm experienced enough with this complex a matter to maneuver straight upstream against the advice of people who know criminal law."

"I don't know about experience, Jules, but I know you're smart enough. And I know Quinn feels good about having you in her corner. You don't feel pressured to defend her because of our friendship, do you? I understand your reluctance. It's a real mess."

"That's not it at all. I suppose I'm afraid of failing both you and Quinn."

"Oh, well, if it's just about fear, then let's go for it," Celia said, turning to face Julia and taking her by the shoulders. "I'll do anything I can to help. It's been awhile since we took on a challenge together. Remember the hamsters?"

Little by cumulative little, both women dissolved into laughter. "We're going to make our mascara run," Julia finally managed. "Stop now."

"Are you girls decent?" Pete called from just outside the bedroom door. "If you're having as much fun as it sounds like, I want to come in."

"We're decent," Celia answered, barely speaking through the tears from her laughter. "We're just talking about the hamsters." She burst out again, and Julia followed, peals of laughter echoing through the house. Pete stood, hands on hips, looking at the two and shaking his head. He had become accustomed to such scenes since Julia moved to Charleston. It was wonderful to see Celia have so much fun.

"Do I get to hear this story?" he asked.

"We can't possibly tell it right now," Julia squeaked. "Later, I promise. I'm leaving this room right now. Hurry up, Cele." And with that, she left the bedroom, still laughing uncontrollably down the stairs.

43

"You can eat dinner at home tonight with us," Martha crooned in delight. "What would you like Mother to make?"

"Mom, would you and Dad mind if I talked to the doctor alone for a couple of minutes?" Mac asked. "There's some stuff I want to know before we go home, and it's hard for me to talk about it with the doctor, let alone in front of you guys."

"Of course, son. We'll take some of these flowers down to the car while you and the doctor talk." Martha patted her son's hand. She was anxious to take her son home. Dr. Grant waited until the door closed behind Mac's parents.

"You have questions?" he asked.

"Yeah, Doc. I want to know what's going to happen when I...you know...will I be able to..." His face was red, but he plunged on, needing to assuage his anxiety. "What about sex?"

"If I were you, son, I wouldn't be giving that much thought in the next month or so. You'll be coming to see me every week, and I'll explain the progress each time you come. There's no reason to think you won't be perfectly normal when the healing is complete, maybe in about twelve weeks. Try to compare it to a broken bone; mending the body is a miraculous but slow process. We want to give it whatever time it needs. Are you with me?"

"I guess so. Are you saying I'll be just like I was before, just like this never happened?"

"I'm saying that could be the case. I have absolutely no reason to think otherwise. I would make you that promise if I could, but doctors don't guarantee. We just do the work and wait for the results. I expect the results in your case to be superb. I guess you won't want to advertise for me?" The doctor smiled widely.

"Yeah, right. I'm hoping no one ever finds out about this. I'm not even telling my friends. I've told a couple of them that I was stabbed in the stomach. That's my story, and I'm sticking to it."

"Good luck, Mac. You follow the instructions the nurse gave you; follow them exactly. Call me if you have any questions. If not, I'll see you at my office in a week." The doctor shook Mac's hand before leaving. "You take care, now."

44

Rose's little gatherings were usually an eclectic collection of people she enjoyed and those she tolerated. Her knowledge of and connection to Charleston's prominent and powerful families was unrivaled, and she brought them together to mix and re-mix a colorful stew of influence, adding at will the seasoning wisdom of her own longevity. Joe Riley was a regular, rarely turning down an invitation to Rose's home. She had been a mainstay of his support from the beginning, her love of the city recognizing his own and taking up his cause.

"You look lovely, as always," he said to Rose, kissing the back of her hand. "I tasted those little things you made with shrimp and crab, and I was wondering if you would consider adopting me."

"Adopting?" Rose responded. "I was hoping you'd ask me to marry you, but I see you've found me out. Is it the wrinkles or the arthritis?"

"If I had half your wit and charm," the mayor responded, smiling, "I'd consider running for public office."

"And if you did," Rose countered, "I'd consider voting for you."

Joe Riley made the Charlestonian accent sound patrician, as though he had taken it up to Boston and had it gilded just slightly. First elected some forty years ago, he was the chosen among the young pups, the up-and-coming sons who would soon be the city's guiding force. Those boys—the Howes, the Rosens, the Gadsdens—chose him from amongst them, and a new leadership was born, one that would span four decades and remain steadfastly popular. He had looked so young back then, bookwormy with a boyish appeal. He still looked intellectual, but the gray hair and preeminent brows had enhanced his image, and his success as captain of the battered but ever-buoyant ship of Charleston assured his place as the city's public face and guiding force. Though officially retired a year earlier, Joe Riley would always be The Mayor.

"I want you to meet a friend of mine before you get lost in the mingling." Rose held Julia lightly by the arm. "Julia McKenzie, this is Joe Riley. Isn't he just as handsome in person as he is on television?"

Julia extended her hand.

"Julia went to college with my granddaughter, Joe, and moved down here last fall. Listen to the accent she's already acquired."

"It's a pleasure, Miss McKenzie."

"The pleasure is certainly mine, Mr. Mayor," Julia smiled. "You preside over a city I've come to love."

"That's always music to my ears," the Mayor responded. "Are you here to stay?"

"Quite likely so."

"Oh, of course she's going to stay," Rose chimed in. "Julia bought the old beach house over on the island from me last fall, and you should see what she's done to it. It does my heart good. And she's opened her own office down on Church Street, you know, and has a growing law practice."

"Oh, yes, didn't I hear that you came from Washington and did some work there for the District from time to time?"

"We did handle some things the District farmed out, overflow from its legal department."

"I'll keep that in mind, with your permission, of course. Our legal offices are bursting at the seams right now, and we occasionally cry for outside help. I could mention it to the new mayor."

"I actually enjoy municipal work," Julia said, "especially in the areas of planning and development. That was a real challenge in the District, and I see that you have your own growth issues, speaking of bursting at the seams."

"Well, if you being here tonight means a little new blood for the city and for tonight's Spoleto planning, I'm grateful. I can always count on Rose to know just the right people."

Julia was pleased. She had seen Joe Riley at a distance, but he was charming in person. It was no wonder that the city had continued to elect him, his popularity never compromised while weathering bombardment from those who wanted more and those who wanted less: more development, less traffic, more preservation, fewer rules to restore and protect the historic architecture. It had become a balancing act. Progress sometimes meant diluting the very essence which distinguished the Lowcountry, whose allure in large part stemmed from devotion to preserving its history and nourishing a life tempo whose rhythm still bathed in the ceaseless sea and whose life blood flowed through sweetgrass and meandering marsh.

The people around Julia were professors at the College of Charleston, real estate developers, doctors, authors, Southern historians and a few attorneys of her acquaintance, most with spouses in tow. It was a relaxed and cordial group; most had been acquainted for much of their lives. Only a few newcomers worked their way into these circles of Charleston society, and those who did usually did so because a longstanding member felt them worthy. Julia was fully aware that she would not be here except for her closeness to Celia and therefore to Rose Pinckney.

Turning, she backed into a discussion on preserving the old forts which dotted the Lowcountry. Julia walked often past the sprawling remains of old Fort Moultrie on her own adopted Sullivan's Island and had learned some of its stories from Henry, a regular to her part of the beach who was spending his retirement attached to a fishing pole.

Julia's growing acquaintance with Charleston's remarkable past had oozed over her bit by bit. She had suffered college history as an irksome requirement, but here the very air she breathed was suffused with the consequences and dividends of a rich and meaty past. One could not escape it, and Julia found to her surprise that she did not wish to do so. She felt it first—a stirring of real interest—as she stood on the seawall looking across Charleston Harbor. Fort Sumter, heretofore only a name from a book, sat peacefully just across the water. This low brick structure covering a sandbar in the middle of the bay seemed an improbable testament to the monumental events of decades past. It looked, to Julia, like a sitting duck.

She had mentioned her observation during a prior evening with Celia and a few acquaintances at Rose Pinckney's house. Rose had sat down beside Julia, taking her hand. "That piece of rock sticking up out of the sea is hallowed ground, my dear, not just for the South but for the country. Southern men and boys died right out there to save the only way of life they knew."

"I certainly meant no disrespect, Miss Rose," Julia had assured. "I just looked across there and thought it looked like such a vulnerable spot. Why would anyone take a stand on that little sandbar at the commencement of a war?"

"Charleston sits at the back of a harbor deeper than it is wide and protected at its mouth from the open sea by Sullivan's Island on the north and James Island on the south, both reaching out at the mouth of the harbor like the encircling arms of a guardian angel. Between those two protrusions sits the little nub of a sandbar upon which is built Fort Sumter. It is the center segment of a defense against attack by sea."

Everyone in the room was listening. Rose's unabashed passion always attracted attention. Tugging on Julia's hand, she walked to the window, looking out at a scene preserved for posterity: across the harbor wall, the sea, the lights of the islands, and Fort Sumter basking midway in the light of a summer moon whose light shimmered across the water like a radiant pathway.

"Imagine being right here at this window, or up on top of the house, watching cannon fire between the fort and the mainland. In 1861, that fort was manned by the army of the United States," Rose explained. "When South Carolina voted to leave the Union, it was insufferable to have that fort, right there in our harbor, in the hands of the Union. On these two sides were men who had differed on the day's issues but who talked and drank together and who knew one another by name. So the gentlemen of Carolina, under the command of Brigadier General P. G. T. Beauregard, took a couple of boats out there and asked the Union army politely to leave. Also without rancor, and after the time it took to receive word from Lincoln, the Union's Major Anderson regretted to respond that the Union army was ordered to hold the fort. Beauregard, ever the gentleman, told Anderson that firing on the fort would begin at 4:30 a.m. on April 12, 1861, giving him an hour to prepare. Deeply divided in loyalties, these men maintained a civility, a decency of spirit, born and nurtured in this fledgling city. We are the heirs, the children of that genteel mentality. And that battered brick fort is a monument to a tradition of wholehearted devotion common to the Old South and a still-young America."

Remembering, Julia smiled as she surveyed the room, grateful to be in it with these extraordinary people. She vowed to borrow another of Rose's books on Charleston's past when the Quinn affair was over and she had reading time for something other than case research.

FRIDAY

45

Friday morning was usually a very busy time for Willa Fallon. She often had help on Fridays and Saturdays to prepare her catering orders for weekend events. Today, however, her two part-time helpers were full-time and working without Willa's direction. Willa was still at the hospital.

Several of Reggie's friends had stopped by, as well as many of Willa's, offering to help with anything she or Reggie needed. His friends were such dear boys, she thought, many of whom she had known as youngsters in the neighborhood where she raised her son. Her friend Bernice had brought her Bible, and it lay on the bed by Reg's feet. Now and then Willa held it, fingering the pages or stroking its leather cover. As word spread of Reg's accident, they kept coming, sitting with Willa in turn, helping the long minutes pass with conversation or just sitting beside the bed while Willa caught a fitful nap.

The nurses reported continuing signs of improvement. The fluid that had accumulated around Reg's brain, they said, was slowly draining away. His vital signs were improving. Willa herself could see that his color was better this morning than the lingering pallor of Thursday night. But her emotions were frozen in a state of static trembling. Her faith was sustaining, but her body was exhausted.

Spots of sunlight dappled the bedding and Reg's bandaged face and head. As if responding to a new morning's effort to rouse him, Reg's eyes and mouth twitched slightly once, then again. Willa was on her feet, studying her son's face, saying his name quietly. His eyelids fluttered, opened, closed again.

"Get the nurse," Willa instructed her friend Bernice. "Something is happening. Hurry." The fingers on Reg's free hand uncurled, seemed

96

to reach. Willa took that hand again in both of hers, barely breathing, clutching at hope. "It's gonna be all right, Reggie," she crooned quietly, not relating to the calm and assurance in her voice. She could feel the pulse in his hand, slow and regular. His eyelids moved again, opened, looking nowhere, and closed. Willa did not know whether to rejoice or despair. What did this mean? Where was the nurse?

And then the nurse was in the room, standing on the bed's other side, watching. "Did he open his eyes, Ms. Fallon?" she asked quietly.

"He did, and then they closed right up again. What does it mean?"

"Let's keep watching, and you go ahead and talk to him, Ms. Fallon. I paged the doctor to stop by. He's already in the building this morning. "Keep talking to him like you were, and I'll lift the cover and rub his feet a little. Maybe he's coming around."

"Praise the Lord," Bernice said, "I'm gonna stand right behind you and pray with my whole soul, Willa. I knew God wasn't goin' take that boy away from you." She put both her hands on Willa's shoulders from behind and closed her eyes. And there they stood when the neurosurgeon entered the room, each in her way willing consciousness into the broken body of Reg Fallon.

Dr. Raines walked quietly up to the foot of the bed, placing his hands on the rail. The nurse and Willa each looked at his face questioningly, but no one spoke except the mother to her son. "You come right on back to us, now, Reggie. You been sleepin' there the day an' night long, an' yo' momma is ready to see your eyes open an' a smile on that face. We all here waitin'. I been thinkin' 'bout makin' you a whole pecan chess pie jes' for yourself. You hear me, Reggie? Can you hear your mama?"

Both the doctor and the nurse noticed changes on the monitor, but Willa saw only the face of her sleeping son. She lifted his hand and stroked the back, squeezing each finger in turn. When his eyes opened this time, he seemed to see her. Though he did not turn his head, his eyes moved slightly to meet's his mother's. His lips moved, but without sound. "There you are, my baby," Willa said softly. "All your friends been waitin' for you to wake up. I'm so glad to see those eyes open." Willa cooed and murmured as if to an infant.

Moving around the bed, the doctor took the place where the nurse had stood, taking the chart from her. He continued to watch the boy's face, waiting for some sign of beginning recognition and comprehension. Alternately, Reg closed and opened his eyes, refocusing at places around the room, finally looking at the doctor.

"Good morning, Reg," the doctor said. "I'm glad to see you awake. You're doing fine. I know you're very tired, but can you tell me how you're feeling?"

Reg managed a small frown line in his forehead, then looked back at his mother. "It's okay, Reggie," she assured him. "You were in an accident, and Dr. Raines fixed your head." She nodded encouragingly, and her son looked back at the doctor.

"Hurts," he said thickly. Out of context, they might not have understood the word.

"What hurts, Reg? Is it your head or somewhere else?" The doctor waited patiently, unsure whether his patient would be able to form either the thought or the words to answer.

"Head," he said, and a moment later, "leg."

The doctor shook his head, approving of Reg's response. "Okay, that's what I would expect to hurt. We'll give you something for that. I'm pleased with how you're doing. The nurses know when they have a celebrity, so you let them know if you want anything at all. You're going to be all right. If you understand what I'm telling you, squeeze your mother's hand," he instructed. Reg did.

The doctor gave Willa a thumbs up. "You haven't been home, have you, Ms. Fallon?" he asked, knowing the answer.

"No, I can't leave him, doctor. He's all I got in this world. I know God don't care where I do my prayin' from, but I feel better doin' it right here."

"I understand, but since things are looking up, maybe you'll let me give you something for sleep tonight. We'll talk it about it when I come by later. We can order the patients around, but it's a little harder with the families. You get something to eat, will you? This boy's going to need you when he gets up and around." He winked, hoping to lighten the mother's heart. "We might have to be shooting some hoops right here in the room in a few days, so you keep up your strength."

Willa managed a weak smile, wanting to believe the doctor. Her son's eyes were open, and he had spoken. Now she could take a quick shower here in Reg's hospital bathroom and put on the clothes her sister had brought her. Things might be looking up.

46

Uneasiness clouded Rose Pinckney's morning as well. She had talked with Celia and with Julia about Quinn's situation. She could no longer put off talking with Quinn. She was sure Quinn had been preparing for it as well, knowing Rose's concern was deep and genuine. She heard Quinn upstairs. She was awake, probably dressed. Rose had just taken cinnamon rolls out of the oven, and their aroma filled the kitchen. They were made from her own grandmother's recipe, another that she intended to share with Quinn. Would there be days in this kitchen to bake and laugh, she wondered. Could those times be counted upon, or were all such moments in jeopardy, shadowed by a threat Rose did not wish to consider?

Quinn took the steps lightly, skipping just like the little girl she was, Rose thought as she listened. They were such familiar steps, recorded over time in Rose's heart as the child had grown into a young woman. Quinn was just as much a part of her as were Celia, Tyrney and Katey. And she would protect her in all the same ways. She intended to protect her fiercely.

"I smelled them all the way upstairs," Quinn said as she came into the kitchen. "If you'd been at school with me, Grams, Krispy Kreme would be out of business."

"It's so nice to have you here. I don't know what I did without you for four whole years."

"You want to talk about it, don't you, Grams?"

Rose sighed, marveling at Quinn's perceptiveness. It had always been so. Rose attributed it to a little girl's need to please an unpredictable mother. Her antenna was ever tuned, trying to sense the mood. It was a wonderful, sensitive quality, but acquired at such a cost, Rose thought.

"Oh, my dear, I feel we must. I want to help, but mostly I want to understand. Can you bear to let me in that place where you've been hiding your secret?"

Quinn poured tea for them both and put a plate with two cinnamon rolls by each cup. "I feel so at home at this kitchen table," she said, sitting in her usual chair. "I always thought I could tell you absolutely anything."

"You can, dear."

"I don't know how to talk about it," Quinn began. "All along, I don't know which was stronger, my need to pour it out to you or my fear that you might look at me the way Mama did." Tears glistened unshed in Quinn's eyes.

"Give me your hands, Quinn Ravenel," Grandma said, her voice quivering but strong. Quinn did so, reaching across the table. "No one has ever made me prouder than you. I feel as connected to you as if I had borne you from my own flesh. You are a precious human being, and I cherish each of the moments we have had together and each that is yet to come. I am in awe of what you have survived. You must understand from this moment that we are in this together. Nothing you have done disappoints me. And whatever we will do now, we will do together. Don't doubt that, Quinn. Don't ever doubt that again."

Rose felt that she had almost been holding her breath to say those words. She had not planned them, had not known what they were, but each of them was true.

Quinn came around the table and sat on the floor, putting her head in Rose's lap. She cried there, sobbing as though her heart was broken, for most of an hour.

47

Julia spent Friday morning on the beach. She woke at eight, checked messages on her office machine, returned important calls briefly and gathered her towel, sandals and folding chair. Almost out the door, she rethought her earlier hesitation to return Detective Legare's call. He had said it was not important, but any new information he might have could help direct the serious thinking she had in mind. Without putting down her gear, she dialed his number and held the phone with her chin, the towel over her shoulder and the chair on her arm. As the phone rang, she filled her container with ice and water.

"Legare," Sonny answered.

"Hey, this is Julia McKenzie. How are you?"

"I'm okay, McKenzie. I left a message at your office earlier."

"Yes, I just checked in. New developments? I almost hesitate to ask."

"Actually, my call was more personal than business." He paused. "Would I be out of line to ask you to have dinner with me, McKenzie?"

Caught totally off guard, Julia almost dropped the beach chair. "Dinner?" she asked finally.

"Well, I've seen you almost every day for the past week, and I didn't want to have withdrawal, so I'm just trying to head that off. After the week's events, we certainly wouldn't lack for topics of conversation. What do you say?"

"Well, dinner...when?"

"How about tonight? Do you already have plans? I know a guy is supposed to think ahead."

"My calendar for tonight just happens to be empty." Julia's mind had finally caught up with the path of the conversation. "I think I owe you dinner anyway, don't I?" She recalled her offhand offer.

"I think you do, but this one is mine. Do you like Anson?"

"Of course I've heard about it, but I've never been. When I want good food, I just go to Celia's house."

"Shall I pick you up?"

"Frankly, I'm headed down to the beach for a while, so I won't get in to the office until after lunch. I've got some thinking to do, so I thought I might as well do it in the sand. Do you want to come by my office later and we'll go from there?"

"How about seven or so. Is that too late?"

"That sounds good. I'll be ready and hungry."

"Thanks, McKenzie. I'm looking forward to seeing you." And he hung up the phone.

Well, Julia thought. Dinner. Out. With a man. Unexpected. But she would think about that later. There was plenty on her mind for now, and she was taking it all to the beach for sifting.

48

Rose was drying tears of her own as she dabbed at Quinn's face with a cool, damp washcloth. "There's nothing like a good cry," she said. "I haven't seen your eyes this puffy since the music teacher gave that part in South Pacific to the Johnson girl. You were so disappointed that you skipped school the next day, remember? We sat right here and ate chocolate chip cookies and butter pecan ice cream."

Quinn laughed through her tears. "How do you remember these things, Grams? I hadn't thought of that for years. I was so angry. Melinda Johnson couldn't even sing. I still don't know why she got that part. That should have been my first clue that things aren't always fair."

"Oh, honey, you had plenty of clues before that. If life were fair, your daddy would be alive and your mother... well, I might as well say it. Your mother would have known what she had in you and cherished you as I do."

"And maybe if life were fair, I wouldn't have been stupid enough to crawl in that creep's window. That would have changed everything."

"What window, dear?" Rose paused, puzzled. "Oh. That's the beginning of the story, isn't it?"

"Are you sure about this, Grams? It's gonna be hard for me to tell you. It's hard for me to even think about it myself."

"I'm sure. You tell me what you can."

"You know, I never even liked him. He was just too full of himself."

"The Howe boy?"

"Yes. He always walked around school like he was all that and then some. I hardly saw him after he graduated. I don't even know where he went to school. Some military school, I guess. He's in the Army now, isn't he?"

"Just like his daddy."

"Well, I was running past his house, just like always, the summer after I graduated. I remember I was thinking about all the things I still needed to do before I left for college. I was pretty excited. He yelled at me when I ran by, and I shouldn't have even looked back. If only I could..."

"No, dear," Rose interrupted. "None of this is about what you did. It's all about what he did. All of it."

"I know that, but thanks for reminding me. You might have to do it again."

"I can do that all day," Rose assured her.

"He said he was locked out of the house. He'd broken a pane out of the window, but he couldn't get through. He asked me to do it because I would fit through the space. If only I...oops!" Quinn smiled. "Anyway, I crawled in his window. I really did that, right into a dark house where I thought I was going to find my way to his front door and let him in and be on my way. But I never got to the front door, Grams, not until later, and then it was too late."

"Too late for what, dear?"

"Too late for me to ever be the same again."

49

Living on the beach was not a dream come true for Julia; it was a dream she had never had. She had visited some of the vacation beaches in Virginia and Maryland, had even spent a week at Nag's Head on two occasions, but the shores of South Carolina were a different experience. And the spot right here on Sullivan's Island was better than she could have dreamed. She bonded with it from her balcony, from her windows, and from right here on the sand. Her new relationship with the sea was changing her mind and her life, and the changes were both gentle and profound.

Though living alone, she was not lonely here. The sea had called to her, whispering as a new friend, cautioning in quiet counsel that to feel lonely was an extravagant squandering of life energy. This was the edge of the world where nothing is alone and everything is part of the ocean of life. The surf, the sand, the air all teemed with living, and the end and the beginning were one. Water touched land; land blended into water, and shifting was the constant. Julia's insecurities had been nothing, she saw here. She was but a grain of sand.

Maybe it was possible, she mused, to grasp these notions looking out across the wheat fields of the Midwest or down the majestic mountains of Colorado, but the voice she heard was here. How long it had been calling her she did not know, but she was finished resisting. She was here to stay.

Looking back over the dunes, she smiled with pleasure. That was her house. She was coming to understand that Sullivan's Island was itself a special place. Once upon a time, it was hard to reach from the mainland, just a finger of land where those folks lived who had no need for daily contact with the city, generally those too poor to afford to live nearer the center of activity. It had once been just an "out" island; now it was "the" out island.

Julia had brought no work with her. It was all in her head, the decision to make about representing Quinn, about whether to follow the guidance of Jordan Guerry or the unorthodox instincts in her gut. She was a lawyer, but she was a woman first. There were no excuses for what MacArthur Howe had done to Quinn, no adequate ways by which to repay him. Quinn's way was pretty close, she thought, astonished that she could admit that, even to herself. But she had looked into the girl's eyes. Quinn was damaged but quite sane. She was a young woman who had thought her options limited and had acted to save herself. That was her story.

Julia acknowledged that she was buying into it on a psychological level, but was there anywhere in the law a defense equally compelling? She knew of none. In the fringes of her legal theorizing, she was toying with the far-fetched notion of stretching a simple self-defense argument to cover what Quinn had done. Her inexperience with criminal matters cautioned her; her gut could not let it go.

Taking a long drink from her water bottle, Julia placed it under the chair and started down the beach. She usually walked all the way around the curve by Fort Moultrie, passing the lighthouse. No pleasure compared to having her toes in the surf and the Carolina sun on her back, she thought. For all the years of her life she had not known it, she enjoyed it the more now.

There in the harbor, Fort Sumter sat at peace, its low profile no clue to its role in history. Relics of a country's battles lay on either side of her as she walked this shore, and here between them she found her greatest sense of calm. Mullet jumped aplenty in the shallow water. She had assumed the fishermen who frequented this stretch of sand were fishing for them, but then she became acquainted with Henry. He knew her name too, now, and she always stopped for a visit when he was there. Seventy-one years old and retired from a high-stress job on Wall Street, he was the source of all her newfound fishing knowledge. The mullet, he said, weren't good to eat, but they attracted the dolphins playing just offshore. He was fishing for sheepshead, herring and pure enjoyment. His leathery skin proved his hobby long-term.

The dolphins were there today, but Henry was not. Julia's fascination had not diminished for the brown pelicans that fished here as well. They were such awkward-looking birds, that big pouch hanging from a beak too large for the head. But then they took flight, cruising just above the swells or scanning the water from high above, looking almost regal, and performing stop-on-a-dime dives Julia thought aerodynamically impossible, beak-first into the sea.

In contrast, little sandpipers skittered along the water's edge in groups of three or four, their slender beaks popping into the sand for tidbits left each time the water ebbed. Acting territorial, one ran aggressively ahead of Julia, chasing another. They strutted toward the receding surf, then darted in hasty retreat when the water changed direction, seeming not to want their toes wet.

Julia sloshed along ankle-deep and content. She passed the sign that read "deadly currents", knowing that someone must have made that discovery the hard way. Was it undertow, she wondered, or rocks just beneath the water's surface that created the danger. She would ask Henry.

Being here always mellowed Julia. She had not forgotten the task ahead of her, but being near the ocean helped keep things in perspective. Quinn's life was at risk, time in prison a real possibility for her, Julia thought. But her own life was calm and steady. She had Celia and her family, including the indomitable Rose. She had the house here on Sullivan's Island which felt more like her home every day. She had a developing circle of friends and acquaintances with whom she felt connected. That was reason enough for her to smile, she thought, recalling that just a short year ago she was overwhelmed by the hollow shell her marriage had become, feeling that without Jack she was without anchor.

Here, Julia did not claim a grasp of life's essence, but as she dwelt on the shore in harmony with the tides, she was less sure that life required the discovery of its meaning. She knew a measure of contentment and pleasure in discovering herself. She was okay, she thought gleefully, despite her mother and her husband who had tried so hard to convince her otherwise. She was, after all, smart enough, pretty enough, good enough. People in her new life liked her for herself. There was no man behind her, no prestigious law firm, no social circle except the new one she was forming for herself. She had never considered that to become one's own person was a goal to which she aspired. Now it seemed her dearest desire. Like the Velveteen Rabbit, Julia finally thought it was possible that those who mattered would love her with all her fur worn off, and that she would likely still love herself as well.

To see the divorce as a gift was a thought Julia had not considered until today. Now, she thought, it seemed clear that she would not be here, not be content, not even be whole, if that event had not marked a different path for her. She would still be waiting for the approval that would finally be enough, finally set her free. It would never have come, she knew now. The validation for which she had waited her whole life could only come from Julia herself, but she could not have recognized that while paddling desperately against the self-negating current of her marriage to Jack. Jack had the capability to walk into the room and wring the joy out of Julia at any given moment, to shatter her world with a carelessly dropped phrase. Others could do almost the same, but he did it best, and he did it most often.

She had felt cumulatively more and more alone in her world as there became less and less she was willing to share. It was too risky to be open, too frightening to be vulnerable. In a journal kept since high school, Julia had written repeatedly during the years of her marriage that she would hold on just another day for Jack to remember that she was worthy of his love, his respect and his long-lost attention. She wondered now if she had been increasingly less worthy as those days blended one into another and she thought less and less of herself, her opinion of herself depending upon his, his opinion of her depending upon her own. She had not seen the circle while in it; she saw it now, thankfully, for the trap it was. Celia had helped her.

Celia had been there for her so many times, never failing to believe in Julia. Now there might be an opportunity for Julia to repay some of her friend's goodness. Her confidence in herself, previously so easy to shake, was gaining foundation. She would revisit Jordan Guerry very soon to try once again to enlist his help in preparing Quinn's defense. He had the criminal law expertise, and Julia was willing to do whatever he required to assist and learn from him. She would have to make him see that pleading insanity was not the answer; there had to be another way.

Realizing she was well past the Fort Moultrie bend, Julia turned back, now facing the sun that had journeyed past midday. It was hot on her cheeks, as it had been on her back, and she bent to splash a few handfuls of salt water across her shoulders. It was just cool enough to be refreshing. The tide was going out and sand fleas, losing their ever-ebbing cover, were forced to move as well. Repeatedly exposed as the receding surf took layers of sand back to the sea, the little critters kept themselves almost invisible by re-burying immediately. Julia saw the nail-sized holes appearing and reappearing, along with their round fringes of sand kicked out as the crabs burrowed. Tyrney and Katey had taught her to catch them, digging quickly as the hole appeared. She did not like the wriggly feel of them, but she enjoyed the evidence of their constant activity. Their frenetic movement made her motions seem still and deliberate.

While concentrating on the little holes, Julia almost walked into a beached jellyfish. Stepping quickly aside, she stopped to look more closely. Though she now understood that most of these beautiful creatures were harmless, she had yet to risk touching. It looked lifeless, though still moist and almost transparent. Not good swimmers, Henry had explained, they were at the mercy of winds and currents and were often forced onto the beach to dry out and decompose in the sun. It seemed such a shame, Julia thought. Such a beautiful creature, so ethereal and full of light. She would happily be one of these in her next life, she decided, modified with mastery of wind and waves so as to live forever riding the ocean currents just off the coast of South Carolina.

It was time to pull herself away, Julia decided, and head for town and the real world. She was renewed, as always, by her time on the sand. She had thought once or twice about bringing her laptop here to work, but it seemed a sacrilege. This place was for body, mind and spirit, unencumbered.

Gathering her things, Julia headed across the sand toward home.

50

"What might my life be like right now if that day had never happened?" Quinn asked Rose. "Would everything be entirely different? Would I be engaged or happily married? Would I be able to at least tolerate my mother? How could those few minutes of my life so change everything?"

"Have you been asking yourself that question for four years?" Rose asked in return.

"Yes, but not constantly. Mostly, it was like a shadow, one I couldn't run fast enough to escape, like when little kids dream of monsters under the bed. It was just a few minutes of my life, but it changed everything."

Rose took both of Quinn's hands in her own, holding them as she would a child's. "You must believe me, Quinn, when I tell you that every moment changes everything. Try as we might to control all those accumulating moments, tumbling one upon the other, some of them catch us unaware. You were altered by that moment just as you have been by each one that came before and each one that has followed, but you are defined by none of them unless you choose to be so. Do you see what I'm saying?"

"Not exactly, but I like the feeling it gives me."

"You are redefined in this moment, my dear, and again in the next. Since we exist only in the current moment, consider how many times you have been new during this very conversation. Some events that might be defining must be weeded out of our psyches, assessed and discarded, because we sense they will not serve us well. Others can be fused into our developing consciousness, held and treasured to make us whole."

"Will I ever be whole again?"

"We need not be defined by moments; we are simply refined by them, again and again. That awful moment can only hold you if you allow it," Rose continued. "Don't allow it. You and life have moved on. Let yourself recognize it. Let me help you. I have already begun to will the damage away from you. I want you to feel it."

"Grams, it was so awful. I've grown up a lot since then, had girlfriends and experienced things, but that picture and that feeling won't leave my head."

"I guess that explains why you never talked about a special boy at school. There haven't been any boys, have there?" Rose asked gently.

"No, there haven't been any boys. I have a couple of friends, but not in that way. I know it's not normal, but I don't know how to get over it, Grams."

"You'll get over it in time, and Celie and I will help you now that we know. I can love you as hard as anyone could, but our little Celie is trained in matters of emotional well-being. She will help you straighten this all out in your head. We must reorganize this information so that you will be able to have a life without the shadow, and I know Celie can help. She's helped me on occasion, and I'm old enough to be her grandmother," Rose quipped.

"Oh, Grams, it's such a relief to have you in on my secret. Are you mad at me for not telling you?"

"Yes, I most certainly am, and don't you ever withhold important things from me again, Babyluv. Not ever. I can hardly bear it that you were in such pain for all this time and I wasn't there for you."

"My fault, Grams. I knew in my heart that it was you I should have come to. It was you I wanted. But all I could think of was to shower that night, and when I went in the house, Mother was there. She saw the torn clothes and the mess I was, and I just blurted it out." Quinn rose from her seat at the table, reheating the water in the teakettle. "I think now I can eat a cinnamon roll," she sighed, "or three. I've cried through lunchtime, so maybe this is dinner. And then I must do something I've been dreading. I have to go see Reg Fallon."

51

MacArthur Howe IV was happy to be home, glad to be alive. He was sitting on the covered patio behind his parents' house reading the Clancy novel he'd started at the hospital and sipping the lemonade his mother had made. She was starting dinner in the kitchen but coming regularly to sit with him, refilling his glass and inquiring about his comfort. He was, in fact, very comfortable today. The pain in his groin had subsided, his mother's attention was soothing and familiar, and he had escaped the hospital's white sterility.

Squirrels played on the lawn near him, already gathering acorns, eating some and running away with others. A blue jay screeched in the oak tree, warning a neighborhood cat walking along the top of the fence. The day was as warm as the hospital had been cold. Mac held the book, but his thoughts drifted. He was bothered by the police detective's last visit, by his reference to the girl. He'd not thought of that girl for years, could barely remember her face. The only reason he recalled her at all was because of that day, the one when he got her into his house. It wasn't much, he thought, just a few entertaining minutes. But if the detective was on the right track about this attack, then it must have been more to the girl. Could she have done this to him? He cringed.

"Are you doing okay, dear?" his mother called from the kitchen window. "I'm just putting dinner in the oven, and then I'll be out."

"I'm fine, Mom."

"Your father should be home soon. Are you up to a game of cards? Would you like that?"

"Sure, Mom, whatever you want. I could use a little more ice when you come out."

"All right, dear. I'll be right there."

That cat was near Mac's feet now, after a cricket. He would have kicked it away, but quick movements usually brought pain. He wanted the girl out of his mind, but the possibilities associated with her nagged at him. Was she, after all this time, extracting revenge? Sure, she'd said 'no', but a lot of girls said 'no'. That's what they were supposed to do. She was nobody, anyway, the little bitch, he thought, returning to his reading.

52

Sonny had made a reservation at Anson, but they would have seated him anyway. He was a regular. He and Julia walked there from her office, just a few blocks as the evening cooled, and were glad to take a quiet table in the twilight ambience of a cozy corner. The warm dampness outside had curled Julia's hair, and she pushed it away from her face with the ends of her fingers as they settled into comfortable suede-covered chairs.

"It's nice to see you, sir," the waiter greeted Sonny, "especially in such lovely company." He smiled, nodding to Julia.

"Yeah, Tony, I don't need any of your ribbing tonight. This is Julia McKenzie, one of those downtown lawyers, who tells me she hasn't been here before. If you make a good impression, maybe she'll come back."

Julia gave the waiter a wide smile. "I already have a lovely first impression," she said, "and if the food is half as good as it smells, I'm sure I'll be back very frequently."

"May I bring you something to drink before dinner?" the waiter asked.

"I'll take my cues from the lady, I think, Tony. Would you like some wine, McKenzie?"

With glasses filled and dinner ordered, Julia and Sonny settled into comfortable conversation.

"I'm glad to hear that Reg Fallon is hanging in there," Julia said. "I'll go by the hospital tomorrow and sit awhile with his mother. She must be beside herself with worry."

"I still can't get over that accident. I shook the boy's hand and wished him well just an hour before. He didn't even seem to have any hard feelings. All he wanted was to go home."

"Earlier today when you came by my office, I wanted to talk more, but the others came. I knew you were feeling some responsibility for Reg being hurt, but you must know on a rational level that it's not your fault. As an attorney, I find the situation intriguing. One could certainly argue that Reg Fallon need not have been in that police vehicle, that he was a victim of police malfeasance. As a person, I want you to give yourself a break. You're a good guy who was doing his job."

"Am I having dinner with the attorney or the person? I must admit I hadn't considered the ramifications of that. You won't sue the City and use my admissions against me, will you?"

"Absolutely not." Julia smiled. "If I learned nothing else practicing with the big boys in D.C., I did clearly come to grasp the line between personal and professional."

Sonny nodded, studying Julia's face. "So we're here strictly as friends, not lawyer and cop?"

"Friends. I can't explain why Reg was in that car or why the guy in the truck wasn't paying attention when he hit them. I don't expect to understand that in this lifetime."

"I like being in a room where you are, McKenzie. It's been a long time since I felt that way, and I don't know exactly how to handle it, so I thought I'd just tell you."

"Well," Julia said, "I guess that's better than your saying I scare you."

"Did I say that?" Sonny raised his brows and shook his head. "Well, I was probably being honest then too."

Julia laughed, enjoying the man's candor. "I don't think anyone in my life has ever been scared of me, so I'm going to enjoy it for the moment, Detective."

"I thought we were over 'Detective' now. Didn't you agree to that?"

"Yes, I did. And I'd ask you to call me Julia, but I kind of like you using my last name. No one ever did that before."

"That's good, because even my dog would tell you that I'm set in my ways."

"You have a dog?"

"Yeah, Tork. He's my best pal."

"What kind of dog is he?"

"I'd guess he's a good part Old English sheepdog, but the rest is anyone's guess. He's big and shaggy and is the only one who truly appreciates my company. You'll have to meet him sometime, although I don't know how he feels about women."

"Why is that? Doesn't he know your women friends?"

"I don't have friends who are women."

"Oh, come on, Det—Sonny. I've heard you're somewhat of a loner, but a bachelor like you in a social town like this has to be noticing the Southern belles."

"I notice from time to time, but that's about all." His tone was light, but his eyes were serious as he looked at Julia.

She paused, assessing. "I don't know the story, but I sense there is one."

Sonny took a long sip from his chardonnay. Julia did the same, giving him time, half expecting to be shut out right here.

"I finally found the woman who could live with me. Her name was Annie. I only had her for a little while, and then she was killed in a car accident. That was seven years ago." He had said it slowly, as though recounting it aloud would make it more real than he wished it to be.

"I'm so sorry, Sonny." And she was. His pain was obviously only mildly tempered by time.

"I can't undo it, so I don't talk about it."

Julia nodded. They were silent.

"I know you came down here from D.C., and the talk is that you're divorced and live alone over on the islands. Why don't you tell me your story?"

Glad for a chance to lighten the conversation, Julia seized it. "And how do you know this, Detective? Oops, sorry."

He did smile. "Lawyers talk. And so do cops. You're not exactly the typical Broad Street lawyer, in case you hadn't noticed."

"I'm not a Broad Street lawyer at all. My office is off Broad, which makes me a Church Street lawyer. Does that put me in a better category?"

"Oh, you're in a different category all right, no matter where you have your office. There's not a cop, or probably a lawyer either, who hasn't noticed you around. And you're getting the reputation of being a decent person in addition to being a pretty woman. That's quite an accomplishment in less than a year for a Charleston newcomer."

"And here you are, you who don't know any women, sitting at a table having dinner with me. Is that an accomplishment as well?" she teased.

"I guess you could say that, but it could be that the accomplishment is mine, McKenzie, you sitting here at this table eating dinner with me."

Julia smiled, the corners of her eyes crinkling. She could not remember when a man had flirted with her, but it seemed that's what Sonny was doing. It was very pleasant, and she was surprised to find herself enjoying the evening.

"What brought you to Charleston from the big city?" he asked.

"My best friend since college is here. So when I was deciding where to take my life, she persuaded me to give Charleston a chance. And when her grandmother, Rose Pinckney, sold me the beach house for a pittance, I was hooked. I never held a paint brush before that house, but I'm getting pretty good, and I know all the salesmen at Sherwin Williams."

"A woman of many talents?"

"Not necessarily talents, but possibly more interests than I knew. I've found I'm okay with a hammer and nails too."

"Now there's an area where I have some expertise," Sonny offered. "I've been working on the boat since...well, I'm always working on the boat."

"Boat?"

"It's where I live. I live on a boat."

"You're kidding. No one really lives on a boat!"

She amused him. "I live on a boat. It's over at the Ashley Marina, real easy for me to get to the station. Maybe one of these days you'll let me show you."

"And then I can meet the dog. What did you say is his name?"

"Tork. And don't ask where it came from or what it means, because I have no idea. It just fit at the time. I found him wandering around one night several years back, just a pup, and he looked about as lost as I was then. Now we're family. How about your family? Any around here?"

"No. My parents live in the Midwest, but we aren't close. Celia's family feels like my own, especially now that I'm living here. They've been wonderful to me."

"And how about this man who let you get away? Is that subject off limits?"

"No. I married him right out of law school and spent most of the last fifteen years trying to be what he wanted. But I'm not, so now I'm trying to be who I am, whatever that is. Celia calls it a great adventure. I've been calling it pretty scary, but it's getting easier."

"Living alone, in my lengthy experience with it," Sonny offered, "at least makes you get to know yourself. I admire you for having the guts to start over somewhere new."

"Thanks, but I'm not sure it was very brave. In a way, I was running away, and I was very lucky to have somewhere to go where there waited a Celia Rutledge."

"That's who you called to get Quinn out of jail, isn't it? Rose Pinckney's granddaughter?"

"Yes. Do you know her?"

"I only know of her, but everyone knows Miss Rose. She might be the most charming little lady in Charleston. I was on her porch just the other night, the night of the Howe attack, letting her know everything was okay. She knows more about this town than anybody."

"I'm discovering what a jewel she is. She's a pillar for Quinn Ravenel right now. Celia was explaining the relationship to me."

"Yeah, speaking of that, McKenzie, how's the case going? I was hoping you'd give that defense to someone else just because I don't want to see you involved in such a mess. There's no happy ending that I can see, no matter who defends her. I'm not doubting your capability; I'm just talking as a friend."

"I appreciate it, Sonny, but I may have to see it through, certainly not because I'm the most qualified to do it, but because I have to do it. I'll explain it to you when I understand it better myself. Meanwhile, I did see Jordan Guerry, like I told you. It didn't go as well as I hoped, but we'll see."

"I'm glad to hear it. He's a good lawyer."

"Why doesn't the newspaper have this story?" Julia asked. "Jordan Guerry hadn't even heard it in any detail. They aren't printing anything except the bare bones: break-in at the Howes' place; original suspect released; new suspect under arrest. Doesn't the press want to know more? It has such potential to be the juicy story of Charleston's summer."

"We haven't made anything public yet except those basic facts. I've made sure our people keep a poker face and say very little. It's currently being reported as just a break-in with injury to one of the occupants of the house. I'll keep it that way as long as I can. You'll understand it better after you've lived in this little town of Charleston for a while longer. Keeping some things under wraps has become an art form."

Dinner came, grilled swordfish for Sonny and seared scallops for Julia. They shared a plate of Anson's famous grits. "It was so good I almost forgot how tired I am," Julia sighed as they finished. "I know you are too. But let's both try to sleep tonight knowing everything about this mess is out of our hands. Quinn is in the care of Rose for now. I think she's a little naïve about her dilemma, but it's probably better than the alarm she could be feeling. MacArthur Howe is going to be okay. And Reg Fallon's life is in the hands of God."

53

Quinn was sitting in the chair beside the hospital bed when Willa Fallon woke from a short evening nap.

"I didn't mean to startle you, Ms. Fallon," she spoke quietly. I've just been sitting here watching Reggie sleep. I hope that's okay. The nurse thought you wouldn't mind."

"We're grateful for any of Reggie's friends to sit here with us," Willa answered. "I tell him just before I went to sleep that we all pray together and he be good as new. How's your grandmother, Miss Quinn? It's been a time since I saw her."

Quinn smiled, pleased at the incorrect association. "She's doing very well," she replied. "I'm so lucky to have her."

"We all lucky to have her, child. She help me keep my business agoin' the last some years. She tell her friends, and they call me, and they tell their friends. She a real good lady. She a pistol, ain't she?"

Quinn grinned, wishing the conversation could remain on this innocent plane, knowing she was more than just one of Reggie's visiting friends. She was the reason he was here, the reason he was hurt. She was the reason he had spent a night in jail. She was the reason his mother was suffering here in a cold hospital room on a hot Charleston summer afternoon. How was she going to tell this woman that it was her fault? She had thought that telling Reggie would be hard, but explaining it to his mother was infinitely more difficult.

"Have you been spending the nights here too?" she asked Willa.

"Lawd, child, I ain't left here since Reggie was hurt. Can't leave him here by his self. But folks been comin' by, jes' like you, bringin' food and newspapers and jes' sittin' with us. It sure do help. It's a comfort and a blessin' to have such good friends, I swannee it is."

"Can I get you anything from downstairs, Ms. Fallon, or could I just sit here awhile longer with Reggie while you walk down the hall or go outside for some air?"

"That's real nice, Missy, but I reckon I jes' keep this spot for the night now unless Reggie wake up and need me. You jes' tell me how you doin'. You done with college now too?"

"Yes, I finished just when Reggie did. I wanted to be back for the College of Charleston's graduation because so many of my friends were graduating, but it happened right before my own. You must be so proud that Reggie graduated so near the top of his class."

"I always proud of Reggie. He's a good boy. I don't know why the good Lawd bring Reggie here, Missy, but his friends stand by him."

"Reggie and I have been friends for so long, Ms. Fallon, since we were little kids. You know that. I want to tell you something about why he's here. God didn't have anything to do with it; it's all my fault." Quinn looked straight at Willa as she made her admission. "I want Reggie to know how sorry I am. I'll come every day until I can tell him myself."

"You not makin' much of any sense, Missy," Willa frowned, trying to see how this girl could be responsible for Reggie's accident. The police had said, she was sure, that a man was driving the other car.

"You know how they took Reggie to jail for what happened to Mac Howe?"

"Yes'm, that be a big mistake of some kind. If'n he not be in that jail, he wouldn't be here in this hospital. That's what I knows for sure."

"And that's why it's my fault, Ms. Fallon," Quinn continued. "I should have been the one in jail. I'm the one who attacked Mac Howe, not Reggie. Reggie would never do something like that."

Willa was sitting forward in the reclining chair now, the blanket draped over its arm. She was looking at Quinn, but she could not yet find the question to ask. Moments passed while Willa studied Quinn's face.

"You tellin' me it be you? They say they find Reggie sittin' right by a knife. They say that knife had the Howe boy's blood on it."

"It was a razor, and it belonged to Grams' husband before he died. I brought it from home, and I guess after I was done I just dropped it somewhere along the sidewalk on my way home. I have no idea why Reggie was anywhere near that razor. I couldn't believe it when I read that he was in jail. I went right over there and told the police what really happened. That must be why they let him go and were bringing him home in the police car. Now do you see why it's my fault?"

"You a good girl, Missy. I been knowin' you with Miss Rose your whole life. You can't be sayin' you'd break into no house with no knife. Why you be sayin' this?"

"Before we all went away to college, Mac Howe did something really awful to me. I went there to hurt him back. I don't expect you to understand, but I didn't mean for anyone else to get caught up in this, certainly not Reggie. I guess he won't ever forgive me, but I have to explain it to him."

There was silence for a minute. Quinn was at a loss for any further explanation or apology, and Willa was trying to make sense out of what this girl had said. She finally processed it to the point of her son being taken into custody for something Quinn claimed she had done.

"You went in that house with a razor?"

"Yes, I did."

"And you cut the Howe boy?"

"Yes, I did. I hurt Mac Howe. I nearly cut off his penis, and then I left, and I dropped the razor and went home and went to sleep. I thought it was all over right then."

"You did what?" Willa's eyes were wide, and if her knees were younger, she would have jumped from the chair. "You cut off his...?" The question was formed in her eyes but did not come out. Reg stirred slightly and made a small sound. Both women watched his face for signs that he was waking, but he was once again quiet.

"We best be more quiet," Willa cautioned softly. "He be needin' his rest."

"I should probably go anyway," Quinn whispered. "I just wanted Reggie to know. I'll be back again to talk to him. Is there anything I can do for you before I go?"

"You say the Howe boy harm you?" Willa asked.

"Yes, he did, and I was just trying to make it right. I never meant to hurt anyone but him."

"He musta done somethin' real bad."

"It was real bad for me. I've been thinking about it for the last four years of my life." Quinn's eyes were full of tears and her lips trembled. She didn't want to cry here in this hospital room; there had been enough crying for one day, and Reg's mother certainly had enough on her mind.

"Lawd a'mercy, he done rape you, child." Willa said it as a declaration.

54

Sonny decided to sleep late on Saturday morning. He certainly deserved it, he thought, after the week he'd had. But of course he woke at 6:45, as was his habit, and could sleep no more. At least his night had not been interrupted by a call from the station.

The water's choppiness confirmed the forecast of a stormy day. There was a tropical depression at sea to the southeast, and the coast was feeling its presence. It was predicted to veer to the northeast and diminish in strength, but the mere suggestion of hurricane potential made Charlestonians take heed. Hugo had seen to that in 1989, tearing through the vulnerable Lowcountry with maniacal force and leaving only devastation in its wake. Sonny had lost a boat to that storm; this one was its successor.

He had everything here that a man could want, he thought, except satellite television. And there were plenty of places where he was welcome to watch a little football during the season. The wives and girlfriends of his pals found him charming and easy to please, so he was always welcome for dinner and a game. He enjoyed the families, the rowdy kids and the teasing between the guys and their wives. He had almost had all that, he thought, wondering if there would have been kids with Annie.

Julia would have liked Annie too. The thought surprised him, their images both in his mind at once. But they could have been friends, both gentle women with quick minds and warm hearts. He had enjoyed the evening with Julia, he thought, fishing inside his head for feelings of disloyalty to Annie. There seemed to be none. Maybe she could see him, and it was okay with her. He hoped so. It wasn't a romance, was probably unlikely to lead to one, but it was nice. He was certainly attracted to Julia, but the new acquaintance they were building was enough. These little sparks he had never expected to feel again were welcome and entertaining. They reassured him that he could still feel. He was alive, and his allotment of the desire a man feels for a woman had perhaps not died with Annie after all. He had to smile, and he hoped Annie was smiling with him.

Tork wanted breakfast and the morning run around the marina. "Okay, Boy," Sonny agreed, "let's get on with it." He poured the big dog's breakfast into his bowl and drank several swallows of orange juice from the carton. It would feel good to run in the wind.

55

Julia had waited only briefly to see Jordan Guerry. She was surprised he had returned her call on a Saturday morning, but it would be good to talk with him again about Quinn's representation.

"I hope you don't mind, Julia, but I took the liberty of discussing this with our senior partner. Mendel's experience is considerable, and I've always respected his opinion. He'll be joining us in a minute or two. Do you mind?"

"No, not at all. I would prefer that discussion stops here, though, Jordan, considering the delicacy of the subject matter. But I'm grateful for another input, especially from someone whose expertise is almost legend. I understand he had bypass surgery a year or so ago. He looks very well now."

"Oh, he's doing remarkably well. The doctors were amazed at the speed of his recovery, and he thinks and acts like a man twenty years younger than his age. There's a treadmill in the corner of his office, and intellectually he keeps us all on our toes."

The door to the office opened after a small rap of knuckles, and Mendel Comings poked his head in.

"Am I welcome?" he asked, "or have you two deemed my advice unnecessary and antiquated?" He smiled broadly, and the man at seventy-something did indeed look trim and well.

"Never, sir," Jordan answered, coming around the desk. "Have you met Julia McKenzie?"

"Oh, yes, I had the pleasure just the other evening at Rose Pinckney's. It's nice to see you again, Julia."

"Nice for me as well, Mr. Comings," Julia replied. "And thank you for offering your opinion on this case. I didn't know Jordan had bothered you with it, particularly on a Saturday morning."

"My dear, it's no bother whatsoever. We tend to be here on Saturday mornings just so that the golf course will seem more pleasurable on Saturday afternoon. Let's sit down and chat for a few minutes. I understand your client graduated from Smith College and was hired to teach at Porter Gaud. She must be an impressive young woman. They hire only the best and brightest over there."

"Yes, sir, she's a smart girl."

"So how did she get into this dilemma, and how do you plan to get her out? Jordan sees no alternative to an insanity defense. Do you concur?"

"Well, Mr. Comings, I certainly see an insanity plea as the practical choice, but my client adamantly refuses to consider it. We have talked at length, and as you know, I brought her over to talk with Jordan as well. She remains totally unmoved. I believe she would petition to defend herself rather than have even the best attorney argue insanity on her behalf."

Jordan was studying the expression of Mendel Comings, who was nodding slightly, his eyebrows knit. He processed Julia's assessment, his fingers marching rhythmically on the corner of Jordan's desk.

"Jordan thought as much," he said finally. "He thought you might bring her around, but you think that unlikely?"

"I can't see it happening, sir, and I've given it a great deal of thought. I'd like to broach an alternative with you if you have the time to hear it."

"Of course. I'm happy to listen. These boys around here tell me that's all I'm good for these days." Glancing at the younger man, he winked. "Right, Jordan?"

"I've already heard on very good authority that you argue the best case in town," Julia injected before Jordan could reply. "Having your ear is a distinct honor for me. I know what I'm thinking is a little unconventional, so bear with me here."

"You go right ahead. I think I've heard it all."

"Well, I'm toying with the idea of arguing straight self-defense for Quinn. I know proving the immediacy of threat to her will be troublesome, and I realize the uphill battle I'm proposing, but Quinn will not hear of questioning her sanity as the means to save her."

Mendel Comings was frowning somewhat, his eyes slightly narrowed. He pursed his lips and rubbed his chin with one hand as he considered what Julia had said. "Now that would be an argument worth hearing, and if you craft it, I want to be there to listen when you present your case," he said finally. "I'll have to stick with Jordan's more pragmatic approach and recommend that you continue to try to convince your client to use it. However, your line of thinking intrigues me. If you go with it, please keep me posted on your progress, Miss McKenzie." He rose to leave.

Julia rose as well, extending her hand. "Well, you haven't encouraged me," she said, "but I certainly appreciate your time and the benefit of your wisdom."

"If you win this case with that argument, you have a standing invitation to join my firm."

Julia smiled. "If I should win this case, I'll probably not need your firm, sir; I'll be infamous."

Comings held Julia's hand in both of his for an extra moment, his laughter filling the room. "You've won me over, my dear. If I were even twenty years younger, I'd be asking you to dinner here on the spot. Since I'm not, call if I can help you unofficially. It's a very interesting proposition. Very interesting." With that, he patted the back of her hand and left the room, chuckling.

Julia looked at Jordan and he at her. It was clear that Mendel Comings, cordial as he had been, had no interest in involving his prestigious firm in the mess Julia's case presented. He, and Jordan as well, were accustomed to winning. He obviously did not consider this matter winnable, especially after hearing Julia's unorthodox plan. Julia would have to decide whether to go it alone.

56

Rose used her cane to get up when the doorbell rang late on Saturday morning. Her knees were bothering her more than usual. It was a beautiful walking cane, intricately carved, that the mayor's wife had brought her from Australia. She grimaced at the pain but admired the cane nonetheless. Opening the door, she faced Adeline Ravenel.

"Good morning, Rose. I brought the rent for August. I hope you don't mind my stopping by."

Rose opened the door wider. "Come in, Adeline. I've been meaning to call you. Would you like a cup of tea?"

Adeline looked at the gold watch on her wrist. "I can spare a few minutes. I'm on my way to do a little shopping at Nordstrom. They're having a fabulous sale."

Rose motioned to a wing chair by the window in the living room. "Sit down then. I'll be right back with the tea. Would you like sugar?"

"Oh, yes, please," Adeline responded, simpering. She removed a small silver compact from her purse and checked her reflection in its mirror. Her hair, Rose noted, was freshly permed and colored. Nothing would keep Rose from thinking it a mousy unkempt brown. Quinn told her last year that her mother had undergone cosmetic surgery to change her nose and remove wrinkles from around her eyes. Rose noted no visible improvement. Adeline had, Rose thought, classically beady eyes and a straight, skinny, boring nose that just suited her.

Rose had thought of this scene, but it was writing itself a little sooner than she expected. Never mind, she thought, she was ready. "Would you mind carrying the tray for me, Adeline?" she called from the kitchen. "I'm feeling like an old woman this morning."

"Oh, of course. I should have thought." Adeline hurried to the kitchen to get the serving tray and carried it back to the coffee table in the living room. She took her seat again, and Rose poured the tea into two porcelain flower-adorned teacups. Adeline watched as Rose stirred a spoonful of sugar into one of the cups and handed it to her on its saucer. The tea was just brewed, she noted, and steam rose from the cups.

"I cannot fathom that it is almost August," Adeline began. "Where has the summer gone? Doesn't it seem like spring was just a moment ago?"

"Yes, the summer is almost over. Our little Quinn will soon be starting her new teaching job at Porter Gaud. You must be so proud of her."

Adeline's face took on a strange expression. "Yes, of course," she replied. "Your garden has been just magnificent this year, Rose. I can't remember a summer since I've lived here when it was more beautiful."

"It has done well this year. I think we last talked out by the garden the night the police were here. Wasn't that an unusual event? Did you ever hear what happened?"

"I did hear. The Howes had an awful break-in, and I believe their son was injured. The paper said there was an arrest, but I haven't followed it very closely."

"If you had followed it a little more closely," Rose spoke slowly and clearly, enunciating each word, "you might be aware that the assailant on that night was a young woman."

Adeline sipped her tea, holding the cup's handle between her thumb and forefinger, eyeing Rose through the steam. "Is that so?" she responded tentatively.

"Fortunately for her, that young woman had friends to help her. She might otherwise still be occupying a cell at the county jail. Her own family did not choose to stand by her. Can you imagine that?"

Adeline, wary now, set her cup on the coffee table and reached to the floor for her purse. She did not wish to have this conversation. "I really must go now, Rose. Thank you for the tea." Rising from the chair, she started for the door, walking quickly on her three-inch heels.

Rose spoke to Adeline's back, her voice clear and strong. "If you don't mind, Adeline, you can just keep going in a more permanent sense. I'll tear up the check you brought, since I neither need nor want your money, and I'll give you thirty days to be out of my guesthouse. Don't take a day longer. I already have a new tenant."

Adeline whirled around, her face red, her breath quick and shallow. "You can't throw me out!" she said, her voice raised. "You have no reason to throw me out."

"I can and I just have," Rose responded, smiling. I'm sure you'll find a place more to your liking. And do it quickly. If you don't, the entire city of Charleston will know just what kind of woman you are."

"I've done nothing to you, Rose Pinckney," the other woman almost shouted. "You have no right to judge me. I never asked for that child, and look what she's brought me: nothing but grief and humiliation. She's finally shown herself for the little tramp she is."

Rose had also risen from her seat and, using the cane, she slowly approached Adeline, whose eyes were blazing with anger. When Rose slapped her with her free right hand, the other woman was stunned. "You are not worth the ground upon which Quinn walks. Mark my words clearly. I've been onto you for years. This time you've gone too far. Now get out of my house, Adeline Ravenel. The thirty days started five minutes ago."

Rose didn't move and didn't take her eyes from Adeline until she was out the door, slamming it loudly behind her. Quivering slightly, Rose nonetheless smiled. My, how many years had she longed to do that? And true to form, Adeline had finally freed her to do it. Looking at the palm of her right hand, she found it reddened and tingly. She hoped its print would remain on Adeline's loathsome cheek until Charleston washed into the sea.

57

Julia was tearing fresh spinach leaves for a salad when Quinn arrived.

"Come on in," she called, drying her hands on her way to the door. "It's open."

"Hey," Quinn greeted her, slipping off her sandals just inside the door. "I can't believe what you've done with this house."

"Thanks. Come on in and see the inside. It's a work in progress, but I'm enjoying every minute I can spend working on it. I'd forgotten that the house is familiar to you."

"Grandma Rose used to bring me here all the time. In the summers, I hardly slept at mama's house at all, and in the winter, we would sit in the sunroom all day on the weekends putting together jigsaw puzzles or doing my homework while we watched the dolphins. Wow," she exclaimed, seeing the kitchen.

"What do you think?" Julia asked. "I'm not finished with the cabinets."

"It's beautiful," Quinn said, looking around the room. "These old floors look great. Did you do them yourself?"

"The handyman and I together," Julia laughed. "I don't think I could have done it alone. I wanted to keep all the hardwood, but the sanding was a horrendous mess. I'm so thankful it's over."

"Here, sit down and get comfy." Julia pulled out a stool at the kitchen island where she was working. "Would you like a glass of wine, or shall we start with iced tea?"

"Tea would be fine. I hope you're not going to any trouble for me. You've already gone out of your way to help me, and I'm very grateful."

"Well, you're part of Celie's family, and she's the reason I'm still sane," Julia grinned, "so I'm delighted for any way to be helpful. And about dinner, I cannot be counted on to make anything beyond a basic salad, as you can see, and I got sandwiches earlier at the deli. If that goes wrong, I have a whole notebook of menus from places that deliver."

"That's great. It makes you seem a little more like a real person."

"A real person?" Julia asked.

"You know, like with shortcomings and all."

"Oh, trust me, I have plenty of shortcomings. Did you doubt that?"

"I'm sorry, Miss McKenzie. I meant that I felt a little intimidated, I guess, coming here to your house. You're a lawyer, after all, and I sure blew my first impression with you, seeing as how we met when I was under lock and key."

"Not at all. My impression is evolving, but you certainly got my attention. I'm anxious to get to know you. Please just think of me as Celia's friend, therefore yours as well, and we'll do the lawyer stuff later. Okay?"

"Okay."

"Let's take this pitcher out to the sunroom and see if the view is what you remember. You need sugar, right?" Julia asked.

Following Julia across the house and into the porch, Quinn stopped to admire changes along the way. It was the old house she knew, but better. Julia was combining big soft pieces of furniture with sleek, contemporary wicker designs. The effect was neither beachy nor pretentious.

"Pick a spot," Julia invited, settling in. "We don't have to worry about the sun coming through the west windows today. It's nice to have these blustery, dark days to break up the summer, isn't it? Oh, see the dolphin? Right there," she pointed, and Quinn saw it. "It makes me so happy to sit here and watch them. It's a version of pleasure I never knew before."

"What do you mean?" Quinn asked, taking a corner spot where she could look out over the harbor.

"Life here doesn't seem to expect anything from me except just to be."

"That sounds," Quinn observed, "like a result of where you are in your life rather than a product of the house or the surroundings."

Julia looked across the room as she sat in a corner opposite Quinn. "Well, that's a pretty perceptive thing for you to say," she smiled, "and probably quite true. Celie says I've slowed down enough now to start enjoying my life."

"Weren't you enjoying it before?" Quinn asked.

"I don't think I ever really knew how," Julia answered. "Or, according to Celie, I didn't think I deserved to enjoy. All the years I was married, I enjoyed things because Jack was enjoying them. Or maybe I just reflected his pleasure, not experiencing any of my very own. Does that make sense?"

"Sure. I took as much psychology as I could fit in my schedule, and it gave me a peek into how complicated we humans are. I gained insight into people in general and into myself too. Those were my favorite classes."

"Really? I liked psychology courses too, but I guess Celie liked them better than both of us."

"She's so good at what she does, partly because she comes across as the warm earth mother we all wish we had, don't you think?" Quinn asked. "As her client, it sure would be easy to transfer attachment to her. Or is that just true for me because I grew up thinking of her that way?"

"No, I see it too. She's a natural at what she does. Usually, trite as it is, a good mother is as good a gift as life can give. If we didn't get one, it's great to find that safe, fuzzy feeling with a confidante like Celie. If she weren't my best friend, I'd certainly pay for a few hours a week in her presence."

"Me too, so I guess we're lucky to have her for free."

"She and I laughed our way through college together, and then we lived on the phone as post-grads at different schools. She's always there for me, even now after all this time. I guess I'm a good poster girl for the fact that men come and go, but a good friend is forever."

The two women looked out at the sea, watching two or three dolphins play just offshore. The wind had picked up again, roughing the surf.

"Did Celie know your ex-husband?" Quinn asked.

"She did, and she let me marry him anyway," Julia grinned. "I met Jack during my last year in grad school. Celie never knew him very well, but I kept telling her he made me happy, which never true. I mistook addiction for happiness."

"Addiction?" Quinn asked.

"I was addicted to his interest and attention. He was attractive and desirable, and he wanted to be with me, or so it seemed. Since I wasn't very high on my own company back then, I was hooked when he was. He had me wrapped around his little finger and his every word." Julia paused. "I'm talking to you like I would to Celie. But I guess you get the picture."

Quinn laughed in delight, a pure, light genuine sound. "Y'all must have been quite the pair when you were in college together."

"I guess we were. Sometimes it seems so recent, those times. We agree that our hearts and spirits are still the same, though our minds are crowded with a lot more life experience."

"It's pretty brave for you to leave a marriage and a home and a law firm several hundred miles away and start over all by yourself. I'm not sure I'd have that kind of courage," Quinn said, which Julia thought a somewhat ironic statement. She let it pass, however, preferring to let the conversation continue uninterrupted by thoughts of Quinn's current predicament. That would come later.

"It wasn't courage at all," Julia shared. "I threw him out because I thought it was the only way to save us. I believed even as I packed his things that he would realize it was me he loved, that we belonged together. He never came back."

"You believed he'd be back?"

"Yes, so you see it wasn't brave at all. It was pure blind desperation, my last attempt to hold on."

"I'm sorry, Julia. That's so sad. Are you okay now? Are you over it?" Quinn asked sincerely.

"I am okay, maybe better than I've ever been. When I told you earlier that I was having a good time, that I enjoy just being here, it was true. I've been insecure personally and competitive professionally, both consuming a lot of life energy unproductively. I think I used my professional competence, winning cases, producing exemplary results, to compensate for the total personal midget I felt I was. But that doesn't work; one part of life doesn't offset another and balance the scale. Now I go to my own little office where I'm perfectly happy, and I come home to this great house where I'm just as happy, and I think maybe this is enough. This is contentment. I found it when and where I least expected it and when I'd stopped longing for it. Wouldn't Celie be pleased to hear me say that?"

"Yes, and you can be sure I'll tell her," Quinn nodded, "every single word."

"Okay, on that note, shall we bring the food out here? Unburdening is apparently good not only for the soul but for the appetite," Julia laughed. "I'm starving."

58

The Howes were enjoying an early dinner on the covered portion of the patio behind their house. Protected from the weather by screen and latticework, they listened to the wind and intermittent blowing rain. The main course was a seafood soufflé from Martha's own recipe, and after a digestive break before dessert, Martha had gone inside to get the pie just out of the oven. CNN played in the background, visible through the sliding door. The colonel liked to keep up with world events.

After his time in the hospital, Mac was enjoying this time with his parents. His leave from Fort Bragg had been extended by the injury, and although he was ready to get back to the base, there was no better care than his mother's and no better companionship than his father's.

"I wanted to wait until your mother was out of earshot to ask you about the girl," the colonel spoke quietly. "Is there anything to this story the detective was spinning about a girl being involved in the attack on you or is it as preposterous as it sounds?"

"I can't make any damn sense out of his story, Dad," Mac replied. "The cops must be pretty fucking stupid to think they can make that fly." He glanced toward the house to be sure his mother hadn't heard the language. "They haven't been around here trying to peddle that trash anymore, so maybe they're on the track of the real lunatic."

"I plan on going by the station tomorrow to see what they've come up with. I'm going to keep on their asses, because we don't want them sitting on this. Those fools down there don't seem to know a crook from a hole in the ground."

"I'd offer to go along, Dad, but I'll leave it to you for now. I am damn curious, though. I hope you can find out something."

"Is there anything you can think of that would make this something other than a random act, anything at all? Have you had a run-in with anyone, stepped on someone's toes, made out with someone's girlfriend? Have you thought of any reason why someone might have been after you personally?"

"Dad, I get along with everybody. I can't think of a damn soul who would mess with me. Guys who don't like my style just don't hang around me."

"I've been over and over it in my mind, son, and I can't see how this happened without any of us hearing anything. It just galls me to think of someone like that on the loose right here in Charleston. No one is safe until he's caught. And when that happens, we'll see that they throw the book at him."

"I'd like just a few minutes alone with him in an alley myself," Mac growled through gritted teeth. "There's nothing the law could do to him that I can't do better."

"God knows you have the right," the colonel agreed. "Every hour of the day I'm thankful you weren't killed. I don't know how your mother would survive if anything happened to you. This was bad enough, but she's holding up amazingly well, don't you think?"

"She's a trooper. She's been hovering over me like a mother hen. I think it does her more good than it does me."

The colonel nodded, smiling. "There isn't a damn thing in the world she wouldn't do for you. She held up at the hospital like an artillery sergeant the whole time you were in surgery, and then when she saw you were okay, she passed right out."

"No kidding?" Mac laughed aloud.

"Don't you let on that I told you. We have to keep that between us, but I thought you'd get a kick out of it. For your mother, the sun rises and sets with you, has since the day you were born. I might as well be a fly on her sleeve since you came along." He chuckled.

"Oh, I think she would react about the same way if we were sitting by your hospital bed, Dad. Better me than you, though, old man!" Not wishing to be serious, Mac teased.

"Watch yourself, son. You're in no condition right now to be giving any guff, even to a geezer like me. The shape you're in, I could knock your ass right across the fence and into the Manigault's back lawn without even breathing heavy."

"Yeah, just give me a day or two."

Martha opened the back door carrying a tray heavy with three servings of rhubarb pie and a pitcher of iced decaf with caramel and whipped cream.

"You're just in time to keep this old man from trying to whip my tail, Mom," Mac said in his best little-boy whine. "Here I am laid up, and he's pickin' on me."

"He won't be picking on my boy if he knows what's good for him," Martha bristled in pseudo scolding. "Now you boys settle down like civilized folks and have some pie and coffee. If you behave yourselves, I might offer seconds."

"Aw, Mom," Mac cajoled, putting his arm around his mother's waist as she set down the tray, "you know you're gonna give us anything we want." And, of course, she was.

59

After their early dinner, Julia and Quinn settled into opposite ends of Julia's L-shaped sofa, feet up, toes almost touching. Quinn was feeling much more comfortable with Julia as the two talked, covering many subjects and discovering interests in common. Both were bookworms and loved old music, though the definition was different for Quinn than for Julia. It had made them laugh when Quinn confessed she thought 80's music old; for Julia, it was songs from the 60's. They each had a well-developed, wry sense of humor about mothers.

"She did so want me to reflect well on her," Julia recalled, shaking her head in disgust. "Why do these women have children?"

"I know mine did it for my daddy," Quinn responded. "Heaven knows she's told me often enough. She never expected to be left alone to raise a child she never wanted. She wanted Daddy, and Daddy wanted me. After he was gone, I was nothing to her but a stone around her neck. She never actually said that to me, but I heard her say it on the phone to one of her friends. I must have been about ten years old then. I wasn't even surprised, though I remember wishing I'd never heard her. She kept cutting into the moments when I could pretend I had a mother who loved me."

"I heard lots of those same things, even though I had my father. He traveled a lot. We never get over those things, do we? It's a wound that doesn't heal. It fascinates me now that I have Celie and her girls to watch. She tells me, and tells me often, that I need to grieve for the mother I never had so that I can move on and be good to myself and find friends who nourish me. I think I've been working on that over the last year. It's not easy. You can start now and finish light years ahead."

"I'm still angry with my mother. Aren't you angry?"

"The anger is fading now. Celie convinced me it wasn't serving any purpose once I'd ranted and acknowledged it and wallowed in it for a while, which I did. And then I cried, mourning someone I never had. It wasn't so much the mother I didn't get, but the little girl who never had her. Part of me was stuck as that little girl because I couldn't move on without accomplishing the very basic task of getting my mother's love. I deserved that love, but since it didn't come, how was I to know that I deserved it? And if I wasn't even worthy of that very basic love of a mother for her daughter, would I ever deserve anything else in my life? It's a hard place to be stuck, particularly if you don't know you're stuck there."

"Is that why you married Jack?" Quinn asked.

"I thought I'd finally found what I was missing."

"When did you start to doubt that?"

"When I couldn't deny to myself that he was sleeping around. Too many people knew, and one of my friends took me to lunch one day and explained the facts of Jack's life as she saw them. It was both enlightening and humiliating. She knew all that I suspected and then some. Her conscience was bothering her because she had been with him the previous weekend. She asked what I was thinking of myself to stay with him. After a few sleepless nights, I began to wonder that myself."

"So you threw him out?"

"It wasn't that clear cut, but yes. I was so naïve as to tell him that it was her or me. Cute, huh?" Julia smiled wryly as she recalled and retold the events of a year earlier. It seemed much longer ago. Even the day the papers came seemed long ago. "We're officially divorced now. The decree came last week in the mail."

"Do you feel like a new woman?"

"I am a new woman. It's amazing even to me how far I've come. You can't ever give up on life because there are so many grand surprises just around those corners, even though the corners are sometimes hard to navigate." Julia sat up and leaned over to get the bottle of wine from the coffee table. "More?" she asked. "I've been rambling on and ignoring your empty glass."

"I do have to drive home, but maybe just a little, thanks," Quinn held out her glass. "I'm not much of a drinker, but this is good, and I'm having a really good time, Julia. Thanks for having me over."

"Listen, let's just have the wine, and you can sleep in the guest room. It's a great night to sleep at the beach with the wind whipping the waves. How about it?" Julia poured. "You know, I just recently discovered how much I like this wine from a local vineyard. Jack would have laughed at me and refused to try it. Who knew I could have opinions and favorites of my very own?"

It was settled that Quinn would stay. She had spent many nights in this house and was feeling at home here again. She called Rose to tell her. "You girls just have a wonderful time," Rose advised, obviously pleased.

"Let me run and get the keys out of my car," Quinn called as she opened the door. "I'll be right back."

The wind was whipping around her as she ran down the steps, but it was a warm, tropical wind, heavy with moisture. The sound of the surf was powerful and rhythmic. Quinn relished the thought of sleeping here again with the sea playing her lullaby.

"I just checked my messages," Julia said as she took her place again on the sofa. "Did you get your keys?"

"Yes. It's windy. I always loved a storm on the beach, especially one with lightning and thunder. Grams used to tell me that it was the gods carrying on. She said the thunder was the male and the lightning was the female. The male would rant and rave and roar, only making noise. Then the female in a flash would strike him dead. She would laugh and laugh at that story. I'll bet you like it too, don't you, Julia?"

"As a matter of fact, I do," Julia smiled broadly.

"Speaking of being struck by lightning, I meant to tell you earlier that I visited Reg Fallon at the hospital last night. He was struck by a bolt of lightning, and it was me. He was asleep, so I confessed to his mother. I feel so guilty about what happened to Reg."

"Quinn, that was not your fault."

"It sure wasn't Reg's fault," Quinn asserted quickly. "What will happen to him now? Will he be able to play basketball? If he can't, I don't know how I'll live with it."

"I meant to go see him and visit with Willa, I promise to do that tomorrow, and then I'll find out as much as I can about it. Blaming yourself won't do any good."

"I am to blame."

"If we follow that crooked course of thought," Julia went on, "then Mac Howe is ultimately to blame."

"Yes, I guess he is. But then Reg fell into the sequence accidentally."

"If you believe in accidents, he did," Julia agreed.

"What would you call it?" Quinn asked.

"I'd call it food for a long conversation another time, Julia replied. We can talk about accidents and coincidence. For now, I'll have to swear Willa to secrecy about your conversation with her. And please don't succumb to the urge to confess to anyone else. We don't want to spread this story around any further. Okay?"

"Okay. Sorry."

"I need to see Reg anyway. I'm the one who handled his contract with the Mavericks, and we're going to need to be in touch with their people. If his basketball career is impacted, there might be some merit to a case against the city for medical costs. He wasn't just coincidentally in the wrong place at the wrong time; he was put in the wrong place because of a mistake by employees of the City of Charleston."

"And by something I did," Quinn added.

"Let's not beat ourselves up tonight. We can save that for another time. Or better yet, let's make a pact to be allies and never allow each other to rag on herself." Julia held up her glass, and Quinn reached over to touch it with her own, tinkling the crystal.

"Done," Quinn agreed, smiling.

"So now that we've broached the subject, shall we talk about it? I need to tell you about my visit this morning with Jordan Guerry and the senior partner at his firm. Are you ready to tackle it?"

"Okay," Quinn sighed. "I can't stop the forces that put this in motion, so let's talk about it before it rolls right on over me."

"First, I have to tell you once again that I am not an experienced criminal lawyer. Jordan Guerry called in Mr. Comings, their senior partner, to advise me against any plea except one involving a mental lapse."

Quinn's mouth opened, but Julia held up her hand, forestalling interruption. "Hear me out. I need you to know that what I propose as a defense is not a traditional one. It probably has few if any precedents in the law, and these guys who have criminal defense experience don't believe it can work. I have no business persuading you to use such a defense. In fact, I'm trying to dissuade you from it based upon the best advice I can find. I called someone at my old firm in D.C. to run it by him yesterday, and he seemed to think I'm the one who is crazy for even considering it."

"But you are considering it?" Quinn asked.

"I am considering it as a last resort if we can't agree on another more orthodox plan. My first responsibility to you as my client is to strongly advise that we hire and take the advice of an experienced trial attorney. It doesn't have to be Jordan Guerry; we can talk to some other people."

"I don't want other people. All the others will think I'm crazy. Even if I am crazy, I'm not going to say so out loud and use it as an excuse for what I did. I'm just not going to do it."

"Well, Quinn, my new friend, I'm going to ask you to think about it overnight. I want to help you, and I appreciate the fact that you think I can, but the consequences of my failure to come through will affect your life more than mine. I would be devastated, to be sure, but you could be in prison."

"Well, Julia, my new friend," Quinn mimicked, "I didn't like the jail, but I know I wouldn't like the nuthouse any better. Let's go for it."

60

Looking out over the stormy harbor, Rose thought of Julia and Quinn cozy together just across the water. It was a good night to be with friends, she thought, and her little Quinn needed one like Julia just now. She and Quinn had spent many nights in that very house, watching the sun set over the city, naming the steeples as nature framed them in lengthening strands of orange and gold. The sky was blustery now, clouds streaming across its starless face, their circular movement promising another night of wind and rain as the tropical depression stalled just off the Carolina coast. Rose enjoyed these nights, feeling enveloped by nature's exuberance. Her soul would soon ride with these winds, she surmised, blending back into the great source from which it came.

Rose had been in other places upon the earth where she felt the presence that was here in the Lowcountry of Carolina. She had felt it sitting atop a mammoth black rock jutting out of the Pacific off the coast of Oregon. And it had touched her as well when she and her husband, rest his soul, had traveled to Nepal and visited a village at the foot of the Himalayas. These were places, she felt, where conduits from the source of life connected to the planes of earth, where a converging of life's essence tumbled out and bubbled over, trickling onto the rest of the earth, diluting as it spread, leaving a density of spirit in these special points on the sphere. There were likely many more, but Rose was grateful, always grateful, to have spent her life right here. Charleston. Home.

The lights across the bay were hardly visible, appearing only as twinkles between bursts of rain. Her thoughts wandered from Quinn to her own great-grandchildren and back again. Tyrney and Katey were so safe, so loved. Rose did not fear for them as she did for Quinn. That fear, she knew, had bolstered her ousting of Adeline from the guesthouse earlier in the day. It was easier to blame Adeline than to question herself or destiny. She had folded the little girl into her care as warmly as she knew how, and it was not enough. In the end, she wondered, had Adeline's mothering prevailed?

If the mother had been away that night, would it have changed the course of things? Would Quinn then have come to Rose for help, finding words of sympathy and support instead of blame? Why on that night in the great scheme of things had fate, whatever she is, written the scene as she did? Quinn was not a violent person, less so than most. Was the young MacArthur Howe by nature a violent boy? Were they not born two children with the same possibilities before them, raised in this sunny locale, loved as youngsters? Now there was the departure point, Rose feared. What had these two children known as love in their young lives? She had a clear picture of Quinn's experience. She knew only a little of Mac's.

Do we all have an equal capacity for violence given the right provocation, she wondered, staring out into the night? What, indeed, would she do in this moment if she were face to face with MacArthur Howe IV? Tonight, she decided, she might respond with appropriate restraint. Four years ago, however, had she been witness to Quinn's anguish in the rape's immediate aftermath, she was not so sure. Most of our individual capacities for violent behavior are, she thought thankfully, vastly untapped.

Turning from the window, Rose made her way slowly up the stairs to her bed. She was glad that tomorrow was Sunday and that she could try to calm her spirit in a church pew.

SUNDAY

61

Sunday morning dawned partly clear, the sun trying to burn its way through the end of the still-swirling clouds as it inched its way out of the eastern sea and up to warm the Holy City. Houses of worship prepared for morning services, and the Sunday Post and Courier was open over many breakfast tables. It did not print any news of value to Willa Fallon. The nurse had left a copy for her when she came to take

Reg back to surgery, but the only news Willa wanted was of her son's recovery.

Several friends would be stopping by after Sunday services, but Willa was alone when Julia opened the door. Seeing the empty bed and the mother's distress, Julia was momentarily stunned, her thoughts racing. Reading the puzzled expression, Willa quickly reassured her.

"Oh, Miss McKenzie, he be in surgery again." She rose and came to embrace Julia, thankful for company. "They decided he be strong enough to fix the knee an' the wrist this morning."

"I should have come sooner, Willa. Here, sit back down and tell me everything that's happened. How are you holding up?"

Willa sighed. "I be doin' the best I can, Miss McKenzie, "the best I can with Reggie comin' and goin' in an' out of operations an' such."

"Did they say when he would be back?" Julia asked. "Do we have time to get you out of the room and down to the cafeteria for some breakfast?"

"Lawd, they done say it be noon before he come back. But if I go, they won't know where to find me if anything..."

"Well, then, I'll just go down and get us some coffee and breakfast and bring them up here." Julia assured her. "And then we can sit and talk. What do you say?"

Willa got back up, almost losing her balance as she stood. "I guess some hot coffee jes' do me good, Miss McKenzie. I'm powerful glad you here."

Julia steadied the older woman and settled her back into the reclining chair. "I'll be right back, Willa. It won't be as good as your cooking, but we'll just make do, won't we?"

Julia made her way to the cafeteria on the lower floor, ordering a pot of coffee, a pitcher of orange juice, an order of bacon and eggs and some pastries to go. She would see that Willa ate the eggs and bacon while they talked. It was obvious that she needed to take care of herself while concentrating on her son's recovery.

As she rounded the corner nearest Reg's room, a doctor emerged, still in surgical cap and gown. "Doctor," Julia called to him, "could you spare me a moment?"

The doctor, a very tall slender man with graying hair, stopped as he pulled the cap from his head. "Yes?"

"I'm Julia McKenzie, doctor. I'm Reg's attorney and a friend of the family. Can you tell me how he's doing?"

"I'm Doctor Raines," he introduced himself, "neurology. I was there monitoring the surgery while the orthopedist repaired the knee. We were fortunate that his condition stabilized for us to do the orthopedic work this soon after the accident. I've just told his mother he'll be back in the room in a couple of hours, barring anything unexpected. I'm very pleased with his progress."

"I know this is somewhat premature, Doctor, but as Reg's lawyer, I have to talk with the basketball people about his condition. Can you advise me what to tell them? Is Reg going to be playing ball?"

The doctor shook his head. "There are no sports in this young man's future," he advised, sounding certain. "The knee will prohibit any activity causing impact. There was not only a compound fracture just below the knee but a virtual crushing of the knee joint itself. It will require several months of care and rehab, not to speak of the trauma to the head and some spinal inflammation and kidney bruising we're watching carefully. I'm sorry to say that he might be very fortunate just to walk on that leg, and then I would predict a slight limp for the rest of his life. I know the story and the future he was expecting. I wish I could give you better news, Ms. McKenzie."

"Well, thanks for being honest with me, Doctor."

Julia would not broach the subject of basketball with Willa. But she would have to spend part of the afternoon back at her office deciding what to say to the Dallas Mavericks on Monday morning.

62

"I knew you'd be holed up in this office," Celia said as she poked her head in the door. "Come on over to the house. I had Pete drop me here after church when I saw your car outside. He took the girls home, and he's going to start a nice lunch, probably one of his omelet creations." She plopped into one of Julia's chairs, slipping her shoes off immediately.

"Feeling bossy, are we?" Julia asked. "I've hardly been working here for an hour, and I have to be sure I'm ready for the preliminary hearing tomorrow. I went over to the hospital first to see about Reg Fallon."

"So how is he?"

"It' not a pretty picture," Julia replied. "I don't think he's ever going to play basketball. I understand from talking to his doctor that he'll be very lucky to walk. Apparently, his injuries are more serious than I realized."

"Wow," Celia looked serious. "How's he taking it?"

"He has no idea, and I sure wouldn't want to be the one to tell him. He's been heavily sedated, I gather, because of the head injury. They were concerned about keeping him as quiet as possible."

"He hurt his head in the crash?"

"I guess there was some swelling around the brain. Now that they have that under control, they did surgery this morning to repair a badly broken knee. If the head injury didn't nail shut the basketball door, the knee probably has. The doctor described it as a multiple fracture and a crushed kneecap. They might have to replace it with an artificial knee joint, which they don't want to do at Reg's age. And if that isn't enough, there's apparently some sort of injury to his spine, and his kidney is bruised. He really is lucky to be alive."

"Jules, that's awful. How's his mom doing? Was she there?"

"Yeah, she's the one I talked to. Reg was in surgery for the knee. She's trying to be strong, but she's a wreck. I would be too in her shoes. She lives for that boy."

Celia shook her head sadly. "Seeing your kids in pain is the hardest thing in the world. I can't even stand it when the girls get their feelings hurt. Is there anything we can do?"

"I guess we can stop by to check on her and maybe take her food. She looks pale."

"Let's get Grams to bake her something great, and we'll take it by the hospital. Better yet, maybe Grams can coax her out of that hospital room for a visit. She and Reg's mom have history way back to when Quinn and Reg played together as little kids. Grams helped her get her catering business up and running. If anyone can provide a little extra strength, it's Grams. I'll call her later."

"Thanks, Cele. I just got a good start on Quinn's case. We had a great time together last night. I see why y'all love her. We drank a little wine and put our feet up and talked, and then she spent the night out at the island with me. When I got up this morning, she already had the coffee made and was sitting on the porch."

"I'm so glad you're getting to know her. I'm worried about her. Am I asking too much of you, my friend, getting you involved in this mess?"

"It's too late now. I'm already in, and getting in deeper. The mess has several ripples. There's Quinn's preliminary hearing tomorrow. And then I must call the Mavericks first thing in the morning to tell them about Reg. I dread it. I wrote the contract between Reg and the team, and now I hope my signing bonus clause will help Reg keep at least some of that money. I'm not sure who's going to take responsibility for Reg's medical expenses. Will the Mavericks cover it? Will the City agree without an action against them? I haven't even started working that out."

"Just think, several months ago you were worried about getting clients," Celia reminded. "Now here you are sitting behind a pile of law books with more work than you want. Are you overwhelmed?"

"A little. I'm trying to organize all of it in my mind today before the week starts. That's why I'm here this afternoon."

"Well, take me home and come in for a break and some lunch. I want to hear more about your time with Quinn. And I want to show you the new honeysuckle that's just started to bloom. It's not your traditional rambling yellow; it's a hybrid compact variety I planted last fall, and you've got to smell these blossoms. Come on," she urged, getting up from her seat and leaning on the desk beside the pile of books. "You look stressed. I'm betting Pete will rub your feet if you come over for lunch."

"Well, that's the clincher," Julia smiled, agreeing with little hesitation. "That's probably the only thing that would make me consider marrying ever again."

"What's that?" Celia asked.

"Finding someone who would rub my feet," Julia laughed, turning off the banker's-style light on her desk. Julia's car, since it was Sunday, was parked on the curb right in front of her office. It was locked.

"You've gotta stop locking this car," Celia argued for the hundredth time. "This is Charleston, not Washington, and it's hot. Now we're going to melt like the sweet things we are as soon as we get in. Don't you know it's ninety-five degrees in the shade?"

"Old habits die hard," Julia replied, starting the engine and turning the air conditioner fan immediately to the highest setting. Celia adjusted her vents to get maximum airflow, and Julia edged the car onto Church Street.

"I think I went on a date," Julia said quietly and without prologue.

"You what?" Celia asked, her head whipping toward the driver's side. Julia smiled, enjoying her friend's reaction. "You think you did what?" Celia asked again.

"I think I went on a date."

"A date? You think you did? When?"

"Friday night."

"Friday night? Day before yesterday? And you're just now telling me? With whom?"

"I've been busy." Julia's smile broadened.

"You've been even busier than I thought," Celia pretended to bristle. "Let's have it. Are you making this up?"

"Why would I do that? Don't you think anyone would want to take me on a date?"

"Okay, enough already. You'd better tell me everything, and you'd better tell me in a hurry. I can't believe you've been sitting on this major tidbit and not telling me, and now you're behaving like a cat toying with a mouse. What's the story?"

"You know that detective who was in my office the other day when you came with Rose and Quinn?"

"Yes."

"He asked me to go to dinner."

"He's gorgeous," Celia squealed. "You went out to dinner with Sonny Legare?"

"I did."

Celia did a little drum number on the dashboard with her fingertips. "I thought he was just there about police business. He is a cop, and you're a lawyer, and he had papers in his hand. But I can see it now. You had your hand on his arm when we came in. I should have caught that."

"Slow down," Julia interrupted the flow. "He was there on police business, sort of. He wanted to tell me about Reg's accident. That was all."

"Obviously not. One day you're talking police business and the next you're out to dinner! Fill in the blanks, Jules."

"Well, we've talked a few times since they picked up Reg. He seems like a nice enough guy. And then out of the blue he called me on Friday morning and asked if I'd go to dinner with him. I think I was too surprised to say no."

"Why would you say no?" Celia asked, still at soprano pitch. "I'd say yes if that man asked me, and I have a husband, two kids and a couple of cats. Where did you go?"

"Anson. It was delicious."

"Did you have a good time?

"I really did. I didn't have much time to worry about it beforehand, and I actually enjoyed myself. I think he did too."

"Did he kiss you?"

"Celia Rutledge, what a question! He did not kiss me. I'm not even sure it was a real date. We do have this case going on, and I think he's a little lonely. Maybe he just wanted company, and I was it."

"So after dinner, you just said goodnight and went on home?"

"He walked me back to my office, and we said goodnight and went home, yes. It seemed perfectly all right at the time. Would you like me to make up a better story? Should I have ripped off his clothes and had my way with him on the desk? That was before I had the books all spread out, you know."

"You're exasperating," Celia answered. "But how long has it been? I mean, you weren't sleeping with Jack for several months before you left, right? And now you've been here a whole year. That's a pretty long time, Jules. And Sonny Legare looks darn good if you ask me, which you most certainly didn't."

"Honestly, Cele, you're the one who's exasperating. It might not even have been a date."

"Oh, it was a date all right."

"Well, it's hard for me to imagine anything beyond sitting across the table. That was nice, though."

"It's progress. Not that I think you need a man in your life, but don't rule it out. Keep your options and your mind open. You've got me and Pete and the girls, but you're young and attractive and alive. I don't want you to miss anything, okay?

"I'm not missing anything." They turned into Celia's driveway, and Julia sat with her hands on the steering wheel for a moment, letting the engine run. "It has been a long time. This isn't anything romantic, but I enjoyed his company. And I really enjoyed surprising you. You should have seen the look on your face."

"I imagine it was priceless. That was definitely a 'gotcha'. I'm just glad for you to have a good time; you know that. We'll have to talk about this some more, lots more."

Julia rolled her eyes and shut off the engine, ready to join Pete and the girls for Sunday lunch. She shifted gears in her mind from men and possibilities to the wonderful little family she already had, not born of her flesh and blood but kindred of her heart.

63

The river was still choppy, so it was unlikely Sonny would catch much, but he had been restless on this Sunday afternoon as his mooring tugged at the dock. Even if the fish weren't biting, he could go out past the Morris Island Lighthouse and head south toward Edisto and Hilton Head. Tork ran back and forth expectantly as he watched Sonny untie the boat.

"Okay, boy, let's head out and see what we can see."

Easing out into the water, Sonny adjusted his controls and turned into the wind. Clouds sailed above the river, relinquishing more and more of the sky to brilliant blue and the influence of a warming sun. His shirtsleeves were rolled to the shoulder, and Sonny kicked his well-worn boat shoes under the seat, flexing his ankles and enjoying the wind in his hair. It had been more than a week since he left the dock.

His usual fishing buddies were busy on this afternoon. Surprised at himself, he had thought of Julia, wishing he could call her. But theirs was too new an acquaintance, he decided, to assume he could call her on a Sunday afternoon and ask her to go fishing. Did she know how to hold a fishing pole or bait a line, he wondered. A woman who was in her element in the courtroom or comfortable at a good restaurant would not necessarily be at home on a rocking boat holding a rod and reel.

A couple of women had mildly interested Sonny since Annie was gone, but in each instance, he was put off by the lady's pursuit of him. Although flattered, he had found himself uncomfortable with the attention and unsure how to cope with the presumption that he wanted to be half of a couple. He had always been a loner, happy on the water, dedicated to his work.

Annie had been the exception. She had encouraged his boys-only outings and embraced his love of work and sports. And he had neglected all of it to be with her. She was such a gentle, enchanting woman, calm and unperturbed by life's ups and downs, her outward persona a perfect foil for the warm and compelling seductress it concealed. Unprepared and then totally abandoning resistance, Sonny had been swept off his feet. The romance, unexpected and consuming, had lasted only months when Sonny proposed, on his knees. It would have been for life. Maybe it was, anyway, for him, Sonny thought. He had not, for the years since he lost her, found any comparable sense of closeness or compatibility with a woman; he had not searched; thinking himself possibly not receptive.

Time had, if not healed the wound, at least dulled its pain. Sonny was accustomed to his own cooking, his own company, and the unwavering companionship of the shaggy dog. There could be more, he knew. He had experienced it, however briefly. Turning over in the bed to find himself nose-to-nose with Tork was less than ideal, far short of turning to the warmth and softness of a woman sharing his bed and his life. The sense of something missing was greatest on lazy Sundays such as this one when he found himself at loose ends, wishing for companionship, conversation, sex. Yes, it was about sex too. He missed it.

There was no one to touch, and Sonny had reveled in the touch of a woman who cared about him. The absence of that special intoxication, the knowing that it waited, eagerly and for him alone, left a hole in his life, an ache just behind his heart.

Daydreaming, he had sailed out of the mouth of the Ashley River and south around John's Island, skirting the coast toward the beaches of Kiawah and Hilton Head. Reaching to scratch Tork behind his big ears, Sonny thought again of Julia.

64

Julia had questioned her capability for this task, but she would see it through. Georgetown Law had purported to give every graduate the basic tools to try criminal cases, and she had certainly assisted with some doozies while with the firm in Washington. Struggling to reinforce her confidence, she recalled her scores on the LSAT and her enviable place in the graduating class of students with minds good enough to get into Georgetown Law, not to mention that she had passed the bar exam with flying colors on her first try, no small feat when compared to some of her colleagues who had tried repeatedly to do so for months after graduation.

Okay, she had been warned away from this by almost everyone who knew what she was planning. Jordan Guerry, an experienced criminal lawyer, had made his opinion crystal clear. If Julia pursued this line of defense, he would stretch his diagnosis of insanity to include her as well as her client. He had, after all, called in the senior member of his well-respected firm to dissuade Julia. Sonny Legare, speaking as a friend who wished her well, simply did not want Julia to risk her tenuous acceptance in Charleston's preferred circles. Grandma Rose remained mum, obviously grateful to Julia but afraid for Quinn. Celia, alone, expressed her usual steadfast support and confidence.

Julia settled into the chair behind her desk, glad that she had chosen the ergonomic model, satisfied she had spent lunchtime with Celia's family. Though she had not expected these long and late hours at her desk, she would at least be comfortable. She would treat the coming dozens of hours as study, she decided, just like preparing for exams in college, at which she had always excelled, knowing just what meaty portions to note and which ones to discard as fat and gristle.

The books on the desktop were sorted into piles, each representing the beginning of a search into one element of the case Julia planned to make. On one level, she looked forward to building the argument in Quinn's defense, convincing and creative. On another, she cringed at the formidability of the task, the difficulty of finding any precedent to cite which would support her contention that her client acted in simple, straightforward defense of herself. Julia knew that she was intellectually capable of building a compelling case; she felt nauseous when she remembered that someone's life depended upon it.

The challenges were multiple: First, no proof of the rape existed, making its use in an affirmative defense troublesome at best. Second, the self-defense argument generally required proof that one was protecting herself against imminent danger, a threat so immediate that the action in question was justified. And third, the obvious premeditation over four years begged an argument for insanity instead of an effort to prove Quinn legally sane and rational.

The lunch she had bagged--two egg salad sandwiches and a bag of chips from the deli around the corner—would now be dinner. The aroma from a fresh pot of coffee just brewing filled the little offices, fortification for a long afternoon's effort. The office was quiet, and Julia would take the work home with her at some point, she decided. With just a select volume or two and a specific focus, she could continue working in her bed before she fell asleep.

Wishing for a legal wizard perching on her shoulder, Julia tackled one problem at a time. Intending Mr. Webster to be her ally, she reached first for the dictionary, thick, red-bound and unabridged. The law might have a pretty clear take on self-defense, but she would jump-start a jury's preconception at the outset, breaking it down further, beginning with her own legal-psychological definition of "self". Webster was a great start, but she had asked Celia for access to her extensive collection of psychology texts as well, thinking to spoon feed her captive jury audience a basic explanation of the self we were defending, the unique individual with physical and psychic boundaries, both of which had been crossed when MacArthur Howe attacked Quinn. Feeling somewhat like an artist, she relished the hours ahead among the words, which had always been Julia's medium of choice.

MONDAY

65

It was exactly nine o'clock when Julia arrived at her office on Monday morning, somewhat tired from working late the night before but relieved to have an early start. She had left the office before eight o'clock the previous evening, but it was midnight when she turned off the lamp on her bedside table and closed the top on her laptop computer. She had completed an outline for the case she planned to make, but there were many substantive portions yet unformed on paper and some still fuzzy and tentative in her own mind.

Sunlight speckled the sidewalk through the trees along Church Street as she set down her briefcase to unlock the office door. It was another splendid morning, the prelude to what the weatherman had called a picture-perfect day with the usual possibility of a thunderstorm in late afternoon. Julia's morning was clouded slightly with the knowledge that she would have to talk with her contact at the Dallas Mavericks organization about Reg.

The answering machine on her desk blinked rhythmically, indicating that three messages already awaited her. Remembering that not long ago she longed for the light to be blinking, she smiled as she touched the playback button.

"I know you're not there yet, but call me when you get a break. I'm just checking in. Love you." Celia's voice.

"Julia, dear, I'd like to meet with you when you have time to add another teensy codicil to my will, if you don't mind. You call me when you can. Thanks, sweet." Old Mrs. Prague who changed her will as often as her clothes.

"Ms. McKenzie, Melanie in Judge Stoney's office. He has a small conflict in his schedule this afternoon and would like to reschedule the Ravenel preliminary hearing from one o'clock to two o'clock. Please give me a call. Thanks." The voice of the judge's clerk.

The machine rewound automatically, and Julia dialed, holding the phone receiver between her chin and shoulder so she could talk as she started the coffee. The change in schedule was a welcome delay, giving her an extra hour in which she might well have lunch with Celia before they went to the courthouse. Celia would be picking up Rose for the hearing, who insisted she attend for moral support, and Quinn would come to Julia's office so they could go together. The hearing should be brief and without complication. As coffee began to drip through into the pot, smelling good, Julia sat down behind the desk to make the calls to reschedule. She noted that the three African violets on her window ledge needed water. They were each blooming profusely in the light from her shady south-facing window, but the lower tier of leaves was drooping.

As the phone rang at Celia's house, Julia's office door opened, its little bell jingling. "Delivery," a young man called.

"Come in." Julia motioned to him. "I'm on the phone."

The young man placed a clipboard on the desk in front of Julia, pointing to a line on which he wished her to sign. The name on his uniform read "Charleston Florist". Julia gave him a questioning look, wondering what he was delivering. He trotted to the outer area, returning quickly with a cobalt blue glass container holding a multitude of sunshine-yellow daisies. "Hey, Cele, can you hold on for just a second?" she said as her friend answered the telephone.

She quickly scribbled her name on the white pad and thanked the delivery man.

"Cele," she returned to the receiver, "it's flowers. A florist just brought me the most beautiful yellow daisies."

"Well, shoot, girl, is there a card?"

Julia was already fumbling to open the small envelope. It fell to the floor, and the card fell out as she retrieved it. "Just wanted you to know how much I enjoyed your company", the card said, and it was signed, simply, "Sonny".

"Jules?"

"They're from Sonny Legare. He sent me a bunch of yellow daisies. How would he know I love daisies?"

"Maybe he's smarter than your usual cop. So it was quite obviously a date then. Julia had a date," quipped Celia in a singsong. "Julia had a date."

"Enough already. I called you before the flowers came. The preliminary has been moved to two o'clock."

"Julia had a date," Celia continued.

Smiling, Julia quietly hung up the telephone, knowing full well that her friend would call back.

66

Willa's friend Bernice was spending another morning at the hospital, sharing the vigil a mother kept over her son as best she could. Bernice had brought the Sunday and Monday Post and Courier for Willa and a double batch of her caramel-pecan muffins to share with the nurses. She was surprised to find Reg awake and as alert as he had been since his admission to the hospital. His smile was weak and his color pale, but Bernice was measurably encouraged when he asked for one of the muffins.

"Smells good," he spoke in a voice raspy from the tubes recently in his throat. But he spoke, and there was once again life in his voice and in his eyes. The head of his bed had been rolled up slightly so that he was no longer lying flat.

Willa radiated relief. Though she gratefully bit into one of Bernice's muffins, she looked as though she could live for days on the sustenance of Reg's improving condition.

"Lawd, Bernice, this boy be needin' some good bakin' to help him mend. Let's ask that sweet l'il nurse if he can have one." She pressed the call button.

Responding quickly, the nurse hurried through the door. "Everything okay in here?" she asked.

"We be wantin' this boy to have a home-baked muffin," Bernice answered. "And we want all you girls to come in here and get yourself one too."

The nurse, brunette and tan in her white uniform, stood alongside Reg's bed, checking the monitors and taking his wrist in her fingers to check his pulse. After a moment, she smiled. "Any sign of nausea at all, Reg?" she asked.

"No. Muffins smell real good."

"Well, I'll bring you another glass of that diluted juice, and you can try a few bites. Chew well and go slowly until we see how it sets with your stomach. You're going to be getting some Jell-O and toast pretty soon, but I can't imagine passing up something that smells that good."

"Y'all come on and get some now," Bernice offered.

"If they're as good as the aroma, we'll soon have a line at your door," the nurse said as she left to get the juice. "I'll spread the word."

Bernice moved to stand by Reg's bed, looking down into his face. "It does my heart good to see you lookin' so much better," she said. "It's been a good while since so much prayin' go up from so many folk, and I can see it do you good."

"I've been better," he grinned weakly, "Thanks for being here with my mom."

"I been knowin' your mother way too long to let her be here by herself. There been lotsa folk here prayin' over you, settin' with you and your mom, lots and lotsa folk."

The drip still trickled fluid into the back of Reg's hand, but the bandaging on his head was smaller. His right leg, not covered by the sheet, revealed a new white cast from mid-thigh to ankle and a loose white sock on the foot.

The doctor's voice preceded him into the room. He was obviously in a jovial mood this morning, bantering with the nurses as he plucked Reg's chart from its box on the door.

"You're looking much better this morning," he began when he saw his patient awake. "Doctor Rudolph did some nice work on that knee yesterday. How's it feeling?"

"Hurts a little, but it's okay," Reg responded. "Am I gonna be able to get up before long?"

"Well, it's a good sign that you're interested in getting up," the doctor replied, "but let's give it another day or two. And we want to be sure it's okay with Rudolph before we hand out crutches. I'm very pleased with the injury to your head, but we'll have to let Dr. Rudolph make the decision about getting up and around. His concern, now that he's repaired and casted that leg, is those areas in your back where there was inflammation after the accident. He thinks they will be okay in time, but we don't want to rush it. So many strands of nerves controlling bodily function are woven through the spine. We just want to treat it with the utmost respect and give it a chance to do whatever healing it is able to do without intercession on our part."

"I didn't know my back was hurt," Reg frowned.

"Well, son, it was of lesser concern in the beginning than the injury to your head, which is doing very nicely now, so we can concentrate on the less troublesome injuries. I'm sure Doctor Rudolph will be by later in the day to talk with you. He can explain more about the knee and the back. Now I'd like to just have you follow my finger with your eyes if you would." The doctor held up his index finger and moved his hand slowly back and forth and up and down a short distance from Reg's face. Reg followed with his gaze, not faltering. The doctor was pleased, nodding his approval.

"Don't you be anxious to move around too much today," he cautioned again, closing the chart after making a notation inside. "If Rudolph agrees, then we can try getting you into a chair in a day or two. I'll be by to see you again in the morning unless you can think of anything else. Dr. Rudolph usually makes his rounds in the early afternoon." He headed for the door.

"I swannee you can't leave this room without a muffin," Willa said, "especially after all you done for my boy."

"Ms. Fallon, I smelled those muffins all the way down the hall, and I was beginning to wonder if you were going to make me leave this room empty-handed," the doctor chuckled, holding out his hand. "I left home without breakfast this morning." With a broad smile, he moved on about his rounds.

67

Thinking one last time about how best to couch the doctor's disappointing news, Julia held her hand on the telephone receiver and took a deep breath. She did not relish this conversation with the basketball organization. She would, if she could, wish the situation away. But too many chapters had been written; too many ripples resonated back through too many lives leading up to the accident, back to the arrest, back to the attack on Mac Howe, back to the rape of Quinn Ravenel, back to...what? How far back could events be traced, Julia pondered, how many influences counted relevant or events causal leading up to the night Reg's basketball career was ended in a midnight auto accident?

Having avoided making this call as long as she could, Julia dialed the number. It was time to see what could be salvaged from a promising athlete's career.

"Good morning. This is the Dallas Mavericks," a pleasant female voice answered.

"Good morning. This is Julia Slaton McKenzie in Charleston, South Carolina. May I speak with Weldon Scott?"

"Of course, Miss McKenzie. One moment, please."

Commentary on the team's current activities and status of players was piped pleasantly into Julia's ear while she waited to be connected to the Mavericks' general manager in Dallas.

"Weldon Scott," he answered shortly.

"Mr. Scott, this is Julia McKenzie in Charleston. How are you this morning?"

"I'm well, Julia. It's a nice surprise hearing from you. How's our man Reg doing? Is he getting ready to report for practice? We're sure looking forward to his arrival."

"That's why I'm calling, Weldon. I'm afraid I have some rather upsetting news to pass on. I wish it were not so, but Reg has been in an automobile accident. He's in the hospital here in Charleston with his leg in a cast and his head bandaged. I saw him myself yesterday morning."

"Is he going to be okay? Are the injuries serious?"

Julia could not be certain if Weldon Scott was expressing a genuine concern for Reg or if his real interest was only in the effect of an injury on his new player's viability. She decided to give him the benefit of the doubt.

"His injuries are serious, I'm afraid. He broke his right knee, and they've been draining fluid from around his brain. According to the doctor I spoke with yesterday, there's no possibility he'll be reporting for practice with y'all next week. I'm so sorry to be the bearer of this news, Weldon."

"I'm sorry too, Julia. I don't know what to say, but my first thought is that I should fly down there with one of our team's doctors and see if we can be of any assistance. In a case like this, that's what we're here for. Do you think Reg's doctor would mind a consult?"

"I imagine not, but I'll check with him this afternoon. Contractually, you have the right to fly in any doctor you see fit, so I'm sure Reg's doctors will cooperate with you. Would you like me to get you a couple of rooms at the Wild Dunes where you stayed last spring?"

"I'd appreciate it. Unless you hear back from me, we'll try to get down there tomorrow afternoon. I'll give you a call when we get in."

"Okay, Weldon. I look forward to seeing you."

"The same here. Thanks for calling, Julia."

Sighing with relief, Julia gently returned the receiver to its cradle. She had passed on the bad news, and now the wheels were in motion, rolling toward a resolution of Reg's contract to play ball in Dallas. She wondered if Reg had yet considered the possibility that an NBA career was unlikely.

68

"All rise," the bailiff ordered in his official tone. The judge swished into the courtroom, his clerk closing the door behind him at exactly two o'clock. Taking his place behind the bench, he adjusted his glasses to sit lower on his nose, peering over them at the participants and then down through the lenses to read the file. "You may be seated," the bailiff intoned, calling the room to order.

Recalling his displeasure at their last encounter, the bond hearing, Julia felt some trepidation appearing before Judge Stoney for this next installment of the same matter. Since her practice rarely involved criminal cases, she had no experience or history with this judge. Trying to appear confident, she took a deep breath and glanced to her left to smile reassuringly at Quinn. She was quite sure that the matter would be scheduled for trial, so all she had to do was get through this hearing without incident. She had done her homework, and the proceeding should be straightforward. Certain objections were to be expected from the State, but she was prepared for each one. They should, she thought, be finished here in fewer than thirty minutes.

The courtroom was almost empty, evidence that media had yet to get wind of the darker nature of this matter. A cursory review of the court docket by any reporter would show simply a brief preliminary hearing in the case of State versus Ravenel on a charge of aggravated assault. The last name, not unusual in Charleston, would cause no undue inquiry, nor would a routine charge of aggravated assault. Still, Julia was somewhat surprised. The reporters she knew in Washington would have been all over this story. Maybe their noses for news were sharper.

She noted as the judge read his notes that Sonny was sitting in the last row of benches near the door. Celia and Rose were two rows back on the other side of the aisle, here to lend moral support.

"This is the matter of State versus Quinn Ravenel, aggravated assault with a deadly weapon, case number nine-one-four on the court's docket," announced the clerk.

"Are the parties ready to proceed?" Judge Marshall Stoney asked in the booming voice that matched both his size and his imposing demeanor.

"Yes, Your Honor," was the response in turn from each table.

"The Court will hear from the prosecution." Stoney looked over his glasses at Alan Cantrell, representing the State.

Cantrell rose. "The State has before Your Honor a motion to proceed to trial on this charge. We have submitted for your Honor's review the portfolio of evidence in this case, including most prominently the fingerprints and the weapon. We would also like to re-address the issue of bond if Your Honor sees fit. The State is not comfortable with this defendant remaining out of custody pending trial." He was finished. Short and to the point. The judge looked to Julia.

"Julia McKenzie for the defense, Your Honor. My client would like to formally enter her plea of 'not guilty by reason of self-defense' and is ready to schedule a date for hearing of her case. We realize the forensic evidence against my client is persuasive, but we will submit a similarly compelling defense. On the matter of bond, we maintain that Quinn Ravenel is no danger to herself or anyone in the community. There is enough confidence in her that the prohibitively high bond was posted immediately. There should be no concern in the community about this defendant."

Cantrell was again on his feet, not surprising Julia.

"Self-defense, Counsel? You are planning to argue self-defense? I have seen no shred of evidence to suggest that such a case can possibly be made. May we approach, Your Honor?"

"This is just the preliminary hearing, Mr. Cantrell. I see no need to delve into the details of the declared defense at this time. I presume we will all be apprised of those details at trial."

"We must beg the Court at least to reconsider this defendant's status pending trial, Your Honor. Counsel correctly describes the evidence against her client as 'persuasive'; we certainly concur. It seems to us that the knowledge of a defendant with her capacity for violence roaming the streets of Charleston should make the community exceedingly uneasy. We move that this defendant's bond be revoked and that she be remanded to the county jail pending trial."

The ball had been hit nicely back to Julia. It was her turn. "Your Honor, we are prepared to move to trial as expeditiously as the Court sees fit and see no reason that bond should not remain in place as previously ordered by this Court. My client has had ample days and nights since her release to show good faith in the matter of presenting herself to this Court when ordered."

"Your Honor," Cantrell volleyed, "this defendant has no supportive family in the community. It is the prosecution's understanding that her bond was posted by a person unrelated to her, making her ties to the community and her connection to it tenuous at best."

Julia's best-laid plans had not counted on such a tactic. Her mind raced, forming a response.

"If I might, Your Honor, I believe I could provide a bit of clarity for the Court." Rose Pinckney's voice came clearly from the third row of benches. She was on her feet, Julia saw as she turned, looking every bit as though she belonged in that very spot appropriately offering some helpful tidbit to a criminal court judge, her silver hair held in its bun by a copper clasp catching the light from the old ceiling fixture.

His Honor could not decide whether to peer over the spectacles or through them, so he removed them entirely, holding them between his left thumb and forefinger. He looked at Rose with mixed recognition and surprise. She remained standing in place, simply looking back at him. Everyone else in the room was for the moment, Julia saw, only an observer.

"Well, Rose, I grant you the floor which I assume you would have whether or not I approved," the judge finally managed, decorum temporarily aside. He had seen in the file that Rose Pinckney was the source of this young woman's bond. That alone took this case from the simply extraordinary to a plane where anything could be expected. He had, however, not anticipated his old friend insinuating herself personally into the matter at this juncture.

"Would you like me to speak right here, Your Honor, or might we have a word in your chambers?" Rose spoke sweetly, smiling across the room at The Very Honorable Marshall Stoney.

"Is there something you wish to add that you would not want to have on record here?"

"Certainly not. I just want to make clear that Quinn Ravenel has plenty of family in this community, and that family is mine. We have known and loved this child since she could barely reach my front doorknob, and we will not have it said that no one is here to care about her." She glanced pointedly at Allen Cantrell, who immediately looked away, feigning a need to study his notes. "I am here to care, Marshall, and I'd like it noted that I care very much." After a pause over an articulate holding of the judge's gaze, Rose simply took her seat. Julia, still standing, turned back toward the bench. Allen Cantrell remained seated. Rose Pinckney was a presence with whom to be reckoned, and only the judge himself could decide how to proceed.

"I will bind this case over for trial," he looked over to his clerk for a date and got a nod, "four weeks from today. The defendant will remain free on her present bond until that time." He rose as the gavel fell decidedly, and the proceeding was over.

No opportunity for protest. Little time to prepare a case. Four weeks?

69

Sonny left the courtroom quietly as soon as the gavel fell. He was chuckling on the street while Quinn was still looking questioningly at Julia, neither having moved from her seat at the defense table.

Rose prepared first to leave, rising from the pew with her hand on Celia's arm. Her expression suggested nothing out of the ordinary, but Celia was trying hard to suppress her incredulity and amusement until they were outside the courthouse. She was once again delighted to be related to this extraordinary woman.

Knowing plenty of paperwork awaited him back at the station, still Sonny lingered near the gate at the park across the street hoping to see Julia and her client as they exited the building. He felt vaguely like a little boy peeking from behind the corner of the barn for a glimpse of the little girl from down the road. And Julia obliged by coming out rather quickly, trailed by her client and the other two women. After a quick look, Sonny walked on through the park and to his waiting car. He would call her later, he decided, maybe to propose a cup of coffee to discuss today's performance.

He drove out of the City proper and down Lockwood Boulevard toward the Ashley River. It was time to go over the paperwork that had piled up on his desk during the weekend. His cruiser had hardly begun to cool when he arrived at the station, and he reached for a handkerchief to mop his forehead as he crossed the parking lot. The afternoon thundershower had not materialized as predicted, but there was still time. It was certainly hot and humid enough to create a strong one, he thought.

Sonny was annoyed but not surprised to see Colonel Howe through the glass partition in the only enclosed cubicle, sitting in the chair across from the Chief. It was inevitable, he supposed, that the colonel try to huff and puff in his overbearing manner to make known that he intended to have an appropriate outcome for the investigation into the attack on his son. Sonny knew he had touched a nerve when in Mac's hospital room he announced that a young woman was being investigated in connection with the incident. Neither Mac nor his parents had reacted well to that possibility, the colonel fairly bristling at the idea of a mere woman having accomplished the attack on his son. The reaction had been interesting but predictable, not giving Sonny any new direction. He assumed the Chief had kept the Howes apprised of the charge against Quinn Ravenel and the resulting preliminary hearing. He also assumed that the only reason the family was not blustering publicly and in the press was that these parents, high profile in Charleston, did not know how to handle the unfolding facts. Publicly, the break-in at the Howes' residence remained a fading story of an unsolved random crime.

Seeing Sonny in the squad room, the Chief motioned for him to join them, no doubt wanting an update on the preliminary hearing. Sonny braced himself to be pleasant, though the colonel rubbed him the wrong way. He knew the type and had fully expected that the man would find his way to the Chief's office soon after their conversation at the hospital. Sonny had no problem with that; the Chief was the expert at smoothing ruffled feathers.

Colonel Howe rose from his seat when Sonny opened the door, extending his hand. "Detective," he acknowledged Sonny in a less than cordial voice.

"Colonel," Sonny responded, shaking the hand firmly.

"Have a seat, Sonny," the Chief gestured toward the empty chair beside the one occupied by the senior Howe. "The colonel was checking on our progress. I thought you might have been over to the courthouse."

"Yeah, I wanted to monitor the preliminary hearing," Sonny responded.

"He's also concerned about any details of this getting out. I told him it won't come from us."

"The judge scheduled it for trial four weeks from today. Not a lot of time to prepare, but apparently neither side feels a need for more time."

The colonel's frown widened. "This girl you mentioned is still seriously suspected?"

"She is," Sonny replied simply.

"So it went smoothly?" the Chief inquired. "No surprises, no glitches?"

"No glitches."

"And no reporters poking around?" inserted the colonel.

"No reporters." Sonny took a moment to decide whether to offer up a detailed recounting of the small courtroom drama he had witnessed. "Cantrell asked for the bond to be revoked, but after a little intervention by Rose Pinckney, the judge left things as they are."

"Rose Pinckney!" the colonel said. "What does she have to do with this?"

"She posted the bond, and she's tenacious as hell about keeping that girl out of jail pending trial. Quite an ally to have, that woman." Sonny glanced at the Chief, supposing he was a little out of line throwing in his commentary.

"You mean to tell me that this crazy woman y'all suspect of nearly killing my son is walking the streets of Charleston as we speak?" The colonel was turning red and raised his voice. "Chief," he continued, looking the man squarely in the eye, "I want this girl in jail. Now."

The Chief was not moved. "That is out of our hands, Colonel. We have no control over how a judge handles bond for a suspect. We just arrest them, and then it's up to the judge."

"Who is the judge?" Howe roared.

"It was Judge Marshall Stoney," Sonny offered, knowing that these men moved in the same circles. They might very well have played golf together during the past week.

"Marshall turned this maniac loose?" The chair scraped noisily on the tile floor as the colonel rose abruptly, heading for the door. "We'll just see about that."

70

"Grams, sometimes even I can't believe the things that happen when I stick with you. Quinn was still laughing quietly as she set the table for dinner. "That man is a judge, after all, and you talk to him like he's just a regular guy."

"He is just a guy, my dear. I made mud pies with Marshall Stoney before we started elementary school. That's how long I've known him. He's done well for himself, and I would think he'd be ready to hang up that robe and step down from the bench, but he claims he still enjoys meddling in other people's lives. And I must admit he does it well. So be it."

"Did the two of you ever go out on a date?" Quinn asked, grinning curiously.

"Well, aren't you the inquisitive one?"

"Did you?"

"Well, if the truth be told, Marshall was my boyfriend when we were freshmen and sophomores in high school. We kissed a few times. Now is that enough detail for you, my dear?" Rose smiled sweetly.

"Oh, Grams, that's so cute. I can just imagine it. I think one of these days you should tell me about the romances of your young life. I can see that the image I have of you is missing some pieces." Quinn was making mischief, and Rose was enjoying it thoroughly. There were many things, some serious and some simply entertaining, that Rose wished to share with Quinn. One thing, however, merited sharing immediately.

The buzzer sounded, signaling that the chicken potpie was ready to come out of the oven. It was another of Quinn's favorites, and tonight she and Rose had created it together, shaking off tension as they reviewed the events of the day. It was nice to see the humor along the way in what was intrinsically a very serious situation for Quinn. Steam escaped edges of the foil covering the pot as Quinn carried it to the trivet in the center of the kitchen table. Slices of cheese and fresh garlic rolls waited in their separate baskets beside the trivet, and Quinn filled glasses with ice and tea, one for each place. Setting the glasses in place, she joined Rose at the table.

"It smells so good, Grams. Next time, maybe I can make it all by myself while you watch. I love having these recipes to follow in your handwriting."

"Of course you can, dear. My handwriting isn't as steady as it used to be, but one day you can put them on that computer of yours and print them when you need them."

"I never thought I'd hear you admit seeing a practical use for the computer, Grams," Quinn laughed in delight. "Soon, I'll have you using it yourself."

"Not likely," Rose feigned crossness, holding out her plate so that Quinn could ladle onto it the thick pie mixture, "but I was thinking you might set that machine up upstairs so I could watch you use it. That big old desk hasn't been uncovered in years, which reminds me of something I've been meaning to tell you."

"What's that, Grams?"

"Well, I had a little chat with your mother a few days ago. It seems she's looking for another place to live."

"Really?" Quinn wrinkled her brow, surprised. "Why would she do that?"

"Well, I don't think she's especially comfortable so close to this old woman any more. In fact, I suspect that after our conversation she might be extremely uncomfortable here."

Seeing the twinkle in Rose's eye, Quinn began to grasp the undercurrent in the older woman's disclosure. The corners of her mouth curled slightly, and she tilted her head, looking questioningly. "What are you up to, Grams?" she asked.

"Up to?" Rose took a bite of her food, concentrating on it as though nothing else was on her mind.

"Grams," Quinn prodded.

Rose chewed deliberately, reaching for a second roll from the basket. "May I have the butter, dear?"

"Come on, Grams. No butter until you tell me what's up with my mother."

"Now that you mention it," Rose spoke slowly, "I do recall that Adeline will be out of the guesthouse by the end of the month. I was wondering if you might know of anyone who would enjoy having a place there to study or curl up alone with a good book? One of your friends maybe? May I have the butter now, dear?"

Quinn passed the butter, her grin spreading. "You threw her out, didn't you?" she sputtered through her laughter. "You actually threw her out!"

"Well, dear, I wouldn't actually call it that. I just mentioned that she might be more comfortable elsewhere, all things considered."

"What things?"

"You know, things like mothers who don't respond when a precious daughter needs them. Things like that."

Jumping from her chair, Quinn came around the table and threw both arms around Rose's crinkled neck. "I love you so much, Grams. I wish I could have been a mouse in the wall."

"I wish you could have been." Rose hugged the young woman back as hard as her arms would squeeze. "I hate to admit that I rather enjoyed it."

"Grams," Quinn said, retaking her seat, "you're awesome."

"Well, it was quite a self-serving move I made," Rose admitted. "It wasn't so very much that I wanted her out as that I want you closer. You know that, don't you, dear? I thought we could totally redecorate the guesthouse to suit whatever use you might have for it. Am I being too pushy?"

"You could never be pushy. But I do have a new lease over on Tradd Street, you know. I'm not sure I can get out of it so quickly."

"You just leave that to me."

"Of course." Quinn laughed again. "My Grandma Rose with the genie in the magic lamp. Everybody should have one."

"No, not everyone. Just people like you who deserve a little magic in your life. Of course I want you to live here in the big house with me, but I want you to have a place of your own as well, so that when I become crotchety and annoying you can have your privacy."

"If that's what you want, Grams, then don't you want to rent the guesthouse to someone else? I don't need any separate space away from you."

"I don't need the income from the guesthouse, and I would just as soon we didn't have the bother of someone else coming and going. Don't discount your need for a little privacy in the future, my dear. Life goes on, and one of these days I suspect you'll want a place to bring a young man where you won't be bothered. You just give it some thought, and I'll call that nice woman who decorated the Pruitt's new addition last year. She did a wonderful job for them."

"You're such an optimist, Grams. I'll admit that I would like to think you're right about my life. Since you're almost always right, I'll take that as a good sign." She smiled so sincerely that it brought tears to Rose's eyes. They had finished the meal, and Quinn rose to clear the table.

"There's one more thing I need to tell you," Rose stopped her with a hand on her arm. "Just put these dishes in the sink and sit back down with me for another minute or two. Maybe you would bring us a cup of that nice hot decaf. Would you mind, my dear?"

"I have nothing to do and nowhere to go, Grams." Quinn rinsed the plates and silverware and quickly placed them in the dishwasher. Pouring two cups of coffee, she returned to the table. "If you keep telling me this kind of story, I'll be in stitches all night. What other secrets do you have to tell?"

"I've left this house to you when I'm gone," Rose said without preamble. "I've taken care of it with my attorney and my family. I know you'll love it and take care of it. So when we work with the decorator, you can think to the future and the way you want the house to reflect your own tastes. I believe with all my heart that you will be very happy here."

Quinn sat still, her lips parted, the coffee cup in her hand midway between her lips and the table, trying to absorb what Rose Pinckney had said.

TUESDAY

71

Julia left her office just before noon on Tuesday morning, leaving a note on the door saying she would return at three o'clock. Her morning appointments had gone smoothly, and she would return in plenty of time to take the expected call from Weldon Scott when he arrived from Dallas. Meanwhile, there were a couple of hours to spend away from the concerns of her practice, and she was having lunch with Sonny Legare. When she called to thank him for the flowers, he had invited her to have lunch on the boat. Sonny was grilling burgers; Julia was bringing southern-style potato salad from Celia's refrigerator.

She found herself looking forward to this time, not even slightly anxious about spending time with Sonny. It was increasingly easy to feel comfortable with him. He had been interested in and supportive of her, and she was enjoying his friendship. The manner of the server at Anson had suggested Sonny usually dined there alone. Julia suspected that he indeed usually kept to himself, as he had confessed, and the fact that he sought her out was both flattering and intriguing.

The potato salad picked up from Celia this morning was still cold, kept so in Julia's mini office refrigerator. She felt a rare twinge of longing to be able to cook like her friend; maybe she would make it a priority, after Quinn's trial, to learn to make a few select dishes. Celia would gladly teach her, had offered to do so often enough. She would take Celia up on that offer. But now she would simply confess to Sonny that her contribution to this lunch was not made in her own kitchen.

It was not hard to find the boat. Sonny's directions were explicit. The Ashley River shimmered blue and calm in the midday sun, and the blue and white boat swayed gently in the breeze blowing softly from the Atlantic, keeping the heat here on the water from being overbearing. The whole Ashley Marina lay quiet and largely deserted in the middle of this weekday, Julia observed. She saw only one other soul on the deck of a sailboat two slips away, obviously preparing to go out for the afternoon. Sonny appeared on the deck of the boat, heading up the short walkway to meet Julia.

"Good directions," Julia greeted him, smiling.

"I try," the detective grinned in return, holding out his hand to steady Julia on the swaying planks. The grill was smoking on the deck.

"How do you keep that thing from rolling around?" Julia asked as they stepped across onto the boat.

"It's anchored right there. See?" he pointed. "Life on a boat has its complications, but they're all worth the trouble. Things get fastened down when I use them and fastened in storage when I don't. It's the extreme version of 'everything in its place'"

Julia laughed, looking around. "Impressive," she noted. "It's the opposite from your desk at the station. From looking at that, I'd never have predicted this neatness."

"Just a product of necessity. Besides, I have total control here. What comes onto my desk at the station seems to grow there and then reproduce overnight. I just try to keep my head above the piles."

Just then a large shaggy dog bounded up the steps from below, wagging his tail. He stopped short of Julia's feet and looked inquiringly at Sonny.

"Julia, meet Tork," Sonny said. "I was beginning to wonder if he was gonna sleep through lunch."

Julia bent to pet the dog on his big shaggy head.

"He's such a good boy, so calm and well-behaved."

"Yeah, just like his roommate," Sonny added. "He's pretty darned easygoing."

Julia handed over the container of potato salad. "Celia made it. I'm not much of a cook."

"Well, lucky for you, I'm pretty good. In fact, my repertoire includes much better stuff than burgers. You'll have to hang around with me more. Maybe I can teach you a few things." Sonny raised an eyebrow and tilted his head, smiling broadly. "Here, take a seat." He pointed to one of the two deck chairs fastened in place under the extended awning. Julia sat down, and Tork immediately took a place at her feet, sniffing her toes curiously.

"I told you he hasn't had much contact with women," Sonny reminded Julia. "You'll have to establish your boundaries."

Dropping her arm to take one of the dog's ears in her hand, Julia rubbed the soft flap between her fingers. "He's just fine. I've never had a dog. When I was little, my mother wouldn't let us have pets. And then I've thought myself too busy to take care of one." Tork lifted his head and licked Julia's wrist, relaying his gratitude for the ear scratching. He had, Julia thought, the biggest brown eyes she had ever seen.

"How do you like your burger?" Sonny asked, unwrapping three fat, juicy patties of ground beef and lifting the lid on the grill to place them above the hot charcoal.

"I'll eat it any way you cook them, although I'm not partial to rare," Julia answered.

Sonny closed the grill. "I've made a pitcher of lemonade, but I've got plenty of beer if you'd rather have that."

"Lemonade sounds wonderful."

Going below briefly, Sonny returned with the lemonade and two clear acrylic tumblers. He poured each glass three-quarters full and sat down in the chair near the grill opposite Julia. "Is it too sour for you?" he asked as she took her first sip.

"No, it's great, just the thing for a day like this." Julia looked across the river, taking in the surroundings that were Sonny's everyday scenery. "What a view," she remarked. "I can see how you'd grow to love it. I already feel real life fading away. How long did it take for you to get accustomed to the constant motion?"

"I always loved it. Does it bother you?"

"No, not at all. In fact, it's soothing."

"I probably missed my calling. I should have been a captain on a fishing boat or maybe a pirate." Sonny grinned.

"I can picture you as a pirate. Black patch over one eye. Monocle always at the ready. Treachery on your mind. Yeah, I can see that."

"Treachery?"

"Well, isn't that what pirates are all about? Didn't they steal and plunder on the high seas?"

"Steal and plunder? Is that how you picture me?"

"Well, I was just following your train of thought, taking it to the next level, you know. Shouldn't you check on the burgers?"

Sonny jumped from the chair, rushing to flip the meat. Mesquite-scented smoke billowed as he lifted the lid, and Julia laughed aloud. "Maybe my kitchen finesse is already rubbing off on you."

"I'm glad you didn't want them rare. They're okay. Just a little on the done side. So what are your strengths then, besides the obvious?"

"What are the obvious?" Julia fished a little.

"You're a good lawyer, a pretty lady, good company. What other talents are you hiding?"

"Didn't I tell you I've been apprenticing with the handyman? I've got my own hammer now and a couple of screwdrivers. If I'd met you back in the spring, I could have shown the calluses on my palms from sanding and painting in my kitchen. I don't cook in it, but it's beginning to look pretty good."

"Are you gonna invite me over one of these days to see this work of art?" Sonny asked. "I might even cook you a meal there, unless it's just for show."

"Okay, I'll admit that I felt a little inadequate today when I had to bring Celia's potato salad."

Sonny glanced back as he moved to take the meat from the grill. "You? Inadequate?"

"It's something women are traditionally supposed to be good at, isn't it? Slaving over a hot stove?" Julia offered.

"I'm not much on stereotypes, McKenzie. I can't really see you in an apron any more than I can see me in an eye patch."

"Good, because I don't own an apron."

Sonny speared the three burgers, placing each on a bun. The usual fixings were already on the table in a plastic bin, along with forks, spoons and napkins. He placed one of the plates in front of Julia, seating himself as he opened the container of potato salad and inserted a large serving spoon. "More lemonade?" he asked as he set the third plate on the floor. Julia had thought he was preparing two patties for himself and one for her, but the big dog ambled to the plate as though having a hamburger on a bun for lunch was the usual fare.

"Just a little more, please." Julia held out her glass. She watched in amusement as Tork ate the top of the bun first, then the meat, and then the bottom half of the bun. "He's a very neat eater for a dog," she commented. "What does he eat when you have broccoli?"

"You'd be amazed at what this guy eats. Neither of us eats broccoli. We have our limits."

"No broccoli? What about those Southern collard greens?"

"Absolutely not. I'm a typical Southerner in almost every way. I love my grits and gravy, but I never could stomach collards. Surely you haven't come to like that stuff?"

"No. I took one bite years ago because Celia is very persuasive. It's one of the few times she's ever led me astray."

"Are you easily led astray?" Sonny asked with a gleam in his eye, taking a bite of the potato salad.

"I'm practicing every day," Julia replied, countering with a mischievous glance of her own, thinking how long it had been since she flirted. "Time will tell if I'm getting smarter."

"I'll just bet you are. How's the Quinn Ravenel matter, speaking of getting smart? Did you successfully pass that case on to a criminal lawyer?"

"Oh, that. You're not going to think me very clever when I tell you that the criminal lawyer wants nothing to do with Quinn's case. I've decided to tackle it myself." Julia eyed Sonny over a forkful of potato salad, waiting for him to express disapproval. Chewing, he was silent, nodding as though he was not surprised.

"I guessed as much," he said finally.

"Why is that?"

"I just couldn't see you turning her over to anyone else. You don't even have a criminal guy associating on the case?"

"I tried. He wanted Quinn to plead insanity and she won't have any part of it. So we're on our own. I've tried to impress upon her the risks of having only me to represent her, but she seems undaunted. I really like the girl. She may be a little naïve, but she's smart and funny and charming. I don't think there's an insane bone in her body."

"If not insanity, what then? I was at the hearing, and I'm afraid to speculate on where you're going with a self-defense argument. I'm one of the few who knows her rape story, and that's only because you've told me. It's an unlikely tale, and I believed every word."

"I believe it too. But will a jury be convinced? And will they let her go?"

"You're in a better position to judge that than I, McKenzie. You must think you've got a shot or you wouldn't be going for it, but I'm puzzled how you're calling it 'self-defense'. It's a four-year-old rape."

"I admit it's a stretch."

"A stretch? Yeah, it's a stretch. Does she realize she's putting her life on the line? Several years in prison is quite a detour for a girl like Quinn."

"I've told her in every way I know how."

"Well, McKenzie, if you've got the guts to make that case, then my hat's off to you. Anything I can do to help?"

"If there is, you'll be the first to know. Thanks. I'm going to be spending every waking moment on this for the next four weeks. I need more time, but that's beside the point."

"I think it's not out of line for me to tell you that Mac Howe's father was in the station yesterday nosing around for information. He still has no idea that this could be anything more than a random attack on his son, but now that he knows a woman has been charged, he's on the warpath. He can't fathom that his macho son might have been ambushed by some girl."

"I've met the Howes. They seem like nice people, not people who would condone what their son did."

"They wouldn't condone it; they just wouldn't believe it," Sonny offered, "any more than Ms. Fallon believed her son capable of the attack on Howe. Difference is, I didn't believe Reg did it. I believe Mac Howe did."

It was a simple declaration, but Julia absorbed it, packaged it gratefully with her own feelings on the subject and took it to heart.

72

Melanie had returned from lunch and was sorting through a pile of paperwork for the judge when Colonel Howe opened the door. Though he was not a regular visitor, Melanie saw him from time to time when he picked up or dropped off the judge from a round of golf. She was surprised when he appeared brusque.

"I need to see the judge," George Howe said.

"He's just finishing up in the courtroom, Mr. Howe," Melanie responded pleasantly. "Would you like me to put a note on his desk saying you're waiting out here for him when he's finished?"

"That will be fine," the colonel answered. "I hope it won't be long."

"Can I get you some coffee or a soda?" Melanie asked as he took a seat in one of the worn leather chairs and picked up a months-old copy of Sports Illustrated.

"No, thanks." He didn't look up.

Minutes passed, during which Melanie continued her work and the colonel sat silently, flipping the pages of the magazine. He was obviously in no mood for pleasantries. His toe tapped rhythmically on the tile floor.

Marshall Stoney opened the door after twenty minutes and motioned for George Howe to come into his chambers. "What's up, George? You ready to get out there and try to improve your game?" He smiled, glad to see his friend the colonel.

"Not today, Marshall. I've got something else on my mind."

"Well, come and tell me. I have twenty free minutes before the next case. I hear Mac went home from the hospital. Howe's Martha?" He clapped his friend on the back and closed the door behind them.

"Martha's doing well, under the circumstances," George replied.

"It must be hard as hell on her," the judge continued, "but Mac is going to be okay, is he not?"

"He's doing very well, thanks. It's the girl who's on my mind. What were you thinking, letting her go free?"

"The girl?"

"Come on, Marshall. The police chief told me he arrested some young woman for the attack on Mac and that you turned her loose on bond. Is that true?"

The judge steepled his fingers beneath his chin, weighing his friendship with George Howe against his vowed impartiality as an officer of the court. "The Ravenel girl. Yes, it's true that she's out on bond—a million-dollar bond. When I set that bond, I had little expectation it would be posted."

"Can't you do something about it?" the colonel continued. "You're the judge."

"There would have to be a significant change in circumstances for me to change the bond, George. I don't anticipate that, though I understand your frustration."

"I'm not sure you can understand," the colonel growled. "Who is this girl? Is she crazy?"

"It's a matter of public record, George. The girl's name is Quinn Ravenel. If I was convinced she's crazy, I wouldn't have offered the bond, even at a million."

"So she has a lawyer and someone to post a million-dollar bond? Who are these people?"

"Also matters of record. Rose Pinckney posted the bond, and the Ravenel girl's lawyer is Julia Slaton McKenzie, neither of whose credentials I would brush off lightly."

"My god, Marshall, how could Rose Pinckney be involved with someone like that? You're the second person who's told me she's involved. Is the old woman losing her marbles?"

Smiling slightly, the judge thought of his long friendship with Rose. "Not that I can see, George. She seems as sharp as always and just as determined to prevail when she sets her mind to something. She was in court with the Ravenel girl, and I must say that the girl could not wish for a stauncher ally."

"What's the evidence against the girl, Marshall?"

"The prosecutor has submitted her fingerprints from the assault weapon and your windowsill, George, not to mention the fact that she doesn't deny committing the crime."

"She doesn't deny it?" George Howe asked incredulously. "Then why isn't she in jail?"

"She claims to have a valid defense, George, and every American is entitled to bond pending trial. You know that."

"This girl admitted to the attack on my son?"

"It is my understanding that she walked into the police station and turned herself in. But you must understand, George, that doesn't constitute guilt under the law. It's not even admissible in court since she simply blurted out some alleged confession prior to being advised to consult counsel. I frankly do not know where the matter is headed, especially with her plea of not guilty by reason of self-defense."

"Self-defense! What kind of crap is that, Marshall?" George Howe's voice reached crescendo as he appeared ready to leap from his seat. "Is she saying that Mac was attacking her there in our home and that she was just fighting back?"

"I've been puzzling over that myself, George. Why don't you talk to Mac and see if he has any history with this girl at all? Could this possibly be a one-time girlfriend, the woman scorned?"

"We've touched on the subject, and he hardly remembers the girl, says they were in high school at the same time. That's all. This is such fucking bullshit, Marshall. There's got to be something you can do to get her off the street."

"I know where you're coming from, my friend, but I'm at the mercy of lady justice, as are you. If we could decide arbitrarily who should be walking the streets, it might be a much better town. But then there might be no one walking the streets but you and me." The judge smiled, hoping to lighten the mood.

George Howe was not amused. "I'm going to see what else I can find out about this," he said as he headed for the door. "It's a sad day when known criminals can keep walking the streets of Charleston." He did not slam the door, but he did close it loudly.

73

The rocking of the boat had diminished as the afternoon lengthened and grew still. Enjoying conversation, Sonny and Julia had not removed the dishes or moved from the table. The chairs were nicely padded and comfortable, and the sun was still above the edge of the boat's awning that shaded them. They had bantered easily over mutual acquaintances, lawyer jokes and the pros and cons of being single.

"I miss just having someone to turn to when something's funny, you know?" Sonny asked.

"Yes, I know what you mean, but I haven't had that for a long time, not even when I was married."

Noting the time, Julia sighed. "I guess I'd better get back to the office.

"Well, speaking of having someone to enjoy good moments with, I've enjoyed this," Sonny pronounced. "I'm glad you agreed to come over here. Do you really have to go?"

"I'm expecting a call this afternoon from the Mavericks' doctor. He's flying in to check on Reg in person. I think I'd better be there when they meet the local doctors."

"I'm sorry, McKenzie. It sure isn't fair, is it?"

"No, it isn't. Not too much of this story is fair, not the part involving Reg or the part involving Quinn. Other than one appointment at four o'clock, I can concentrate on her defense while I wait for that call."

"I haven't asked much about the legal argument you're making, McKenzie, but I'm wondering if there's any research I could do to help, like pulling up old records for you. Did the Howes get the rape charge dropped? I'm surprised I don't remember it at all."

Julia was startled at the assumption Sonny was making. Quinn had told him at the start, of course, out of breath at the station, that she had attacked Mac. Julia had later told him that the reason was the rape. Now that he was convinced Julia was plunging fully into the girl's defense, he was trying to connect the dots.

"Sonny, there was no rape charge."

"No charge?"

"Her mother talked her out of it, and she told no one else until now. Not anyone. Not for the four years since the rape. I should have explained this all to you before. That's why it's so complicated."

"Her mother talked her out of it?"

"If you didn't understand before why I was so angry at the woman, now you see."

"Was Quinn examined by a doctor?"

"No."

"But, McKenzie, if there was no charge and no one was told, then there is no evidence that the rape happened at all."

"That's true. Just Quinn's word."

"So you're just going to go into court and declare that Quinn's defense is a wholly unsubstantiated story that she was retaliating for an unreported rape four years earlier?"

"That's the plan."

Sonny looked across the river, concentrating on the far bank and then on the gentle lapping of the water nearer the boat. "McKenzie," he said finally, leaning forward and reaching his hand across the table to place it atop Julia's, "you've got to charge him."

"What?"

"You've got to charge him with the rape. Charge him now. Don't wait another day."

"But it's been four years."

"There's no statute of limitations on rape in South Carolina, McKenzie. You're the lawyer; look it up."

"Okay, if that's so, how will it help us?"

"How could it hurt?"

Julia looked at Sonny intently, processing his suggestion, enjoying his large, moist palm on her hand.

"I'm thinking," she said.

74

Arriving in Charleston by air offers an unrivaled overview on a clear day of the maze of meandering marsh that is the Lowcountry of South Carolina. From above, water is the prevailing feature, slithering in and through the habitable terrain, carving out its own pathways and leaving no doubt that the entire land mass is at its mercy. Those warm, wandering fingers of water which offer beauty and recreation and nurture can just as easily team with the mother Atlantic to wreak havoc.

Weldon Scott enjoyed approaching the Carolina coast by air. He always inhaled deeply upon landing and filled his lungs with moist Southern air, hoping to breathe it over a couple of rounds of golf at the magnificent Wild Dunes golf course while he was here. It was a rather unremarkable arrival if one did not know Charleston, the little airport pleasant but generic and tucked away in the trees north of the peninsula. His first visit years previously had taken him down the old, commercial Rivers Avenue wallpapered with dingy commerce and strip malls to get to Charleston proper. The new Mark Clark Expressway now circles from the Ashley River on the airport side across the northern neck of the peninsula, by the paper mill, crossing the Cooper River and bridging the mainland to the beaches of Mount Pleasant and the islands of Sullivan and Palm. Weldon considered the expressway incongruous with the provincial nature of the area, but it did offer a new ease for moving around the city. It was the route he and the doctor would take to a villa reserved for them at the Wild Dunes, a comfortable golf and beach resort carved into the far north end of the Isle of Palms some years back when such a concession to commercialism was considered by the environmental community a pivotal assault against Mother Nature.

"Breathe a lungful of the South, Doc," he said as the two men crossed the few yards on the tarmac between the express flight and the airport.

"Yeah, who needs a sauna?" the other replied. The humidity on this Tuesday afternoon was near one hundred per cent, not unusual for a Charleston summer day. Dallas could be humid, but the southeast coast was another atmosphere entirely, saturated with reminders of the ocean's nearness.

"Let's get our bags and get closer to the sand and the greens," Weldon suggested. "I predict you're going to enjoy dinner here tonight, and you'll be a convert before this trip is over."

"Weldon, old man, you could do tourist promotion for the Charleston Chamber of Commerce. I'll try to remain open-minded right up until the heat stroke," the younger man joked as he mopped the perspiration already trickling down his cheek. Chuckling, Weldon Scott thought ahead to an appropriate dinner plan, thinking that including Julia McKenzie could help to impress the young Doctor Claude Baker with the charms of Charleston. She could brief them on Reg Fallon's condition and make it a very pleasant evening as well.

Bags in hand, the men stepped into a waiting taxicab, nicely air-conditioned. Claude Baker loosened his tie, laying his arm across the back of the seat, and leaned into the corner, stretching his long legs as much as possible. He had the height to play ball himself, but not the talent, much as he had wished it so. His affiliation with the team as one of its staff physicians was as close as he would get to involvement in the sport past the college level, where he had played at Stanford. That part of his life had gotten him past the door and into the interview with the Mavericks. Weldon Scott had gotten him onto the golf course.

"Our courses in Dallas have nothing on this one at the Dunes," Weldon assured his friend. "It's a beauty. We're going to broaden your horizons this week, Doc. You'll be vacationing down here with one of your young lady friends before the year is out." Enjoying his bout of smugness, he pulled the cellular telephone from his pocket and dialed Julia McKenzie as the taxi pulled onto the Mark Clark.

75

As the late afternoon sun cleared the roof of the hospital building to stream through Reg's west-facing window, he and Quinn were deep in conversation. It was the first time Willa had left the hospital since the accident, but Reg was so much more himself today that she was comfortable leaving him with his friend Quinn for a couple of hours. She had sensed, anyway, that the girl wanted to talk to Reg alone.

"It's great to see you, kiddo," Reg reached his free hand toward Quinn, and she came to sit on the bottom of his bed, pulling her legs up to sit Indian-style.

"I'm not hurting you, am I?" she asked, careful not to get too near the leg cast.

"Heck no. This thing is like concrete on my leg. My only pain is in this hand where the IV is, and I still have a headache." The head of the bed was rolled up, and Quinn noted that the bandaging on Reg's head was smaller than before. "I could get bored with this hospital stuff real fast, so talk to me. Tell me what you've been up to. I heard about your job at Porter Gaud."

"I was pretty excited to get that job," Quinn bubbled, forgetting for a moment the reason for her visit. "I can hardly wait to have my own class full of little kids."

"So you're going to do what you always wanted. I never doubted it for a moment," Reg grinned.

"Me? How about you, big man! You got the job of a lifetime. Who knew you could get rich playing a game you've been playing since we were kids. I'm so proud of you. When you get out of here, I'm taking you to dinner to celebrate our success. How about that?"

"Can't wait. Being here in this bed isn't what I had planned for the end of the summer. I guess this is going to make me late for training in Dallas. I'm waiting for the doctors to come up with a timetable for me to get back on track. They've mentioned rehab, but they haven't said how much or how long."

Quinn remembered. "I have to tell you something, Reg." Her expression darkened, and tears came to her eyes.

"Hey, kiddo, what's the matter?"

She had not considered where to begin, so she started with the part of the story Reg would understand. "I'm the one who hurt Mac. It's my fault you're in the hospital."

"What are you talking about?"

"I dropped that razor by the sidewalk after I cut Mac with it. Why were you sitting by it?"

"You what?" Reg was not making any sense of Quinn's story. "You cut Mac Howe? Quinn? I don't get it."

Quinn took a deep breath and looked at Reg squarely, steadying her voice. "Okay," she started again. "I'm the one who did it. You're the one who got picked up for it. I came to the jail to tell them the truth as soon as I found out they arrested you, but then you were in the accident when I was in the jail. It's just a nightmare. I'd do anything to undo what's happened to you."

Reg was studying Quinn with a mixture of surprise and confusion. "Are you telling me that it was you who attacked Mac Howe?"

"Yes. It was me. I cut his penis nearly off."

"Quinn, why would you do that?"

"I don't want to talk about this, Reg. I'm going to tell you because I owe you an explanation. Reg raped me before I left for college four years ago."

Mouth open, eyes wide, Reg winced, trying to sit up straighter in the bed. "You gotta be kidding me." Quinn said nothing, just looked at Reg while he tried to process her story. Reaching out, he took both of Quinn's hands between his, one purple and bruised and still attached to an intravenous line.

They sat quietly, each looking at the other. "There's nothing you could have said that would shock me more. I always knew you had guts, kiddo, but..." He stopped, not sure what else to say. "Couldn't you just have called the cops?"

"See why I didn't want to talk about it?" Quinn looked at their hands. "It's too complicated."

"That bastard raped you, honey? How and when?"

"He just did, Reg. It was about a week before we went away to college four years ago. I never told anyone."

"How could you not tell anyone?"

"Just trust me that I did what I had to do then, and I did what I had to do the other night."

"If you had told me, I would have killed him for you myself. I can't believe that happened to you. I'll still kill him for you as soon as I get out of here, since you didn't finish him off. How about that?"

Quinn almost smiled. She knew Reg meant every word, and she knew, looking back, that he would have made the same offer, just as sincerely, four years earlier. Reg Fallon was a good guy, her friend from childhood who had reached down his hand while she tentatively climbed to the top of the jungle gym.

There was an army of support upon whom she could have depended, but she had not done so. She was younger then, she was hurt, and she was afraid. "Thanks."

"Well, what's going to happen now? Are you saying the reason they let me out of jail is that you told the cops you did it?"

"That's what I'm telling you."

"So how come you're not in jail?"

Now Quinn did smile. "I almost spent that first night there, but Grandma Rose bailed me out. I spent most of a day in a jail cell, Reg. It was awful, wasn't it? Did you hear the rats in the wall?"

"Of all the experiences we could possibly have shared, that is the least likely." Reg laughed aloud, then stopped himself abruptly, holding his ribs. "That hurts."

"I'm sorry." Quinn was laughing too. "Are you ever going to be able to forgive me for getting you into this mess?"

"You didn't get me in this mess. I was a young black man in the wrong place sitting drunk as a skunk in the rain on somebody's front step. It's worth being in this hospital just to think of you doing what you did." Reg shook his head, smiling broadly without laughing. "I always loved you, kiddo, but this gives new meaning to the word 'revenge', doesn't it? I don't even have a headache anymore!"

"This is the best I've felt about what I did since I knew you got blamed for it."

"Well, good, Reg responded. "That makes two of us."

174

76

It was late, for Julia, but she was still going by to talk with Celia before heading across the river for home. The conversation over dinner with Weldon Scott and the doctor was pleasant enough, but nothing could be settled until the doctors conferred and agreed about Reg's prognosis. They would see him in the morning, and Julia had promised to be at the hospital. It was a visit she would like to avoid.

Pulling into Celia's driveway, she was glad she had asked her friend to wait up. It was almost ten o'clock. Celia opened the front door as Julia climbed the porch steps.

"Hey, girl," she said quietly, an indication that Tyrney and Katey were settled upstairs. "Come on. I've made us margaritas, frozen, extra salt. Go curl up and I'll get them."

Julia dropped her purse by the door, shedding her shoes, and plopped gratefully into the plush softness of Celia's family room. Celia followed, and the two women settled comfortably into Celia's plaid sofa with their feet on the big square ottoman.

"Okay, tell me. What's going on?" It was so good to have a friend, Julia thought, so different than the relationship she had had with Jack. Celia was always happy to see her, eager to share her time, her worries and her world. Maybe, she thought, this kind of bond existed only between women friends, a companionship of heart and spirit which men were not able to experience. Somewhere in the back of her mind, she was aware that she hoped not.

"I had lunch with Sonny and dinner with the guys from the Mavericks."

"Do tell! And which was more exciting?"

"I had a great time with Sonny. He cooked hamburgers for me on the deck of his boat at the marina, which makes the first time I've ever had a meal on a boat. But that's not the best part. He had this idea, and I need to try it out on you. He thinks we should file charges now against MacArthur Howe for raping Quinn."

She waited patiently for Celia to digest the proposition, one that had been on the back burner of her mind all afternoon, simmering through her appointment, through dinner. Julia took her first sip of the margarita, licking the salt from her lips, appreciating the sweet lime aroma and taste.

"Why?" Celia asked finally, brows furrowed.

"Well, as our friend Sonny said, 'why not?'" Julia shared Sonny's thoughts with Celia. "I just can't quite get a grip on the idea. I looked it up this afternoon, and there is indeed no statute of limitations for charging rape, not in South Carolina. The more I think about it, the better I like it. It establishes officially the reason for what Quinn did."

"But how exactly does that help?"

"We think so much alike," Julia grinned. "That's exactly what I asked when Sonny suggested this."

"Well?"

"Well, that's why I'm here. Let's play this out in theory and see where we can take it."

"Okay," Celia continued the story. "They take Mac down to the station and question him. He denies it. Do they let him go?"

"I don't know. It's up to the prosecutor at that point, just like it was with Reg and Quinn. You gotta remember that this is not my area of expertise. I think he will be charged with rape based on Quinn's allegation."

"And then?"

"Then he goes to sit in the jail until someone posts bond, which I'm guessing wouldn't be long. These folks have the money, right?"

"They most definitely do, and they know all the right people. So now he's out on bond, just like Quinn. It sounds like some sort of stand-off, except that Mac has bandages to show what Quinn did to him, and Quinn has nothing but a four-year-old story." Celia felt obliged to present the dubious side of the picture. So far, she was not convinced there was anything to gain from this course of action. "So are we better off somehow at that point?"

This was exactly what Julia needed. Celia was always a good devil's advocate. "Well, now I can argue Quinn's case from a little different angle. How could it hurt us to have a rape charge pending?"

"Better late than never?"

"Ouch. I don't like that perspective, but yes, better late than never." Julia was chewing the inside of her cheek, a habit born in her childhood when she was deep in thought. "Don't you think our case is strengthened at some basic level, especially to a jury, if there is a rape charge?"

"Maybe. I'd like it lots more if he could be tried and convicted before you have to use this in Quinn's defense."

"Well, if he's charged, his preliminary hearing wouldn't even happen until next week, and Quinn is set for trial in less than four weeks."

"This is about her life. Won't the judge put off her trial until after Mac's based upon the relationship between the cases?"

"Probably not. That's just not how it works. If that kind of legal ploy was effective, think what a mess could be made of the justice system. One could bring a false charge as a delaying tactic."

"So once again I'm questioning the benefit of charging him at this point. Wouldn't that get the whole story on television and in the papers? Some reporter would certainly smell a story as soon as he saw the Howe name on the same court document with the word 'rape'. Quinn never wanted anyone to know, remember?"

"I haven't suggested this to Quinn. I wanted to run it by you first."

"I'm concerned about Quinn's state of mind. She's maintaining this stoic, upbeat attitude that can't be genuine. I'm afraid she hasn't come to terms with the seriousness of what she did or the repercussions that may be coming, but it's going to catch up with her. She's been way too cool."

"That's your area of expertise, and I'll defer to you, Cele, but if we're going to file a charge, it has to be soon. Can you be with me when I talk to Quinn about it?"

"Sure. When?"

"Much as I wish it were not so, I have to be at the hospital tomorrow morning to see what the doctors and Weldon decide about Reg. I'd rather eat dirt than be there when they tell him he can't play ball."

"Are you certain that's going to be the decision?"

"I am."

"I have appointments until noon and then another at four o'clock. I'm sure nothing would please Rose more than to have us come for lunch. How about that? Then she would be there as support for Quinn as well."

"Can you try to arrange this in the morning and leave me a message? I'll check it from the hospital."

"We haven't made a decision, have we? Which way are you leaning? You want to file a charge, don't you?"

"Except for the publicity you mentioned, I can't see a downside. But let's sleep on it."

Julia groaned as she uncurled her tired body out of its comfortable position. It had been another long day. The stiffness she felt was more a product of tension than any actual physical exertion, she knew, reminiscent of the grueling hours she had often kept in Washington. Charleston's pace was infinitely preferable, and she vowed to return to it as soon as possible. The margarita had warmed to liquid in her glass, but she drank the last sip anyway on her way to the kitchen, following Celia.

"Be careful crossing the bridge, Jules," Celia cautioned. "And we'll talk in the morning." The hug she gave Julia at the front door was welcome and lovingly returned. Each knew she would sleep only fitfully with Quinn's dilemma weighing heavily, decisions to be made and apprehension to be kept at bay.

WEDNESDAY

77

The sun was just burning its way through the remnants of a pre-dawn thunderstorm on the East Battery along Charleston Harbor, one of those rains that cleans the air for a brand-new day. A tourist walking along the harbor peered through his binoculars toward Fort Sumter and the sea beyond. Clinging raindrops warmed, merged with others on the leaves of the oleanders lining the seawall and fell to the warm earth below.

Rose had already been out to pick a few of her yellow roses for Willa Fallon, shaking off raindrops gently as she brought them up the back steps. The teakettle was whistling merrily, but Rose did not hurry. She was content this morning, knowing Quinn was safe upstairs, knowing she had told her about the house, more confident this morning after a good night's sleep that her faith in life was usually rewarded. Quinn was in good hands with Julia McKenzie. Celia had said so.

Rose heard Willa's old Chevy come to a stop by the house on the Water Street side. Maybe, she thought, Willa could have a new car now that her son was going to be a basketball star. She smiled at the thought, opening the front door, smelling the harbor's salty presence, to stand and wait for her friend to round the corner.

"Good morning, Rose." Willa appeared on the sidewalk and made her way slowly up the steps to embrace Rose on the stoop. "I'm so glad you asked me over."

"You've been on my mind every day and night since I heard about Reg's accident," Rose replied, returning the long hug. "Come in here and let's catch up. I've made us some tea and goodies. Julia told me you weren't taking care of yourself at all, so let's rest awhile and gobble up a few calories, my dear friend. Here," she motioned, "you sit over there and put your feet right up on the hassock. I'll get the tea."

"Lawd a'mercy, Miss Rose, no need for you to be a'waitin' on me. I ain't used to it."

"Well, you can get used to it, at least for this morning," Rose insisted, going to the kitchen for the tea. "I want to hear all about Reg."

"He be doin' better, Miss Rose, God be praised. This is the first time I've left him. I been prayin' over that boy till my prayers was 'most dried up."

"I've been doing the same," Rose assured her, pouring the tea. "Here, help yourself." The plate held fresh poppy seed muffins and several of the cinnamon rolls baked the day before. "Quinn told me Reg seemed much better yesterday. I was so thankful. I thought I might pry you away from the hospital for an hour this morning. I'm so happy you came."

"That child Quinn sho' grow into a pretty little thing," Willa observed. "I remember her and Reggie makin' mud pies out behind your house when they wasn't knee high to a grasshopper. My, they's growed up so fast." Willa shook her head. "Don't it jes' beat all that our babies grown up and graduated from college. We did all right, didn't we, Miss Rose?"

"We did indeed, Willa; we did indeed. You worked those fingers to the bone cooking and baking for the likes of folks like me so that Reggie could go to college. You've paid your dues and then some. And the convergence of events that brings us here together this morning just baffles me. It seems your Reggie and my little Quinn are both victims, in different ways, of MacArthur Howe. Quinn feels responsible for what's happened to Reggie, and I can't help feeling responsible for what happened to Quinn."

"You, Miss Rose? Lawd a'mercy, you the best thing in her life when she be a little girl. You can't be blamin' yourself."

"If only she had come to me, Willa. If only I had known, I could have helped her. Now there's so little I can do. You and I never were very good at being helpless, were we? It's just the worst place to be, and that's how I feel with Quinn. I would like to say that I trust the system of justice to do right by her, but I don't. I'm trying to put my faith in God and Julia McKenzie."

"I swannee, that Miss McKenzie be a blessin' in all our lives. Thank the good Lord you sent us to her last spring when we was dealin' with the basketball folk from Dallas. She done go to my Reggie in the jail, she did, and she come to the hospital too. She'll take good care of our chillun', Miss Rose, I do declare she will."

"It's reminded me to treasure each day when we have only our simple little difficulties about which to complain. I think back to the morning before Quinn was arrested when I was cranky about my arthritis. My, what I would give to have that arthritic old morning back again."

"And I" Willa recalled, "to be a'waitin' up for Reggie to come home from his party so's I could box his ears for drinkin' too much beer." Sipping the tea, both women smiled, finding comfort in sharing their uneasiness. Willa's eyes fell on the walking cane beside Rose's chair, thinking of the spry little woman Rose had been until recent years. She resented being at the mercy of time and the relentless process of aging. But it was at least a bane assigned across the board, unlike the blindside wallops which had impacted the two young people loved by Willa and Rose.

"We got to cling to our faith, Miss Rose. I keep a'prayin' for your Quinn and you for my Reggie, and then we leave it up to the good Lord. We done come this far doin' jes' that, ain't we?"

"Yes, we've come this far, and it's been quite a journey for us both, has it not? But I'll admit to you that I've been asking a few pointed questions to the good Lord this past week, Willa."

"I done did the same thing too, and I don' mind sayin' so, but there's neither one of our babies dead or in the jail today, Miss Rose, so we best be offerin' up a mite of thanks. It could be worse, and jes' a couple o' days ago it was." Willa's eyes crinkled at the corners as she looked forward to seeing her son sitting up in the bed today.

"I needed that little nudge, Willa. There is a measure of gratitude in this old heart, even under these circumstances. I just needed a friend to pry it out of me." Some of the twinkle returned to Rose's eyes as well. Her little Quinn was, after all, here in this very house. She could hear the shower running upstairs now and the music coming from Quinn's iPod.

"We're going to be all right, aren't we, Willa?"

"One way or another, I swannee we are. And these here muffins ain't hurtin' a bit neither. I could sit here and eat these until..."

Willa was interrupted by the sound of the doorbell. It could, at this time of the morning, be the mailman bringing a package too large for the box, Rose thought. Or maybe he was just checking in on her, as was his frequent custom. Whatever the case, Rose found the handle of her cane and slowly got to her feet.

"I best be goin' on, Miss Rose." Willa started to get up.

"You stay right where you are," Rose responded. "I suspect it's just the mailman." Willa settled back down, still enjoying the comfort and company of an old friend whose acquaintance and help she had cherished through many hard years of raising a boy alone.

The bell had just rung for the second time when Rose reached the door. Preparing to remind the mailman that she was old and slow, she was surprised to find George Howe standing tall and imposing on her porch.

"I apologize for not calling first," he began, seeing Rose's surprise, "but I found myself needing to see you on a matter of some importance. I hope you don't mind."

"Well, now that you're here, Colonel, you're certainly welcome to come in. I was just enjoying a cup of tea with my friend Willa Fallon. I believe the two of you have met?" she asked as she ushered the colonel into her sitting room.

"Yes, yes, I know Ms. Fallon." The colonel was polite. He had not expected the Fallon boy's mother in Rose Pinckney's living room. It appeared every bit a simple morning tea between friends.

"Please sit down, George," Rose offered. "May I pour you a cup of tea?"

"Oh, no, thanks. I don't mean to intrude. Would you rather I came back a little later?"

"I was jes' a'leavin' anyway, Mr. Howe," Willa said, setting her cup down and reaching for her purse. "I need to be gettin' on over to be with Reggie," she reassured Rose who was preparing to protest her leaving.

"Let me wrap up a few goodies for you to take to him," Rose insisted, heading for the kitchen. "A strapping boy like him on the mend can surely afford to gain back a pound or two."

Willa followed along to the kitchen, thanking Rose for her friendship and her concern, the two women exchanging puzzled looks over the unexpected appearance of George Howe at Rose's door. Rose assured her quietly that whatever the purpose of his visit, she could handle it. "You put these roses in Reggie's room. He might not enjoy them, but I know you will, and you give that boy an extra hug from me."

"I be checkin' in on you a little later, Miss Rose," Willa called back over her shoulder as she closed the front door.

"Are you sure you wouldn't like a cup of tea?" Rose asked again as she took her place once more across the coffee table from the colonel, securing the handle of her cane on the arm of the overstuffed chair.

"No, thanks. I won't stay. That was the mother of the Fallon boy who was first thought to have attacked Mac, wasn't it?" he asked.

"What a tragic mistake," Rose answered, shaking her head. "I've known that boy since he was just a youngster, and his mother too. Such good, hard-working people shouldn't have to suffer this way just when things were going so well. It's a terrible shame, don't you think, George?"

The colonel cleared his throat, wanting to get on to the business he had with Rose Pinckney. "Well, speaking of mistakes, Rose, the reason for my visit is to find out for certain if you are really behind the bail that was posted for the girl who claims to have attacked Mac. I find it hard to believe, and I was hoping you could dislodge that rumor from my mind."

Rose had not expected this confrontation, not even when she had seen it was George Howe at her door. She studied him before she responded, noting the hard set of his jaw and the flicker of anger in his eyes. "There's no rumor, George," she said finally. "It is quite true that I am as good as family to Quinn Ravenel, and I certainly came as quickly as I could to her rescue. I assume you would have done as much for your child in a similar situation."

"Rose, my only child would never be in a similar situation," the colonel asserted quickly, his voice steady but the anger clearer in his gaze. "It is my son who was the victim of this girl. Surely you can't be defending what she did?"

"And surely," Rose replied just as emphatically, "you cannot defend the actions of your son who raped her."

The silence was deep and heavy between them, as though a weighty object had been dropped there and its waves were resonating, leaving the whole room off balance. He realized after a moment that he had stopped breathing, stopped thinking, stopped moving at all. His first stirring after an intake of breath was to blink his eyes. Yes, he thought as in a fog, Rose Beauregard Pinckney was indeed still sitting quietly across from him, straight in her chair, her gaze direct upon his face.

78

Julia got to the hospital before Weldon Scott arrived with the Mavericks' doctor. She found Reg just finishing his first real breakfast since his hospitalization. The doctor had decided that he could have cold cereal, eggs and grits today, and he appeared to be enjoying every bite.

"Hey, Miss McKenzie," he greeted her with a smile. "I'd offer you a bite, but this is my first real meal in this place. They've let me have a few bites of stuff people brought by, but even hospital food tastes good after all that Jell-O and dry toast."

"I'm sure it does. You look much better than when I saw you last. How's the head?"

"My head hurts less all the time. And the knee only hurts when I bump it around. How are you? Thanks for coming to see me."

"Where's your mother this morning?"

"She finally gave in just this morning and went over for tea with her friend Rose. I'm sure she'll be back here before long, though. She called the nurses' station once already to make sure I was okay."

"You're a lucky man, Reg Fallon. She's a jewel."

"You don't have to tell me that, Miss McKenzie. I'm so sorry for the toll this has taken on her. I think she nearly worried herself to death over the last few days."

"I know, but now you're doing better. Nothing will do her more good than that."

"I'm ready to have some crutches and try to shoot a few hoops. The night nurse said she could put a hoop on the top of the door if I'd give her an autograph." He smiled.

"Well, we should know more pretty soon. Mr. Scott is in town, and he brought in one of the Mavericks' doctors to have a look at you and talk to your doctors. They should be along shortly."

"Really? Mr. Scott is here? How did he know?"

"I called him. We are under an obligation to let them know if anything should interfere with your contract with them. I thought this qualified, don't you?"

Nodding, Reg had to agree. "I hadn't thought about talking to them. Thanks for taking care of it."

"No problem. Heaven knows you've had enough to deal with. It's so good to see you feeling better. That's quite a cast on the leg. I remember having a cast on my arm from my shoulder to my fingers when I was a little girl. It got really itchy and annoying before it came off."

"You broke an arm? How?"

"I fell out of a mulberry tree."

"I'm trying to picture you in a tree, Miss McKenzie. I wouldn't have thought you a tomboy."

"I had a special spot out on the thickest limb of this tree where I hid when I wanted to be alone, which was pretty often. I could climb there from my bedroom window. After I fell out, my mother had the tree cut down. I was heartbroken."

"Aw, I'm sorry. My mom learned to use a saw just so she could help me build a treehouse. We made windows and a roof, and it took us all of one summer when I was about seven. Everyone thought she was the most awesome mom in the world. I guess she probably is."

The laughing of deep male voices signaled the arrival of Weldon Scott and the two doctors. Weldon came right to the bed to shake Reg's hand, finding only the left one free and unbruised. "It's good to see you, Mr. Scott."

"And you as well, Reg, although I'd rather you were arriving for training in Dallas. This is Doctor Claude Baker, one of the team's doctors. He needed an introduction to Charleston, so I brought him along." The doctor smiled warmly and shook Reg's hand gently.

"Great to meet you, Reg. I've heard nothing but great things about you. How you feelin', man?" he asked.

184

"Much better, thanks. They tell me I was pretty bad off the first couple of days, but I'm gonna be okay now. Right, doc?" he asked, looking to Dr. Raines who held his chart.

"I'm extremely pleased with how you're doing, Reg," the doctor answered. "I've explained the different aspects of your condition to Doctor Baker—the head, the bruising along the spine and around the kidney--and he'd like to look at the leg and the x-rays. He's probably more of an expert than I am on injuries to the spine, so he's asked for another MRI to help evaluate the back. You're not having much back pain, right?"

"I'm getting to know what positions cause the pain, so I avoid them. The best position is on my left side when I can get turned over that way."

"How much pain meds are we using now?" Doctor Baker asked Dr. Raines.

The neurosurgeon checked the chart in his hands. "Stopped the IV drip yesterday, and we're using Vicodin by mouth. This guy says he's comfortable enough with just that."

"Well, your lawyer here tells us that the City or the County of Charleston will likely be paying all of your medical expenses, so we won't concern ourselves with that, although I did want you to know that we're carrying plenty of insurance to cover this if that should fall through. It sounds like the county will be very fortunate if you don't sue them for a lot more, but that's between you and Julia."

Reg looked surprised. "I hadn't given much thought to all that. I guess you're just taking care of all this stuff for me, aren't you Miss McKenzie?"

"That's what I'm here for," Julia smiled.

"Well, thanks again."

Weldon Scott cleared his throat, uncomfortable with broaching the subject of Reg playing basketball. There was no easy way to tell him that playing was unlikely, but it was part of his job to confront the disappointments of his players as well as protecting the team from contractual glitches. This situation was going to involve both. He had liked this kid from the beginning, coming to Charleston with the scout to watch him play high school ball and then following his four-year star career at the College of Charleston. It should not end this way, here in a hospital bed before it was begun, but it did appear from the detailed accounts of Doctor Raines and Doctor Rudolph and from extensive review of the records that there was no possibility this boy's damaged knee would tolerate the punishment inflicted by a career in professional basketball. Even more problematic, Reg did not appear to expect such news. Weldon did not know how to cushion the disclosure, knowing it would be for Reg a profound disappointment.

79

When Quinn bounded down the stairs, she found Rose still sitting in the living room sipping her tea.

"Good morning, Grams," she said as she kissed the older woman on the cheek. "I thought Ms. Fallon was coming over this morning."

"Yes, my dear, she has come and gone. I was happy for you to sleep a little later. We had a nice visit, but she was anxious to get over to the hospital to be with Reggie. She was telling me how impressed she is with the lovely young woman you have become."

"I'm surprised she would still think that now, Grams," Quinn said, pouring herself a cup of tea and plopping down into the chair occupied just minutes before by George Howe. "I thought I heard a man's voice earlier. Was someone else here?"

"We had a surprise visit from MacArthur Howe's father, Quinn. Isn't that interesting? I am ever so grateful that he has gone before you came down."

Quinn jerked up straight, eyes widening, and sloshed her tea over the side of the cup and into the saucer. "Mac's father was here in this house? This morning?"

"He was indeed."

"Why?" Quinn was intense now, regretting sleeping late, anxious to know the reason for the visit. "What was he doing here?"

"He was miffed at a rumor that I was involved with the little criminal who attacked his son." Rose stated this matter-of-factly but with a slightly bemused expression. She had herself still not totally assessed the conversation with the colonel.

"Miffed?" Quinn's voice had risen an octave. "He came here to say he was miffed?"

"There was nothing much to it, dear, so let's not blow it out of proportion. I've been acquainted with him and Martha for some years, you know, and I think he came here without thinking it through. I gave him a little food for thought, though, I believe. I don't think he'll be coming to see us again for quite some time. I hope you won't be upset with me."

"Upset? Why would I be upset with you?"

"Well, dear, I told him what his son had done."

It was a development coming too quickly upon the heels of others. Quinn sank back into the chair, not knowing how to react. The procession of events, incessant and alarming, was unraveling her life thread by thread, laying it open to be inspected and judged by far too many. It was as though at this moment another man had the same awful knowledge and power over her as the younger Howe had had on that years-ago night. And yet it felt as though a circuit had been completed by this most recent link in the chain of those events. Rose had closed the circle by bringing into it the only man of any importance in the life of MacArthur Howe. A flash in Quinn's gut saw this as a blow that would cut as deep as the razor she had held in her hand. The small smile from somewhere deep inside could not reach her lips, and although she had just awakened from a good night's sleep, she was overcome by exhaustion.

"I think maybe we'd better tell Julia what I've done," Rose thought aloud. "I'm not sure she will approve, but what's done is done. I've spoken out of turn before, and I suppose I will do so again." She watched as Quinn sat low in the chair, looking deflated.

"Are you all right, dear?" Rose asked.

"Things just keep happening, Grams. I feel like I'm not in control of anything anymore."

"Oh, my, I'm so sorry My words just came tumbling out."

"It's not that, Grams. I just feel so helpless. What have I done? I'm going to jail, and I'll be a convict instead of a teacher. I'll be," her voice broke, "locked up in a little gray cell for years. No one will ever look at me the same again. After all my waiting and planning, I have no control over anything at all."

Tears welled in Rose's eyes as well, and she felt Quinn's despair, had felt it before her and willed it away. Control of this situation was out of reach for both of them, she knew. She had not protected Quinn from MacArthur Howe and could not protect her now. The realization was agonizing, and she cried with Quinn as they huddled together on the paisley sofa in the sun.

"I've found that it's not control that matters anyway, dear," Rose managed through trembling lips. "It's hard work and undiluted faith. You and I are capable of both in large and potent doses." She stroked Quinn's hair, brushing it away from her face. "That will get us through this. It has to."

80

Heartened after her visit with Rose, Willa opened the door to Reg's room with her foot. Both her hands were full. The yellow roses were in one, and her pocketbook and the goodies from Rose's kitchen in the other. She was startled to walk into a roomful of people. Dr. Raines was at the bedside; Julia and the Mavericks' Mr. Scott were at the end of the bed; and a stranger was on Reg's other side. Initially fearful, she quickly realized that her son was talking and apparently in good spirits.

"Hi, Mom," he greeted her.

"Good morning, Mrs. Fallon," Weldon Scott spoke warmly, moving to help Willa put down what she was carrying. "Julia tells us you've been keeping a mighty steadfast vigil over this boy. Here, I'd like you to meet Claude Baker; he's one of the doctors for the team." He introduced the one stranger in the room, a tall, slender black man somewhat older than her son.

Doctor Baker shook Willa's hand with both of his. "It's good to meet you, Mrs. Fallon, although it would be better under other circumstances."

"You come all this way jes' to see my Reggie?" Willa asked.

"I think Mr. Scott is using Reggie as an excuse to get in a few rounds of golf out at the Wild Dunes, Mrs. Fallon," Doctor Baker grinned, "and he brought me along so he wouldn't have to play alone. Seriously, though, we wanted to see how Reg is doing. Now that I've had a chance to talk to Doctor Raines, I think we have a better handle on it."

"My boy be doin' all right," Willa confirmed. "He look better an' better all the time."

Julia watched the others hedge around the issue. "Now that you're here, Willa, maybe we can talk about Reg playing ball this year. I think the doctors have made a joint assessment, and they seem to agree that Reg can't be showing up for basketball practice any time soon. Is that correct, gentlemen?" Julia asked, looking from one doctor to the other, hoping to ease gently into a realistic discussion of the diminished possibility Reg would play professional ball and unwilling to wait longer for someone to broach the subject.

"We do seem to agree," Dr. Raines began, glancing to the other doctor for confirmation, "that this knee injury alone would preclude any high-impact activity in the near future. There will be long-term rehab and physical therapy. There's also a high probability that at some point the knee joint should be replaced. Would you concur, Doctor Baker?"

"Absolutely. And the physical therapy should start as soon as possible.

Reg was enjoying the conversation and the company around him, but Willa was already jumping to conclusions, wanting with all her might to shield her son from a diagnosis that would shatter his dream.

Julia had become privy during dinner the previous evening to the judgment of Weldon Scott and Claude Baker. A professional sports franchise, even one with nice guys in charge, was not interested in throwing good money after bad. Their priority was ensuring that their players were in good health and ready to play. They would ride out an injury with a player as talented as Reg if his value to the team was seen as long-term, but a shattered knee before a recruit had stepped onto the court in a Mavericks uniform appeared definitive. Dr. Baker had said as much the night before. Her job was to insure the best financial outcome for her client.

"The team is taking care of all your medical expenses for now," she assured both Fallons. "It's almost a certainty that the city or county will have to reimburse them. We'll get into that next week. Financial concerns should be the least of your worries. That's all under control."

"When can I start practice?" Reg asked, looking toward the more familiar Doctor Raines.

The doctor was afraid that his patient had not yet considered the seriousness of his injuries as they related to a sports career. It was a shame to have to break it to him just as his spirits were up, but the arrival of team representatives had taken the timing out of his hands.

Weldon Scott put both his hands on the metal rail at the foot of the bed. "We don't see you playing ball this season, Reg, and the doctors seem very cautious about predicting the future. I've seen and am a big believer in miraculous recoveries. Just for now, however, I'm sorrier than I can say that we have to consider the possibility you simply won't be playing professional ball. The doctors reluctantly concur that your knee probably won't take it. We talked with Julia yesterday evening about a financial agreement per our contract that will allow you to keep a good part of the signing bonus. That should open other possibilities for you, further education perhaps? You're not, after all, just a jock. You're a very smart guy."

He had put it right out there, Julia thought, not taking her eyes from Reg's face as Scott spoke. She had seen the shadow cross his eyes as the words touched him. She checked Willa's reaction, sharing the chagrin in her expression as she moved closer to her son's bedside. The mother, she knew, would feel the pain as deeply as her son. She had bought into his dream as surely as if it was her own.

Reg did not know what to say. It was clear that he was stunned, that he had indeed not considered this possibility, beyond basketball, beyond the years he expected to play the game he loved, whole and healthy, providing for his mother all the things he wished for her, repaying her love and care with comfort beyond her wildest dreams. He was a ball player, an athlete. His future was in the stadiums of the NBA. Reg had never dreamed of being a fireman, an astronaut. All his dreams played out on shiny hardwood courts under bright lights in front of screaming fans, eyes on the rim, nothing but net. The picture began to blur by unshed tears gathering at the corners of his eyes. Weldon Scott looked toward the floor, but Julia could not look away.

81

When Julia returned to her office, Celia was sitting behind the desk, tanned bare feet on the desktop, toes wiggling, leaning back in the chair engrossed in a recent issue of Psychology Today.

"Okay, here's your cell phone on the desk while you're out galivanting around," she said as Julia opened the door. "I've been adding numbers to your contact list. And I brought lunch."

Julia smiled weakly, still badly in need of distraction after the hospital. "You're such a bossy friend." Picking up the small black phone, she ran her fingers over the screen. "I thought you had an appointment this morning."

"She cancelled. Did you say you were unspeakably grateful that I take care of you like this?"

"Okay, don't tease me, Celia Rutledge. It's been a bad enough day. So, yes, I'm glad you're here."

"What's been bad?"

"I've been at the hospital. They told Reg that he can't play ball."

"Oh, I'm sorry, Jules." Celia took her feet from the desktop, sitting up straight and placing the open magazine face down on a pile of files. "How did he take it?"

"Not well. I'm not sure he believes it yet. It will take some time for this to sink in. Poor kid. I thought we were eating lunch with Quinn and Rose."

Celia took a deep breath. "Grandma Rose told Colonel Howe that his son raped Quinn."

"What?" Julia's head snapped up from examining the phone. "She did what?"

"Okay." Celia's expression grew more serious. "I've been trying to find you for two hours. George Howe paid a surprise visit to Grandma Rose, just appeared at her front door and asked to talk to her."

"When? Today?"

"He had left just before I called her this morning. When he accused her of befriending a criminal, our little Grams told him who the criminal is. I guess he was stunned, told her she's a crazy old biddy, and left."

Julia sat down slowly in the chair across the desk from Celia. "Whatever possessed her to tell him that?"

"You know how she is, Jules. I guess he was calling Quinn vicious and crazy, and Grams just dropped her little bomb on him. She's not one to put up with much these days, and I don't think she had time to wonder how it would affect Quinn's case. That's why I'm here waiting for you; I don't know either. What's the fallout from this?"

"Well, the plot certainly thickens." Julia replied. "I'm temporarily dumbfounded. My immediate thought is that our incentive to file a rape charge just went up. This little secret is spreading too far and too fast. I've had too much coffee, and I need a ladies' room break. Call and tell Rose we're coming over. Let's eat."

"Didn't you just call me bossy?" Celia quipped.

"Okay, would you please call Rose? And may we please eat whatever scrumptious thing you've brought here for my totally undeserved pleasure?" Julia rephrased. "Please?" she looked back over her shoulder with her best imploring expression.

"Grams said that after she told her about the colonel, Quinn went right upstairs to her room crying and curled up in a ball. Grams was hoping she went back to sleep."

"Well, Cele, wake her up," Julia called as she closed the bathroom door.

82

George Howe had walked from his home to Rose's house that morning. It was only a few blocks. When he stormed out after talking with Rose, he looked for his car, remembering only after a brief search that he had not driven. Thoughts roiling, he started toward home and then turned back, opting to walk along the battery wall toward White Point Gardens. He did not notice the heat or the tourists, numb and blinded by his anger at Rose Pinckney's accusation. It was hard enough to swallow the possibility that a mere slip of a girl had caused the unthinkable injury to his son; it was an outrage for a respected Charleston woman, one of supposed means and substance, to align herself with this girl, suggesting his son was a rapist. His son was a military man, a patriot. He was born to a family of integrity and honor, the colonel's family, the son who would carry on a tradition grounded in duty and principle. He was Martha's son, and Rose's words must never reach her ears.

Walking slowly, running his hand absently along the iron rails and up across the rough top of each concrete pillar, the father pictured his son, handsome in his uniform, elbow bent in a sharp salute. He had been promoted to the rank of first lieutenant while at Fort Hood, and his prospects were excellent for rising quickly through the ranks.

The colonel had walked, while immersed in dark and vexing muse, too soon to sort it rationally, into the park itself, occupying the tip of the peninsula. White Point Gardens was a landmark of mixed tribute, its liveoaks and palmettos a backdrop to the beauty of the harbor, its polished old Civil War cannons a reminder that this spot had not always been a scene of tranquility. Foregoing a seat on one of the benches lining the park and offering a clear view across the bay, the colonel walked deeper into the dappled shade, passing the statue of William Gilmore Simms, renowned southern author and historian. Choosing to sit on the concrete steps of the old gazebo, George Howe faced away from the harbor and toward the historic houses along the East Battery, looking but not seeing them through the haze in his mind.

Perspiration had formed on his head and neck and trickled down his face and chest unnoticed. Struggling to regaining control of his racing heart, he formed a slow resolve to be untroubled by the ramblings of a crazy old woman whose unfathomable tale had, for him, no ring of truth. Could this whole torturous mess be put to rest by the courts and the police in whom he had so far found no promise for a quick or resolute end? Or did it fall to him to take charge? He had always believed in and protected his country, his honor, his family. Running his fingers through his hair, his palm came away wet. It was too hot to sit here seething, he decided, pulling himself up to head toward home. He would try to put this out of his mind for the moment, shake it off and give no indication to either his wife or his son that he had heard the old woman's baseless rambling.

83

Julia and Celia sat on Quinn's bed, each with her legs crossed under her. Rose sat in the chair, thinking that they could, but for this twist of fate, be three girls having a slumber party, giggling together, sharing secrets. Here they were instead, sharing grown-up pain, each taking unto herself a portion of the heartache dealt to Quinn.

They had cajoled and comforted, coaxing and finally persuading Quinn to sit up in the bed. She was propped on her two pillows now, holding a cool, damp washcloth on her eyes and forehead. Rose had not been willing to wake her when Celia called, so the three had come together to the bedroom, Celia carrying a pitcher of bloody marys, Quinn's drink of choice on the infrequent occasions when she had something alcoholic. They had decided that this early afternoon called for whatever measures would get them through it.

When they entered her room, Quinn was curled under her quilt, nothing visible but the top of her head. She did not move when Julia and Celia piled onto the bed, nor did she respond to their gentle pleas in any way except to finally shake her head back and forth, signaling her wish to be left alone.

"Should we just let her sleep?" Rose asked quietly, worried. She had seen Quinn awake, crying as she climbed the stairs an hour earlier, not consolable.

"Absolutely not," Celia responded, knowing that now was the time for fierce and aggressive support. The weight of the secret Quinn had carried alone for four years had come crashing down, and they could not allow her to drown as the waves of anguish and guilt broke over her. This, if ever, was the moment for a loving mother, Celia thought, but here they were, the three of them, offering the love they had.

Celia finally crawled to curl herself around Quinn, forming her body to cup the other from behind, nuzzling her face into the back of Quinn's neck and hair, pulling her close with an arm around her middle.

She would not have been surprised at a robust rebuff, Quinn pulling away or throwing the cover aside and running to the bathroom. But instead, presently, the girl's shoulders began to shake as she sobbed into the pillow, her whimpers ripening to a wail as she turned and nestled against Celia. Wishing she could reassure the other two women in the room that this was not out of the ordinary under the circumstances, she could not turn away from Quinn, concentrating her energy and focus on being the sister, the friend, the comfort Quinn required. She had never, she thought, been so grateful for her professional training.

Tears streaked down Rose's cheeks, and Julia went quietly to crouch beside her, offering tissues, otherwise at a loss for any way to help. They had maintained those positions for minutes, many minutes, while the sound of Quinn's pain rose and then, slowly, subsided. Her breathing quieted, still jerky and rasping but becoming more regular. Celia pulled her face back slightly, brushing the hair from Quinn's swollen cheeks and eyes, offering just the hint of a smile as a test.

"We made bloody marys," she offered as an almost whisper. "I'll bet even Grams will have one."

A ragged sigh rose deeply from Quinn's chest, seeming to involve her very heart. "More Kleenex."

Julia jumped to supply the whole box, and Celia dabbed at the wetness around Quinn's eyes. "I think we could use a wet cloth here," she said softly, still not moving away. "This baby face is all red and puffy." Julia was getting the cloth, wondering if she should go down to the kitchen for ice. "Could we plump up these pillows and sit up for a nice bloody mary?" Celia asked. "When have any of us starting drinking right in the middle of a day? Doesn't this seem like the day?"

Quinn nodded. "Okay."

Julia poured and stood beside the bed, holding the glass and the wet cloth.

"We're gonna have to sit up, sweetie. Let's nest you against the pillows." Quinn was limp, and Celia arranged her like a rag doll, fluffing, tucking, cooing calmly as she worked. Julia set the peppery red drink on the bedside table, and Celia put the cloth in Quinn's hand and guided it to her forehead.

There they were, four women, each now holding a drink in her hand, waiting for a cue from Celia. "To us," Celia offered, holding up her glass, "together." The others held out their glasses and took a first sip,

Quinn raising hers with a quivering hand, saying nothing, dabbing at her eyes with the cool cloth.

"You gonna be all right?" Celia asked, tucking the quilt around Quinn's feet. "How's the bloody mary? I made it myself."

"I know. Yours are the best," Quinn replied, sipping again.

Celia had debated offering an anti-anxiety medication, but she opted to wait, hoping they could restore Quinn's spirits with undiluted support and reassurance. It was obvious that Quinn had come face to face with the seriousness of her situation. She was afraid.

"We're not going to let anything happen to you," Rose assured from her chair in the corner of the room, hoping with each confident word that her statement was related in some way to the truth. If intentions mattered, it was gospel.

"I'm so scared," Quinn admitted, her hand clutching the glass. Her eyes met Julia's. "I'm going to go to jail for this, aren't I?"

"I'm doing everything in my power to see that you don't," Julia answered sincerely. "I came here today specifically to offer an idea. Are you up to talking about it?"

"Julia's got a plan," Celia offered, trying to sound positive and excited. "It's something we can actually work on rather than just waiting for life to happen to us."

"What can we do?" Quinn asked. "I've gotten us into this. I'm scared to death. Y'all are worried sick about me. No one in this town will ever look at me the same after this gets out. I'll be that girl who was raped. I'll be the crazy one. I'll never be a teacher. People will skirt far around me on the sidewalk and snicker. Even if I don't go to jail, my life is pretty done." Her lips were trembling again, and her eyes were tearing.

It was time for Julia to step in, be the lawyer as well as the friend. "You're not crazy, Quinn. You were the victim of a crime, and you were taking back the power for your own life. You were defending something, weren't you, trying to save something? What was it?" Julia paused, waiting, hoping for the quick instinctive response.

"Myself."

Julia let the words hang there in the air of the old high-ceilinged bedroom, assuring that the others absorbed the logic of her question and Quinn's answer, straightforward and without frills. It was the entire foundation for the case she was building, the clear rationale behind Quinn's defense. She wanted Celia and Rose, in that moment, to grasp the moral, if not legal, validity of Quinn's position, hoping it would mimic her desired reaction from a jury.

"Exactly," she said finally, with satisfaction, "and if anyone deserves to be looked at as crazy, it is MacArthur Howe. He is a rapist, a common criminal walking the streets and receiving a regular paycheck from the government of the United States. No one has known until now. No one but you. Would you not like for the world, his friends, the Army, all those people on the sidewalk, to know what he really is? Doesn't he deserve that?"

"I thought I was giving him what he deserved."

"That hasn't gone quite as planned, has it? My friend at the police station suggested that we file a formal rape charge against him. You could have done it on the night it happened. You could have done it the next morning, or the following week, though it becomes more troublesome over time to prove. You could have done it the day after you graduated from college. You could have done it on the day you crawled through his window with the knife. Quinn, you can do it today."

"What?"

"You can charge him with raping you. It doesn't matter that all this time has elapsed. The law doesn't set a time limit on reporting a rape."

"But … well … why would I? Too many people already know. I don't want this to be the main story line of my life."

"He hurt you; you hurt him back. His move. Your move. Now there's a charge against you under the law of South Carolina. Let's file your own charge. It's our move, and I can find no overarching reason it shouldn't be this one. It's a bold, confident move, one that establishes on paper your reason for doing what you did. It's not a legal justification, certainly, but it's laying groundwork we badly need. That's why I wanted to talk to you. Are you up to discussing the idea?"

Slowly, Quinn sipped her drink, her reddened eyes revealing that she was processing. Julia pressed a little further.

"We're going to use this at trial anyway. It would be a bombshell then, which I've been thinking is good, not for you personally but for the case. It somehow legitimizes the accusation if we press charges openly, right now, prior to trial. Am I making sense to you?"

"So that means I'm saying right now to the whole world that I was raped. It'll be on paper for anyone to read?"

"They will ask you for every last detail at the time we file a charge. I'll not leave your side," Julia added, grasping at any opportunity for reassurance. There was so little.

Quinn wiped her eyes once again with the damp cloth, finished her bloody mary in three large swallows and nested the empty glass crookedly between two lumps in the quilt. "I never wanted anyone to know." She said it so softly, so full of deep and undiluted despair.

"No one is ordering you to do this, baby," Celia said. "It's an option to consider. You could run away, never look back. You could go into an emotional tailspin, which lets him win. Or you can recognize the truth—that you were the victim of a criminal act and a hurtful experience—and then fight like hell to get past it."

"I'm so tired right now," Quinn admitted. "I don't know if I have the strength to fight any more."

"That's why you have us," Rose piped in. "We're your army. No one will ever speak or think badly of you without answering to me. People here know and love you. They're your friends, my friends, parents of children who have known you for years."

"That is also true of Mac and his parents, Grams. They have friends who will believe him too."

"Sometimes in life we have to throw down the gauntlet and meet a problem head-on," Rose replied. "You tried to handle this all alone, and now it's time to call out the artillery and the press and run up the flag. You're my beautiful, talented Quinn. There is no shame for you in having been molested, nor is there any in having fought back. The scarlet letter will be on MacArthur Howe when we are through, Babyluv. It will not be on you."

Quinn continued to look forlorn, totally disheartened. The morning's events had for some reason put her over the edge. "I don't need him to have a trial or go to jail. I just want it to go away now. I want to be left alone. I don't want people to think of me as 'that girl who got raped'."

"It's not about what people will think anymore, Quinn," Julia added reluctantly. "It's about your life. We're going to have to convince a jury to go against the letter of the law. Under the law, you're guilty of assault, possibly to the extreme of trying to take someone's life. We have to make the jury feel compelled to base their ruling on a higher authority, a moral authority. The judge will instruct them not to do so. It is his job to see that the law is followed to the letter. It is ours to see that your life goes on. You have to decide, and do so quickly, if you are willing to give strength and legitimacy to this case by filing a rape charge. You are strong enough to do this. I already know that about you." She paused, hoping she had been persuasive, realizing that she had in the last few minutes convinced herself. MacArthur Howe was a rapist. She wanted to go after him.

Quinn sighed deeply, finally tilting her face up to meet Julia's eyes for the first time.

"Do you remember," Julia went on, "when you were at my house we promised to stick by each other? I'll do everything I can to help you. All three of us will lend you our strength. We have to hold hands and believe."

"Okay," Quinn said. And holding out her empty glass, she added in little more than a whisper, "More please."

84

Summer's relentless heat clung to the land as the sun dropped lower over the city. It was a typical waning afternoon, white puffy clouds drifting along the horizon, a couple of sailboats in the harbor, and a shrimp boat just returning with its day's catch to be enjoyed at one of the local waterfront restaurants. The water and sky were almost the same blue at this time on a clear day, though near the shore stirring sand and a multitude of tiny saltwater creatures clouded the surf.

In the rocking chair on the porch, Julia reviewed the events of her day, thankful to be here for an evening alone. It had been a stressful day, pocked by unnerving episodes with both Reg and Quinn. Instead of the usual hot tea, Julia had settled onto the porch with a crystal wine glass and a bottle of pinot noir, its cork removed and resting on the gray porch floor. Slender strands of luminous orange and gold were just beginning to grow across the western sky, extending tentacles of a sun reluctant to give way.

A lone ring-billed gull, large and plump, perched like a statue on the rocks just beyond a clump of sea oats, waiting expectantly for his next meal. Julia had learned to recognize the bird from his black-ringed yellow bill, and she liked to think this was the one who frequented her section of beach because she regularly provided him with bits of canned sardines to supplement his diet of unwary fish and little beach rodents too slow to escape when spotted by his beady eyes.

The colors were spreading as the sun descended over the skyline of Charleston proper, a patch of fiery orange making the spire of St. Phillips appear a solid stone sentinel standing watch over its city. There were no skyscrapers on this horizon, no reminders that a world full of bustle and smog existed. The steeples were the prominent markers, along with the requisite rigs of the seaport now standing motionless for the night. Catching Julia's eye, a green anole lizard darted up the white porch pillar just in front of her, stopping to extend his pink throat fan. Julia smiled. He was flirting, she had learned, using this colorful signal to attract a mate.

"It's not me, little fellow," she said softly. "But I'm flattered nonetheless."

Julia sighed deeply with her first sip, listening to the wind and water that were now the background music for her life. She was sitting on her own porch behind the Sullivan's Island dunes overlooking the Charleston harbor, immersed in a new place of charm and beauty, knee-deep in the lives of its people. It was both unanticipated and remarkable. Contentment had crept upon her unaware, settling over her while she was sanding floors, acquainting herself with new people and surroundings, applying a concentrated effort to building a law practice.

There was plenty of reason for concern. She thought of Quinn's predicament and her precarious state of mind, the improbable task of the girl's defense weighing heavily upon her. After a glass or two of the pinot and a much-needed interlude here overlooking her cherished seascape, she would devote the rest of her evening to working on the case.

Reg Fallon's misfortune also haunted Julia. It seemed inadequate to call it that, but some quirk or plan of fate was responsible for his loss. He possessed an undeniable talent, one that would likely have brought him fame and fortune, well deserved in Julia's assessment. He had worked and practiced tirelessly, never taking his skill for granted, sincerely grateful for the opportunity it would provide for him and for his mother. He went to a party with his buddies, had a few beers, went for a walk to clear his head and sat down, against all odds, beside the bloody weapon used in the commission of a crime to which he was totally unrelated. She had seen in Reg today the first signs of what would surely play out as grief over a loss, a dream unrealized through no fault of his own.

Julia had always been troubled by life's not playing fair. That questioning had pulled her slowly but surely back from the religious indoctrination of her childhood. She had, she was sure, a grand and deep faith, much of it yet untapped and unexcavated, but her faith was not blind. It rested somewhere in the belief that she was required without qualification, without whining or cowardice, to give her best to life. In return, life would meet her when she had come the whole way of which she was capable, taking over with open arms.

The cases of both Reg and Quinn tested this theory. She was ever receptive to a chance to knead her convictions with new input, didn't mind knowing that her understanding of life was always evolving. But what good was a perfectly good mind, able to assess logically, if critical life events defied analysis? This was true in the cases of both Reg and Quinn. Julia was perplexed and not content to be so.

After her third glass of wine, she found herself wishing for a friend, a little conversation. The answering machine picked up at Celia's house. Without a second thought, she dialed Sonny Legare.

"Legare," he answered after the first ring.

"Legare, it's McKenzie," Julia smiled as she took on his tone of voice, brusque, deep and all business.

There was a momentary pause. She had surprised him. She grinned.

"Well, hey, McKenzie." His voice lightened immediately. "Could you feel me thinking about you?"

"Good thoughts, I hope. I was just wanting to hear a friendly voice, yours in particular. I admit I tried Celie first, but she's not home."

"I'll take being second choice after your best friend as a compliment, McKenzie. In fact, I might call her myself to thank her for not being at home."

"Well, I wanted to thank you for your advice. I had a very difficult afternoon with Quinn, but she and I will be down to the station in the morning. She's agreed to file a criminal complaint. The more I think about it, the more I know it's right. So I definitely owe you one. You sure you weren't a lawyer in a previous life?"

"Not a chance. But I like the idea of you owing me. Does that mean my chances of spending a little time with you on the weekend have just improved?"

"Done," Julia agreed without hesitation. "What do you have in mind?"

"I can promise you that I've given it considerable thought, McKenzie. Would you be up for dinner at a grungy little seafood place where the food is so good you don't notice the atmosphere?"

"You may find that I'm more adventurous than you know, Detective Legare. How will we dress?"

"It's a jeans place at all hours, or a pair of shorts, one of those dimly lit places, but they usually have a great little country band on Saturday nights. Is that way outside your tolerance limit?"

Thinking of the music she could hear from her stereo, she had to laugh. "Again, Sonny, you might be surprised. I've spent my share of time, admittedly not recently, in places off the beaten path. I was young once upon a time, you know."

"And you still are, McKenzie," Sonny said quickly. "Young and beautiful and quite capable of reminding an old guy like me that life might not be quite over after all."

"I was just sitting here thinking what I've messed up in my life, and I sure hope it's not over. You know those moments when you can hardly contain yourself because life is so exciting?"

"Yeah, I've had a few of those."

"I want there to be more." Julia asserted it without thinking.

Listening to the quiet at Sonny's end of the line, she wondered how much the three and a half glasses of wine had mellowed her. "Detective?"

"Sometimes you just leave me speechless, McKenzie, and that's not easily done."

"Okay, well, that accomplished, I'd better admit that I'm ever the teensiest bit tipsy."

"That may be a condition I'll want to encourage in the future. It's not my sense that you're possessed by the southern coyness which afflicts a lot of the women of my acquaintance, but it might be that a couple glasses of wine just fan that refreshing honesty of yours."

"Okay, I'm corking the bottle now so that I can get ready to be with Quinn in the morning. Will you be there when we come down?"

"Wouldn't miss it. You should know it's not going to be easy for her. And probably not for you either."

"Okay, well, thanks again for lending your ear. After the fact, I'm glad it was you instead of Celia."

"I'm glad too, McKenzie."

"Goodnight, Sonny."

"Goodnight, McKenzie."

THURSDAY

85

Quinn was as pale as white bread dough and trembling from head to toe as they left the squad room. Julia held her arm, concerned that her knees might buckle before they got out of the building. It had been an agonizing ordeal as Quinn was subjected to recalling the rape in graphic and excruciating detail, especially necessary, Julia knew, in pursuing a charge this old. Every scrap of recollection could matter.

Sonny had chosen to take a seat behind Quinn during the questioning, attempting to spare her any unnecessary discomfort. The only faces she would see as she spoke were those of Julia and the female detective he had chosen to take her statement. Although she had paused occasionally and dabbed at tears once or twice, Quinn had been almost stoic as she described the events of four years earlier in the bedroom of MacArthur Howe. She appeared to have steeled herself for the difficult morning. Julia had not been prepared for the brutal details. If she had known, truly known, she might not have asked Quinn to relive it. She fought nausea as they walked outside, praying to deliver Quinn safely back into the care of Rose Pinckney before she herself collapsed.

86

Weldon Scott and Claude Baker had teed off at nine o'clock on Thursday morning on the spectacular course at the Wild Dunes where they were staying. The young doctor had to admit that the warm, gentle breeze off the Atlantic Ocean did not interfere with his shots, especially as his ball had landed cleanly on the green for eight of the nine holes they played.

"I never should have taught you this game," Scott joked as they pulled the rented car alongside the curb near Julia's office. You're gonna be full of yourself now, aren't you?"

"If you feed me a dinner tonight as good as last night's, I might let you come close to winning tomorrow before we go home. It doesn't seem right to beat you that badly, old boy. I was feeling your pain around the seventh hole when your ball landed in the sand trap. It just hurts me to see you suffer like that."

"I know it does. I'll try to recover while you dig out the change for this parking meter. You can probably shake some out of the big head you've grown this morning."

"Don't be surly now, Mr. Scott, sir," Baker grinned as he dropped coins into the curbside meter and turned the handle to buy two hours of space.

Julia had needed two hours to recover from the ordeal with Quinn at the police station. Thankful for her minimal but sufficient stash of make-up in a desk drawer, she had repaired her mascara and added a touch of blush to her cheeks before the two o'clock appointment with Messrs. Scott and Baker. Checking her watch and her desk, she assessed herself prepared. When the door opened, she greeted the two men as though it had been a normal day in her world, one not scarred by listening to a victim recounting the brutal details of her rape. But they had gotten through it, both she and Quinn.

"I can see that you gentlemen have been on the course," Julia observed, noting the sunburn on both their faces and forearms. "How was it?"

"I'll pass that question off to our friend Mr. Scott," the young doctor teased. "How was it?" he repeated.

"I had to let the kid beat me, Julia. I didn't want him to pout and go home. You know how temperamental these young guys are. But I'd venture to say he realizes that he's now played a real golf course."

"Do you play?" Claude Baker asked Julia.

"I never learned, she answered. "But the people I know who do are positively rabid about the game. Come on into the library. Can I get you some coffee before we get started?"

"That would be great, thanks." Weldon Scott walked to the pot. "I can get it myself."

"None for me, thanks," Claude Baker responded. "I'm still on a high from my spectacular victory this morning." He glanced at Scott as he brushed by him on his way into the library, suppressing a grin. "Some days you just can't lose for winning."

"Someone should save this little punk from himself before he explodes," Scott implored Julia. "Can't you do something about him?"

A little levity in the room helped Julia's spirits. She had never known Weldon Scott to be anything but upbeat and positive. "Would you like me to break both his legs?" she asked in her most innocent voice.

Now Scott laughed, raising an eyebrow as he peered into the library at Claude Baker. "Did you hear that?" he asked around the doorjamb. "And I can attest that this woman has a very serious side."

"No question about it," Julia concurred.

"Thanks," Scott winked.

"Yes ma'am," came from the library. "I guess I've been told."

Taking places around the table, Weldon and Julia opened their respective files on Reg Fallon's agreement with the Mavericks. It would be an amiable discussion, Julia knew, in the manner of her previous dealings with Weldon Scott. He had so far been generous and up front, no holds barred, cutting straight to the bottom line in each stage of their negotiations. She expected no less today.

"Reg keeps three-quarters of his signing bonus," she began, scratching on a legal pad. "Are we in agreement there?"

"We are," Scott replied. "Your insistence on insuring that part of his income when we wrote this contract has paid off for him in spades. It's a clause I sometimes resist, but even I am satisfied that we agreed to it in this case. That money will put him in a position to buy some time and assess his options. He deserves that. He's worked hard for it."

"Thanks, Weldon. He has. You can't pay someone to give up a dream, but let's hope this will help him find another dream."

"Do you have any idea what he might do?" Claude Baker asked Julia. "I looked at his grade point average, and he's not just some dumb jock. He could do almost anything he wanted with brains like that."

"I'm going to recruit some help to remind him of that in the next few weeks," Julia assured them. "Are you going to see him again before you go back to Dallas? I think that would mean a lot to him. Maybe he'd talk more openly to you guys now that he's had a little time to absorb what's happened."

"We're planning to stop by to see him tomorrow before we leave town," Weldon said. "I really do like the kid. If you think of anything I can do after we're gone, anything at all, don't hesitate to call me. It's always a pleasure hearing from you anyway, Julia. You know that."

"Well, let's put this on paper, and I'll take you boys over to Bubba Gump's for that late lunch."

87

Sonny was surprised and somewhat pleased that Julia had taken his advice and moved on it so quickly. Here he was, some forty-eight hours after giving it, on his way to bringing Mac Howe down to the station for questioning on a charge of rape. It would be an interesting moment, he thought, announcing matter-of-factly to the cocky young man that his choices were to come for questioning or be placed under arrest then and there based upon Quinn Ravenel's allegation. It would be even more interesting if the father was at home. He did hope, however, that Mac's mother was out of the house. It was not his wish to upset Martha Howe.

There on the old historic peninsula, Sonny enjoyed a clear view across the harbor, noting that it was clear enough to see the guardrail and the antenna at the top of the black and white lighthouse on Sullivan's Island. Partly because of his job and partly because of his nature, Sonny was an observer of detail. He had memorized the outline of the horizon.

This old city with its history and its foibles and quirks was as much home to him as the marina on the Ashley River. He had blended into it growing up, though not on the side South of Broad Street, and was now a part of its political landscape. His face was familiar in the historic district as well as west of the Ashley, and he was greeted by name at Joe Riley Stadium as congenially as at the open-air market among regular sellers of craft and art. It was his town; he was comfortable here. Coming up through the ranks, he had not pressed to be the chief of detectives, but his rise to the position was a natural result of his insistence upon excellence in the department. Fellow officers looked to Sonny long before he had the position in name, and they had grown comfortable with him as their official leader. Though his routine duties involved mostly overseeing the department, he could confront uncomfortable situations involving Charleston notables when special handling was required. As in the situation today, he was frequently reminded that deviant and criminal behavior crossed all social and economic lines. Saints and sinners, he liked to tell his colleagues, existed in every stratum of society. His deeper belief, however, was that neither the saints nor the sinners were born to their respective stations but were trained, intentionally or not. Circumstances of one's birth did contribute; having advantage and opportunity might be factors; mothers and fathers were key.

It was difficult to look at the Howes and assign blame for the actions of a rapist son. They were pillars of the community, respected and contributing members of Charleston's cultural core. There was no question that they loved their son every bit as much as Reg's mother loved hers. How, then, was the arrogance born in a young man's mentality which allowed him to assume himself entitled to behave as he had on the day he raped Quinn Ravenel? It was, Sonny decided, not for him to know. Closing the cruiser door in front of the gray stucco house, he took a deep breath, un-pocketed the warrant and headed for the front door.

Walking along the same piazza where he had last investigated the assault, Sonny's mind traveled back to recall the ambulance pulling away, sirens blaring and lights flashing, the chief putting Mac's shocked parents into the car, the profuse amount of bright red blood soaking into the bed. It had been a savage and surprisingly calculated attack, precisely executed. He was more surprised by its equally cruel aftermath, still unfolding as he rang the bell. It played the Westminster chime as he waited. There was only one car parked at the house, a new Mustang convertible that he presumed to be Mac's. As he prepared to ring the bell once again, the door opened and the young MacArthur Howe appeared, supported by two crutches but looking much improved.

"You're looking pretty well," Sonny complimented. "Why the crutches?"

"Doc says it keeps stress off...places," Mac replied, none too warmly. "I have an appointment with him tomorrow, so maybe he'll let me off them. What can I do for you, Detective?"

Sonny held out the warrant, which gave him the authority to arrest, and Mac, looking puzzled, took it as he balanced his weight on one crutch.

"Would you mind if I came in?" Sonny asked. "You could get off your feet, and I'll explain the papers."

"Be my guest," Mac replied casually, backing away with the crutches to make way for Sonny to enter. It was cool and quiet inside as Sonny followed Mac down a hall and into the paneled family room, all oak and masculine in decor with black leather furniture and pictures on the wall of men in uniform.

"Have a seat," Mac gestured with a crutch as he sat on the sofa. He had made no move to look at the warrant.

"I'm going to have to ask you a few questions," Sonny began, leaning slightly forward and clasping his hands between his parted knees. "Quinn Ravenel has filed a first-degree aggravated rape charge against you. Under the circumstances--you just getting out of the hospital and all--I didn't want to send the boys over to haul you down to the station, so I came myself. The prosecutor has looked at the particulars of the complaint, and the judge has issued a warrant. You're holding it in your hand. Is there anything you'd like to tell me?"

Stunned momentarily, Mac recovered quickly. "Who the fuck do you think you are?" was his response, his voice raised. "Don't you people think I've been through enough? You can't arrest me. I haven't done anything. I'm the damn victim here, or have you forgotten that part?" He was fumbling for the crutches, trying to get back on his feet. "I shouldn't have let you in here in the first damn place. Get out of this house before I throw you out." He had pulled himself upright, waving one crutch in the air for emphasis.

"I'm just doing the job I'm paid to do," Sonny replied evenly. "I don't think you're up to throwing me out, so why don't you just sit back down." Sonny had not moved, his fingers still woven together, his posture relaxed.

The sound of the front door closing broke the silence, followed by footsteps coming down the hall.

"What's going on here?" the colonel asked. "Is everything okay, Mac?"

Now Sonny got to his feet.

"Dad, this fucking son of a bitch says he's here to arrest me. That girl has accused me of rape, for god's sake, has actually filed a charge against me."

The colonel wished mightily now that he had chosen to discuss with Mac his conversation with Rose Pinckney the day before. He had managed to contain his initial outrage, categorizing Rose's charge irrational, and was thus largely unprepared for any formal accusation against his son. It was a preposterous development, but one requiring his immediate effort at containment. There must not be a scene. He stood stock still, looking straight at Sonny, struggling to maintain his composure.

"This is an obvious and desperate attempt to discredit my son, detective, a flimsy ploy to deflect the blame from the girl who broke into this house. I expect we'll be needing our attorney to take care of it. Shall I give him a call?" His voice was steady and matter-of-fact, revealing nothing of the alarm creeping up the back of his neck. Martha could be home at any minute, he thought. Flipping up the top of his old metal address pad by the phone, he found and dialed the number for Comings and Guerry. His call was answered on the first ring. "This is George Howe. I need to speak to Mendel Comings."

There was a pause. "No, he can't call me back. I need to talk to him right now."

Another silence. The senior Howe stood as though at attention, his fingers tense around the telephone receiver at his ear. "Mendel? Thanks for taking my call. There's a police detective standing in my living room threatening to arrest my son on some trumped-up rape charge. I need you to help me out here."

The colonel listened intently for a minute or two. "Yes, I'd appreciate it, Mendel. Thanks again." He held out the receiver to Sonny, who walked across the room to take it.

"This is Sonny Legare."

"Sonny, Mendel Comings. I understand we have a problem."

"We do. I have a warrant."

"Sonny," Comings continued, "I'd really appreciate it if you'd let me present my client at the station first thing in the morning. You and I both know he's not going anywhere, and I'm in the middle of a messy negotiation here in my office as we speak. You have my word we'll be there at whatever time you suggest. Can we handle it that way? I'll owe you another one."

Sonny glanced at the young MacArthur Howe, whose face was still reddened by anger. There was no point in exacerbating an already-tense moment, and what Mendel Comings proposed was an accepted practice when a defendant could afford a reputable attorney. Comings was always as good as his word. "Done," Sonny agreed. "How about nine?"

"Thanks, Sonny. I'll see you then."

Sonny placed the receiver back in its cradle. "Your lawyer says he'll have you down at the station in the morning. I'll see you then, gentlemen. Thanks for your time." Sonny strode briskly down the hall and out the front door, closing it quietly behind him, welcoming the heat and humidity as less oppressive than the animosity inside.

88

Rose had looked in on Quinn several times during the evening, slipping to the side of the bed to stand watch for a few minutes at a time, worried, wanting to touch her, brush her hair from her face. But Quinn was breathing evenly, curled with her hands together under her chin and had not changed position, drained and exhausted.

Sunlight had streamed across the bed when Rose tucked her in, making light patterns on the quilt. Rose sat quietly in the rocker until Quinn was asleep, just as she had done so many nights when the little girl slept in this same bed. Now that the sun had set, Rose could see a sky full of stars out the window as she closed Quinn's door part of the way, preparing to go to sleep herself. The ceiling fan directly over Quinn's bed hummed rhythmically as she slept, and Rose had taken the telephone off the hook so it would not ring, wishing for Quinn as many hours as possible of peaceful, uninterrupted sleep. Maybe that would restore some of the life force which Rose had seen slip away from her little Quinn in the recent difficult hours. It had seemed to her in the late afternoon that the girl's very soul was limp from the morning's corrosive recall of the rape.

The heat would not be diminished on this night, without even the hint of a breeze from the sea to loosen its hold. Though the atmosphere was saturated with moisture, there was no brewing storm to help dissipate it before the morning, so this day would blend into the next without significant relief from the heat of a southern sun. Quinn was cool under the quilt, lulled by the sound of the fan, sleeping deeply, her subconscious engaged in active sabotage of her will to forget.

FRIDAY

89

The colonel and his son strode into the Charleston police station on Friday morning as though preparing to review the troops, looking for all the world like men in charge.

"Is Mendel Comings here yet?" the colonel asked the desk sergeant gruffly. "He's supposed to meet us."

"No, sir, I haven't seen Mr. Comings. You're welcome to have a seat and wait for him."

They were early, George Howe knew, anxious to get this annoyance out of the way. But they chose to stand, not willing to sit on the molded plastic chairs provided for people who had business at a police station. The room was quiet, save the sounds of an antiquated fax machine transmitting information and a telephone ringing constantly somewhere deeper in the station. One young man, shabbily dressed and slouched almost horizontal, occupied an orange plastic chair, flipping through a magazine.

George Howe resented each of the scant minutes until Mendel Comings arrived, but he was cordial when the door opened, aware that he depended on this man now to clear the way for his son down a path on which the colonel had no expertise.

"Good morning, George, Mac," Mendel Comings greeted each of them with a quick handshake. "Good to see you."

Looking to the desk sergeant, Comings greeted him warmly as well. "How's it going, Wayne?" he asked. "When's that baby due to arrive? Isn't it any day now?"

"Yesterday was the due date. My wife is getting anxious, so I sure hope it's soon. She's been pretty cranky these last couple of weeks."

Mendel Comings laughed a deep, resonant laugh and slapped the officer on the back. "Hang in there, Wayne. It'll all be worth it. Do you have a room we can use for a little while? I told Legare I'd be in to surrender my client this morning."

"Sure, I'll buzz you back. Will the usual suite be all right?"

Laughing again, Mendel Comings shook his head in mock disapproval. "Ah, ever the comedian, Wayne. Can we expect the usual lavish TLC?"

"Always at your service, Mr. Comings. Help yourself to the coffee back there, such as it is."

Turning the handle in response to the buzzer, Mendel Comings stood back and motioned for his clients to enter the dingy, ill-lit hallway with multiple doors on either side. Waving his thanks to the young sergeant, he led the two men to the second door on their left, partly open. "We could have met at my office first," he said, gesturing to the metal chairs around a small rectangular table and closing the door behind them, "but I know you want to get this out of the way as quickly as possible. I'll try to expedite things for us. There are certain formalities to be dealt with, and they require that we be here at the station."

"You said you were here to 'surrender' your client, Mendel. I didn't like the sound of that," the colonel said, sitting. "What did you mean?"

"Just that we're appearing voluntarily in response to a complaint that's been filed, George. Don't be put off by the terminology. All we are concerned with here are the facts, and I thought we should go over them briefly before we call in the detective." Pulling a yellow legal pad and old-fashioned fountain pen from his briefcase, he slid his chair comfortably under the table. "Now. Fill me in, Mac. I'm looking over the complaint. One Quinn Ravenel claims you raped her." Having stated it simply, he looked expectantly to Mac, his pen poised.

"That's total bullshit, Mendel, and..." the colonel began, then stopped as Comings held up his hand.

"I need it from Mac, George. Please just let him tell me in his own way. No offense."

Sitting back in his seat reluctantly, the colonel sighed, placing his hands palms down on the table in front of him. "Okay, Mendel. Whatever you say."

"Mac?" Comings prompted again.

"I know who this girl is, Mr. Comings. She was a couple of years behind me in high school. We never really dated, but there was a time or two when we hooked up."

"Hooked up?"

"You know, we fooled around a little."

"You'll have to be more specific than that, Mac. Let's tell it exactly like it is. No lawyer likes being surprised down the road by a client having to adjust his story. Did you have sex with this girl?"

Glancing sideways at his father, Mac needn't have. George Howe was looking straight ahead, his eyes fixed on the far wall as though studying some small speck of dirt.

"Yes, sir," he answered. "I had sex with her."

"More than one time?"

"I think it was just once, but I can't be absolutely sure. That was several summers ago, and there were a few girls while I was home on leave that year. I wasn't exactly keeping notes."

Scribbling, Mendel Comings maintained a totally unreadable expression, nodding as he asked the simple, pointed questions. "She was, as you recall, a willing participant, Mac?"

"Absolutely. I don't have to ask more than once, Mr. Comings. You know how girls are."

"You would then be pleading not guilty to the charge of rape?"

George Howe's head snapped from its locked straight-ahead position. "Of course he's pleading not guilty," he growled. "This is my son we're talking about, Mendel, for God's sake."

"I've asked Judge Chastain to be available so that we can post bond," Comings said, unruffled. "After that, I'll have to turn you over to another attorney. It's unfortunate, but I had a brief discussion with Miss

Ravenel's attorney on this matter some days ago. I highly recommend you use Collie Rivers. You know him, don't you George? He's on the bank board with you."

"You can't be Mac's lawyer?" George Howe's eyes were wide, and he was on the edge of his seat, his hand clutching the metal arms of the chair. "Are you taking sides against us, Mendel, after all these..."

"Hold on now, George. That's not it at all. Julia McKenzie came to someone at my firm for advice on her case, which is at least tangential to the case against Mac. He called me in to talk with them, so I know some things about her case that would make it unethical for me to be Mac's attorney. It's not exactly a conflict of interest, because our firm chose not to be associated with Miss McKenzie to represent the Ravenel girl, but it would be ethically inappropriate for me to use the information I gained in confidence. Even we lawyers," he smiled, "have our code of ethical behavior, George. You understand that."

"Collie Rivers isn't much older than Mac, Mendel. I'm not comfortable trusting this to a youngster."

"He's by no means a youngster, George. Collie has been with me for twelve years, and he's the best litigator I have. You couldn't be in better hands. You can, of course, consider another firm to take over from here. It's up to you."

"We'll give Rivers a chance, Mendel. I don't like it one bit, so I expect you to keep a close eye on how he's taking care of this. I don't want amateur hour when it involves my family." The senior Howe looked to his son for objection, finding none. "Are we on the same page, Mendel?"

"It seems so," the seasoned attorney responded congenially. "Now if we're ready to proceed, let's call in the detective, shall we?" He can take your statement, and then we'll get on over to the judge's chambers. He may let Mac out on his own recognizance, but there's a good likelihood he's going to require some amount of bond. Are you prepared for that, George?"

"Whatever it takes," George growled, sitting back in his chair, his jaw clenched. "And Mendel, we don't want people getting wind of this ludicrous charge against Mac. Isn't there a way you can force it to be kept quiet?"

Mendel Comings stopped taking notes and raised his head to look at the colonel. "I don't know, George. That's an unusual request, one usually made by the victim of a rape instead of the accused, and the victim has made no such petition. I'll see what I can do when we talk to the judge."

90

Judging from the expression on Reg's face when Sonny opened the door, he might well have lost his best friend. Sonny knew what he had lost was something equally devastating; he had some experience in letting go of a dream.

"I thought I'd come by and see if you'd give me the time of day," he began, extending his hand toward the bed. Managing a half smile, Reg took it, shaking as firmly as his still-bruised hand would allow.

"Why wouldn't I give you the time of day?" he asked.

"It's hard to tell who you might be blaming right now for what's happened," Sonny explained. "I feel partly responsible. Wouldn't blame you if you were damn mad."

"I am, but I can't decide who to be mad at. I'm sure workin' on it, though."

"What's the latest?" Sonny asked. "Have they said when you can go home?"

"What's the point? They pretty much said I can't play ball," Reg replied solemnly. "If one of the injuries wasn't enough, they can name another one. I'm not seeing a light at the end of this tunnel."

"That's gotta be hard to swallow, Reg. I know we're not exactly friends, but I've watched you play. I was part of the fan club. When the boys brought you in that night, I couldn't find a reason to let you go. This is the most convoluted damn mess I've ever been involved with."

"How's Quinn? Do you know?"

"Julia McKenzie tells me she's hanging in there, but I don't see how a jury will let her off."

"Yeah, well if someone should hang for this whole thing, it's Mac Howe," Reg responded bitterly. "I wouldn't be here if it weren't for him. But Quinn is the last person in the whole world who deserves what he did to her. I'd kill him myself if I could get my hands on him, Detective Legare, and you can take that right back to the station and write it on the wall. He's lower than scum."

"Agreed," Sonny concurred readily. "I had the pleasure of telling him he's been charged with rape."

"You charged him? I didn't know that was in the works. How can you charge something that happened so long ago?"

"With rape, there's no time limit. But let's talk about you. You look a lot better than when I saw you last, although I gotta say you look like you could use a beer."

Reg almost smiled. "I'll bet the doc would really go for that idea. He's fed me enough Jello and toast to last the rest of my life. I could sure go for a greasy burger and fries."

"Can I pull up this chair?" Sonny asked.

"Be my guest."

Sonny pulled the institutional hospital chair with metal legs and vinyl seat to the side of Reg's bed and settled onto it backward with his arms folded across the back, his legs straddling the seat. "I've had some disappointments in my life, but this has got to be the mother of all letdowns."

"That's putting it mildly."

"You got a girl?"

"A girl?"

"You know," Sonny said, "some special girl whose shoulder you can cry on right now."

"Wish I did. I've sort of neglected my social life for basketball. Some of my friends are coming by, but a lot of them are just now going off to their own new lives. They've got jobs and places to go."

"So there are plenty of good friends?"

"There's a bunch of guys I've known since forever and another couple of people I've gotten close to in college. There are a few girls too, but we're just friends. I haven't taken time for much of anything but the game. I thought there would be plenty of time for girls later. And now it's later, isn't it? Who knew later could sneak up on you so soon?"

"I discovered that the hard way too, Reg. It felt like being struck by lightning when my wife was killed in a car crash. Just a bright flash in one moment, and your whole life is changed."

"I didn't know that, Detective Legare. I'm sure sorry. I guess losing someone you love is in another league from my finding out I can't play a game."

"The flash leaves you stunned just the same, I'm sure."

"I don't even remember the flash. Headlights crossing the median. Then I'm here. What happened to the people in the other car anyway?"

"One guy, the driver. He's dead."

"Dead?"

"Well, you're one rung up the ladder from that. Does it make this hospital room seem any better at all?"

"Okay. This is better than dead."

"That's a start. I know you haven't had much time to process all this, but when you were a little kid, what did you want to be when you grew up?"

"I wanted to be Michael Jordan," Reg answered without the slightest hesitation.

"Okay, what else? Don't we always want to be a fireman or Superman or a doctor at different times? I wanted to be a vet at one time so I could hang around the animals. And I think I wanted to fly airplanes or be an astronaut. Wasn't there ever an alternate life in your mind?"

Reg did give it a minute, thinking back. His eyes narrowed, and he grinned. "I remember wanting to be the President of the United States when I was probably about twelve or thirteen. My mom played me old tapes of JFK, and I wanted to be him for a while."

"Hell, I wanted to be him myself," Sonny said. "I think most everyone did back then. I remember the day he was killed. Everyone was in shock for weeks, maybe months."

"That's how my mom talks about him. Did she send you here to give me a pep talk?"

"Absolutely not. I haven't talked to your mom since right after the accident. How's she holding up?"

"She's a rock."

"Yeah, you're lucky to have a mom like that. She thinks you walk on water. She was telling me that your scholarship to the College of Charleston wasn't for basketball. It was academic. So you're a smart guy."

"All through school, my mom said I had to do the best I could because a career in sports is only for a select few people. She believed I was one of those, but she also said I had to prepare for a life after basketball. And look, this is that life, and I'm not prepared. I'm not prepared at all."

"Are you going to get through this and find another dream to follow?"

"I don't have another dream."

"Maybe you do."

"In every dream I have, there's a basketball in my hand."

"It's time to find another dream, Reg. I'm not much into giving advice or meddling in other people's lives, but I've been slung into your life by circumstances that make me feel some responsibility for what's happening to you."

"You knew when you had me in the jail that I would never have done something like that?"

"I've been in this business for a while. Sometimes, you just know. You're not that kind of guy."

"No, I'm not."

"Yeah, like I said, I feel guilty." Sonny hung his head forward and ran his fingers through his hair. "I've been over and over it in my mind. What could I have done? I could have driven the car that took you home that night."

"So maybe you're a better driver? Maybe your reflexes are quicker? Or it could have killed you, Detective."

"I might have saved us."

"We might both be dead."

"Do you mind that I'm interested in what happens to you now? I want to know what you're gonna do."

"You don't need to feel responsible for me. You did what you could. You treated me okay. You were doin' your job, and I was in the wrong place at the wrong time."

"That's a fact. What were you doin' there, anyway?"

"I was at a party. We were celebrating getting real lives and going away to start them. Some start, huh?"

"Do you believe in destiny, Reg?"

"Destiny. Yeah, I thought mine was basketball."

91

The in-basket on the judge's desk was full to overflowing, and he pushed aside file folders to make room for his cup of steaming coffee. Since this hearing was scheduled hastily at the request of counsel, no courtroom was available. Mendel had suggested that chambers would do nicely. There were only five of them: the judge, the two Howes, Mendel Comings and the prosecutor.

Chambers suited the judge just fine. His vacation had left him behind in his work, as expected, and the spectacular scenery of an immense Alaskan wilderness still paraded about in his head. The Honorable Wynfield Eldridge "Bubba" Chastain had just returned from one of his forays to exotic places, indulging his fascination with a whole world opened for his exploration now that he could afford the habit.

These chambers, created by knocking out a wall between the original office and a storage room, were spacious and comfortable, remodeled and decorated at the judge's expense to his taste and liking. A state-of-the-art plasma television was set into the wall above a well-stocked bar, frowned upon by part of the courthouse elite and regularly enjoyed by others. The substantial desk and matching bookcases were made from specially chosen Brazilian cherry, the furnishings plush and luxuriant in overstuffed suedes and sumptuous wide-wale corduroys. He had not shared with the decorator that his aversion to leather dated to a torn recliner where his father snored away his stupors in a t-shirt and underwear.

Bubba had grown up on the very wrong side of the tracks, his parents the hapless owners of a shabby liquor store on a corner whose bars on the windows and door made little sense beside the flimsy, termite-eaten frame. Food wasn't high on the "needs" list, as long as there was alcohol, and any paltry profit was quickly consumed by the bottle. Bubba was aware of the dry spells, periodic suspension of the liquor license, lots of fighting and throwing things in the house and pointing fingers and blaming. Selling to a minor was a frequent infraction. Bubba was never clear on the others. The tailor who now came to his office was compensation for those days of Salvation Army thrift store clothes, the wall of books a cherished redress for all the childhood days at a small table in the back of the library. It had been his refuge and his salvation, feeding a keen, raw intellect which would gain the young, unpolished Wynfield Eldridge Chastain admission, fully funded, to Harvard University and Law School, and from which he graduated with honors and a ravenous desire for the good life as he had only glimpsed it.

Other of his travels in recent years had acquainted him with parts of the African continent and helped him develop a special fondness for the American Pacific Northwest. Its rocky, unruly coastline surprised him with its contrast to the familiar wide sand and shallow surf of a temperate Atlantic Ocean. The Pacific was seductive, its sounds and sights magnetic to Bubba Chastain, the crashing waves and wild eddies calling him to return time and time again. He had last year purchased part ownership in a sturdy A-frame on a cliff overlooking an untamed bay near Yachats where he planned to return four times each year to enjoy the dramatic collision of Oregon land and sea.

"How was your vacation?" Mendel asked Judge Chastain as they took seats in the handsome chairs around the cherrywood desk. "Did you get in some golf?"

"I couldn't have looked down long enough to focus on a golf ball. But I saw some damn breathtaking parts of Alaska. Anyone thinking of drilling for oil in that wonderland can't have seen it. It was incredible."

"Was it a cruise you took?" Mendel tried to refresh his memory, knowing the judge had told him.

"I flew in there and toured around by car and an occasional helicopter. Nothing like it. And now I have to pay for it by digging myself out from under the pile on this desk."

"Nothing's free, is it?" Mendel joked, "speaking of which, thanks for freeing up a few minutes for us on this matter. We'll get out of your hair, Your Honor, if you're ready to set a bond and schedule a prelim."

Squinting as he looked at the file his clerk had prepared, the judge noted the charge with surprise. Glancing at Mendel with a raised eyebrow, his curiosity piqued, he prepared to dispense with these formalities so that he could tackle the pile on his desk before his afternoon roster.

Alan Cantrell had been assigned this case as well as Quinn's, Mendel Comings noted, wondering if that was a purposeful or coincidental move on the part of the prosecutor's office. "How's it going, Alan?" he asked the younger man. "Have you and Sissy set a date yet?"

"As a matter of fact, I gave her the ring last night, Mr. Comings, so now you can consider yourself an official matchmaker." Mendel had introduced Allen to a new junior member of his firm at a party the previous Christmas, and the two had been inseparable since.

"Now I won't be able to get any work out of her because she'll be planning a wedding. I swear, Alan, you're more trouble than you're worth." Mendel was obviously pleased with himself, thoroughly enjoying the role he had played.

"Okay, if y'all have finished your personal business, let's deal with the matter at hand," the judge chastised in an almost-convincing gruff tone of voice. "I see that we have a rape charge before us and need a bond set. Do you have anything to say on the matter, Mr. Cantrell?"

"We are, of course, amenable to bond by the defendant, Your Honor. We are well aware of his longstanding ties to this community and do not believe him to be a danger. I do have to ask for a bond in an amount commensurate with the seriousness of the charge."

"Mendel?"

"We would defer to the judgment of the Court, Your Honor," Comings said simply. The legal community in Charleston was a small and tight-knit enclave, its charter members familiar with its workings due to each knowing and accommodating the styles and idiosyncrasies of the others, breeding a shorthand among them which facilitated their regular interaction and lent a unique efficiency to Charleston's legal mechanics. Some had called it clannish and exclusionary. Those of the inner circle called it comfortable.

"Bond is set in the amount of twenty-five thousand dollars." The judge was looking at his calendar. "I'm scheduling a preliminary hearing for a week from today, on Friday morning, if that is acceptable to all." Looking up and finding no objections, he made a note.

"Anything else, counsel?"

"Just one thing, Your Honor." It was Mendel Comings. "If Mr. Cantrell has no objection, defense would ask his honor to seal the file on this matter pending further investigation."

"That's a little unusual, isn't it, counsel?" asked the judge. "What your reasoning?"

"We contend, of course, that this is an unfounded and totally baseless charge, Your Honor, brought by the accuser in an attempt to establish grounds for her defense in a separate but related matter. That being the case, we see no reason to have the name and reputation of my client tarnished unnecessarily. We would be happy to stipulate that we would withdraw this request at the time of the preliminary hearing if Your Honor finds the charge to have any basis in fact whatsoever."

The judge pursed his lips for a moment or two, and the others could hear the tapping of his foot under the desk. "Any objection, Alan?" he asked.

"No, sir."

"Done," the judge decided, and stood. Many other matters awaited his attention. "Gentlemen," he said by way of obvious dismissal.

92

Just enough coffee had dripped into the pot to pour her first cup when Julia's office door opened, tinkling the little bell. Turning with both her cup and the pot in her hands, she smiled in surprise to see Mendel Comings in her doorway, backlit by a bright morning sun filtering through the trees and onto Church Street.

"I thought I'd better come over and see where an up-and-coming young lawyer hangs her hat."

"Mr. Comings. What a pleasant surprise. I knew if I kept making really good coffee that someone important would eventually come by. And here you are."

"Beautiful and charming as well? Didn't I invite you to join my firm, Miss McKenzie?" Mendel Comings closed the door behind him, putting both hands in his pockets and looking around Julia's little space. "Although I must say you've created a nice space for yourself right here. Last time I was in here, a few years ago, it belonged to old Martin Lamboll."

"I haven't heard much about him," Julia responded, "although a couple of people mentioned this was a law office before. It was empty and neglected when I moved in."

"Old Martin never gave a nod to anything related to aesthetics or technology. He had a secretary who was with him for the entire forty years of his practice, sitting right over there at a metal desk that looked like Army surplus. Used a manual typewriter. When he needed a copy of something, she walked over to the courthouse to make one. He was a good lawyer, rest his soul, but he was crotchety as hell as he got older, set in his ways, and this place was dark and musty and smelled like stale tobacco. Not that my opinion is worth much on ambience, but you've transformed it."

"Well, thanks, that's very nice of you. I've enjoyed making it my own little space." Julia was flattered by the compliment. "Do you have time for a cup of coffee?"

"If you can spare a few minutes for me, that would be great, thanks. Black is fine. But I can sure come back later if you're busy."

"Not at all. I'm happy to see you."

Comings took one of the seats in the waiting area, stretching his long legs out in front of the chair and leaning back. "I wanted to come by personally to make sure you don't have a problem with someone over at my firm representing the young MacArthur Howe. The colonel called yesterday afternoon saying he needed representation, so I agreed to meet them at the police station this morning with a judge to bond him out, but then I explained that I couldn't be Mac's counsel because I already have knowledge of the situation."

Julia held out the coffee, steaming and black. "I hope your offering me advice hasn't cost you a good case."

"I've represented the colonel in a couple of matters, mostly related to his retirement and financial planning. Our little talk last week—yours and mine and Jordan's--left me knowing just enough to make it unethical for me to take this on. The colonel was not happy."

"I'm sorry, Mendel."

"Oh, it's not a problem at all for me. I just thought I should make sure it's okay with you if I pass the case on to Collie Rivers. I've assured the Howes that Collie is perfectly capable, and I give you my word that our conversation remains in complete confidence. Would you be agreeable to his having the case?"

"Of course. It's awfully good of you to run it by me. I've no doubt you'll keep my confidence."

"I'm pleased to hear that. Never want to leave any doubts hanging like loose threads between colleagues, especially those I might be courting to my own firm in the future." He winked, and Julia thought for a fleeting moment how delightful it would be to have a mentor like Mendel Comings if one were to cultivate a practice based on courtroom litigation.

"I seem to recall your offer being contingent on my winning this particular case, counsel, and that's anything but certain."

"Well, I'm not betting against you, Julia McKenzie, nor can I see with any degree of certainty how this whole drama will play itself out. If it were not a direly unhappy human tragedy involving some very decent people, it would be a fascinating legal scenario. I'll be watching with interest, might even have to pop over here again to see how you're holding up. Strictly personal, of course. No prying. Just a fatherly concern, with your permission, of course." Mendel Comings stood and handed the empty cup back to Julia. "I know the strain you're under. Don't let it get you down."

"I'll try my best," Julia responded, taking the cup. "I must admit I'm feeling the pressure."

"Take it from one who's let the pressure win, my dear. Life is too short and too precious." Julia knew he referred to his reminder of mortality when stress had caused his heart attack.

She walked to the door behind him. "Thanks again for keeping me in the loop. I'll look forward to working with Collie."

"And thank you for the coffee," he replied. "You can rest assured I'll be back one of these mornings for another cup. You take care now."

93

Martha Howe enjoyed her Friday morning prayer group. The women often brought knitting or embroidery projects, busying their fingers as they talked, and it was an opportunity for the hostess to showcase her home and her baking skills. Martha was certain that she was leaving this morning a pound heavier than when she arrived, thanks to Molly Hanlon's raspberry tarts and the heavy cream they had used in the coffee. Molly always served real cream and raw sugar. Her figure remained so slender that the women claimed she ate nothing between their weekly get-togethers.

The group avoided malicious gossip, though it was tempting now and then to pray over someone's misfortune immediately after it was discussed in elaborate detail. Such was not the case this morning when they had talked of Martha's son and his recovery from the awful attack. It was disturbing, they all agreed, to know that in their midst, right on the peninsula, there had prowled a thief bold enough to crawl through an open window on the East Bay. Thank goodness, they remarked, Martha's son had foiled the possible theft of Martha's valuables and that he had not been seriously injured in doing so. Martha assured them that her Mac was recovering nicely at home from his wounds, back to almost his old self, ever her joy. They had offered prayer for his continued recovery and for strength and blessing upon his mother.

Feeling strengthened by the support of her friends, Martha inhaled deeply of the summer blooms along the Hanlons' front walk. Molly tended her flowers with such skill that her lawn and garden were featured almost every summer in one of the Lowcountry gardening publications. On her next visit, Martha thought, she must ask for a cutting from Molly's peach-colored double impatiens that bordered the walk. She could fill a container with them on the back patio where they would flourish even through a mild winter. The patio was where Mac and the colonel were probably having their lunch, she thought, a meal she always prepared for George on Friday before she joined her prayer group. She was going to stop by the supermarket on her way home to buy a lean pork roast to make for dinner with parsley potatoes and curried carrots, one of her son's favorite meals. She would bake a pie for dessert, also a favorite of the men in her life, from the rhubarb and strawberries growing in her own garden.

Those men were lingering over the lunch Martha had made for them, but neither had much of an appetite after their morning at the police station and the courthouse. The guidance by a good lawyer had insured the arrest itself was a tidy and almost-painless procedure, as civil as possible. Mendel Comings had prepared the judge for a quick bond hearing, and the whole distasteful process was over before noon, well before Martha could be expected at home. Now, they knew, she would have to be told. Martha kept immaculate account of the family's affairs; the colonel had written a large check. There seemed no way around it.

"Let me tell her, son, and then we can fill in the blanks after we see how she takes it," the colonel decided. "I don't want to tell her, but I sure as hell don't want to take the chance she'll find out from someone else."

"Can we try to make light of it, Dad, laugh it up like it's all a big joke?"

"She would see right through that, I'm afraid. We'll explain that it's a plot by the girl and her lady lawyer to make it seem like there's an excuse for what she did to you. I think your mother will understand that. It's the truth, after all."

"Okay, Dad, whatever you think."

"I'm glad you told me about the girl, son. Like you said, it's surprising that you remember her at all. I know all the girls were after you in high school. You were bound to take advantage of some of the stuff that was offered. Hell, I did the same when I was young, well before I met your mother, of course. You'll find a woman like her yourself one day."

"Are there any others like Mom?" Mac asked with a smile. "I think she may be one of a kind."

"That she is, but you'll find a nice girl too one of these days. In the meantime, a guy has to sow his wild oats. Your mother will shake her head, but she'll understand. She knows you're a normal, red-blooded boy."

"What's that about a red-blooded boy?" Martha asked as she came out of the kitchen onto the patio. "You can't be talking about the two of you. And you certainly won't be red-blooded for long if you don't eat better than this. You didn't touch half the sandwiches, and look at the salad; it's still covered. Is something the matter with the food?"

"No, Martha, it was wonderful as usual," George assured. "We probably should have eaten inside where it's cooler. This heat always interferes with my appetite."

"Mine too, Mom. How were the ladies?"

"Oh, everyone is just fine. They all send their love, and Esther McCandless wants you to meet her granddaughter when she visits from Sumter next week if you're still here. You'd like that, wouldn't you, dear?"

Martha smiled sweetly, knowing full well that her son avidly avoided deliberate pairings by his mother and her friends. "I'm sure she's a very nice girl, every bit as pretty as the picture Esther has in her wallet."

The colonel rolled his eyes at his son but resisted replying, offering instead to help clear the lunch dishes and take them to the kitchen. "We have a little something to tell you, Martha, when you have the time." He spoke casually, offering no clue that the matter for disclosure was of any serious import.

"What is it, George?" she asked. "I'll be right out. Is there any iced tea left in that pitcher?"

"There's plenty, Mom," Mac called after her. "Most of the ice is melted, though."

"I'll bring some more, dear. You sit still." The heat of the day had melted the ice and was wilting the leaves on the first row of blue hydrangeas that brushed the patio screen, an indication that the automatic sprinkling system needed an adjustment for these hottest weeks of the year. Mac made a mental note to take care of that for his parents. "I'm going to start the dinner, and then we'll sit down and visit a bit." Martha placed a tall glass of fresh ice on the table in front of her son and disappeared back into the kitchen. The colonel sat back down with his son to wait, anxious to get this conversation behind him.

94

"Julia McKenzie, it's Collie Rivers over at Comings and Guerry. How are you this morning?"

Julia was prepared for the call, thankful for the heads-up from Mendel Comings. "Yes, Mr. Rivers, I've been expecting your call."

"Oh, please call me Collie. I expect we'll be on a first-name basis quickly before this mess is over."

It was an amicable beginning, Julia thought, but the man's reputation kept her wary. This was just a prelude to the onslaught of legal skirmishes and lawyer-to-lawyer haggling that was about to begin between them. She was quite certain he thought her an inferior opponent, inexperienced and ill at ease with criminal defense. But her infrequent contact with him on previous occasions had proven him charming and decidedly engaging, someone who might have piqued her interest were he not married with teenaged children. Celia had filled in those details, along with the fact that the first name he used was short for Collinsworth, given to him to preserve the family name on his mother's side.

"You're calling because you've been retained to represent MacArthur Howe?"

"I am indeed. I wanted to first make sure that the charge y'all filed against Mac is a substantive one. I got just enough background from the Howes to know that you were representing the Ravenel girl for the assault charge, so I can see how this would be a good move for you. What can you give me?"

"I can tell you that the charge is not only substantive but quite legitimate. Your client raped Quinn Ravenel the summer before she left for college."

"Is it going to be your contention that she was exacting a rightful revenge?" His tone remained friendly and matter-of-fact, a colleague on a simple fact-finding mission. She could imagine him scribbling on a legal pad as they spoke.

"I'm in the early stages of my own research on this subject, Collie, but it will be our contention that she was defending herself."

There was momentary silence on the line. "Well, I wanted to mention to you that Judge Chastain agreed to seal this file pending the preliminary hearing, which he set for next Friday. I don't see any point in making this mess public knowledge, do you? It seems like that might serve your client's interest as well."

"It does indeed, Collie," Julia answered, surprised and pleased. For the moment, Quinn's fear was being addressed, and not by her own counsel. "Who did the prosecutor assign to the case? Do you mind my asking?"

"Not at all. Alan Cantrell was there for the State this morning."

"That's interesting. Alan was at the table when Quinn was charged as well. I guess that's not a problem."

"Maybe the powers that be decided to keep it all in the family, so to speak. I'm willing to see how that plays out. You?"

"Tentatively, I have no problem with it" Julia responded, still puzzling over the sealing of the file.

"Listen, Julia, it's going to be nice working with you, even as adversaries. We'll be talking soon."

"Okay, Collie. Soon." And they hung up the phone.

The file had been sealed, Julia thought. That was too easy. But it was the rape charge that was declared private, and only for another week. Nevertheless, the piece that would be a juicy tidbit for the prying eyes of an investigative reporter was currently inaccessible. She would take it as a gift and offer it as such to Quinn, who had never intended for anyone to know.

What should their position be on keeping this whole story under wraps, she wondered anew, placing the receiver in its cradle. Was it even possible, now that the circle of those with knowledge of the facts was growing daily? Quinn, of course, valued the secrecy. She had meant to have a quiet little life teaching kindergarten in the fall with all this behind her. She had planned to run down the street that night in the rain and home to enjoy the liberation she had found after four haunted years.

But now the first goal of MacArthur Howe's new attorney was to seal the court record, keeping the whole matter secret. Interesting. She scrunched her brows together and wrinkled her nose, speculating. Whose priority was it to keep the matter concealed? Collie Rivers would seem to have no reason for squelching publicity on what could be a high-profile case, enhancing his reputation as a trial lawyer. The interest in secrecy, then, had to be the clients'. The Howes were apparently intent on keeping this matter under wraps. Well, she thought, so much the better for Quinn.

There was no doubt in Julia's mind that her young friend and client had told her the truth: MacArthur Howe had raped her. She was sure that Mac's parents had just such faith in his denial. It appeared to be a classic impasse, a stalemate with all roads leading to a very public trial by a Charleston jury. The thought nudged at Julia again that names and reputations were somehow at the crux of this matter, that here in this town the patina on a family name and address were paramount. No one wanted to risk the conclusion by his fellow Charlestonians, or the ensuing whispered exclusion, that his cherished place here was shallow or his Southern character an affected veneer. Julia had discussed it with Celia, whose perception came from inside the societal box and who acknowledged the peculiarity with a mixture of amusement and acceptance. She had finally conceded one afternoon, when pressed by Julia to analyze and unravel Charleston's cultural quirks: "It is what it is."

And so it was, Julia smiled.

95

The wraps on MacArthur Howe's penis had been removed before he left the hospital, but today there were still a considerable number of stitches remaining, most of which would dissolve in time. He had been caring for it as the doctor directed, cleaning it gently with diluted antiseptic and salt water several times daily, treating it with a newly-acquired appreciation. He could, he knew, have lost it.

"How's it going?" the doctor asked as he closed the examining room door behind him, opening Mac's chart. "Any problems, or are you just here so I can admire my work?"

"I'm happy you can find humor at my expense, Doc," Mac grinned slightly, sitting on the end of the examining table with one of those paper sheets across his lower torso and thighs. "I think I'm doing okay, but I'm anxious to hear what you think." Not exactly comfortable being handled and probed by male hands, Mac nevertheless sat still and patient, waiting hopefully for the doctor's reassurance.

"Looks good," the doctor pronounced, having examined Mac carefully from the tip to the base of the organ in question, "maybe even better than I would have predicted at this juncture. Any problems urinating?"

"No. Seems almost like before now that the swelling is down," Mac replied.

"The swelling that's left seems confined to the area immediately adjacent to the cut itself," the doctor observed, "which is as I would expect. That's where most of the scarring will be. But it should be aesthetic only, Mac. I'm hoping there will be no effect on your ability to function normally. Only time will tell for sure, and the time for that test is still somewhere in the future."

"You think I'm going to be back to normal?"

"I think it's probable. But let me be very clear that we don't want to engage in any activity that would increase blood flow to the penis yet, Mac. Nothing remotely sexual. That could be critical to total recovery, so don't pull out those Playboy magazines, and keep your distance from any woman besides your mother!" Though he smiled as he spoke, Mac understood that the doctor was very serious about this particular caution.

"So can I ditch these crutches, Doc?"

The surgeon thought for a few moments. "Just keep them handy. If you feel any sense of strain whatsoever in the groin area, use them. Come back to see me again in ten more days, and call right away if anything seems awry," the doctor dismissed this patient to move on to the next. "Just keep doing what you're doing."

Mac flung aside the paper cover and reached for his boxer shorts before the door closed behind the doctor. He was inordinately relieved.

Upstairs, above the suites for medical offices and in the west wing of the hospital, Reg Fallon found little reason for relief. He was alive, and his body was mending, but he had no sense of where his life was going. Sometimes, he felt as though time was suspended in that moment when the headlights had crossed the median, the whole rest of his life held hostage by that singularly inexplicable event. At other times, he sensed himself falling endlessly, careening uncontrollably through layers of despair with no foreseeable landing. The dream was shattered, as broken as the knee. He was losing the battle to hide his desolation from his mother; she saw through his bravado, knew his heart only too well and was therefore co-bearer of his pain, her heart breaking with his. He could not save her from it; he had no idea how to save even himself.

Lost in his own wilderness, he missed the quiet opening of the door to his room and was not aware of the man standing there until Joe Riley cleared his throat ceremoniously, slightly embarrassed to be witness to Reg's solitary tears, confirming the critical state of mind of one of Charleston's native sons. Rose Pinckney had called the Mayor not an hour earlier; his visit to the hospital was his response.

He stood still just inside the door, waiting for Reg to regain his composure. He had seen this young man on the court many times over the years, handling a basketball like a master, never rattled, always coming through under pressure. It was a quality of character that Joe Riley admired.

Moving toward the bed, he took a position on the bedside chair much like that taken by Sonny Legare in the same spot the day before, turning the chair so that he could straddle it with his chest to its back. Reg Fallon was a son of Charleston; Joe Riley intended to remind him he was not alone.

96

Both Mac and the colonel had tried to dissuade Martha from accompanying them to the lawyer's office, doggedly downplaying the nature of the situation, but she was adamant. She wanted to hear for herself what Collinsworth Rivers had to say. If her son needed a legal defense, she required assurance that it would be the best. She would have preferred their usual representation by Mendel Comings, but the men had explained to her that he was unavailable. His services would be expensive, she knew, but she deemed no price too high to preserve the safety and good name of her son.

There was no receptionist at the desk on Saturday mornings. The offices of Comings and Guerry were largely empty on the weekends, occupied only by those who chose to spend uninterrupted time at a desk or who had scheduled appointments. By noon, most members of the prestigious firm were well into a round of golf on one of the local courses. At ten-thirty, when the Howes arrived to see Collinsworth Rivers, the closing of the heavy oak door behind them echoed through the quiet offices, alerting the attorney that his newest clients had arrived.

"Come on back," Collie Rivers called down the hallway from just outside his own office. Walking to meet them halfway, he extended his hand, first to the colonel and then to his son. "Mrs. Howe, it's so nice to see you." He spoke to the small woman bringing up the rear, taking her offered right hand in both of his in the genteel manner to which a Southern gentleman seems born. And Collie Rivers was, if nothing else, the epitome of this genre, his Southern roots extending back as far as those of Rose Beauregard Pinckney and possibly beyond. His father still sat as Chief Judge of the Circuit Court, and the political and social influence of the Rivers family wound inextricably back through the history of Charleston and the Lowcountry. It was possibly the only reason Martha Howe was willing to entrust him with her son's welfare. His name was his qualification.

Still, she assessed him as he held her hand in both of his, trying to measure his character in his eyes and his bearing. He was young, but he was a Rivers. She would give him the benefit of the doubt until he gave her reason to do otherwise.

Seeming poised and totally relaxed, Collie guided the trio into his office, offering seats around a gleaming black modern desk trimmed in brass and totally clear of clutter. It was the space of an organized individual, surfaces polished and bare except for family photos framed in rich woods, and a handsome clock whose pendulum marked the minutes of his life with its arc and its audible ticking. The one folder on his desk, topped by a legal pad and silver pen, was labeled "Howe" in bold, black script, his own handwriting.

"I've just started a fresh pot of coffee," he began, taking his seat behind the desk. "It'll be ready shortly. Shall we cover the facts of the case while we wait?" He looked up, businesslike but smiling, treating the matter at hand as though it were a routine traffic offense. "I understand we have a preliminary hearing on Friday, which is why I thought we should meet today. I'd like more than a day or two to prepare."

"Thanks for making time for us on a Saturday," the colonel responded. "Mendel said he was certain you can take care of this for us without undue delay or publicity."

"I'll do my best," Collie continued. "Now let me see if I have the facts correct. This charge was brought by the young woman accused of breaking into your home and attacking you with a knife. Is that right, Mac?" Uncapping the silver pen, the lawyer prepared to take notes, looking directly at MacArthur Howe for answers.

"Oh, she's not just accused. I guess this proves she did it," Mac replied. "And now she thinks she can get herself off by crying 'rape'. It's total crap to think I would have to rape a girl." Mac shook his head as he spoke, his eyes shrugging off the accusation. "It's a crock of ..." he stopped mid-sentence and looked at his mother in the chair to his left. "Well, it's just a crock, Mr. Rivers, if you know what I mean."

"Yes," Collie grinned slightly, "I know what you mean. I have the police report from the night of the attack at your house. I also have a copy of the girl's sworn statement when she filed the rape charge. It's compelling reading." He passed several printed pages across the table to MacArthur Howe. "Why don't you look this over while I get the coffee." Pushing his chair back, Collie skirted the desk and left the room, leaving the three Howes alone with the printed transcript, a generic-looking black-on-white Xerox copy.

The pages lay on the desk in front of Mac, silent, screaming accusations. After almost a minute, he picked up the pages tentatively, his thumb and forefinger on the top left corner of the stapled pages, holding them gingerly and moving them slowly to his lap as though he feared contamination by their contents. He had not expected so concrete a confrontation with the accusation against him. Quinn Ravenel had told her story, and it was here on the paper in his hand. Would her recollection of it match his? Could he read it and hide his recognition of that day four years earlier? The cover page said simply "Statement: Q. Ravenel". It was dated the day before yesterday.

"Are you going to look at it?" Martha asked her son. "Is it just too painful, dear? Would you rather I read it aloud so we can all hear it together?"

"No, Mom. I'll look it over." Mac flipped the cover page and began to read in a sort of dreadful fascination, taking care to keep his expression nonchalant. He now wished fervently that his mother was not in this room, her eyes full of concern fixed on his face. It was almost as though, as he moved down the page, she was with him in the scene as Quinn described it, foiling his pleasure. Quinn's memory of it was better than his own, he thought, containing far more detail than he could have recalled. He had certainly made an impression, left an imprint she had not forgotten. Quelling the stirring in his groin, he read on, turning the page.

"Are you all right, dear?" Martha asked, reaching over to place her hand on Mac's left knee.

"I'm fine, Mom," he answered, resisting the urge to brush her hand away.

Collie returned to the room carrying a tray with cups, cream, sugar and a carafe of hot, fresh coffee. "You folks help yourselves," he said, placing the tray on the front edge of the desk, easily accessible, and pulling his chair back under his own side of the desk. He looked at the younger Howe, noting the deepening color in his face as he read. This young man, the son of socially prominent Charlestonians, was his client. The parents were concerned and protective. The case could prove explosive. He needed up front a clear understanding of the facts.

"Does anything you've just read sound remotely related to an incident you remember, Mac?" Collie asked evenly as Mac finished reading and closed the folder, returning it to the desk.

"Mr. Rivers," Martha Howe exclaimed, "my son would not behave in any way but as a gentleman. He knows how to treat a lady, and I will not sit here and allow you to suggest otherwise." Her small hands were clenched into tight fists around the handle of her handbag, and she leaned forward as though to challenge with her body any affront to the character of the child she had raised.

"Now, Martha…" the colonel began, somewhat surprised at the vehemence in his wife's outburst.

"It's okay," Collie intervened, holding up his hands, palms forward and fingers spread. "You've hired me to be the best possible advocate for Mac. It's my job to make sure we're ready for the hard questions, Mrs. Howe. I'd like to suggest that you and the colonel go out in the waiting area with your coffee while Mac and I talk. It's just going to make you uncomfortable, and I know your son doesn't want that any more than I do. How about it, Colonel Howe? Mac can fill you in later."

Hesitant but seeing the lawyer's point, George Howe conceded quickly, wishing once again that he had been insistent about Martha staying at home. "Come on, my dear," he offered, holding out his hand to his wife, "let's you and I leave these boys to take care of things. Mac is in good hands, and Collie's right; there's no sense in getting you all upset."

The deep frown on Martha's face lessened almost none as she considered, looking from one man's face to the next. Finally, shaking her head slightly from side to side, she rose from her seat, taking her husband's hand. "We'll be right here," she cautioned, fair warning that this mother had no intention of abandoning her son.

Mac grinned awkwardly at the lawyer as the door closed behind his parents. "Sorry," he grimaced. "She can be pretty stubborn when she sets her mind to something."

Collie nodded knowingly, smiling back. "I've got one just like her. Wouldn't trade her for the world. But that could have been awkward, and I just didn't want our conversation to be anything other than totally candid." He looked pointedly at Mac as he said this, reaching across to put his hand flat upon the transcript of Quinn's statement. "Now," he continued, all business, "tell me about this girl."

When Quinn woke slowly at almost noon on Saturday, Rose was waiting in the rocker beside her bed, sipping tea and watching as a mockingbird picked at the ripe mulberries outside the bedroom window. The sun at midday streamed through the leaves and bathed the room in a golden light that seemed incongruous with the darkness occupying space in the mind of Rose Pinckney, who had spent every hour of the night and day with Quinn since she woke screaming at two o'clock on Friday morning. She had slept the remainder of that night in the girl's bed beside her, listening as her trembling abated, her ragged breath returned to a regular rhythm and the tension finally drained away as she slept after taking the Valium Celia had left earlier in the day. Rose had convinced her to take a second tablet before bed on Friday, insurance against another round of nightmare excursions into the past.

She did look rested, Rose thought as Quinn wiggled her toes, stretching them out from under the quilt. Her arms uncurled from around her body, as though her need to wrap herself in them was over, and a wide yawn formed as her eyes opened, focusing on the swirl pattern textured into the high ceiling above the bed. Seeing or sensing Rose, she turned her head.

"Hi, Grams," she sighed sleepily, stifling a second yawn. Rose's heart ached as she forced a smile.

"Good morning, Dear. I was thinking as you slept that you still look just like that little girl who spent her first night here in this bed sixteen or seventeen years ago. Do you remember that night?"

Quinn smiled. "Of course I remember. It was the night before I started kindergarten. I was so excited, and I was driving Mama crazy."

"You had packed and repacked your little backpack with all your new crayons and pencils. And you wanted to take that little white stuffed bear. I helped you sneak it in with your things, and you giggled all through dinner."

"We had hot dogs. You let me help cook them on the grill out in the garden."

"I wanted to be part of that evening, so I thought a little cookout would allow your mother to share you with me. When she agreed for you to sleep at the big house, I was too pleased for words." Rose smiled, recalling.

"She had to leave for work before the bus came, so she left me with you on those mornings. I remember going to sleep in this bed that first night, snuggling under the quilt you gave me, thinking I was the luckiest little girl in the whole world."

"And I was thinking that the good fortune was mine, little one, to have you bring such light into my life."

Quinn's expression changed, the darkness returning to her eyes. "And look what I've brought to your life now, Grams. Look what a mess we're in."

"It's a bump in the road of our lives, an obvious obstacle, to be sure," Rose assured quickly, "but it's just that. We'll get through it; don't doubt that for a moment, Quinn. I will not permit any other ending."

98

"Did you expect that I'd be driving a beat-up old pickup truck?" Sonny asked, opening the door of his two-year-old Expedition, roomy and clean on the inside, for Julia. "Even we redneck cops have our civilized side, you know."

"I just said it was a nice car," Julia hedged. "I've only seen you in the police cruiser before now."

Closing the door, Sonny walked behind the car to get in on the driver's side. "I would have come over to Sullivan's to get you, McKenzie."

"Oh, it's okay. I did intend to spend the afternoon at the office anyway. There's so much work piled up on my desk. I've been spending a lot of time on Quinn's defense at the expense of my other cases, so I used the past few hours to get things under control. My phone didn't ring at all, so it was a very productive day. And look," she added, pulling the little black phone out of her purse, "I've muted the cell for the night."

"Just so I can have your attention? I'm impressed."

"I'm even thinking of hiring a part-time secretary for the office. Notes on the door saying I'll be back are pretty quaint even for Charleston, don't you think?"

"I think you should put me on speed dial, McKenzie."

"You do? Well, if you can keep my mind off work for the evening, maybe I'll think about it. Where are we going, anyway?" Looking out the window, Julia saw the beginning of another beautiful sunset, this one painting pinks and purples across flat-bottomed clouds on the horizon to her right as they crossed first the Ashley River and then the picturesque little bridge over the Wappoo Creek onto James Island.

"It's called Gatlin's. I helped Eddie Gatlin when he started building it fifteen or so years ago. It's not on the beaten path. No yellow page ad. No commercials. They don't even have a paved parking lot."

"So no one will be there but you and me?" Julia joked.

"It's always packed, especially on Friday and Saturday. It's built out on a pier along the Stono River over by Buzzards Roost Point. Eddie is an ex-cop who got shot walking in on a robbery in progress. He nearly lost his leg, so after that he said he was going to do what he's always wanted: open up this little place on the river and play the guitar."

"Is he part of the band?" Julia asked.

"Sometimes. He plays when he wants, but the band is good without him. Their lead singer sounds like ...well, I don't suppose you ever heard of Marty Robbins, did you?"

"And I don't suppose you ever heard of Luciano Pavarotti?" Julia replied.

"So you're into classical, I guess."

"Oh, so far off base. I discovered George Jones before I was twenty, and I'll bet I know more of the lyrics to George and Tammy's stuff than you do. It's dangerous to make assumptions, Detective Legare. Didn't they teach you that at cop school?"

"I'm thinking right now that just being in this car with you is dangerous, McKenzie. You are full of surprises, all of them pleasant."

"There's no better way to wallow in the aftermath of a broken heart than to sit with a box of Kleenex in one hand, the fingers of the other wound around a bottle and Vince Gill on the stereo. That would be the picture of me during my last month in Washington a year or so ago. I think I wore out Vince and my 'repeat' button during May and June of last year."

"Tell me about it. I remember those days."

"Oh. Of course you do, Sonny."

"Did you really have a broken heart, McKenzie?"

Julia had to think a minute for the answer. "I don't think I knew enough about what was in my own heart at the time to recognize whether it was broken. I felt rejected. From the little you've told me, I think your heart was broken. You lost something you knew and wanted. I lost something I only imagined and never really had."

"Pretty deep stuff," Sonny nodded. "I loved her, and my heart was broken. People did everything they could for me, but no one wanted to get near my grief after I lost her, like getting too close to the fire might get you burned. And you, McKenzie, you walk right up to it and hold your hand near the flame."

"Maybe I feel the warmth from the fire."

They were quiet after this, not wanting or needing to define the parameters of the conversation. Julia looked out at the lengthening colors as the sun's red-gold ball crept down toward the horizon, leaving the higher clouds in the western sky increasingly inky and India blue, beginning to blend with the twilight.

"I see the first star," Julia said, pointing to the southwest. "Do you want to make a wish?"

"Did it last night on that same star," Sonny replied, "and now I'm a believer." He grinned ever so slightly, and Julia watched him as he glanced her way while guiding the Expedition into a bumpy gravel parking lot.

"I've had she crab soup downtown, but nothing like this," Julia said after her third spoonful from the bowl. "Who does the cooking for your friend Eddie?"

She had been introduced and was sitting in a comfortably padded booth across the table from Sonny. The glass wall from floor to ceiling was broken only by beams every three feet around the entire perimeter, allowing a spectacular view across the copper and coral mirror of the Stono River and into the setting sun. Enough light remained for Julia to see the water below, lapping calmly at the riverbank beneath them, reflecting a soft glow from the room above where they sat. The band was tuning instruments quietly, and the hum of conversation and laughter permeated the large open space filled by people of every stratum of Charleston's society. Sonny had stopped on their way in to greet a fellow detective, sitting at the long, curving bar, wearing a baseball cap on his head backward. In the next booth, Julia recognized an assistant prosecutor with his wife. In the line waiting to be seated, she had spoken to a friend of Celia's, someone from her circle of practitioners of psychology.

"Miss Triss does the cooking," Sonny told Julia. "A couple of the downtown restaurants have been courting her for years. She doesn't believe in anything but real butter and heavy cream. Can you tell?"

"If that's the difference, then I'm converted," Julia answered, continuing to spoon the soup from the bowl. "This is so good I could eat it for my whole meal."

"Eddie says she uses the good sherry in the soup."

"There's sherry in this?"

Sonny smiled, a wide, relaxed expression Julia enjoyed seeing on his face and in his eyes. "Does that mean you want to send the wine back?"

Julia put down her spoon and took her first sip of the wine that Sonny had ordered and tasted. It was passably smooth, just bordering Julia's limit for the dry varieties. "I think we'll keep it," she smiled back.

Eddie came by a couple of times during the meal, squatting beside the table, asking about the food. It was obvious he enjoyed what he was doing, relishing the familiarity of his regular clientele, providing a warm, laid-back atmosphere where they could gather for an evening of good food and easy company. The band was ready as they finished the main course. The sun was gone, and the moon had risen, yellow and almost full, over the mouth of the Stono River where it emptied into the Atlantic Ocean. Julia's wine glass was empty, and their waiter stopped to fill it, inquiring about dessert. Julia shook her head.

"Let's give it awhile," Sonny suggested to the waiter. "I don't think we can leave without one of Miss Triss's desserts."

"I don't think I can leave at all," Julia added. "I've eaten so much that I feel like a rock in this seat. You'll probably have to lift me out with a crane."

"I don't think it will come to that, ma'am," the waiter assured her. "People usually dance off the meal when the band starts. Can I get y'all some coffee?"

"That would be great," Julia acknowledged, and Sonny nodded as well.

"So was I right?" he asked, "about the food?"

"I ate so much I can't even breathe," Julia answered. "I'm not sure I've ever had a piece of salmon that good."

When the waiter brought their coffee, Sonny had excused himself. Julia was unobtrusively refreshing her lipstick and enjoying the band's first number. The members were all over forty years of age, she guessed, one totally bald, one whose beard was largely gray, and each very capable with his instrument. The drummer, she was certain, was an investigator in one of Broad Street's most successful law firms, moonlighting to make use of his artistic talent. They launched first into a lazy, haunting rendition of Ebb Tide, a version where Eddie was dazzling on guitar, a different persona in his ragged t-shirt with the sleeves cut off. The pianist was a woman, her fingers confessing a longstanding love affair with the keys, her thick red hair almost to her waist.

Once again, Julia experienced the limb-looseness of three glasses of wine. She felt mellow and content, under the influence of good music and good company. Under the table she removed her sandals, pushing them beneath the seat, letting her bare feet rest on the oak plank floor. It was cool. She felt the grains on the bottom of her toes, wondering if it was sand or salt, not caring. Sonny returned, sliding into the booth across from her just as Eddie fingered the last chords.

"He's pretty good for an old cop, isn't he?"

"He's great. His style reminds me of Chet Atkins, and you know that's no small compliment."

"I'll let you tell him yourself. He'll like that."

"I like everything about this place," Julia shared her approval. "I'm having such a good time that I forgot for a while about the real world. All the files back there on my desk seem so far away."

"Is it going okay?" Sonny asked. "Are you feeling okay about Quinn and her chances?"

"I'm scared half to death. I'm in way over my head, and I suppose you're aware that I barely made it out of that room at the station yesterday morning still standing. You've heard stories like that before?"

"It never gets easier."

"I heard her words. I understood it perfectly in my head, but it was so painful that when we were done I felt like a rag that had been shaken by a bulldog for about three days. I went back to my office, locked the door and cried for an hour or so before I could pull myself together. That's partly why I had to spend part of today working."

"I'm sorry you had to put yourself through that, McKenzie. I wanted to protect you from it, but I knew you needed to be there with Quinn."

"We did the right thing. I'm sure of it now."

"And I'm sure we should drop this subject and begin the discussion of my totally mediocre dancing skill. I figure if I admit right up front that I'm not much good, you might give me a break and dance with me anyway."

Julia smiled, happy to lighten the mood again. "The last time I danced was possibly three or four years ago at a horribly boring event at the Washington Hilton. I think in the years since, I probably expected never to dance again."

"Now that would be a shame and a waste, wouldn't it, McKenzie? They're bound to play something nice and slow so we can try out these feet."

It had been years--many years--since Julia Slaton McKenzie had been in such a place as this. It had been her favorite kind of hangout all through college, smoky little places where the beer was cheap and the atmosphere relaxed. She recalled watching couples dancing back then, their movements slow and synchronized, wondering how one seemed to know the exact next motion of the other's body. She learned later that it was not so much a learned skill as a willingness by one partner to sense the other's signals and respond so that the two appeared as one in motion, a fluid extension of the pulsing bass.

Several couples were already on the floor, and Julia felt a shiver at the base of her spine as she watched them. It seemed such an intimate interaction, bringing to the surface a longing she had kept at bay and one that washed over her now with surprising intensity. It had been so long since she was touched.

The band played a faster number and then, with a short bridge sequence to change key and tempo, they began a steel guitar intro to the old romantic Together Again, slow and rhythmic. Sonny was looking at Julia, the question in his eyes. She slid out of the booth. Sonny glanced down as he joined her.

"Bare feet? I did mention my clumsiness, didn't I?" Most of the women on the dance floor were barefoot.

"I think I'll risk it," Julia answered, smiling, realizing for the first time that she had to look up. Sonny took off his shoes as well. Still, as she moved tentatively into his arms, the top of her head was at his earlobe. Leaving inches between them, both wondered if it was like riding a bicycle. Julia curled the fingers of her right hand around Sonny's left and placed the palm of her left hand gingerly against the right side of his chest just below the shoulder. They began to move slowly together, testing the feeling. Toes brushed a few times as they adjusted.

Julia didn't look up. But she did, a few measures into the song, adjust her hand in his so that her little finger slid gently, comfortably between his first and second fingers. They grew quickly less stiff as tension gave way to relief and then to the pleasure of moving easily together, surrounded by the melody, steeped in the sentimental lyrics ...

... you're back in my arms,

right where you belong

and nothing else matters ...

we're together again ...

...excavating a feeling so old, so new. Sonny moved his hand ever so gently from between Julia's shoulder blades to that spot near the small of her back. It almost took her breath away. Her left hand crept up Sonny's chest and over his shoulder to settle in that indentation in the back of his neck. She traced up and down it slowly to the music as the inches between them closed. His chest was broad, and she let herself lean into it softly, feeling the length of him against her, feeling the gentle pressure of his hand on her back, aware of the front of her thigh touching his as they moved. Julia nestled her cheek against the curve where Sonny's neck met his shoulder, and she knew he must feel her warm, salty tears on his skin. It had been so very, very long.

SUNDAY

99

Attending church was not an option for Rose Pinckney on this Sunday morning. Her soul required sustenance and fortification, and her fingers longed to clutch the back of a wooden pew as she rose with a congregation of the faithful to sing some old standard sacred rendition led by a choir in robes of cream and crimson. She drew strength from the familiar surroundings and faces, the stained glass, the tall pipes from which poured those sounds of solace unique to an organ at the hands of a devoted practitioner of gospel music.

Quinn sat quietly beside Rose this morning because Rose had insisted that she accompany her. They would both benefit, she had coaxed convincingly, from deliberately drawing closer to life's quiet center and a faith which had sustained Rose for a lifetime. They would receive the smiles and greetings of friends, sit among those who shared their faith, and brush against and grasp the hands of fellow Charlestonians. Quinn wore a linen skirt and white cotton blouse with sheer sleeves that ruffled gently at her wrists. She looked fragile and vulnerable, Rose reflected, listening as the pastor talked of love and forgiveness, of a creator who has no capacity for animosity, of the faithful who should devote no space in their hearts and minds to grudges or ill will. Rose heard the words and processed them with ambiguity. She knew that Quinn was not hearing the words at all.

It was the same creator, nicknamed "destiny" by some of life's less theology-inclined philosophers, who determined that at the end of the sermon the departure path of Rose and Quinn would intersect that of George and Martha Howe at the rear of the cavernous sanctuary just as the multiple lines of Sunday worshippers converged to shake the hand of the pastor on the steps of the old church. Rose was holding Quinn by the hand, sharing steadiness, as she turned this way and that to greet friends, nodding across the aisle, kissing a young man on the cheek. When she looked up, just before the open doors into the summer heat, she and Martha Howe were shoulder to shoulder in the exiting crowd. George's arm circled his wife when he saw Rose so near, forming a protective collar to keep her from the harm of an encounter with this long-time acquaintance now turned family foe. Both women were startled, each meeting the other's eyes with unasked questions pooling between them. Awkwardness gave way after a few instants of silence.

"Martha." Rose spoke first.

"Rose." Martha Howe acknowledged the greeting.

"We should talk," Rose asserted firmly, not dropping her gaze. And then she tugged at Quinn's arm, moving the two of them forward and into the brightness of another sunbathed Lowcountry afternoon, the smile returning to her face as the pastor put his hands on her shoulder and Quinn's at once, embracing his flock, dispensing blessings uniformly on those who passed across the threshold and down the old stone steps.

100

Weldon Scott was wrapping up the hour he'd spent at his desk, catching up after the trip to Charleston and preparing for a round of golf before dinner, when Doss Kincaid poked his head in the door.

"What's shakin'?" the reporter asked in his usual jovial manner, acting as though he was always expected and welcome in the office of the Mavericks' General Manager. "I knew that was your car out there. Working on a Sunday afternoon? I hope there's a story there."

"I'm heading out to the golf course, Doss. You want to come?"

"Wish I could, but I'm on a mission. I need something juicy. I'm bored. My editor is bored. Our readers are bored. What can you give me?"

"Hey, man, this is the off-season for us. What do you want from me?"

"I want a story, something I can sink my teeth into. I want excitement, drama, theater for the front page of the sports section tomorrow morning. I've been over to the Cowboys' front office, and they're so boring it's killin' me." Weldon smiled reluctantly, hard pressed not to be amused by the young Kincaid who was always full of entertaining rhetoric, whether in person or in print. He and the sports reporter had developed a congenial relationship, a product of their jobs, which occasioned frequent interaction, and of Doss's enthusiastic devotion to the sports scene in Dallas. It was always better, Weldon had found, to maintain a good rapport with the press regulars, of whom Kincaid was by far his favorite.

"I'd give you something if I had it, my friend," he offered apologetically. "If there were any excitement, I wouldn't be heading out to hit the little white balls around with a stick."

"Man, I'm dyin' here," the reporter continued with more than sufficient animation. "Don't you have something I can use, some little tidbit I can embellish? How about a new whiz kid discovery at some obscure Midwestern high school? Or one of your guys getting arrested for something? Hell, I'll even take some minor injury that's gonna sidetrack a bench-sitter at this point."

Weldon Scott stopped putting the papers on his desk into the file folder and looked up.

"Doss, old buddy, I think maybe I can help you out."

"I'm all ears. Shoot." Eager, the reporter immediately pulled out his pencil and flopped into the armchair in front of Weldon's desk.

"You're going to owe me for this one, Kincaid. It's big, and I'm giving it to you on a silver platter."

"Don't keep me in suspense here. Let me see for myself just how big it is."

Weldon sat back down behind his desk, checking his watch. His scheduled tee time would require that he leave the office within ten minutes. "It's not a feel-good story. In fact, it's downright depressing."

"Well?" The reporter was more than ready.

"Reg Fallon can't play ball." Weldon led with his best impact statement, watching the expression develop on Doss's face. It took only a moment. The reporter was quick, accustomed to processing information and moving on.

"I'm not hearin' you. Say that again."

"Reg Fallon was in an automobile accident. His injuries are so serious that he can't play basketball. He's in the hospital in Charleston. Now do you owe me for a scoop, Kincaid, or not?"

Mouth open, the reporter searched Weldon's face for a sign that this was a ruse, finding none. "How come I don't already know about this?" Skepticism winning, Doss expressed his doubt that such a story could pass into his waiting hands on a random foray to the Mavericks' headquarters. He had been in the news business, however, long enough to know that sometimes that was exactly how things happened.

"I just got back from Charleston yesterday."

"I guess you wouldn't pull my leg about something like this, would you?"

"No, I guess I wouldn't. I wish I was."

"Damn, Weldon, I'm not believin' this. What's the story?"

The general manager glanced again at his watch. "The kid was in a car accident last week. I took Claude Baker down there to have a consult."

"And?"

"And Reg Fallon has some back trouble, a badly broken leg, a head injury. I guess he's lucky to be alive."

"You're telling me that as far as you know, this story hasn't been reported? You haven't discussed it outside this office? You haven't called S.I.? And neither has the Fallon boy? Is that what you're telling me, Weldon?" Doss Kincaid was incredulous.

"That's what I'm telling you, Kincaid. Claude Baker knows. Now I've got to get out of here. You can come by tomorrow and we'll talk some more."

"Was the kid driving the car?"

"No. It wasn't his fault. As I understand it, he was riding in a cop car."

"A cop car? Why?"

"You know, Doss, I don't really know the whole story. I'm only concerned with the part that affects me, which is the part where Reg Fallon can't play ball. The rest of the story may be very interesting, but I don't know it. Now I'm out of here."

Doss Kincaid jumped out of the chair, following so closely on the heels of Weldon Scott that he nearly tripped as the office door closed behind them. "Is the kid still in the hospital? Is there any reason why I shouldn't leave for Charleston on the next flight?"

"Check with his lawyer, Doss. Julia McKenzie. Nice woman. She's listed.

MONDAY

101

Breakfast on the flight from Dallas to Charleston was of no interest to Doss Kincaid. He had wanted an earlier flight, but it was full, so he fidgeted as the plane made its approach to land, anxious to get to the hospital and talk to Reg Fallon before someone else broke the story. This was big, not only in Dallas, but also for basketball fans nationally. He thought it unlikely that the news could remain under wraps for more than another twenty-four hours, was surprised he hadn't heard it as he monitored ESPN while he waited to depart Dallas/Fort Worth International.

He asked for more coffee when the flight attendant collected trays, knowing he needed no more caffeine but wanting it nonetheless. Coffee was his mainstay, the liquid staple that kept his reporter's blood flowing during long and odd hours when he followed a story or sat at his keyboard trying to make one flow properly before delivering it to his editor. Deprived of the black stuff for eight hours, Doss always got a pounding headache. He was addicted, just as he was to seeing his by-line above a story that was the envy of his colleagues. He loved being first on the scene. His assignment was sports; his passion was news.

Doss was out of his seat before the plane taxied to a total stop, meriting a glare from the same blonde flight attendant who had brought him extra coffee. He winked, bestowing on her the charm that regularly opened doors and flattened barricades. Shaking her head, she smiled back. He had known she would.

The doors opened, and Doss bounded down the steps and across to the terminal, carrying only his laptop computer and a small overnight bag. He had learned not to check bags; it slowed him down. His rental car was ready, and he signed his name and grabbed the keys, flashing a smile to the rental agent who thought better of trying to sell him extra insurance. The man was obviously in a hurry. The car was a mid-sized red model, but Doss hardly noticed, sliding behind the wheel and depositing his belongings on the passenger seat. He was counting on his experience as a reporter to get him to the hospital. He would get on the major thoroughfare into Charleston and look for the blue signs marked "H".

102

Collie Rivers had his feet up on the corner of the desk as he ate his lunch in Mendel Comings' large and comfortable office. The deli had delivered pastrami and cheese on rye with extra lettuce, and he ate it along with a large, whole dill pickle as Mendel jogged rhythmically on the treadmill in the corner of the room. It was a regular lunchtime for the two twice or three times in a week, one man ingesting calories as he talked, the other burning them off as he listened and injected an occasional comment or question. An almost father-son relationship had developed while the seasoned attorney mentored the younger, and it persisted after Collinsworth Rivers earned his own reputation as a sought-after litigator. Each man respected the other immensely and enjoyed the easy companionship these midday breaks provided.

"I know it doesn't make sense, Mendel. I've tried to explain it away to my own satisfaction, but my gut won't buy it. He's guilty as hell."

The sound of the treadmill hummed on, marking the steps of Comings' Reeboks on its revolving rubber track. The expression on the runner's face changed little, but Collie knew he was absorbing every word and processing each in his usual analytical fashion even as his feet moved deliberately on the track. Waiting patiently for a response, Collie washed down the last of his sandwich with a diet Pepsi, sipping from the can as he folded the empty sandwich wrapper into a mustard-dotted paper airplane.

"You gotta trust your instincts, Collie. But you're not saying you can't defend him, are you?"

"I can defend him."

The treadmill slowed slightly. "How much did he tell you? Do you want to run it by me?"

"I want your take on it."

245

"Okay, I've got a sketchy idea of the Ravenel girl's story. Tell me Mac's version."

Collie removed his feet from the desk and leaned forward, folding his hands on the desk. Mendel slowed his pace, preparing to end his noontime workout with stretches and a second bottle of water.

"He comes across like a decent enough guy. His parents are good folks who obviously believe every word he's told them. He admits having had sex with the Ravenel girl during that summer four years ago, but he says it was just a casual encounter, one of many with a number of girls who were interested in him. My gut says there's something wrong with his story."

"Your gut is usually accurate, Collie. What do you think is wrong?" Mendel's steps were slowing further.

"He's slick," Collie replied, his eyes narrowing as he considered his reaction to his client. "He's confident and doesn't come across as angry or violent or aggressive, though he's obviously somewhat enamored with the effect he has on women."

"And what effect is that?"

"He seems convinced that women find him enormously attractive, that he can have most any one of them."

"Do you think that's the case?"

"Well, Mendel," the younger man rolled his eyes, "I can't presume to speak for most young women, but I guess he's a good-looking guy, carries himself well, seems confident."

"Then what stops you from believing the Ravenel girl was just one of many who fell for him, Collie? You're building a great case for your client so far." Mendel stepped from the treadmill, taking several large swallows from the water bottle and beginning some long, slow lunge motions.

"There's just something askew, Mendel. I wish I could put my finger on it. I get the sense that right behind his eyes there's some recollection of the incident with this girl that doesn't match the story he's telling. I read her sworn account. It's detailed, even after four years. It grabbed me by the throat. I wanted to throw up when I finished it. And when I look across the desk at MacArthur Howe, I can put him in that picture. I can see him in her story." Collie stopped talking, his eyes fixed on Mendel Comings.

"Did you confront him with it directly? Did you make him understand that what he tells you goes no further, not to his parents, not to the judge or a jury, and did you impress him with the fact that you don't like surprises?"

Collie thought about the questions, drumming his fingers on the desk. "We're meeting again tomorrow. I'll give it one more try."

"Just satisfy yourself, Collie. That's all you can do. Your client would be better served if you knew the whole truth. But it's not always what we get, is it? If you believe him, so much the better. If you don't, you're left working on the good old Constitutional principle that every man is entitled to a defense. And, of course, the good old principle of every trial lawyer that winning is better for one's reputation than losing." Mendel grinned as he spoke. "I respect your instincts, you know. And I will tell you behind these closed doors that I concur with them, based upon the few facts I have."

Collie's eyebrows raised, and his fingers stopped their movement. "Do you have a take on this case?" he queried, wanting more. "Doors are closed."

"You know I talked briefly with Julia McKenzie about her client before I got the call from George Howe. I don't know much, but it was a little too much, which is why it's your case, Collie."

"That's all?"

"Well, I've known the Howes for many years. They're good people."

"And what about their son?"

Mendel stooped to untie the laces of his running shoes. "I don't know a thing about him."

"Is that all?"

"Yeah, Collie, that's all."

103

"Don't do this, Martha," George implored once again. "You'll upset yourself, and then I'll be upset, and so will Mac."

"Mac need not know about it, George." Martha looked pointedly at her husband, making it clear that she wished him not to speak of the visit she was preparing to make. "This is between Rose and me."

"It's just not necessary, and there's nothing to be gained."

"If I thought that to be true, George, then I would stay at home and spare myself this visit." Martha slipped on her low-heeled pumps and collected her small purse and keys from the foot of the bed. "But Rose and I have been acquainted for many years, and I will not shy away from an opportunity to straighten out this mess. I have always found Rose to be a reasonable woman. My mind is made up, George."

The colonel threw up his hands, abandoning his attempt to dissuade his wife from a move he thought extremely unwise. He remembered none too pleasantly his own conversation with Rose Pinckney a few days earlier, one in which he had intended to prevail upon her but which had proven a shock to him instead when the first hint of the bombshell rape accusation had come from Rose.

"If you must go, Martha, then let me drive you."

"I'm perfectly able to drive myself, dear," Martha replied, and the finality in her voice assured George that negotiation was ended on the matter, now requiring the disclosure he had not wished to make.

"I have something to tell you first," he admitted, standing beside the open bedroom door. "I should have told you sooner." George did not want the disclosure to come from Rose.

"What is it, George? Can it wait until I get back?"

"No, it can't wait. I already talked to Rose Pinckney."

Martha stopped halfway to the door, raising her eyes to meet those of her husband.

"I didn't want to tell you, Martha. I went there last Wednesday morning after I found out she posted the bail for that girl. I was angry, and I went to her for an explanation."

"Did she give you one?" Martha asked, frowning as she absorbed George's confession.

"She told me that she considered the girl family. And she accused our son of accosting the girl. That was the first I'd heard of it, Martha, and I was so outraged that I just walked out. And then the detective came with his warrant."

"You knew of this horrible hornet's nest the middle of last week?"

"I knew only what Rose had said. I considered it the raving of an old woman desperate to find an excuse for the behavior of a girl she took in and treated as family, nothing more. I still believe it to be just that, which is why I beg you not to confront her, Martha."

"You've kept this from me for all this time?"

"I wanted to protect you. I never expected what Rose told me to be anything more than trash, the likes of which you shouldn't be exposed to, my dear. It will be over soon, and our lives can go back to normal. Won't you just leave it alone and let me take care of it? You look so pretty. Why don't I take you out for a nice lunch, and we can forget all about Rose Pinckney?"

104

The rolling stainless steel cart holding lunch trays sat outside Reg Fallon's door when Doss Kincaid finally found the hospital room. He had followed the signs to Saint Francis Hospital, only to find no record of Reg being admitted there. Doss berated himself; he had wasted precious time following highway signs and his instincts. Who knew Charleston, SC, was big enough for more than one hospital and a medical school as well.

A slight and tired-looking woman came from the room at Roper Hospital carrying a tray cleaned of everything but one stick of celery. Reg's appetite had apparently returned. She slid the tray into its slot among the others and proceeded down the long hall, pushing the unwieldy cart ahead of her, peering between the eye-level tiers to avoid a collision. She passed the door, and Doss saw the placard that read "Fallon, R." At last, he sighed impatiently, he had found the young basketball star. He had slipped quietly past the nurses' station, waving nonchalantly as though he were a regular. Doss was practiced at blending in, looking like part of the scenery or one of a crowd. He had learned early in his career as a journalist that it was often best to maintain a high awareness and a low profile.

"Excuse me," came the voice from just behind him as he reached to open the door. He turned. "Was you lookin' for Reggie?" The voice belonged to a plump, older black woman whose eyes and mouth were etched with smile lines and who took a proprietary stance between Doss and the door.

"I was indeed, ma'am," Doss admitted.

"I am his mother." Willa Fallon extended her hand, which Doss took in his own, shaking gently.

"I'm mighty glad to meet you, Ms. Fallon. My name is Doss Kincaid, and I work for the Dallas Morning News."

Willa's eyes narrowed. It was not a surprise that a reporter had come; Julia had prepared her for a visit from someone in the press at some point, though they continued to hope against that eventuality. "You here to make a news story of what's happened to Reggie." It was not a question. Doss interpreted Willa's statement as resignation to the inevitability of Reg Fallon's misfortune becoming public knowledge.

"Reg Fallon is news, ma'am. He already has lots of fans around the country who are waiting for him to play ball. I'm surprised someone from ESPN or Sports Illustrated isn't already here. Has no one from the news been by to talk to you or your son?"

"No, sir, Mr. Kincaid. Miss Julia done tell us to expect you, but you be the first one."

"Miss Julia?"

"She be Reggie's lawyer. And she be a good friend, too."

"Would it be okay if we went inside and talked to Reg, Ms. Fallon? Is he up to a visit?"

"He be doin' real good, Mr. Kincaid. But I don't want nobody getting' him upset. He be upset enough as it is, what with him gettin' arrested in place of Miss Quinn and all."

"Arrested?" Doss stepped back.

"If you goin' write about this, you can't talk bad about my Reg or Miss Quinn. They neither one to blame. It's the Howe boy who raped her, and both these chillun' jes' caught up in his awful doins. I won't have you blamin' my boy for any of it."

Doss tried instant mental replay of what Reg's mother had just said, unsure he had the words in order, very sure he had no idea what most of them meant. He was following a sports story; she was offering a tale of something totally different, throwing around names and events, none of which made any sense or seemed to have any bearing on Reg Fallon's injuries or his now-doubtful career.

"I'm certainly not here to blame anyone for anything," Doss offered in reassurance. "I was just hoping to see how Reg is doing. I'm one of his biggest fans."

"Well, ain't nobody a bigger fan than me, Mr. Kincaid, and I swannee he don't need his miseries spread around by no newspaper man. We be prayin' our way through it, so you best git on yo' way."

Doss was more than reluctant to concede that he had come this far only to be waylaid by a protective mother. He was six feet two inches and at two hundred pounds could easily have brushed past Willa Fallon and into the hospital room, but to alienate Reg's mother seemed not the best course of action. He opted for his best boyish grin, backing away from the door and holding up his hands, palms out, in surrender. "I'll give you my card, Ms. Fallon. Would you kindly take it in to Reg and ask him if he'll talk to me? I flew in from Dallas just to see him. I can wait right out here. He may remember me from his press conference in Dallas when he signed with the team. Please, Mrs. Fallon? I'll just be a friend unless Reg agrees I can be a reporter."

The new tactic seemed to soften the mother just slightly. She studied the business card and then looked back at Doss, still standing squarely between him and the door.

"You come here from Texas jes' to talk to my Reggie?"

"I did. I wish nothing but the very best for your son."

"Well, you jes' wait right here." Willa opened the door and disappeared into the room, glancing back at Doss Kincaid as the door closed behind her.

105

It was almost three o'clock when Martha reached the top of the steps, pausing on the stoop at Rose Pinckney's door to look out over Charleston Harbor. She was glad she had chosen to drive the couple of blocks between their houses, recognizing that the humidity was oppressive, leaving the tourists along the seawall wilting. A haze hung over the harbor, nearly obscuring Sullivan's Island, and settled heavy like a midsummer cloak over the bay and the low-lying Fort Sumter.

Martha's heart was heavy as well, troubled by the secret George had kept. He had come here to speak with Rose and had chosen not to share that visit with her. Were there other secrets, she wondered, other events or concerns her husband was keeping from her because he considered her in need of protection from life's stresses? It was, she knew, his way of caring for her. He had done it for the length of their relationship.

Martha raised her hand and knocked firmly in the center of the tall door, taking a deep breath to feed her resolve and composure. Rose could be a difficult and stubborn woman, but Martha was prepared to appeal to her sense of reason and fairness. She would call upon their long-time acquaintance and ask for her help in putting behind them this unbearable trouble between the children. Rose knew that Martha's son had been raised to be a gentleman, a young man of honor imbued with the values of his parents. Despite Rose's best efforts, the little waif she had befriended was obviously not a young woman of integrity. Rose need not be blamed for her lack of character; Martha was not here to point fingers. She was here to save her son, his reputation and his career from undeserved and unnecessary damage.

"Come in, Martha," Rose spoke cordially as she opened the heavy door. "I'm so glad you've come." She seemed sincere, Martha thought, paving the way for a friendly negotiation which could end this unpleasantness.

"Thank you, Rose." Martha stepped inside, into the cool of Rose's foyer where she placed her pocketbook on the floor by the small entry table. "I appreciate your taking time to talk."

Rose ushered Martha into the living room, aware of the tension between them and sorry that MacArthur Howe was Martha's son, that this pleasant, friendly little woman would have to deal with the fact of what her son had done, to face it and suffer because she had been an undeniable contributor to the man he had become. Martha Howe had always been passive, Rose recalled, a poster representation of the genteel but acquiescent southern lady who molded herself and her life to the wishes of the men who were important to her. Somewhat a waste, Rose thought, of one's life, one's time and one's unique talents. She made a mental note to remind her granddaughters once again of their own singular value.

"I've made us a pot of tea." Rose poured a cup for each of the women as she took her usual seat on the plump sofa, placing her cane against the arm. Martha adjusted her skirt primly across her knees and reached for the cup and saucer, stirring a spoonful of sugar into the hot tea.

"How have you been, Rose?" she began. "You're looking very well."

"I am well, thank you. This heat always takes something of a toll on my energy, but it's part of Charleston's character. And you? How are you, Martha?"

"I'm doing fine considering the ordeal my son has been through. It's been somewhat stressful, as you can imagine, spending all that time at the hospital. But I'm so grateful now that he's going to be just fine. I've been on my knees morning and night thanking the good Lord for that."

"Having and loving a child is the greatest gift and the greatest burden, isn't it? It is indeed a blessing for you that Mac is doing well."

Martha saw no reason to detour around the subject that was foremost in both their minds. "His recovery is a blessing for you, as well, Rose. If he had not survived, your little friend Quinn Ravenel would be charged with murder. I would be mourning my son, and she would be on her way to spend the rest of her life in a prison cell. You must have come to recognize that she deserves that, haven't you? I'm so sorry you're involved in this." Martha had not flinched or lowered her gaze. She was certain of her position, comfortable with her confidence in her son.

Rose sipped her tea before responding, seeing Martha's assurance and reluctant to destroy it. Martha had done her best, as she saw it, to raise a son. She had doted on him, Rose knew from years of occasional social interaction. MacArthur had been the center of her world, and Rose hated to inflict a seismic shift. But Martha and George had, despite their intentions, not raised a decent human being. They had raised a rapist.

"And I am sincerely sorry for your pain, Martha, but I must explain to you what has become clear to me. Your son raped Quinn Ravenel. She was a virgin. She is a dear girl, not deserving in any way of what he did to her. I had no knowledge of it at the time, knew nothing, in fact, until Quinn took her revenge on that night a few weeks ago. Had I known, I would most certainly have handled it differently."

Martha was silent, not shocked but unsettled by Rose's directness. "You can't believe my son is capable of something so awful. There is no truth in this girl's story, Rose, and she must be suffering from some mental illness to have attacked Mac as she did. Have you questioned her? Did she have some schoolgirl crush on my son which he did not return?"

"There was no schoolgirl crush. There was no relationship between them at all. Mac deceived Quinn by pretending he was locked out of his house. Quinn was just passing by. When she crawled through the window to help him, he raped her. I am as sure of that as I have ever been of anything in my life."

Martha considered. She had come prepared for a confrontation of sorts. Rose had taken the girl Quinn under her protection and been a pillar in her raising. It was only natural that she would wish to deny failure. She had a vested interest, a significant investment of time and affection in Quinn Ravenel. "There must be something I can say to divest you of this preposterous belief, Rose. I know my son. What do you really know about this girl?"

"I know her heart," Martha replied simply.

"And why did she not confide in you at the time she claims this rape occurred? Why did you find out only now, years later? Is it possible you don't know her as well as you think?"

Rose sighed inwardly, only too aware that she had struggled with this very question. "If I had known then, Martha, it is possible your son would have been in greater danger than he is today. I would have been outraged, as I am now. I am not sure I would have been able to contain my fury."

Somewhat taken aback, Martha saw that Rose was adamant in her position, convinced by this girl that her son was a rapist. It was possible, she thought, that George had been right in his pleas that she not confront Rose Pinckney. There might be no bridge across their differences. Rose's eyes flashed her resolve.

Quinn's footsteps had been silent on the steps. She padded quietly, her white leather sandals now softly slapping the gleaming hardwood that stretched into the parlor where Rose and Martha sat. She did not sit down, standing simply and straight at the end of the sofa. Rose was surprised. Quinn had agreed that she would remain upstairs while Mac's mother paid her visit. Martha was stunned.

"I've been listening." Quinn showed little expression, her gaze fixed on Martha's face as the woman tensed in surprise and discomfort. Quinn wore her usual faded jeans, topped by a white cotton sleeveless shirt, no make-up and a pearl comb that held her blonde hair away from her face at each temple. Her arms hung tanned and slender at her sides, the fingers still.

"Mac raped me, Mrs. Howe. I can understand why you would choose not to believe it; you're his mother. But what I'm telling you is true." Holding Martha's gaze, she continued, her voice soft but sure. "Do you remember the broken window, the one in his bedroom? Didn't you need to have it repaired?" Quinn's eyes narrowed as she studied the mother's face. She lifted her right arm, pointing to a small red ridge on its inside just above the elbow. "He did a good job getting rid of the glass before he asked me to crawl through and help him get in the house. This is from the one fragment he missed. I look at it every day. It's my only visible scar." Martha did not respond, her eyes first on Quinn's and then dropping to focus on her own hands, one clutching the other tightly. The color had drained from her face.

"I must go," she said finally. "It's time for me to start dinner."

"You can't put this in print," Reg stated with finality. "I understand that my accident is news, but that's as far as you can go. Quinn Ravenel is my friend, and it's her secret."

It had taken only a minute or two for Willa Fallon to open the door and allow Doss Kincaid into the hospital room. Reg did remember him from the Dallas press conference and was happy to discuss sports with the young newspaperman. They had talked for more than two hours, during which time Reg had extracted Doss's promise that select revelations would be kept in complete confidence.

"I know you didn't understand before, but do you get it now?" he asked the reporter.

Doss was shaking his head, astonished at the story that accompanied Reg's injury. "I get it. I just don't see how we can print a version of the accident story that won't lead to more questions and eventually to the whole bloody mess coming out."

"Then you can't print it at all," Reg replied firmly.

Doss looked up. "I guess when you don't show up to play ball in Dallas, no one will notice?"

Willa had been in and out of the room, listening to bits and pieces of the conversation and enjoying her son's absorption in the discussion. The two had been alternately serious and shaken by laughter that prompted Reg to steady the cast on his leg. Doss Kincaid was only a few years older than her son. They talked of basketball and girls and Dallas and eventually of the reason Doss was in Charleston.

"Y'all don't need pay me no mind," Willa interjected, "but Miss Julia might be wantin' to hear all this. She done told us the news people be a'comin'."

"She's right, Doss," Reg concurred. "Miss McKenzie is the one we should talk to. Like I said, this is not a secret I'm interested in keeping for my own reasons, but I can't betray Quinn's confidence. I've already told you more than she'd like, but I have your word you won't print it."

"You're killin' me here, Reg. This is a big story. If just a whisper of it gets in the wind, reporters will be all over it. I can't believe it's not all over the papers already. What's up with that? Don't you people have press down here?"

Reg smiled. "This is Charleston, man.

Clutching her briefcase in her left hand and holding the leather cell phone loop between her teeth, Julia pushed open the door and flipped the switch for her ceiling fan as the scent of home enveloped her. It was possible, she thought, that she could still go for a walk in the surf before sunset, swinging her arms as she kicked up droplets of salt water ahead of her. She felt no need for dinner; her need was for respite.

There was plenty to ponder, and Julia wanted to do it here, apart from her files and her reference materials. She glanced at the pieces of mail she had brought from the box, tossing some pieces onto the kitchen counter and some into the trash can, holding the lid open with the foot pedal.

Julia was worried, more than a little, about defending Quinn. Her search for precedent in the shelves lining her library had produced nothing. Collinsworth Rivers seemed confident. Quinn's state of mind had become increasingly fragile. Rose, ever her protector, surely did not need the acute stress she was suffering. Reg Fallon, collateral damage of Quinn's revenge, left Julia haunted by the expression she last saw on his face.

Tucked away in her mind, Julia still felt the warmth of her last evening with Sonny. Going there and away from her research and her apprehension tugged her toward a lighter timbre in her spirit. She was drawn to him, she conceded, gifting an unexpected dimension to her days. She was grateful.

The light was blinking on her answering machine. Julia debated, opting to check the messages although her toes could already feel the sand between them. The first message was simple and straightforward: "This is Doss Kincaid, Miss McKenzie. Reg Fallon gave me your number. Please call my cell phone." And he gave her the number. Pleasant voice. No association in Julia's mind. The second was more imploring: "Please call me this evening, Miss McKenzie. I'm a reporter from the Dallas Morning News. I won't take much of your time. It's important. Thank you. Doss Kincaid." He repeated the number for her. The message had been left just fifteen minutes before Julia's arrival at home. A reporter, Julia thought. It had been only a matter of time.

Collie was lost in thought on Tuesday morning when the buzzer paged him back to the present and his appointment with MacArthur Howe IV. He had once again been analyzing his approach to his newest client, determined to put Mac so at ease that he would trust his attorney with the truth.

"Yes, Rebecca," he answered, certain that the receptionist would announce Mac's arrival, right on time.

"Mr. Howe is here to see you, Mr. Rivers."

"I'll be right there, Rebecca. Thank you." Collie stood and straightened his tie, checking the knot at his collar. The perfectly pressed pale blue Oxford shirt was representative of his usual dress: conservative, neat and typical of the well-appointed Charleston lawyer. There were a few flashy dressers in the cadre, but Collinsworth Rivers was definitely not one of them. He was traditional in his dress, his practice and his approach to life in general, all of which had served him well as he climbed the prestigious ladder of success in Charleston's circle of criminal defense attorneys.

Collie opened the door into the reception area and strode across the room, extending his hand. "Good to see you, Mac," he offered cordially. "Come on back."

Mac followed Collie down the now-familiar hallway. "Did you see that Braves game last night?" Collie asked, turning to Mac and trying to set the tone. "That was some pitching, wasn't it?"

"Almost a shutout, right? I can't believe I went to sleep during the seventh inning," Mac responded.

"I was ready to go to sleep, but my dad came over to watch with me, and he kept me awake until the end." Collie suppressed a yawn. "He's the reason I'm a rabid Braves fan."

"My dad and I went to a few games down in Atlanta when I was in high school. He's a pretty enthusiastic fan too."

"Didn't you play football in high school?" Collie asked.

"Yeah, all four years. Kept me in shape for the Army, or so I thought." Mac grinned, patting his abdomen. "All those sit-ups, and I still wasn't prepared for the rigors of training. It's brutal."

They had reached Collie's doorway, and the lawyer stood aside and motioned for Mac to enter, following behind him and closing the door. "I've never been as physical as I should be," he admitted. "I play racquetball twice a week, but that's about the extent of my exercise. I'm envious of you guys who are in shape." Collie was trim and looked sufficiently fit, but Mac basked in his admiration, taking the seat offered and stretching his long legs out in front of him under the desk. He appeared relaxed, Collie thought, more comfortable than he had been at their last meeting on Saturday morning.

"I don't want to take too much of your time this morning, Mac. I just wanted to go over a couple of things with you before the preliminary hearing. I want you to be assured that you can tell me absolutely anything in confidentiality. The lawyer/client privilege guarantees your secrets are safe within the walls of this office."

"I understand," Mac replied quickly, obviously not taking time to ponder Collie's assurances.

"I know you're put off by this whole situation, and I know it's awkward to discuss, but it would be even more difficult if you leave out anything which could catch me off guard in the courtroom. Surprises are the last thing a lawyer needs in the middle of a case. It's not my job to judge you; it's my job to see that a jury judges you not guilty."

Collie looked pointedly at Mac, trying to convey his sincerity as a confidante without appearing suspicious of the story his client had offered. It was a tricky balance. Mac appeared not to notice.

"I don't have any secrets, Mr. Rivers. I told you everything on Saturday except how fucking mad I am at that girl. She's got my dad furious and my mom upset, and if this doesn't go away quietly, it could affect my career. I'm an officer, you know, and the Army takes this kind of thing seriously. I sure as hell don't want them to get wind of it."

"Well, then, we need to dispose of it as quickly and quietly as possible. Ideally, the judge won't find enough reason to let this go to trial, in which case it will all be over on Friday at the preliminary hearing. It's my job to try to make that happen, and it's yours to tell me everything that might help me do that."

"Like I said, Mr. Rivers, I told you everything I can remember. I had a little fun with that girl a couple of times. She was such a tease, always jogging by my house in those little shorts and that cut-away shirt. Girls like her think they're hot stuff. They think they can get away with bloody murder and walk away scot-free. But this time, it's not gonna happen that way. This time I'm gonna make the little bitch pay for what she did to me."

Once again, Collie got that twinge in the back of his neck, a sense that behind the words of this client there was a truth not reflected in his words. There was a callousness in the eyes of MacArthur Howe, a sliver of inexplicable disdain as he spoke of Quinn Ravenel and "girls like her". Anger would be normal after an attack such as Mac had suffered, but there was a slightly more deep-seated innateness to his attitude, a subtle but unsophisticated rawness to his expression. Collie scribbled with his pen, but his mind raced ahead, grasping at ways to pry inside the mind of his client.

"So you never had an official date with this girl? Is that correct?"

"Absolutely not. She's not my type."

"How did you come to find the opportunity for casual sex, then, Mac? Did she somehow make it clear that she was interested?"

"Oh, it was clear all right. You've been around, Mr. Rivers. You know how girls act when they want it. She definitely wanted it."

"So how did you find the right opportunity? Was it in the back seat of your car or what?"

"She came to my house a couple of times. She'd just stop by when she was running and flirt with me. Mostly I wasn't interested. But when a guy is really horny and a girl is offering, what's the harm?"

"So she definitely offered? She went willingly inside your house with you and had sex?"

"She's a tease. You know the type. I knew her game, and I can play as well as any. She wanted it, and she liked it. I'd like to remind her of that."

"No reminders, Mac. You do know you have to keep your distance from her, don't you?" Collie looked up from his legal pad, startled at the thought his client might engage his accuser apart from the pending legal proceedings.

Mac rolled his eyes, smiling. "Yeah, yeah, don't worry. I'm not going near her. Last time she was anywhere close, she nearly killed me."

109

At least, thought Doss Kincaid, there was shade on the Church Street sidewalk where he waited. Heat felt different in Charleston, he had decided as he sat on the doorstep of Julia McKenzie's law office on this Tuesday morning. Eighty degrees in Dallas was warm but pleasant; here, even in the morning, perspiration beaded on his forehead and trickled down his chest under his shirt, making the damp cotton stick to him. He had made himself as comfortable as possible, using Julia's door as a backrest as he perched on the step up to her office, reading the sports section of the Post and Courier he had purchased from a box at the corner of Broad and Meeting Streets.

"Good morning. Mr. Kincaid, I presume."

Doss jumped to his feet, brushing the seat of his pants, eager to make a good impression. Julia stood just in front of him, waiting to unlock the door. Doss was a full head taller, and she looked up as he straightened, noting his charming good looks. He was classically attractive, tanned and muscular with the soft brown eyes that reminded her of Sonny's dog. Disarmed, she found herself smiling. Driving over the Cooper River, she had steeled herself to brush him off quickly. The last thing she needed right now was some pesky reporter poking around in an already-messy situation and taking time she could not spare. Faced with the eager young Dallas reporter, her animosity mellowed. He extended his hand."

"Please call me Doss." His smile was charming and open. "I'm sorry I bothered you at home last night. I must admit I'm pretty anxious to get my teeth into this story, and Reg and his mother would have no part of it until I cleared it with you."

Julia smiled again as she thought of this young reporter tangling with Willa Fallon. "She's as good as mothers get. I know she can be pretty tenacious where Reg is concerned."

"That's an understatement, Miss McKenzie. If I needed a bodyguard, I'd call Ms. Fallon first! I couldn't have gotten past her into that hospital room without making myself look like a complete fool."

Julia motioned Doss to a seat while she started the coffee. "Like I told you, Mr. Kincaid--Doss--I have clients coming at 10:00. We have twenty minutes to talk, and then they'll be coming. What can I tell you?"

"I came here to talk to Reg about his injuries and how they affect his basketball career in Dallas. What I've discovered is a story with far more facets than a simple sports story. Reg was riding in a police cruiser when the accident happened. He shouldn't have been there. He's a good guy whose life is now way messed up because some jerk raped a friend of his, she took revenge, and Reg got caught in the crossfire."

"That's an impressively succinct summation." Julia assessed. "I gather you and Reg had quite a conversation."

"Thanks. It's my job." His smile was genuine and infectious.

Julia considered the options. If she refused to discuss the matter with Doss Kincaid, other curious reporters would soon follow. She wondered once again if publicity might be helpful, though Quinn loathed the possibility. It was difficult to predict public reaction to such a matter if it was splashed brashly across the *Post and Courier* and discussed in lurid detail on Live 5 News. Would sympathies lie with Quinn or with Mac? Julia would prefer that the story was told, if at all, by someone sympathetic to both Quinn Ravenel and Reg Fallon. In either case, however, Quinn's story would no longer be just her own.

"Do you think it's impossible to keep a lid on this?" she asked, almost rhetorically. The answer was becoming less certain by the day.

"Reg Fallon was on the cover of Sports Illustrated just a few weeks ago. This story has legs, and I'm just the first guy who wants to tell it. You can run me off, but I won't be the last."

Julia held out an empty cup, signaling Doss to come and fill it as she poured her own. "Help yourself to the cream and sugar. Here's the thing. My client—the one you call 'the girl'—is in fragile emotional condition, as you might imagine. She never meant for the story of her rape to be known, or, for that matter, her identity as the attacker who took her revenge. Incredible as it may seem, she thought to keep her secret, extract her measure of justice and go quietly on with her life teaching kindergarten here in Charleston next month. I'm still open to any plan which could make that possible."

Doss nodded, lifting his cup slightly in a mock toast in Julia's direction. "Unlikely."

"I might have a proposition for you, since you're already privy to the story. You seem like an adventurous guy. How far would you go in pursuit of a story?" She raised an eyebrow questioningly.

"I'm all ears." Doss had filled his cup nearly to the brim, all but inhaling the straight black liquid he'd been craving while he sat on Julia's step. He had drunk two cups at the acclaimed Mills House where he'd spent the night, too restless to appreciate the superb surroundings.

Keeping Quinn's secret was still paramount. But exposure was obviously as deeply feared by MacArthur Howe and his parents, as evidenced by their request for privacy to Judge Chastain. Was there leverage here, Julia wondered, aware of the time crunch before Celia, Quinn, Rose and her expert witness arrived at ten o'clock.

"Could I appeal to you to take a calculated risk, Mr. Kincaid, in the interest of preserving the privacy of a very nice girl who could use a break? I'll give you every scrap of information on Reg's condition, arrange continuing access to his doctors, and assure you an exclusive interview, if you will agree to release this as a sports story without information which would lead to questions beyond Reg, the team and the injury." She looked levelly at Doss.

"Miss McKenzie, I'd like to help, but..."

"Wait. There's one more thing." Julia stopped him before he finished, still formulating a plan whose outcome she could not predict. She plunged ahead. "In return, I'd like you to drop by the home of MacArthur Howe IV and his parents before this day is over and present yourself as an inquisitive and determined reporter sniffing around the periphery of what you believe might be a scandal. You'll be received badly; I'd go prepared to run."

Doss Kincaid's crooked grin smacked of interest and amusement. "You don't know a thing about me, Miss McKenzie, and you're trying to enlist me in a shady scheme to save some girl and... and what exactly?"

"Mr. Kincaid," Julia paused before answering. "I can't be sure."

110

Martha seemed to be studying the pattern on the yellow floral wallpaper in the master bathroom, her eyes focused on a spot just below the border in the corner above the shower. George would have thought her contemplating a redecorating project if it were not for the telltale streak down her cheek and the tissue clutched tightly in her fist. She sat on the closed toilet, so deep in thought that she did not hear her husband approach, was not aware that he peered at her from the bedroom, puzzling over her quiet concentration and tearful moment of solitude. Not wishing to startle her, George spoke softly.

"Martha?" he asked tentatively. "Are you all right? Is something the matter?"

Surprised to find that she was no longer alone, Martha Howe dabbed quickly at the corner of her left eye, trying to erase traces of distress she was not yet ready to explain.

"George, don't sneak up on me that way."

"I didn't sneak, my dear. You were lost in thought, and it was obviously not a pleasant thought. What's troubling you?"

Martha had risen and tried to brush past her husband and out of the bathroom. "It's nothing. I was just having a blue moment."

The colonel took his wife gently by the shoulders, holding her out from him and looking her in the eyes. "You're troubled over Mac's situation, aren't you? I should never have allowed you to see that meddling old Rose Pinckney."

Martha's gaze dropped to the floor and her whole body slumped as she leaned into her husband's chest, her effort to stem the tears giving way to full-blown sobs as she pressed her hands against her face. She had been sniffling, sitting alone with her unsettling thoughts, pushing them back from the forefront of her consciousness, wishing her night of fitful sleep had not been strewn with the debris of her son's denials and the haunting, sincere eyes of Quinn Ravenel, his young nemesis, the embodiment of everything a mother fears for her son.

Fear for Mac had not been part of Martha's thoughts throughout most of his young life. She had, of course, suffered a mother's normal concerns for his health and safety. She had borne the fears common to a military wife and mother. But her pride in her son and her enjoyment of him had been the overriding fact of their relationship. It had never occurred to Martha Howe that she might have guided differently, that her doting attention could be paving the way for a young boy to grow to be an egocentric and selfish man, one whose regard for those around him withered in the light of his blistering absorption with his own appetites.

When Mac was little she had bandaged the scrapes almost before he felt them. She had asked what he wanted and provided what she thought he wanted before he asked. He knew, before his fourth birthday, that his happiness was hers. She lived and breathed to see him smile, delighted in his smallest excitement. He was not allowed dissatisfaction. The moment she sensed his discomfort or desire, it was satisfied. The whole world was his to take if she could help provide it for him.

Images were changing now in her mind, pictures flashing behind her eyes. She had given permission by the very way she lived her life in front of him, by the model she was for woman. She had been the coat thrown before him to ease his way to whatever he needed, whatever he wanted. She had turned her life into his stepping-stone—his and his father's—to make life easier, happier, free of unnecessary stresses. She had been the eager provider of comfort, always ready with assurance that her men's every word was boyishly acceptable, their every thought worth hearing, their every guffaw at the pool table in the family room charmingly forgivable.

"There, there," George Howe spoke comfortingly. "It's going to be all right." He patted his wife on the back, uncomfortable as always with her emotional display, having no ability to relate to or deal with it. He would wait it out, as was his custom, maintaining his uneasy composure while Martha expressed her distress in the way common, he thought, to women.

Martha was obviously suffering, deep in the 'what-ifs' and 'if-onlys' that preyed upon her when she dwelt upon the past and the choices she had made. She had followed her heart in the raising of her son, had simply loved and protected him and kept him from harm and frustration, scorning the guidance of both the standard and the trendy childrearing publications. Vague and unnamed doubts now prickled at her. Had her love not been enough, her guidance flawed?

Mac had not known until first grade the initial denial of his every wish. Miss Vandyke, twenty-five years in that very classroom, spotted quickly the result of six years of absolute parental indulgence. She saw a patently spoiled child, intelligent enough but self-absorbed, acquainted with neither caring about nor sharing with his classmates. He hit little Sarah Fisher on the second day of the school year because she picked up what he wanted before he reached it. It was the red baseball bat, and Sarah proved quite good with it during the ensuing months. But on that day, Mac clearly did not understand anyone else's right to anything he desired.

The class, the playground, the world all revolved around him. He had been given no tools for knowing differently. The teacher's tactful but pointed pleas for parental intervention had fallen on deaf ears. And by the end of first grade, Miss Vandyke knew that her mission to show him any other way had failed.

He had made friends because it suited him. Popularity among a certain group would become important to him. During those year, he saw and somehow incorporated into his personality the ability to make those friends, to attract a peer group. He wasn't exactly a bully, nor precisely warm, but he began then to develop a natural manipulative charisma. It suited him. He saw the usefulness of "friends", and it pleased his mother.

"How can it be all right?" Martha managed finally, her words trembling against George's now-tear-stained shirt. "How can this be happening?"

"It's all a mistake, Martha. Just a mistake. You've got to get hold of yourself, both for your own sake and for Mac's. You don't want him to see you like this, do you? You know how that will upset him."

Martha inhaled a long, ragged sigh, failing once again to exhale normally, her breath turning to another choked sob. She clutched at

George's shirtsleeves, holding on as though they were lifelines. Lack of sleep contributed to her uncontrolled tears, and Martha had not eaten breakfast or lunch, her appetite suppressed by the creeping fear that gnawed near her stomach and constricted her throat.

"I'm afraid, George. I saw Quinn Ravenel. I'm afraid of this trouble my baby is in. I'm so very, very afraid."

111

Lunch at the bar in T-Bonz was a habit of Sonny's once or twice a week. The daytime bartender, known to the regulars simply as Hoss, was a wealth of information on all sorts of people and happenings. Everyone talked to him; he had one of those faces that invited unburdening and confession. It was Sonny's opinion that Hoss had missed his calling as a priest, but he expressed that notion for the sole purpose of amusing his old friend. He and Hoss had graduated high school together, fellow mediocre students and football teammates. And Hoss always managed to wrangle a piece of coconut crème pie for Sonny from Kaminsky's next door. The two establishments were connected, and patrons of T-Bonz often ended a meal with one of Kaminsky's delectable desserts.

Hoss got his usually reliable scuttlebutt from the grapevine that ran through and around the open-air market across the street. The artisans and regular sellers there seemed each to consider Hoss his or her personal confidante, and he retained in his memory the latticework of hearsay and tales which formed a fairly legitimate portrait of Charleston's eastern peninsula and its everyday affairs. Sonny found him an invaluable covert resource.

The bartender saw MacArthur Howe come in. Sonny followed his glance, taking note. Mac was alone and waved off the hostess to take a seat at the end of the bar closer to the door, sitting gingerly, Sonny noticed, as though awareness of his injury still controlled his movement. Hoss sauntered in that direction, pointing at the new arrival with his left forefinger.

"Bud," Mac ordered, nodding to the bartender.

Hoss winked and clicked his tongue, his standard acknowledgment. The low drone of lunchtime conversation rose and fell, peppered by laughter. Glasses were refilled and patrons came and went, some consuming a full meal and others making a lunch of the appetizer fare such as the pecan-coconut shrimp or the crab dip. Mac, Sonny observed, ordered no food at all and was drinking his fourth beer in an

265

hour, making a little small talk or saying an occasional hello, but mostly appearing withdrawn, seeming intent on scrutinizing his finger's nonstop tracing along the rim of his glass. Sonny, though interested, decided to leave him under Hoss's capable supervision. The piles on his desk needed attention, and he headed for the men's room on his way to the door, stopping here and there to slap a back or greet an acquaintance.

He wondered later if Mac's confronting him was intentional, a consequence of the four beers and a bad morning with a good lawyer. The door swung open to the men's room, and the swagger modified slightly by the limp was evident when Mac came in. Sonny was just fastening his pants, his back to the doorway, his guard down. His first glimpse of Mac was in the mirror, and it seemed his expression was already crystallized into an insolent belligerence when he entered the restroom.

Sonny would simply have washed his hands and left, thwarting any attempt at conversation. But Mac stopped as the door closed behind him, assessing Sonny with the narrowing of his eyes, the set of his mouth. He watched as the detective ran water over his hands and dispensed the paper towel. He stood squarely in front of the door, wordless but not moving, as Sonny prepared to leave the room. Their eyes met, neither turning away.

"Excuse me," Sonny said, approaching the door.

MacArthur Howe did not move.

"I'm just tryin' to decide if there is any excuse for you," Mac paused expressively, "detective," finishing with a sneer in both his expression and his inflection.

Sonny Legare was not easily baited, desensitized by years of taunts from petty hoodlums and verbal abuse from more sophisticated thugs than Mac Howe. He returned the scowl levelly, showing neither irritation nor anger.

"You're in my way, Howe," he stated simply. "I'm through here."

"You're through, all right," Mac scoffed. "You're through in this town. You took the wrong side when you came to my house with that warrant."

Sonny considered the options. The kid was under the influence of a few beers, emboldening him further than when they had faced off in the Howes' home. Still, Sonny had developed a distinct dislike for MacArthur Howe, an aversion fed by the kid's arrogance, his cocky attitude, his obvious disdain for traditional authority. He would not allow

Mac's bravado to make him appear intimidated or unnerved. It was the classic bully approach. Mac was an amateur unaware.

"Move," he directed, deliberately editing provocation from his tone.

Mac stood still. "You're nothing but a stupid cop," he declared with all the contempt he could muster, "taking sides with that girl. She's a tramp. And you're nothing but a flunky with a badge."

Sonny had listened through Quinn Ravenel's statement when she filed the rape charge. He had looked at her face when she left afterward, her tears suppressed, her spirit ravaged by the recall of an incident his gut told him she had not fabricated. His restraint was legendary, his temper notoriously controlled. He frowned without pretense, allowing his animosity to surface. They were alone in the room.

"And you're nothing but a mollycoddled, yellow-bellied, lily-livered excuse for a man," Sonny returned evenly.

Mac's color deepened instantly, and his lunge for Sonny was quick but ineffective. His right fist had just balled and aimed for Sonny's left cheek when the detective reacted, grabbing the arm above Mac's wrist and using his free open palm to pin the younger man against the door. His adept response was obviously unexpected. Mac's eyes widened, his surprise unmistakable.

"There's no one here now but you and me, kid," Sonny said softly close to Mac's face. "I don't know who you think you're impressing, but there's nobody here to applaud. You done?" He paused for effect, allowing Mac to absorb the words and to feel his back firmly against the door.

"I'm gonna have your badge and your balls for this." Mac spat the words toward Sonny's face. "I'll get you for police brutality. I'm already injured, remember?"

"Go for it," Sonny responded.

112

Feeling as though he had been outmaneuvered at his own game, Doss Kincaid found himself enlisted in Julia Slaton McKenzie's plan with little reservation. Her enthusiasm for her client was contagious, as was her conviction on the subject of MacArthur Howe's guilt. Still, Doss thought, his dedication to the ethics of news collection and reporting should have insulated him from involvement in such unabashed chicanery as Julia proposed. He had come to Charleston in pursuit of a sports story. The broadening of the tale had whetted his appetite as a reporter. His agreement to visit the Howes was not a departure from that purpose, though he recognized it as a fishing expedition. His tentative cooperation with Julia's mission to suppress a part of the story most certainly was.

The door had opened as he left Julia's office, and he had held it for the group of women who were Julia's next appointment. They appeared solemn, and Doss wondered if at least one of them was in trouble with the law, though they looked utterly respectable. Maybe, he thought, it was a family matter requiring legal advice.

The petite blonde young woman who brought up the rear held his gaze for longer than the moment it took for her to pass as he held the door. She was lovely, he thought, making a mental note to ask Julia for an introduction when he returned to remind her that she was in his debt. Lacking reason to linger further, he nodded across the room to Julia and closed the door behind him, the girl's half-smile still clear in his head as he stood on the sidewalk along Church Street.

The four women inside were looking to Julia for direction. Rose had Quinn firmly by the arm, and Celia prepared to present the stranger to defense counsel.

Miranda McQuaid was a presence, would be so in any room, Julia thought when they were introduced. Celia had described the woman, expressing her admiration, but Julia had expected someone bolder in appearance, someone larger and less utterly feminine. Miranda, even in pinstripes and with her graying hair in a bun, exuded a glowing softness, a lace-and-satin fragility belied only by the intensity immediately apparent in her gray-blue eyes. Celia was right; Miranda McQuaid was a woman who made an impression.

She held Julia's hand for an extra moment, meeting her eyes directly. A practicing psychiatrist and professor of women's studies, Miranda was in her early sixties, small-boned and delicate in appearance, sought-after in her field by reputation. Her chosen area of expertise was that of women and rape. Celia had proposed her as someone who could help both Julia with the case and Quinn with the aftermath of her four-year-old experience. Rose had flown her in from Los Angeles.

"I'm delighted to meet you," Julia said sincerely. "Celia speaks so highly of you."

"That's very kind," Miranda replied, warming Julia with her smile. "I'm always eager to help with a situation like you have on your hands.

From what Celia has told me, you're trying to make a case for pure self-defense. That's fascinating. I'll help you in any way that I can."

"Thank you so much." Julia returned the smile. "Why don't we sit in the library. Would you like coffee?"

Miranda shook her head. "I'm a big fan of plain water. Could I trouble you for a glass of that, Julia? I would suggest that Quinn sit here in the outer area for a few minutes while you, Celia and I lay some groundwork. Quinn knows enough about rape already. Would you mind, my dear?" she asked the youngest of them. "You and I will talk at length a little later. I have both reading material and my own thoughts to share with you."

Before Quinn could object, Rose offered to sit with her in the waiting area. "You and I don't need to go over it any more, Babyluv. Let's let the shrinks brief Julia." She smiled at Celia, knowing she cringed at her use of the slang.

Slipping her light suit jacket from her arms, Miranda McQuaid hung it over the back of a chair, letting it hang behind her as she took her seat at the table and looked around Julia's library. "This is a lovely room," she commented, "but I am always comfortable in a space filled with books."

Julia returned to the library, joining Celia and Miranda at the table. She brought a pitcher of cold water, a glass, and two cups of coffee. "I can't say how much I appreciate your help. I've been struggling with this case for two reasons: I am not a criminal defense attorney and I do not have, thankfully, a sufficient understanding of rape as a traumatic experience."

Celia reached for one of the cups of steaming coffee. "I've assured Julia she's as capable as anyone I know.

Miranda McQuaid, calm and self-assured, folded her hands together on the table. "You ask the questions, Julia, and I'll give you my best answers. When you need more, just ask. This is my subject."

"Okay. Let's start with my most difficult challenge. The criminal defense attorney I consulted adamantly insisted that the only defense for Quinn is one of insanity. He seemed thoroughly convinced that it is unlikely to convince a jury that Quinn's action was rational, especially after she had four years to premeditate. Can you help me with that?"

Miranda barely hesitated, her material apparently all at the tip of her tongue and in the forefront of her mind. "The moments of the rape remained fresh and present for Quinn," Miranda began slowly. "Do I understand correctly that she told no one but her mother?"

"That's right," Julia replied.

"And her mother encouraged her to feel shame?"

"Also true."

"She had, then, no outlet for her rightful rage, no counseling to help deal with or diminish her pain, no validation from outside herself of the damage she had suffered. The memory, kept untarnished in a compartment in her mind, never faded, never changed. On the day Quinn lashed out in her own defense, she was psychologically in the same moment as on the evening of the rape four years ago. The part of her memory, which saved that event intact, was stuck in time. It was in that moment when she struck back at her assailant, defending herself as surely as she would have four years before in the same room had she had the means to do so."

"I understand, but won't we be accused of simply playing word games? Are you not just using the insanity defense and calling it by another name?" Julia played devil's advocate now, having gone over it repeatedly in her struggle to knit this defense plan together.

"Not at all," Miranda explained, sure of her subject. "In fact, it would be much crazier for a rape victim not to react in this way. The mind and the psyche are innately protective of their ability to function. They will take appropriate adaptive measures to preserve their own existence, to prevent fragmentation of the self. Those measures, in post-trauma such as rape, often and reasonably include the boxing up of the trauma memory, a sealing off from the painful recall as effectively as possible to keep it from eroding or contaminating the whole and healthy psychological self. Does that not appear to be excruciatingly sound behavior by the subconscious, counsel?" Miranda challenged, tilting her head just slightly.

Julia considered. Miranda was definitely good, and she would make a convincing witness in Quinn's defense. What holes could be made in her logic?

"You're saying, if I understand you, that Quinn sensibly isolated the memory of the rape all this time in order to live a life, keeping her rage in check to protect the whole?"

"It is a unique post traumatic response, unlike the behavior of a soldier back from war with no explicit target for his rage, sometimes lashing out indiscriminately. Quinn had a target."

Understanding expanded rapidly for Julia. "I see."

Miranda shook her head, obviously relieved at Julia's quick grasp of her train of thought. "Rape is a special case of traumatic injury," she continued. "It is different for a woman who is experienced in sexual matters than it is for one who is not."

Julia was puzzled. "Explain, please."

"Women throughout human history, without consciousness of doing so, have learned to draw a separation between the psychic spiritual core and the sexual physical self. They have had to. Throughout ages of male dominated cultures, what would woman have become if her sanity depended on her ability to decide her sexual fate? She would have no sanctuary, not in the world and not in her self.

"Woman has had to understand, on some essential level, that she is more than her sexual self. When it becomes necessary for her own protection, a woman instinctually draws the line. She senses but does not feel, knows but does not internalize. Every woman who has consented to sex for any of the many and various reasons women do so understands. Rape has many, many degrees and comes in many disguises.

"A woman develops this sense, this capacity to keep her essential self separate, only when experience teaches her to do so. It is, sadly, a common experience, world wide and across cultures.

"A woman without sexual experience, however, would be unable to separate her sexual self from her essential self. Never having crossed that line, she would not know how to draw the boundary. Her whole essence would be exposed to the violation; she would experience it as a harm to her core being, a psychic devastation."

"And this was Quinn's experience?"

"Exactly. Quinn is a classic case such as I have just described. As a virgin, she had no frame of reference to help her categorize the rape experience as sexual only. She had not had reason to make a psychological distinction between her essence and her physical sexual self, leaving them as one and putting her whole self at risk. The rape was not of her body only, not just a physical violation. It was a violation of her simple, integrated self, of her whole being, of her undifferentiated spirit."

Julia had goose bumps and could sense that a jury would be affected in the same way, particularly a jury of women, Quinn's true peers. She had never given serious thought to rape, had not been presented with a reason to do so. And now that it was thrust upon her, Miranda had in just a few minutes made Julia cringe with her insight into the psyche of woman. Her understanding had broadened and her resolve deepened. Quinn Ravenel, she thought anew, had been criminally injured, devastatingly damaged, and it was Julia's job to help her prove her behavior sound and just. Four years earlier, MacArthur Howe had taken her innocence and could not return it. Quinn's life was forever changed, and she had recognized that and tried to salvage what remained.

"Will you say, as an expert witness on the stand, exactly what you've said here today?" Julia asked. "Will you make a jury understand?"

"I'll say exactly that and whatever else you think helpful," Miranda assured. "I'll do everything I can, but it's your job to make a jury understand."

113

As late afternoon ripened into early evening in Charleston, Doss Kincaid stood atop the battery wall looking across the bay. His gaze was on the shipping lane, his eyes absently following a cargo ship as it made its way out of the harbor toward the open sea; his mind was on the improbable interview he was mentally drafting for the unlikely possibility that he should get past the front door at the home of MacArthur Howe IV. He shook his head, unaware that he did it overtly, still somewhat perplexed at how he had been seduced into being an active accomplice in Julia McKenzie's admittedly rudimentary gambit. She wanted the Howes to believe Doss was on the trail of a big story, that he had the scent and intended to pursue it like a retriever pup on the trail of a wounded gosling.

Ordinarily, Doss would be doing exactly that. Tonight, he wondered what he was doing, how he intended to handle the information which had come to him. It was a potentially riveting story. It was currently all his. And Doss Kincaid had never withheld a story for any reason other than legal or liability issues for his paper. Until now.

The sun was still warm and orange over the city as he turned from the railing and descended the steps from the battery walk to the sidewalk along East Battery Street. He would leave his car, he decided, here where it was parked along the street, and walk the couple of blocks to the home of the Howes and their son. He had circled the area earlier, locating the gray stucco house with white trim using the directions given him by Julia McKenzie. It was a handsome house, like all the stately homes along the Charleston harbor--not ostentatious but solid and quietly elegant, its white molded trim providing a soft, pleasing contrast against the slate gray.

Doss was still mulling his approach to the family as he crossed the street, looking down East Bay toward Broad Street where the horse-drawn carriage was now turning the corner. He had maneuvered his way into more difficult situations, he thought, had coaxed answers and even interviews from some infamously intractable and tiresome folks whose actions or predicaments had provided stories his Dallas readers were anxious to scrutinize and monitor in great detail. Doss could make people feel at ease. He had charmed doors open with his smile and held them open with his foot. He had wheedled and manipulated and, on occasion, threatened a story from a reluctant public figure. His editor described him as relentless. It was both a compliment and an eye-rolling, head-wagging censure. The elder editor groused, grumbled and grudgingly admired the young Kincaid who was as tenacious a newsman as he had known.

Was he the consummate reporter here, Doss wondered, or just a willing pawn in Julia McKenzie's scheme? He had promised her only that he would not submit a story for print until they had talked again on Wednesday morning. He would keep his word.

He could hear the bell ring somewhere deep in the house when he pushed the button, the melodic sound of the traditional Winchester chime making him smile because it seemed so appropriate. He could hear the soles of shoes on a hardwood floor as someone approached the front door from inside. After a solid click, the door opened and Doss found himself facing a man twice his age and almost his height, trim and straight in his bearing, dignified with his graying hair and imposing presence. The man exuded military demeanor.

"Yes?" The colonel obviously expected a sales pitch.

Doss stepped back slightly and rested his weight on his back foot to convey an easygoing initial impression. This was a man accustomed to respect for his time and his space, Doss quickly assessed.

"Doss Kincaid, Sir," he began. "I was hoping to catch Mac at home."

"Mac?" George Howe's tone had not changed. If he was irritated at the interruption in his evening, it was not yet obvious. "He's in the family room. What was the name again?"

The reporter extended his hand. "Doss Kincaid. I wanted to come by and see if he felt like shooting the bull for a little while."

The colonel was slightly puzzled. He knew Mac's friends. But he would certainly want to be gracious to any of his son's acquaintances.

He shook the young man's hand warmly and stepped back from the doorway.

"Come on in. We were just watching a baseball game back here. You a baseball fan?" Doss was following the father down the long hallway, his mind rushing ahead to the next step, surprised that he was inside the house.

"Sure am," he answered. "Did you see that game last night? Thirteen innings."

"That's why I've been yawning all day," the colonel chuckled. "Mac dozed, but I couldn't give it up and go to bed."

Doss stopped in the archway as the colonel entered the room where Mac was stretched lengthwise on one of the leather sofas, his head propped on a gray-striped suede cushion for better viewing of the big-screen television across the room. He was barefoot but wearing sweatpants, Doss noticed, presumably to stay comfortable in the house Doss had already felt air conditioned to the point of chilly. The smell of something cooking reminded him he hadn't eaten since breakfast.

"Someone here looking for you, Mac," the colonel announced, stepping out of the line of sight between his son and Doss Kincaid. Mac looked up, obviously surprised, and swung his feet down to sit upright, looking at the reporter. His father expected Mac to recognize a friend and take it from there, offering a seat. George Howe, although curious about the unfamiliar visitor, was ready to leave the two young men alone to talk and join Martha in the kitchen while she prepared dinner. It was probably a good idea anyway, he thought, recalling her alarm and anxiety from earlier in the day. She had been nearly inconsolable, and George was relieved to hear the normal sounds of dinner preparation coming from the kitchen.

Mac did stand. He could have been trying to place Doss Kincaid in his memory, obviously coming up blank. It was Doss who made the first move, stepping forward into the room and extending his hand toward MacArthur Howe as though the meeting between them was expected and had been pre-arranged.

"Doss Kincaid, Mac. Good to see you. I was talking with your local sports star, Reg Fallon, and he said you could probably shed some light on a little project I'm doing. I'd sure appreciate a few minutes of your time if you can spare them before that dinner I smell." He had kept smiling and made his tone as casual and engaging as possible.

Caught off guard, Mac shook the reporter's hand as he processed the introduction Doss had offered. Reg Fallon. What could a friend of Reg possibly want with him? "I'm not sure I understand," Mac said, not yet offering Doss a seat in the family room.

"I'm told you graduated a couple of years ahead of Fallon, but you played against him on an opposing team in high school." Doss was still hoping to put Mac enough at ease to initiate a conversation. "And now you're military? I thought of that myself at one time, but I'm not sure I have what it takes, you know? It takes a lot of guts to go off into a dangerous world wearing that uniform. I admire you." Playing to Mac's ego, he also kept the father at bay for another minute, though George Howe stood puzzled, aware now that this young stranger who had wriggled his way into their home was not one of his son's buddies.

Mac looked toward the television screen as cheers caught his attention. "Home run," he said as the baseball sailed across the fence and into the stands.

"Nice one," Doss agreed. "No way that was going to be caught."

"Sit down." Mac finally motioned to the leather recliner. The game was going to a commercial break, so he turned his attention to the stranger. "Tell me what I have to do with Reg Fallon."

"Thanks." Doss sat. He carried no pad or pencil to give away his identity as a newspaper reporter. "I was talking to Reg in the hospital. He's really laid up, isn't he? Doesn't look like he'll be playing any ball for the Mavericks or anyone else."

Doss left that statement hanging there in the room awaiting whatever response it might invoke, hoping it would lead to a conversation peripheral to his real area of interest, giving him room to maneuver gingerly around the subject until he was forced to show his hand. He had played his ace, getting himself into a chair in the Howes' family room. Now he was holding his cards as close as possible to the vest, knowing he was bluffing, counting on his reporter's finesse to advance him in the game. As always, his competitive instincts had kicked in. Now that the game was on, he proceeded carefully.

"Really?" Mac responded, surprised. "What's the matter with him?"

"I thought you'd know. He was in a serious car accident. I'm surprised it hasn't been on the front page of the local paper, let alone in the pages of Sports Illustrated.

"I'm sorry to hear that, but I still don't see what that has to do with me," Mac asserted, frowning slightly.

"The accident happened when Reg was in a police car. He was in that car because he was suspected of the attack on you, Mac, an attack later confessed to by someone else. It's a fascinating story, not just in sports circles but a great human-interest story as well. I was hoping you could shed some light on the whole thing."

Both Mac and his father looked perplexed. "You're not a cop, are you?" Mac asked finally.

"Why would you think that?" Doss replied.

"I don't understand why you're here."

"I'm a reporter for the Dallas newspaper. This whole story is going to be reported somewhere, by someone, soon. I'd just as soon it be my story on tomorrow's front page."

Still unclear, a picture was forming in the colonel's mind. This guy was a reporter with the whiff of a scandal that he intended to print.

"I think you'd better leave, Mr. Kincaid. I'll show you back to the door where I mistakenly allowed you in here."

Doss stood, though unready yet to let go of his advantage. "Wouldn't you just as soon tell me your side of this story so you don't come out looking bad?" He looked directly at Mac. "Reg Fallon seems to think he got caught up in a story that had nothing to do with him and everything to do with you having raped a young friend of his."

Mac lunged from his laid-back position, temporarily forgetting his healing wound. His right fist connected with Doss's cheek soundly. Doss went down at the colonel's feet, sprawled across the fringe of the Persian rug, his foot catching the cord to bring a table lamp crashing to the floor.

"What in the world?" Martha's voice was full of alarm as she rounded the corner from the hallway into the family room, a white tea towel in her hands and a look of total dismay on her face. "George," she exclaimed, noting the young man slumped across the hardwood holding his jaw. "George," she positively shrieked this time, a blatant plea that her husband prevent another blow by her son who was leaning over the stranger with clenched fists.

"Mac, that's enough," the colonel barked emphatically, stopping his son whose arm was pulled back for another jab. "Let him go."

"Mac, are you all right?" Martha cried, running to her son, oblivious to the young man who lay on the floor. "What's happened here?" Rushing past her husband, she grabbed Mac by his right arm, feeling his muscles taut, seeing the anger displayed in red on his face and in the set of his jaw.

Doss Kincaid rose to lean on his elbow, thinking he should have taken Julia's caution more seriously.

114

Julia's voice was almost gruff when she answered her phone on the fourth ring, just before the machine would have picked it up.

"Ouch, McKenzie! You don't sound your sweet, gentle self. Anything I can do?"

"Oh, Sonny, I'm sorry," Julia apologized, meaning it. "It's been such a long day."

"I saw the light still on in your office. Are you alone in there?"

"I am. I've been working on Quinn's defense and lost track of the time. Now I see that it's dark, and I have a headache and a sinking feeling that I'm in way over my head."

"I'm parked right outside on Church Street, McKenzie, and I have aspirin in the car. Can I come in?"

Julia smiled, feeling the tightness in her chest and the pounding in her temples. "Please," she said. "Please come in. I'll unlock the door."

Padding to the door in her bare feet, Julia felt the knots in her shoulders and neck. She had been working at her desk for hours, marking references and shifting heavy volumes as she filled a yellow legal pad with notes, alternately finding hopeful passages and discarding discouraging precedents. Her research had so far produced a potpourri of positives and negatives, feeding Julia's continuing ambivalence about the wisdom of building a case on simple self-defense. The earlier visit by Miranda McQuaid provided her most hopeful groundwork, a stunningly welcome foundation for building Julia's heretofore patchwork thesis.

Sonny stood leaning on the doorframe when Julia opened the door, grinning and holding a bottle of aspirin. "Was this my ticket to see you?" he asked. "Cause if it was, I'll start carrying them in all my pockets."

Julia smiled back, opening the door wider to allow Sonny to enter. "You don't need a ticket," she responded. "You've got a reserved seat in my office."

277

Sonny's eyebrows raised in surprise and appreciation. "That's music to my ears, McKenzie. What have I done to deserve that? Is it just my southern charm?"

"That and the fact that you keep showing up just when I need you, like right now."

"You need me? Little old me? Consider me totally at your service."

"I need a break. And that aspirin. And a little distracting conversation wouldn't hurt either. Think you're up to that, Detective Legare?" Julia held out her hand, palm up, forming a cup for the aspirin.

"That and more, counselor," Sonny answered. "I can make you a fresh pot of coffee and talk your little ear right off, so why don't you sit down and lighten up. I'll get you some water for the aspirin, or do you have something better to drink in the little fridge in the bathroom?"

"I have a couple of bottles of water and some Pepsi. Take your pick. I'll drink anything you bring me." Julia dropped into one of the armchairs in her waiting area, extending her nicely-tanned legs across to the small coffee table and crossing her ankles on the current issue of Southern Living magazine, the one she had perused a week earlier for ideas to decorate the house at the beach.

Sonny returned with a can of Pepsi in each hand, popping off a top for Julia and placing the soda in front of her on the table. "Now I was serious about the coffee. Want me to start a new pot?"

"Unless you want some, I should probably stop now. I've already logged enough caffeine to keep me awake well past midnight. Just sit down and tell me some stuff having nothing to do with the law or anyone's troubles."

Sonny sat in the chair across the table from Julia, leaning back and stretching out his long legs as he removed the top from his can. "That limits my choices, McKenzie, but I'll try to think of something we can talk about." He sipped from the can and pretended to be deep in thought. "How about you and me and what we're gonna do this weekend. There's nothing troublesome about that, is there?"

"Not if I can get a handle on this case before then," Julia replied.

"We're gonna have to talk about it before we can move on to the lighter conversation, aren't we?" Sonny asked, looking resigned. "Go ahead and get it out of your system. Why don't you just unload all the stuff you're stewing over."

Julia tipped her head back slightly, swallowing four tablets with one gulp of the soda. "What was I thinking?" She let her head rest on the back of the chair, closing her eyes. "I'm not a criminal defense lawyer."

"McKenzie, it's time to let it go for the night. It's almost nine o'clock, and here you are lost in these books. There are more hours tomorrow after you get a good night's sleep."

Julia didn't open her eyes or move her head. She sighed deeply and lifted the can to her lips for another sip. "I know. I've found some things we can use, but I've found more that can be used against us."

Sonny set his can on one of the green marble coasters and leaned across the table, taking one of Julia's small feet gently between his hands. "I've been told this is very relaxing, McKenzie. Do you mind if I give it a try?" His hands were warm on Julia's foot, his thumb beginning a circular motion on its sole, alternating firm pressure and gentle travels up and down the bottom of the foot.

"Do I mind?" Julia exclaimed, letting out her breath in a long, slow sigh. "I knew someone back in college who could do that. He was a med student, and he could put me in a trance with those hands. I've missed it ever since."

"Well, then, we've discovered another reason why you need me, McKenzie. You just breathe slowly and let me try to compete with your memory of that med student."

He was definitely competing, Julia thought, his technique already surpassing Josh's as she recalled it. Her absorption in the research faded as Sonny traced deliberate circles on the bottom of her right foot. She remembered the feel of those hands on her back as they danced, the pressure of Sonny's warm fingers along her spine. Something like a chill shook her from neck to toe at the recollection, and Sonny looked up quizzically. "Not cold, are you?" he asked.

"Not at all," Julia replied, "Just some little spring unwinding, I think."

"Not surprising, McKenzie. You're playing a pivotal role in the hottest story in this town right now, and hardly anyone knows it's happening. I'm sorry you can't enjoy the challenge the way you could if you weren't personally involved with the principal players."

"If I wasn't personally involved, I wouldn't have the challenge at all. Have you forgotten that I fell into this through the back door because I happen to be friends with the wrong people?" Julia smiled slightly, thinking fondly of those friends.

"I remember. If you're not careful, you're liable to make a name for yourself in criminal defense. Then you'll be hanging out over at the station on a regular basis, and I think I could get accustomed to that."

Raising her head from the back of the chair, Julia peered out of one half-opened eye, grinning at the compliment. "Well, Detective Legare, I could sure get used to this."

"Are you telling me the way to your heart might just be through the soles of these little feet, McKenzie?"

"I don't know about my heart, but my stress level has dropped dramatically in the last ten minutes."

"Nice ankles," Sonny observed, "and very cute little toes. I wouldn't have expected a woman as smart as you to have such pretty feet."

Aware that he was flirting with her, Julia kept it light. "I guess you know that was a really stupid thing to say, don't you?"

"Yeah, I know. Was it so stupid you want me to stop what I'm doing?"

"Oh, no," Julia responded very quickly. "Don't stop. As long as you keep doing that, you can say any old dumb thing that crosses your mind."

"I've been told that's one of the things I'm really good at."

"Is it, now? And would you like to enlighten me on some of the others, Detective?" Maybe flirting was another of those skills like riding a bicycle, she thought, that just comes back when you need it.

"Things I'm good at? That might be information you're not quite ready for, McKenzie."

Julia was forming an appropriate retort when the moment was interrupted by the telephone. Its ring seemed out of context, and Julia found herself uncharacteristically able to ignore it. Sonny's hands had momentarily stopped moving, but when he realized her intention, he resumed their soothing motion, taking Julia's inaction as a compliment. After three rings, the machine answered automatically. Julia's voice pleasantly filled the room, her recorded message instructing the caller to leave his name and number after the beep.

"It's Doss Kincaid, Miss McKenzie. I've been to see MacArthur Howe, and I just wanted to ..."

Julia's feet were on the floor as soon as she heard his voice, covering the distance to the telephone in seconds and pressing its receiver firmly to her ear. Sonny looked down at his now-empty hands, still formed as though holding Julia's foot, amazed at the split-second reversal of her demeanor; she had literally vaulted from her seat, suddenly oblivious to Sonny's presence.

"Doss, Doss, I'm here," she spoke breathlessly into the receiver. "Don't hang up."

Sonny watched Julia's face as she listened. The person on the other end of the line was obviously important; she had been more than determined not to miss this call. Leaning back in the chair, Sonny sipped from his can, studying Julia's expressions as she talked.

"You did it?" she almost squealed with delight, piquing Sonny's interest further. "Yes, of course. Come on by. I'll unlock the door."

When she turned back toward Sonny, Julia clapped both hands over her mouth like a little girl who had just committed an act of pure mischief. Her eyes were wide, and she stood stone still, looking across the room with an expression Sonny could interpret as either elation or something akin to panic. "Well?" he asked.

"Oh, my gosh," Julia managed after a moment. "He did it."

"I don't know whether to leave right now or offer to stay and hold you up, McKenzie."

Finally dropping her hands, Julia took a deep breath and walked quickly to unlock the door once more. "Don't leave. In fact, I'd really like for you to stay. If you hadn't gotten me so relaxed and comfortable, I was going to tell you about it."

The door opened before Julia could explain further. Doss Kincaid was a sight, the left side of his face decidedly swollen and inflamed along the jaw line and in front of his ear, a few droplets of blood just drying on the left shoulder of his white polo shirt. Julia gasped.

"Doss! What happened?"

The grin was slightly crooked, a result of the swelling. "I was ambushed. I'm here to collect my interview. Does it look like I earned it?"

"He hit you?" Julia was astonished.

"I think your words were 'be prepared to run', weren't they, Miss McKenzie? I guess I should have taken it literally."

Remembering Sonny, Julia turned. He was already on his feet, offering his hand. "Sonny Legare," he introduced himself. "Let me get you some ice for that."

"Oh, Sonny, thank you." Julia was collecting herself.

"Doss Kincaid," the reporter responded. "I'd appreciate that."

Pulling a third chair closer to the coffee table, Julia offered it. "Here. Sit. I'm so sorry. This is my fault. Do you think you should see a doctor?"

"No, no. I'm really fine. I don't suppose you have a beer?"

"No, but I can see why you want one. Tell me what happened. I'm still stunned that you really did it."

"Really did what?" Sonny held out a Zip-loc bag filled with several cubes of ice. "I've missed a chapter or two somewhere, haven't I?"

"Doss, my friend Sonny is a detective with the police department. But I've put him to the test, and he's an okay guy anyway." Julia grinned and turned to Sonny. "Doss is a sports reporter for the Dallas newspaper. He came here to do a story about Reg Fallon, and I sort of roped him into something. I offered him everything I can get for him about Reg's situation if he would help me with Quinn's case and keep it to himself."

Sonny was puzzled. "How could he help you with Quinn's case?"

"Isn't it obvious? By taking a punch or two." Doss volunteered. He had not, Julia observed with relief, lost his sense of humor. "This lady sent me over to ask for a little interview with these Howe folks. She set me up, and I fell for it. This girl better be worth it because I'm sure going to have some shiner in the morning."

"She's worth it." Julia looked suddenly serious. "She's pretty and smart and she doesn't deserve for her life to be ruined. She's been through enough."

Doss looked to Sonny for confirmation of Julia's biased opinion, raising an eyebrow in question. "Seems right to me," Sonny said. "Are we off the record here?"

"Why not!" Doss replied.

"I was there when she described the rape. When she was finished, I wanted to put the razor back in her hand and let her go ahead and kill the son-of-a-bitch. Off the record, of course."

"Oh, of course," Doss slurred his retort. "I'd expect nothing else at all!"

Doss's story about Reg Fallon was front and center in the Wednesday morning Post and Courier, accompanied by a file photo of the star athlete shooting a nothing-but-net basket. The by-line was shared, and a local reporter had indeed provided many details to flesh out the story in the wee hours of the morning while Doss nursed his blackening eye and swollen cheek. It was artfully written to draw attention to the fact and seriousness of Reg's injury in a car accident and the impact on his career and to draw attention away from scrutiny of the accident itself. The story had already been picked up by online versions of all the country's sports pages.

The colonel waited in the parking lot at the offices of Comings and Guerry, his car motor running to support the air conditioning and the radio as he sat behind the wheel. The morning news reporter spoke of a new tropical depression forming far to the east, just off the coast of Africa. Those storms often tracked across the warm waters of the Atlantic to strike fear in the hearts of residents on the islands of the Caribbean and make landfall as hurricanes along the coast of the southeastern United States.

George Howe's mind was not on the weather forecast. He was anxious to see Collinsworth Rivers, waiting without an appointment, too anxious to observe the proper protocol. His level of concern had increased fourfold since the previous afternoon. The morning newspaper lay on the seat, read and re-read. He had taken it from the house before Martha saw the front-page story: Reg Fallon. It was getting too close to home, too near touching his family. It was time for damage control, time to put a lid on this situation. George had experience with minefields and recognized one when he saw it.

The morning was hazy and hot, warmth already emanating from the concrete parking lot, the air temperature nearing eighty degrees before eight o'clock. The colonel struggled to remain cool in every way. Where was Collie Rivers this morning? It was his intention to catch the attorney in the parking lot as he arrived, but his patience was taut as he felt his left foot involuntarily tapping on the floorboard. He had, he thought, let this situation ferment far too long, and this was the morning to quash its ripening. His family's peace and place in Charleston was threatened. His wife was distraught. His son, of whom he was so proud, was wounded physically and waiting in an unfortified position for reinforcement or rescue. It was time for the colonel to deliver both.

Charleston had been good to the Howes, the colonel mused. It had, in fact, provided a backdrop for the best years of their lives, a haven where his wife could raise their son while George was away on his various assignments. It was home now, for all of them. Martha had her circle of women friends; George had his golfing cronies, and Mac had the security of a stable place to which he could return at his pleasure, where he could bring his buddies or, one day, some special girl who would add a new dimension to their lives. Martha would like grandchildren; she had made it abundantly clear to Mac over the past two years. A baby, she had cooed, would be the perfect addition to her world.

The baby she had raised in the house along East Bay Street had provided Martha with the purest pleasure of her life. She had, while Mac grew, thoroughly immersed herself in Charleston, making friends for herself and for her son, learning to accept his and her husband's love for life near the ocean. Having grown up in the Midwest, Martha was initially uneasy near the water. She had adjusted, enjoyed owning the house on the prestigious Easy Bay Street, but an appreciation for the sea, its encompassing aura and its moods, had never matured in her. She tried, and she tolerated, but when Martha Howe looked out over the harbor, she still felt the urge to turn away. She was out of her element here, always would be, cowed by the depth and the breadth of the dark water. She lived near the sea because it pleased the men in her life.

The colonel had spent many of his younger years as an Army brat in places like Fort Ord on the California Coast, Patrick Air Force Base in Florida and at the Sigonella military installation on the island of Sicily. He had grown comfortable near the water. Charleston's laid-back atmosphere, its staid old rhythms, had felt right to him since his father had bought the East Bay Street house when he was a youngster. He had taken for granted that he would raise his family there, that regardless of his military travels, Charleston would be home. His friends were "old Charleston"; he fit among them. His son would do the same, and he would not have that future threatened.

His troubled reverie was broken when he recognized Collie Rivers exiting the white BMW convertible several spaces from him in the parking lot. The car was the conservative attorney's only concession to excess. As he stepped out, reaching in to get his briefcase, the colonel turned the key to his ignition and jumped from his own car, intending to waste not a minute before getting Collie's attention.

"Good morning," George began before Collie had even straightened to push the handheld button to lock his car. The younger man turned, finding the colonel almost directly behind him.

"Well, good morning, Colonel Howe." Collie returned the greeting, hiding his surprise. Unaccustomed to being accosted in the parking lot first thing in the morning, Collie nevertheless maintained his professional but amiable composure, revealing nothing of his annoyance at the colonel's unscheduled appearance. "What brings you here this morning?"

"Have you seen the paper?" the colonel asked, holding out the copy he clutched in his hand.

"I have indeed," Collie replied evenly. "I read it over breakfast."

"Everything is getting out of hand here, Collie. The reporter who did the story on Reg Fallon was at my house last night. We've got to put a stop to all this. We've got to do it now."

Collie Rivers studied the colonel's face for a moment, taking in the obvious signs of insomnia and ongoing stress. It was in the eyes and the set of the jaw; it was in his voice, raw and agitated. "Come on in the office, Colonel Howe, and let's talk for a minute. My first appointment isn't due for another hour."

"Thanks," the colonel replied, his tone signaling sincerity and relief. He followed the attorney into the back entrance to the law firm of Comings and Guerry. It was quiet as they passed the kitchen and the conference room, the only sound coming from behind a closed door along the hallway, voices and laughter, discordant in the colonel's mind. There was no laughter in his current world.

Collie turned into his office, placing his briefcase on the desk, hanging his jacket on the back of his chair and offering George a seat. "Let me get us some coffee, Colonel Howe. Black, right?"

"Right. Thanks." George realized that the headache just pushing at the edge of his temples would probably be stopped by a dose of caffeine. He had left home without a single cup. He waited impatiently, his hands clasped tightly and his foot tapping rhythmically until Collie returned.

"Now," Collie began, sitting behind the desk and taking out a pen and yellow legal pad as he took his first sips of the coffee from his black ceramic mug inscribed with the name of the law firm. He looked expectantly across the desk. "What's on your mind?"

"Listen, Collie," George Howe leaned forward intently as he spoke, "my son is military. I'm a retired colonel in the United States Army. My wife has friends here in Charleston. We have to put an end to this foolishness. It can't go on."

"I'm not sure I understand," Collinsworth Rivers replied, offering it as a query.

"That reporter was at the house, Collie, some young punk from Dallas nosing around in our business. He knows too much. There can't be a trial. There can't be any more people who know about this stinking situation. There can't be more articles in the paper. We have to stop this. Now."

Collie's pen was poised above the pad, but his hand had not moved. This was not a substantive disclosure, not the bombshell admission he had almost expected from his client's father. The man was here at his office first thing in the morning, arriving unannounced to intercept him in the parking lot, only to express his discomfort at the possibility of his son's dilemma becoming public knowledge. He was not concerned about prison; he was concerned about reputation. Collie's left eyebrow rose slightly as he digested the nature of George Howe's dismay.

"I'm not sure what you're asking from me, Colonel Howe. You've retained me to defend your son against a rape charge. I'm not trained in public relations, sir. I'm an attorney. I can defend him to the best of my ability; I cannot make the matter go away."

George Howe was undeterred, his voice rising a level. "She's the one who should be behind bars right now. Why should we be sitting here having this conversation when it's the girl who broke into my house and nearly killed my son? Why is she walking the streets while my son is still recovering from what she did? Why is his good name, and mine, for that matter, on the line because of some hair-brained accusation she trumped up to justify her actions? This is all preposterous, and you're supposed to make it go away. Isn't that what I'm paying you for? I've been as patient as I can, but if you can't take care of this thing, I'll have to go back to Mendel and ask him to find us someone who can."

Collie saw that George Howe was not in a circumspect frame of mind on this morning. "I understand your concern, Colonel Howe," he said. "Maybe we should check to see if Mendel is in his office yet this morning." Without hesitation, he pushed the button on his intercom to speak to the receptionist.

"Yes, Mr. Rivers," the voice responded.

"Stephanie, is Mr. Comings in yet this morning?"

"Let me check, Mr. Rivers."

There was a brief silence, and then the pleasant feminine voice: "He's in, Mr. Rivers. Would you like me to send him over?"

"Yes, please, Steph," Collie responded. "Thank you." Looking across the desk, he maintained a calm demeanor with the colonel. "Let's see what Mendel has to say, shall we?"

George sat back in his chair, making a concerted effort to ease his posture and his attitude. He was as braced as a soldier on the battlefield, an apt reflection of his state of mind. The door opened, and Mendel Comings poked his head through the space, a questioning look in his eyes.

"Good morning, gentlemen," he greeted them with a voice full of warmth and depth. "How can I be of service this fine morning?"

Collie kept his seat as George rose to shake Mendel's hand, resettling into the next chair to make space for the elder attorney. "Thanks for coming over, Mendel," Collie expressed his gratitude. "We were just discussing Colonel Howe's concern over his son's case. Why don't you tell Mendel what you've just told me," he offered, opening the way for George.

Sighing deeply, the colonel leaned forward again, conveying the clear impression he felt he could make Mendel Comings understand his position by speaking clearly and close, his eyes holding those of the attorney. His tone was urgent, his words coming slowly and carefully chosen.

"Mendel, our lives can't hold up in this pressure cooker for much longer. Martha is falling apart. Mac slugged a reporter who got past me into our house last night. I don't know where the guy got his information, but I think it came directly from the Fallon boy. Now there's the article in this morning's paper, and that's bound to lead to more questions and poking around in our lives by people who have no business there. I know you've gotten the court's records kept private until Friday, but then what, Mendel? Then are we all going to be fair game? Is everything going to come out—this ridiculous rape charge, the real nature of Mac's injury, the whole nasty mess exposed for the world to gossip over? Is that what's coming?"

Mendel thought before responding. Always difficult to read by his expression, the attorney was able to maintain a poker face in most situations, revealing nothing of his thoughts until he spoke. "There was no mention of your family or the Ravenel girl in the newspaper, George. The article was all about Reg Fallon getting hurt, basically a sports story."

"It's just a matter of time," the colonel repeated with urgency. "I just told you that reporter was in my home last evening. If those people are hell bent on sniffing around, they'll manage to find something to print, even where nothing exists."

"It seems to me, George, that your chief concern here is that the whole matter resolve itself without further public knowledge." Though it was a statement, he looked to George for confirmation before proceeding.

George confirmed the assumption immediately. "Yes, Mendel. Is that possible?" The strain on his face manifested itself in the tightness of his jaw, the lines seemingly imbedded in his forehead, the intensity in his eyes. He was simply a father now, intent on protecting his only son.

"We're not talking about a civil matter that can be dropped or settled between two private parties, George. Each of the charges—the rape and the attack on Mac—is now a criminal matter deposited squarely in the hands of the State of South Carolina. Even if the parties did not wish to proceed, the State does not simply let serious charges go. Hearings are scheduled on both matters. We don't have the right under law to now say 'just forget it'."

"Is there no way out?" George asked, his voice dismal.

"Collie is spending considerable time with Mac tomorrow, George." Mendel's voice was quiet but firm. "He's as good a lawyer as Mac will find, but he's not a magician. "It's past the time when anyone can just wish this away." Collie's intercom interrupted. "Yes, Steph," he answered, taking his eyes away from the colonel's face.

"There's a call for Colonel Howe that I thought I should put through, Mr. Rivers. It's on line three."

"Sure, thanks. He can take it in here." Collie punched a button and handed the telephone receiver across the desk to George Howe.

"Yes?" George spoke into the receiver, surprised and taken aback that he would receive a call at the attorney's office. No one knew he was here except his son. He listened, his eyes narrowing and his brows increasing their furrow. "I'll be right there, Mac," he said shortly, handing back the receiver and bumping the chair awkwardly aside in his haste to turn toward the door.

"It's Martha," he said. "The ambulance is taking her to the hospital." And he was gone.

Willa Fallon had become familiar with the chapel at Roper Hospital, accustomed to stopping on her way to see Reg, like this morning, or on her way home. She was more comfortable in a pew at her own Church, but her prayers would be heard, she knew, just as clearly from here.

She sat with her hands folded neatly and her head bowed.

"You been good to me, Lawd, so good, and I mean no disrespect for whatever plan the Almighty have for me an' my Reggie. I know you love him, Lawd, and I know Your hand be on him. But he be sufferin' so. He cry in the night, Lawd; I know he does. It wasn't about the fame or the money. He just always thought he'd be playin' ball, and the disappointment is breakin' his heart. I'm not askin' for me. I'm askin' if you can't jes' make one more miracle like you done so often in my life. Let my heart break, Lawd, but please reach down and help my Reggie."

She had spoken aloud, softly, her words barely audible in the little chapel. Sounds in the hospital were muffled here, the bustling muted. Willa was alone with her thoughts and her faith.

Reg's telephone had been ringing since seven o'clock when the switchboard was allowed to put through calls to patient rooms, a result of the Post and Courier story. It had been a non-stop conversation with sports reporters from across the country, both television and print media. The latest call, however, was different. It was almost ten o'clock, and Weldon Scott had made this call to Reg as soon as he finished conferring with the Mavericks' owner over the morning newspaper.

"Reg, it's Weldon," he started.

"Hey, Mr. Scott. How's it going?"

"I've read the morning paper. You're back on the front page, young man."

"I sure would like to change the story, Mr. Scott."

"I sure would like to help you, Reg, and that's the reason for my call. I've been talking to Mark Cuban this morning, and we have a proposition for you."

"A proposition? What's that, Mr. Scott? I suppose you want to enter me in the slam dunk competition."

Weldon Scott ignored the remark, seeing no point in wallowing with Reg Fallon in the pool of impossibilities that now faced him. "The Mavericks want to offer you a job, Reg. I'd like you to come to work as my assistant as soon as you're able to get here." Scott had not known what reaction to expect, but he had decided to lay out the offer bluntly and without preamble. It was not, he knew, the dream career path Reg had expected, but it was an alternative he hoped the young man would consider. He could be close to the sport he loved. Would that be too painful? Weldon did not know the answer.

Reg was stunned, not speaking immediately.

"Reg?"

"Yeah." He was trying to jump in his mind from the cliff where he'd been hanging to the spot where Mr. Scott spoke, holding what he meant to be a net.

"Mr. Scott, I'm not looking for you or anyone else to give me a job because you feel sorry for me. You know I can't play ball. What use would I be to you there now? I don't mean to be ungrateful, but no, thanks."

"This is not an offer we're making out of pity, Reg," Scott returned. "I've talked to the coaches and the guys around me here in the office. They all agree that you would be an invaluable addition to our humble little group. We're not athletes like you, but we all love the game. You not only love the game, but you've been there. You understand it. You've held the ball and held your breath watching it arc toward that perfect nothing-but-net shot from halfway down the court. You feel it in your bones and know it in your head. Any team in the league would be fortunate to have a guy like you in the front office, and I'm surprised you haven't already been called by half a dozen of them. I was knocking myself up the side of my head for not thinking of it sooner. Mark was all in as soon as I brought it up."

"I never intended to sit behind a desk, Mr. Scott. I don't know if I could handle being that close and yet that far away. Do you know what I mean?"

"All I'm asking is that you give it some thought," Weldon Scott responded. "I know it seems out of left field, but I had to give it a shot before someone else in the league beat me to it. I know we'd get along famously, and the office next to mine has been vacant since Ted Amosson left last spring. I just hadn't found the right person. I need someone who can relate to the players and the coaches and help me with a little PR work. I know you'd rather be shooting hoops, but this is an opportunity to be close to the game and earn, if I do say so, a good salary that would help buy your mama a nice house for you to visit. I'm holding out whatever carrot might work here. Are you turning me down?"

There was a long pause, during which Weldon Scott realized he sincerely hoped this talented young man would take the offer. "Can I get back to you, Mr. Scott?"

"I'd like nothing better, Reg. We're talking a couple of hundred thousand a year here, more or less. And the fringe benefits are pretty good: expense account, hanging with the social elite in Dallas, good golf, lots of pretty Texas girls. It's not a bad gig."

"Thank you, Mr. Scott. I just have to give it some thought. The future has been a total blur since I woke up here hooked up to machines."

"I understand completely. Just don't give up hope, Reg. This job might not be your dream, but it might be a good place to land until you get your bearings. It can be pretty damned entertaining around here. And who knows? You might just like it."

"I'm so surprised I can't even think of questions, Mr. Scott, but I'll call you back later today or tomorrow, and I'm sure I'll have some questions then."

"Okay, Reg. I'll be waiting to hear from you. And it was good talking to you, kid. I sure wouldn't mind having you around."

"Thanks again, Mr. Scott."

Alone in the room, Reg Fallon was left with the whirling thoughts planted by Weldon Scott's offer. Of all the options he had considered, this was not among them. Did he want to be so close to the game he loved and now could not play? He did not have the answer. He wanted to talk about it. He wanted his mother. He didn't know she was just downstairs, talking to God.

117

George Howe had remained in good physical condition, so he was only slightly winded after running across the parking lot at the hospital, into the building and down the corridor leading to the emergency entrance. He assumed that his wife would still be there where the ambulance had delivered her, and that Mac would be with her. His thoughts were racing and jumbled as he trotted across the shiny tile floor and into the bright, antiseptic environment that was all too familiar since Mac's very recent hospital stay.

What, he wondered for the hundredth time, could have happened to Martha? Had she had a more serious one of her fainting spells? Surely not a heart attack or a stroke, he prayed, though the stress of Mac's injury and the ensuing drama had taken its inevitable toll, sapping her strength and making her seem fragile and older than her years in the past three days. George berated himself for not taking Martha's state of mind more seriously. He should somehow have seen what was coming and headed it off, shielding his wife from harm. And he should surely have forbidden her visit with Rose Pinckney or tagging along to the police station.

"Dad," Mac's voice reached him as soon as he rounded the corner into the emergency waiting area.

"Mac," the colonel responded, rushing to his son's side. "What happened?" he asked immediately. "Is your mother alright?"

"I don't know, Dad. Mom made breakfast for me, and then it was so quiet in the house that I went looking for her. She was on the bed, and I didn't try to wake her the first time. But then it just didn't seem right, and when I went back to ask if she was feeling okay, I knew something was wrong. She was so white, and she was barely breathing. I couldn't wake her, so I called nine one one."

"Thank God you were there, son," the colonel said. "Let's just thank God that you were there."

"I should have tried to wake her the first time, Dad," Mac almost whispered. "Mom never naps. But I know this whole mess is hard on her, and I just wanted to let her rest."

"It's okay, son," George reassured his son again. "Where is she now? Can we go in there?"

"They keep telling me I have to wait here. It's been more than an hour."

"Let me see what I can find out." The colonel grasped at the chance to feel less helpless. Glancing around the waiting area, he walked to the nurses' station.

"Excuse me," he said to the young woman in flowered scrubs at the reception window. She smiled, accustomed to constant interruption by a flow of anxious relatives of the emergency room patients.

"Yes, sir. How can I help you?"

"My wife is here somewhere," he offered. "Martha Howe. Can you tell me what's going on?"

The nurse lifted two files before stopping at the third. "Mrs. Howe?" she asked.

"That's right. She's my wife."

"Yes, sir. She's being treated right now, and I can only tell you that the doctor will be out to talk with you as soon as he can break away."

"Can't my son and I go back to her?"

"I'm sorry, sir. The doctors are with her, and you wouldn't want to be in the way when all their attention is on your wife. She's in good hands, and the doctor will update you as soon as he feels he can." It was a speech she made with empathy in her voice, even though she made it twenty-five times during a normal shift.

"Can you tell me what's the matter with her?"

"I don't know that, sir," the nurse replied. "I'm certain they're running all the tests right now. Would you like something to drink while you wait? There's coffee and tea right around the corner with the soda machines."

"Thanks," the colonel answered. "Just make sure they tell us how she's doing as soon as they can."

Doors opened almost simultaneously at opposite ends of the waiting area. Mendel Comings strode through one and a doctor through the other. All eyes went to the doctor.

"Are you folks here with Mrs. Howe?" All the others in the waiting area were sitting.

"Is she all right?" the colonel asked anxiously, rushing to stand in front of the young doctor. "Can we see her?"

"Let's sit down here so I can tell you what we know so far." The doctor guided the colonel and his son to a grouping of chairs around a table strewn with magazines.

"May I join you?" Mendel asked, coming to stand behind the colonel's seat, his hand resting lightly on the other man's shoulder.

"Thanks, Mr. Comings." It was Mac, but his eyes were fixed on the doctor, and both his face and the colonel's were intent on the question that hung perpetually in the air of this room. The doctor addressed it.

"I'm Doctor Moore, and I'd rather you wait a little while longer to go in to see her. We're still assessing her, and I wouldn't expect her to regain consciousness for a while yet."

"She's not conscious?" The colonel's voice was surprised and fearful. "Why is she not conscious?"

"It was a powerful amount of the drug she ingested, sir. We pumped out as much as we could, but her system had already absorbed a good deal, more than I would like. There's nothing to be done now but wait."

"Drug?" the colonel asked blankly.

"I'm sorry, sir; I thought you knew. Mrs. Howe's coma was caused by an overdose of her prescription medication for anxiety. The paramedics brought the bottle that was beside her on the bed. It was filled only a couple of days ago. The bottle was empty."

Mendel looked across at the chagrin on Mac's face. Mac looked at the bewilderment in his father's eyes. Moments passed, and the doctor rose from his chair. "I need to get back to her, gentlemen," he said. "I'll keep you informed.

118

Waiting had become a fact of life for Quinn. She waited for the telephone to ring, for more developments in her fast-changing life, for something out of her control to jolt her once again. Rose had cajoled her to sit outside in the garden this morning behind the old East Bay Street house. It was a steamy Charleston morning, but Rose thought Quinn could use some color in her cheeks. Pallor did not become her, Rose said, and a little southern sun would do them both good. There were flowers to cut, and they could keep their hands busy, she thought, until Julia called for them to come.

The sun was warm on her skin, Quinn thought, recalling all the sunny days she had spent with Rose here and at the beach house. They had been golden days, full of carefree play and delightful discoveries. Here in the garden she had dug and learned to plant, felt the squiggle of earthworms, touched the dew on a newly-opened blossom. There had been such peace in those days. They were idyllic, Quinn thought now, free of worry or concern, safety taken for granted because Rose was there. Rose had always been there, had been her refuge and her security since they met seventeen years earlier.

The ringing telephone interrupted, startling Rose so that she nicked the knuckle of her left thumb with the pruner, wincing as the blood appeared. "You don't have to get it, dear," she said as Quinn jumped to get the portable phone from the kitchen. "If it's important, they'll leave us a message."

But Quinn was on her feet and halfway up the steps before Rose's sentence was complete. "No, I've got it, Grams." She was always slightly astir with nervous energy these days, a far cry from the laid-back young woman of earlier in the summer when her whole focus had been on the new apartment and starting to teach in the fall.

Phone receiver to her ear, she descended the steps more gingerly, listening. "Yes, of course we'll come. We've been waiting."

119

Julia had barely hung the receiver on the hook when her bell tinkled, announcing Sonny. "I thought it was time for me to come by for my daily dose of excitement, McKenzie. My life is boring compared to yours, so I hope you don't mind my living vicariously through you."

"Very funny," Julia replied, knowing as she spoke that she had come to enjoy Sonny's sense of humor. "And I hope you don't mind my living so close to the edge that I might need a stable, boring tug back to ground now and then."

"Are you insinuating that I'm stable and boring?"

"Oh." Julia realized what she had said. "I meant it in the most complimentary and admiring way."

"Nice recovery, but I think I should be deeply wounded. I'm gonna have to work on being much less predictable, more like you."

"I'm not predictable?"

"McKenzie, I haven't been able to predict a single thing you've done or said since we met. You keep me so off balance that I don't currently know my way anywhere except to your door."

The flirting again. Julia liked it. It was certainly a welcome relief from the tension building as she awaited the arrival of Rose and Quinn, their dependence on her weighing heavily.

"What's in the bag?"

Sonny had stopped by the Broad Street Deli and picked up one pastrami on rye and one chicken salad on white bread, two bags of chips and two whole, fat dill pickles. "It's lunch," he announced, holding the bag out in front of him. "Can't blame a guy for coming prepared, can you?"

"Absolutely not, especially when I'm famished." Julia realized that she was. "Let's go in the library and use the table. May I use you as a sounding board?"

Sonny raised an eyebrow, wondering how much could have developed since only the night before. He had read Doss Kincaid's piece in the morning paper. Surely a fist to the jaw of the young reporter enlisted by Julia to entice the threat of publicity was enough drama for one twenty-four-hour period, especially with the preliminary hearing now fewer than forty-eight hours away.

"Do tell," he inquired curiously, spreading the contents of the white paper bag on the library table as Julia sat down. "Like I said, I'm braced every day for whatever spice you can bring to my dull little life."

"Okay, enough. Let's eat. I've just called Quinn and asked her to come over here as soon as she can."

"Really?" Sonny emptied the bag. "Is this routine preparation for Friday?"

"Yes," Julia responded, folding the paper wrapping back on the chicken salad for her first bite. "although nothing in this case has been routine for me. No sense thinking we should start now, is there?"

"I guess not."

Julia took a bite and chewed, her sigh indicating that the sandwich was satisfying. Sonny started on the pastrami, waiting patiently for further disclosures as he opened the two bags of chips, pointing the mouth of one bag toward Julia.

"No matter how hard I try, I can't figure out how to manage this hearing on Friday morning."

Sonny chewed before responding. "What do you mean exactly?"

"It's the picture I have in my head of that moment when Quinn and Mac are in the courtroom at the same time. I can't fathom the effect on her, and I don't know how to prepare her for it. Can you imagine it, Sonny"

"I'd rather not," he replied immediately.

"There have been all sorts of attempts over time to protect rape victims from this, but the right to face one's accuser prevails. I would walk through hot coals to save her from it."

"Need I remind you that you're already doing that, McKenzie?" Sonny asked with a wry smile. "After Friday, the details of this whole mess will come out, right?"

"I'm assuming so."

"There you'll be, smack dab in the middle of the front page of the Post and Courier going toe to toe with the firm of Comings and Guerry. If you can't feel the heat now, just wait until this goes to trial.

Do you remember way back when you came storming into the station that first night? I had the good sense and foresight to warn you away even then."

"Yes, you did. I remember it clearly."

"You were on a mission for Willa Fallon. And the nightmare was just beginning for Reg."

Julia studied Sonny's face, looking for signs that he still felt responsible in some part for Reg Fallon's accident. "You can't let that go, can you?" she asked, shaking her head. "If you had found Reg that night yourself, would anything be different? Wouldn't you have put him in the police car and brought him in for questioning?"

"I don't know. I've been over and over it."

"And there you are with your own hot coals, Detective. We're all going to have scars, aren't we?"

"Let's lighten up before we cause indigestion." Sonny had not meant to bring Julia down. "You're supposed to be the rock when your client gets here. You can remind her that this is just a passage to next summer when this mess will be a memory."

"I can't remember when I've been quite so excited at the prospect of something."

"Now that hurts me, McKenzie." Sonny creased his brows and swallowed so that he could poke out his lower lip in a little-boy pout.

"What?" Julia was perplexed.

"Well, McKenzie, I was sort of hoping you were excited by the prospect of our first real kiss. I know I'm just a lowly Southern cop with rough edges, but I've been preoccupied with that possibility since you walked through the door that night pretending to be a criminal lawyer."

"Pretending?" Julia retorted quickly. "Pretending to be a criminal lawyer?"

"And what about the kissing part?" Sonny continued. "Didn't you hear the part where I've been waiting for you to kiss me?"

Julia's expression lightened, a half-smile forming as she forced her own lower lip forward. "Detective, if I was pretending to be a criminal lawyer, I can probably pretend just as well that I'm not interested in kissing."

She made that sincere expression with her eyes, one that would come from a two-year-old girl with blonde hair and crystal-blue eyes who could without guile deny that there were still remnants of the chocolate chip cookies at the corner of her mouth. "Besides, I was quite sure you'd have kissed me by now if you really wanted to."

"You don't say," Sonny smiled, mock surprise in his voice. "That little bit of information might just keep me going for another day or two."

<h2 style="text-align:center">120</h2>

Quinn helped Rose from the passenger side of her little Volkswagen. They had found a parking space at a meter just half a block from Julia's office, and Rose insisted she could easily walk that distance. Quinn, had she been alone, would have run down the sun-dappled sidewalk in search of a speedy cure for her anxiety. How, she wondered, could she survive the next few days?

"Are you okay, Grams?" she asked, steadying Rose on the side opposite the walking cane.

"I'm just fine." Rose adjusted her balance with the cane and looked down the street, getting her bearings. They covered the half block slowly, and Quinn stepped ahead to push open the door, linking her arm through Rose's as she stepped up into Julia's waiting area. Sonny and Julia looked up, just finishing the sandwiches and the light-hearted banter which felt to Julia like the flirting she had not experienced since Jack.

Sonny got up immediately, crumpling his sandwich wrapping into a ball, brushing crumbs from the library table with his napkin into the paper bag. "We'll have to continue this conversation later, McKenzie," he said, sounding suddenly very professional.

Rose touched Sonny's arm as they passed. "It's very good to see you, young man," she said. "And I'm pleased to see you keeping such good company."

Quinn barely heard, but Sonny winked, smiling. "I try, Miss Rose. And I must agree that Julia McKenzie is mighty fine company. I'm trying to ingratiate myself so she'll let me keep dropping by."

Rose looked across the room as Julia patted her hands dry with a paper towel, refreshed after the pleasant break for lunch. "I'll put in a good word for you," she said.

"I'd appreciate that," Sonny replied, and smiled broadly at Julia as he closed the door behind him.

Quinn had remained tense, oblivious to the pleasantries and fixed upon steeling herself against events tumbling one upon the heels of another, braced for whatever might happen next. She looked questioningly at Julia, who waved them into her office. "I'll be right there," she assured them. "Would you like something to drink?"

"Nothing for me, thanks," Quinn answered. "How about you, Grams?"

"I'm fine."

Julia began talking even as the three women settled into their chairs around her desk, noting Quinn's obvious anxiety. "Please excuse the mess I've made on this table." She noted that her piles had migrated from one end of the table to the seat of one chair and onto the floor as well.

"Your office is lovely, Julia," Rose reassured. "You've done such a good job with it. "It's a peaceful little spot just before you burst onto Broad Street where every second door used to be a law office."

"So I hear," Julia responded, noting Quinn's tense posture.

"It's an art gallery now, but the Rosen boys had their offices right there at the corner on Broad Street years ago," Rose continued, making small talk. "Their daddy was a force to be reckoned with in those days. And Joe Riley was just a young whippersnapper with big ideas. The karma is good here."

"Let's count on that karma." Julia replied. The prospect of confronting MacArthur Howe hung over the room like a fog. "We have to address the most stressful part of Friday's hearing, don't we?" She directed the question to Quinn.

Tears kept barely at bay these days ran slowly down Quinn's cheeks, her crying soundless. Rose handed her a handkerchief and moved her chair closer.

"I can't think of an easy way to prepare for the courtroom where we'll walk into the same room with Mac." Julia looked directly at Quinn, gauging what strength was left in her spirit. "I hope you were helped as much as I was by talking with Miranda McQuaid. She's a wonder and a wealth of just the understanding we both need. Celia is planning to spend the night with the three of you tonight after she picks up Miranda at the airport. Has she told you? The four of you are going to build a protective bubble around Quinn with the light of a rainbow and the concrete strength of our collective faith."

121

Willa Fallon had to park several blocks down Broad Street, near the corner with Orange. Tourists took much of the parking in the spring and summer. Her bulky old Chevy was difficult to maneuver into a parking spot parallel to the sidewalk, but she had learned to do it. It would do her good, she thought, to walk a little, using the time to let her gratitude sink through her pores and down into her very bones. An involuntary smile formed as she locked the car and fished in her pocketbook, her pudgy fingers feeling for quarters to feed the meter. She was thankful for the coins, for the shade along this side of Broad Street, for the afternoon breeze that touched her cheeks and helped evaporate the perspiration trickling down her neck and watering the flowers on her blouse. Reggie was alive. He was not in a wheelchair. And she had seen him smile.

Willa hoped to find Julia in her office. She would enlist her help encouraging Reggie to take the job offer extended just this morning by Weldon Scott. Willa might not, she conceded to herself, always recognize the answers to her prayers. Sometimes the manna from heaven snuck by her unacknowledged, which was why she always offered a blanket thanks in her daily prayers lest God think her ungrateful for a blessing that had passed unnoticed. But Willa thoroughly grasped this morning's blessing; Weldon Scott was the messenger. God must have started working on it before she even left the chapel, she thought, feeling the smile on her face and wishing good will on each of those she met on the Broad Street sidewalk.

Glancing into the shady park as she passed City Hall, Willa was surprised to see a familiar face, though in her euphoria it took her a moment to place it. "Mr. Kincaid," she exclaimed in greeting, turning toward the bench where he sat just inside the gate. "I declare you done foun' one of Charleston's choice little spots."

Looking up, Doss smiled and rose from his seat where he had been watching the pigeons for more than an hour, taking in the sultry beauty of a quiet park in the midst of this bustling southern city, absorbing the sights and sounds as tourists mixed with local lawyers on this historic corner and the horse-drawn carriages blended past and present in a way he sensed could only be done in Charleston.

"Ms. Fallon," he said, surprised as well.

"Lawd a-mighty, what done happen to you?" Willa drew back at the sight of the young reporter's face, his left eye still puffy and turning shades of purple and blue.

Doss touched his cheek gingerly, needing no reminder of his still-painful injury. "I had a little encounter with someone's fist," he answered, grinning as he tried to brush off discussion of his meeting with MacArthur Howe. "It's better now. How's Reg doing? I'm going by to see him later."

"Mr. Kincaid," Willa was nearly bursting with the news, "that nice Mister Scott done call him this mornin' and ask him to come to work in Dallas. He be sittin' at a desk an' not playin' ball, you know, but it be a good thing, Mr. Kincaid, a very good thing. I'm a'goin' to tell Miss Julia about it right now."

"You're going to Julia McKenzie's office?"

"I think she be of a mind to help me talk good to Reggie about this job. He don't know what to think. I know it do him good to have somethin' to fill his head while his body heal up."

"May I walk with you?" Doss asked. "I should probably say goodbye to Miss McKenzie before I head back to Dallas."

"You jes' come right on with me, Mr. Kincaid. And if you goin' down to see my Reggie, I'd be mighty beholden if you speak up for Mr. Scott and the job he done offer Reggie." She looked sideways imploringly at Doss, hoping to enlist every ally to help bring Reggie out of his despair and back to believing that life offered him a future.

"You know I'll do everything I can, Ms. Fallon. In fact, I'll lean on him hard. I'd love to have Reg in Dallas."

Realizing that his statement was very true, Doss described to Willa some of the places in his hometown where he would like to take her son, some of the things they could enjoy together, as they walked the rest of the way to Julia's office. It occurred to Doss that he and Reg Fallon would quite likely be good friends if both were in Dallas. He would enjoy playing local guide to the young basketball star, sharing his favorite hangouts, introducing him to attractive young women with whom Doss was acquainted. They spoke the same language; it had been apparent when they talked at the hospital before Doss became more deeply involved in the tangle of unlikely events that had so impacted Reg's life and career.

"Reg doesn't have a serious girlfriend, does he?" Doss presumed to ask.

"He don't, for sure, Mr. Kincaid, and I sure 'nuf wish he did. I would dearly love for some special girl to be a-makin' over him right now."

"I've been looking for that myself, Ms. Fallon," Doss grinned. "Maybe Reg and I could do a little looking together. Of course you'd have to come to Dallas now and then to keep tabs on us. And then I could introduce you to my mother."

"I'm sure I'd like that," Willa nodded, knowing that she would.

The welcome mat on Julia's step greeted them with its inlay of Carolina jasmine vines and yellow trumpet flowers so common to the Lowcountry and its woodlands. Celia had given it to her the day she opened her office. The oak door swung in as Doss pressed its handle, and he and Willa were embraced by a rush of cool, the air-conditioned oasis leaking out into the humid summer heat.

They were unexpected, and the three women deep in conversation at Julia's library table were obviously startled. The door was open between the library and the waiting area, and Doss immediately noted that one of the women at the table was the blonde who had caught his attention in this office a couple of days before. Her eyes, though now filled with tears which streaked down her face, were as blue as he remembered, her blonde hair wrapped into a loose knot at the nape of her delicate neck and tied with a ribbon. Whatever the legal trouble, it was causing her to cry. A box of tissues sat on the table in front of her, and something in Doss wanted to take her in his arms and comfort her.

"We should have called, Miss McKenzie," Doss acknowledged immediately, both he and Willa feeling as though they had intruded upon a private discussion. Julia wished she had closed the library door. Her usual prudent tendencies had been somewhat derailed by Sonny's visit.

"Excuse me," Quinn whispered, pushing back her chair and the wisps of hair around her face. "I think I might need to go to the powder room and regroup for a minute or two."

"Are you all right, dear?" Rose asked quickly. "Do you want me to come with you?"

"I'll be fine, Grams." Quinn responded. She stepped behind Julia's chair and walked through the door where the library joined the waiting area, not meeting the eyes of the young man but looking up at Willa Fallon. "How's Reg?" she asked quietly.

"He be doin' better, sweet girl. I got good news about Reggie. You dry them tears an' I'll tell you. God be good to us, Miss Quinn, and He goin' take care of you too." The stocky black woman shook her head with certainty, feeling her empathy and faith expand and encircle the young woman even as she curbed the impulse to take her in her arms.

Quinn reached out to touch Willa's hand before she disappeared into the bathroom, closing the door softly behind her.

Doss looked puzzled. "Did you call her 'Quinn'?" he asked, looking down at Willa.

"She be Reggie's friend since they kids," Willa confirmed. "She sho' don' deserve the mess she be in now." Looking through the doorway, she smiled at Rose. "I'm glad to see you. And you, too, Miss Julia. I'm sorry we jes' bust in here like that. I guess I was jes' so excited today that I done forget my manners altogether."

"Come here and sit down, Willa. Tell us what's happened with that boy of yours." Rose assumed for Julia and Quinn that Willa was welcome in the room and the conversation. She did not recognize the young man.

Willa moved to sit down at the table beside Rose, and Doss stood tentatively, not certain what he should do. Like Willa, he realized he had acted spontaneously in coming to Julia's office unannounced. He was accustomed, as a brash reporter, to placing himself where he was sometimes unwelcome, but here he felt suddenly awkward and inept, unsure whether to excuse himself quickly or wait for one more look at the pretty blonde girl who had once again caught his eye and his attention.

Julia came to his rescue. "Doss, come on in and meet one of the most special people in Charleston." Julia stood up and smiled, making Doss feel promptly more at ease. "Miss Rose, this is my friend Doss Kincaid. Doss, meet Rose Pinckney."

Rose allowed her attention to stray temporarily from Willa and smiled across the table, her eyes wrinkling at their corners. "Mr. Kincaid," she acknowledged him rather formally, wondering who he was and why she could not place him.

"Doss is visiting from Dallas. He's a reporter for the Morning News, and he wrote the story about Reg that was in our newspaper yesterday morning. He also got to know MacArthur Howe briefly on Tuesday evening; thus the black eye." Julia knew she had now piqued Rose's curiosity.

"Is that so?" Rose asked immediately, the expression in her eyes growing attentive to Doss. "How is a reporter from Dallas connected to someone like MacArthur Howe?"

"Well, I'm happy to say that we have no connection at all, the only one being his fist with my cheek. I'd call our only meeting brief, enlightening and distinctly unpleasant." Doss grinned, a punctuation to his understatement.

"And this is my friend Quinn Ravenel," Julia continued, turning to the door as Quinn returned.

Quinn remembered him. They had passed in Julia's office before. Doss remembered too. But this was the girl around whom all the fuss revolved? This was the girl for whom he had finessed his way into the Howes' family room? Pieces were quickly falling into place. For her story, he now had a black eye? He would gladly do it again, he thought. She exuded a gentle warmth. She was the rape victim, but she seemed for all the world a normal, appealing young woman. Her scars were invisible.

"Reg told me you've known him since you were kids," he alleged, thinking on his feet. "Would you consider helping me fill in some background for my article about him? I'll bet my editor would extend my stay for that. I've already picked his mother's brain. I sure would be grateful if you could spare me just an hour or so. And your lawyer might even vouch for me." He looked imploringly to Julia.

"Reg might appreciate you helping this guy, Quinn. One day I'll tell you how much he's grown on me."

122

The Ben Sawyer Bridge opened for boats at any hour, either a symptom of Southern shortcoming or a testament to the alchemy of a consummate Southern sanctuary where time proceeds at a pace akin to the native drawl, punctuated by open drawbridges and steeped to saturation in the sweet scent of pluff mud and rich, resonant history. Julia loved the Ben Sawyer, not only because there she was almost home but because there was something especially picturesque and seductive about the panorama, something that drew her to linger and appreciate, to place herself on the canvas and dream.

Julia's day had been replete with all the elements of a steamy Southern novel: the tension of Quinn's upcoming testimony, drama for both Reg and Quinn in their respective plights, and even a hint of romance as she was further drawn to Sonny Legare--romance or comic relief, she thought with a smile as she extended her legs from the open car door and walked once again to place her elbows on the rail of the old drawbridge to enjoy another sunset over the Charleston skyline. How, she wondered again, could nature produce one after another of these exquisite watercolors on the dusk sky, each of them tinted differently and drawn over the earth as though elicited from the imagination of a celestial artist with infinite palette and sublime brush stroke.

The sailboat responsible for opening the bridge had passed and slipped gently down the Intracoastal Waterway away from the city. Its white sails stood out clear and clean against the deep, opaque blue of the water. Below, wading in the marsh grass where receding tide was leaving edible creatures, a heron stalked gingerly about so as not to step on the choices which were his dinner. This was peace at its finest, Julia sighed, where nature was clearly supreme. She breathed deeply of the pungent marsh air and thanked life and Celia for bringing her here.

The cellular telephone rang in her pocket, reminding Julia that she was not alone in the world or immune from intrusion as long as she carried it. Not recognizing the number displayed, she swiped to answer. "This is Julia."

"This is Reg Fallon, Miss McKenzie. I got this number from your machine at the office. I hope it's okay that I used it."

"Of course it's okay, Reg. You're quite probably the only celebrity client I'll ever have."

"I'm hardly a celebrity, Miss McKenzie, but I do need your advice again."

Julia chose not to disclose that Willa Fallon had told her earlier of the Mavericks' offer to Reg, letting him instead broach it as he wished. "I could come by the hospital first thing in the morning, Reg. Would that be soon enough for us to talk?"

"That's great. I'll be waiting to see you."

"And I'm looking forward to it, Reg. Take care." Julia had almost replaced the phone in her pocket when it rang again, startling her as it sounded and vibrated in her hand. Relieved she did not drop it into the water below, she answered again.

"Are you in the middle of something, McKenzie?" Sonny's voice was a pleasant surprise.

"Yes, as a matter of fact, I'm standing in the middle of the Ben Sawyer Bridge watching a spectacular sunset. How about you?"

There was a momentary pause. "You're not really in the middle of the bridge, are you?"

"Yes, I am. It's about the fifteenth time I've parked my car at the foot of the bridge and walked up here to look over the world as seen from the seventeenth post along the rail." She waited for a response.

"You've counted the posts?"

"Yeah, and this one is mine. I feel about this post like one of the pelicans must feel when he perches on his favorite piling."

"What about the traffic? You're just standing there while the cars go by?"

"Are there cars?" Julia asked with tongue in cheek. "I didn't notice."

"If I'd known you were this desperate for entertainment, we could have gone to see a movie."

"No movie could compare with this, Sonny. The sun is setting over the city, and it almost takes my breath away as the colors change and mute and tint the clouds."

"Don't get hit by a car, will you, McKenzie? I know it's beautiful over there, but I'm growing too fond of you to lose you to a reckless driver."

Julia immediately thought of the way in which Sonny had lost his wife, wanting to reassure him even as she basked in his real concern. "I'm being very careful; I promise. Now what's up with you?"

"I couldn't help wondering about the rest of your day. You always leave me hanging, McKenzie. Is that part your strategy to keep me coming back for more?"

"Detective, you seem to keep coming back, and I don't even have a strategy."

"You obviously don't need one. I'm calling you after hours for the feeblest of reasons while you're standing on a drawbridge. Maybe I need a movie and a beer."

"If I weren't totally exhausted, I might be tempted to come back to town just for that beer. Can we do it soon?"

"You know that I'm putty in your hands, McKenzie. Any time you're free, I'll come running."

Julia laughed aloud. "That sounds so pathetic it's almost believable."

"Believe it. Wanna test me?"

"I think I'll save that test for when I'm up to it. I just had a call from Reg Fallon. I'm going to see him first thing in the morning. He wants to talk about a job offer from the Mavericks to work as Weldon Scott's assistant."

"Wow. That's a great option for the kid." Sonny sounded suddenly serious. "I'd sure like to see something wonderful happen for him."

"Let's keep our fingers crossed," Julia replied.

"Okay, then, McKenzie, I'll let you get on home and tuck your pretty little self into bed. It sounds like you have another full day ahead."

"Yes, I do. I'm glad you called, though. I'm growing accustomed to that little tingle I feel when I hear your voice, Detective."

"You're a merciless tease, McKenzie. May I assume it's okay, then, for me to check in with you tomorrow?"

"You may. Goodnight, Sonny."

THURSDAY

123

The morning on Thursday brought no sun and arrived with thunder rolling across the Lowcountry in waves, beginning before dawn and rumbling in from the south, rippling low and then finding its voice and cresting with a bellow almost simultaneous with the next flash of bluish light. Julia thought again, applying mascara carefully, that thunderstorms here had their own character, behaving like none she had known in other locales. Rain came in spurts and had rinsed the atmosphere several times since the middle of the night, mixing its distinct ozone scent with coastal fragrances and blending it all with one hundred per cent humidity. Julia could hear the forecaster predicting clearing for midmorning, knowing the sun's return would lead to a steamy Carolina afternoon. She had resigned herself to the obvious: her curly hair would not be compliant in this hothouse environment.

The umbrella, she discovered to her dismay, was not near the front door. She had most likely left it in the car, which was little comfort. Now she would arrive at the hospital wet.

Driving over the drawbridge, she thought of last night's conversation with Sonny and their warmly developing friendship. She enjoyed being near him and had indeed wondered what his lips might feel like on her own. Something in her felt the desire to bring him comfort and pleasure. Or was it more likely, she wondered, that she felt comfort and pleasure in his presence and wanted more? In either case, a chemistry between them was now undeniable, and she was surprised to find that it felt no different than when she was fifteen or twenty-one. Julia smiled, turning on the car radio to check the latest weather forecast. The rain had stopped.

Julia was lost in thought all the way across town, her thoughts drifting freely between Sonny, Quinn and her upcoming meeting with Reg Fallon. It surprised her to find a parking spot as soon as she entered the lot at the hospital, now a regular stop on Julia's agenda. Checking the sky, she decided to carry the umbrella, little consolation as she checked her mirror. Damp curls crept out of place and toward her face and neck.

Reg was sitting in the chair surrounded by copies of sports publications of every sort and looking absorbed. He welcomed Julia with a smile.

"Hey, kiddo," Julia greeted him. "Nice to see you out of that bed. Have you decided to read your way to recovery?"

"Mom brought them to me last night. She's all excited about Mr. Scott's offer and decided I should start the research for my new job right away. I think there's a copy of every sports magazine she could find in Charleston. She told me she'd seen you and mentioned the job offer."

"Well, then, let's hear all about it," Julia suggested as she settled into the other chair. "I think your mother is already decorating your new office. Have you decided to take it?"

"That's why I wanted to talk with you, Miss McKenzie. I want your opinion, and I was hoping you would discuss the offer yourself with Mr. Scott as soon as you have time."

"One thing is certain. You'd have access to the team's doctors and specialists for great guidance through your recovery and rehab without even leaving the facility. It's not Charleston, but you'd make friends quickly there, surrounded by sports people and athletes."

"Doss Kincaid offered to show me the ropes in Dallas. He seemed sincere."

Julia had to smile. "I can tell you some stories about Doss Kincaid. No doubt he'd take you under his wing."

"Now that I've thought about it, I suppose I have to consider this seriously. At least I'd be close to the game, which could be both a blessing and a curse. It's not like my options are great."

"You know I'll be happy to call Weldon Scott. What specifically do you want me to ask him."

"I'm not even sure of the questions," Reg replied. "You don't think he'll be offended that I've discussed it with you, do you?" Reg asked, suddenly frowning. "I don't want him to think I'm being greedy or anything. I wonder about moving and the expenses and the timing and what they would pay me. He mentioned a couple hundred thousand. That's more than some of my friends are going to make starting out."

"I think, Reg, that you'll be great at whatever you decide to do. You're not just an athlete, you know. You're a smart guy with a college education and a knack for relating to people. How about if I just ask Weldon to fax me a proposed contract, and we'll take it from there?"

"When I was going to play ball, I understood that job. I never thought much about a job of any other kind. I don't want pity. I think he's trying to help me out."

"I think he may be, Reg, but I know that he's savvy enough about the business of basketball to be doing what he knows will be good for the franchise as well. He's making you this offer because he believes you'll bring something valuable to the Mavericks in any capacity. I, of course, thoroughly agree."

"Thank you, Miss McKenzie."

It was clear to Julia that Reg's wounded spirit was preparing to mend, though it would probably be in fits and starts, and she made a mental note to convey her thanks to Weldon Scott. He could have written off the young basketball player the moment he learned of the injury, failing to consider the value of the young man separate from his athletic ability.

"I have a meeting over at the courthouse, Reg, but I'll get back to you later this afternoon after I talk to Weldon." Julia gathered her handbag and umbrella, noting that the sky had cleared while she sat inside. "Didn't I hear that you're going home in a couple of days?"

"Maybe. I'll have to come back here every day for physical therapy, but I can sleep in my own bed."

"I know how happy that makes your mother," Julia smiled, thinking how grateful Willa Fallon must be. "Give her my best, will you?"

The corridors were bustling with activity this morning as doctors just finished rounds and breakfast trays waited on carts to be wheeled away. Julia spoke to a nurse whose face was familiar; she had cared for Reg during his recovery. The elevator came slowly, forcing Julia to stand still, reviewing all that was on her plate.

With the exit in sight, sunlight assured her that she had no further need for the umbrella. Looking down to tuck it into her handbag, she almost collided with a man coming out of the hospital chapel. He reached out instinctively to keep her from falling, and she found herself body to body with Colonel MacArthur Howe.

The moment was uncomfortable at best. Julia apologized and retrieved the leather sandal which had slipped from her left foot when it contacted the colonel's solid shoe. There was nothing for them to say, no pleasantries to be shared, no small talk appropriate. "Oh, I'm so sorry," were the only words spoken, these by Julia, during the brief encounter before each awkwardly moved aside and walked away.

Julia was outside the door before the image of Colonel Howe refocused in her mind. He had been distinctly haggard and unshaven, his eyes red-rimmed inside dark circles, his expression strangely vacant. He had seen her without seeing, she thought, not certain he had recognized her in that moment. Slowing her steps, Julia wondered if she should turn around and go back to the hospital. Why, she wondered, would the colonel be at the hospital? Had he spent the night there with someone, as it appeared? Had Mac had a relapse of some kind? And even if she were to retrace her steps, how would she get answers? Hospital personnel were as unlikely to satisfy her curiosity as was the colonel himself.

Rose Pinckney, she recalled, had been on the hospital board of directors for many years. Surely there would be someone from whom she could extract a piece of information, but Julia did not feel comfortable asking it of her. Bridging that obstacle, she pulled the cell phone from her handbag and dialed Celia.

124

Rose Pinckney felt like the Cheshire Cat as she looked out her front window to see the rental car disappearing around the curve on East Bay Street. Quinn was in the car with Doss Kincaid, on her way to get ice cream.

Doss had followed up his plea of the previous afternoon with a telephone call to Quinn on Thursday morning. He was, he claimed, doing an in-depth piece on Reg Fallon, planning to run it as soon as the team announced Reg's hiring in the new capacity. He cajoled Quinn into give him just an hour or so, shedding light on Reg's childhood in Charleston. Rose had encouraged the meeting, feeling the nice young man was owed at least a little time in return for the black eye he had suffered as Quinn's lawyer's henchman. Rose had an unfailing instinct about people, and she liked Doss Kincaid.

"God bless 'em," she whispered, calling once again upon her faith in life, love and Lowcountry magic.

"She's quite a lady," Doss was saying as White Point Gardens passed on the right. "I don't think I've ever met anyone quite like her."

"That's because there isn't anyone like her," Quinn responded, finding it easy to agree. "I came here when I was five years old, and I met Rose and Reg in the same first year here in Charleston. Now look at the trouble I've caused them both."

Sensing the melancholy undercurrent, Doss moved quickly to head it off: "I didn't hear the story that way. Reg talks about you like a kid sister. That's how I knew you can tell me things that will help flesh out my story. Didn't he say you just graduated from college?"

"Yes, just this spring. I have a contract to teach kindergarten, but that seems as unlikely right now as Reg playing basketball again."

Doss glanced sideways, seeing the distress in Quinn's eyes.

"I'm strictly an outsider, of course, but I get the feeling that there are so many people in your corner it's all going to work out. Even your lawyer loves you. How often does that happen? She collared me into service. So I guess you'd have to say that I'm in your corner too."

"I don't think I've heard the full story about all that. I see the bruise, so I guess, like Grandma Rose said, I should thank you."

"I can tell you the story, and it might even make us laugh over ice cream. I can be a pretty funny guy if you give me a chance." Doss grinned as he finished, a contagious expression to which Quinn responded without thinking.

"Thanks," she smiled back.

125

Afternoon sun now flooded Martha Howe's hospital room with beams of brightness, their slant slipping further across the room as the orange ball descended lazily toward the horizon. That aura was in utter contrast to the angst between these four walls, its distinct presence draped like a throbbing web of trepidation and despair.

Colonel Howe lay with his eyes closed in the recliner on one side of the bed, and Mac sat in the upright chair on the other side, leaning forward with his forehead on the edge of the bed and both his hands holding gently to his mother's arm between her wrist and the taped tube feeding fluid into her unstirring form. Talking had virtually ceased between the two exhausted men; there were no more words, none that would give adequate expression to the nightmare each hoped he was having. The nurse's last visit prompted the usual inquisitive and hopeful looks, but she simply nodded and patted Mac's slumping shoulder before leaving, now recognized as meaning there was in Martha Howe "no change". The doctor would be by again around dinnertime. There was nothing to do but wait, no interest in reading or useless chatter or listening to the television drone on about the rest of the world. Nothing mattered here but the rhythm of Martha's pulse as it was displayed on the heart monitor and the slow rise and fall of her chest as breath flowed faintly but regularly in and out, her life dependent upon that gossamer ebb and flow.

126

No music would have sounded sweeter to Rose's ears than that of Quinn's lilting laughter when she opened the front door. Doss Kincaid closed the door behind the two. Rose could see them from the kitchen table, and as they crossed the living room she thought Quinn's step to be lighter than at any time of late, her bearing less burdened, her tone less troubled.

The young people stopped speaking as they realized, upon entering the kitchen, that Rose was talking on the telephone. Smiling a warm welcome, she raised one finger as though to say she'd be finished shortly. Nodding, Quinn asked quietly if Doss would like a glass of iced tea.

"That'd be great," he whispered back. "Are you sure it's okay for me to hang around for a few minutes?"

"Sit," Quinn replied, pointing to one of the chairs around the table.

"Celia, dear, Quinn has just come home with that charming reporter from Dallas in tow, and I don't want to let him get away. I'm planning to prevail upon him to stay for dinner. It's the least I can do after what he's been through here. Maybe it will be extra incentive now that the smell of my strawberry-rhubarb pie is coming from the oven. And wouldn't it be a shame if that extra serving of salmon with crabmeat stuffing marinating in the refrigerator ended up going to waste? It won't keep until tomorrow." Smiling sweetly, she eyed Doss across the table.

Celia could picture the scene in Rose's kitchen. The young reporter, she thought, was way out of his league. She hoped he was hungry. "How's the big bruise coming along?"

"Oh, he's recovering nicely. I'll give him your regards, and you give mine to Julia. I'm happy I was able to help. It's sad to think of Martha in the hospital, but now I know to pray for her."

"Thanks, Grams. We'll talk later."

127

Julia had turned on her cell phone's vibrate feature while she was at the courthouse. She had felt the pulsing in her pocket more than once, so it was not a surprise that Celia had called. Though she had been absorbed by preparation for tomorrow's preliminary hearing, her curiosity had not abated. The collision with George Howe, disheveled and haggard leaving the hospital chapel, had left her puzzled.

Settling behind her desk after the short walk back to her office, Julia raised a glass of iced tea to her lips with one hand and called Celia on the office phone with the other. Thinking, after the fourth ring, that her curiosity might have to wait for satisfaction, Julia was glad to hear Celia's voice, answering with a breathless "hello".

"You sound like you've been running around the block."

"I've been running girls back and forth from the mall and dropping off their friends all over the peninsula. And of course I've been waiting for you to call. It's been more than two hours."

"Did you find out something about why the colonel was at the hospital?"

"Martha Howe was brought to the emergency room yesterday by ambulance. She was diagnosed with an overdose of some prescription drug. Can you believe it?"

It took a moment for Julia to respond. "Wow, Cele. That's beyond anything that occurred to me. Is she going to be okay?"

"Grandma Rose says that her prognosis isn't good. They're apparently monitoring her around the clock, but she's in a coma. They resuscitated her at the hospital, but she hasn't regained consciousness."

Another silence followed. "Resuscitated? Does that mean she wasn't technically alive and breathing?"

"I guess it does. But she's breathing now. She's just not conscious. That's all I know."

"I don't know what to say, Cele. I've been all focused on taking down Mac and saving Quinn, and something like this comes out of the blue. I wasn't prepared to process any more information."

"I guess it gives one pause."

"I'll say. Is there any more that Rose found out? Anything you haven't told me?"

"Nothing more, Jules. No one is saying she took the pills on purpose. Or that she didn't. But there was that story about Reg Fallon front and center in yesterday's paper. Imagine the impact that must have had on her since the very reporter who wrote that story was in her house the night before asking questions. And there isn't, I assume, anyone with whom she could have discussed her distress. It must have made her son's situation seem like a ticking time bomb."

"Gosh, Cele, I guess I wouldn't have hoped that Mac's mother would be hurt by the fallout, no matter how badly it all ended for Mac himself."

"Another case of those trite old sayings about all the moss gathered by a rolling stone. Mac started that stone rolling years ago when he raped Quinn. Now it's seemingly fallen into the water, and the ripples are starting to radiate and expand."

"I think the old saying is that a rolling stone gathers no moss," Julia replied with a giggle. "But your point is made anyway."

128

Rose Pinckney had never been to Dallas, Texas, so she asked many questions and listened raptly as Doss described his city. He'd been born there and had been away only to attend college, so he described Dallas and Texas as "home". Rose determined his accent less a drawl than a twang, subtle, still satisfactorily Southern, and his vocabulary to be both unpretentiously extensive and unaffectedly sophisticated. He was comfortable in his own skin, she sensed, and was altogether at ease with her and Quinn by the time they sat down to dinner. Quinn had handed him the dishes. Doss had set the table.

"You mentioned getting to know something of Boston when you were away at school," Rose recalled as she passed the basket of bread. "Where did you say you went to school?"

"Bowdoin College. It's in Brunswick, Maine."

"And your degree is in journalism?" Rose probed further.

"Actually, I have a major in English and a minor in political science. This job at the Morning News came as a surprise, but it seemed a pretty good way to start my working life, getting paid to write about sports. I go to games, talk to players and coaches, get invited to all sorts of events. And then I write about it after having enjoyed it all, and they give me money for it. What's not to like?" He smiled, self-deprecating.

"Your parents are in Dallas?" Rose continued.

"They are. My parents insisted I needed a college experience vastly different from life in Texas. Brunswick, Maine, certainly fit the bill. All that snow. The people who didn't get my accent. Northampton was only an hour away, and during the last two years there a few of us spent enough time to get to know a little of Boston. As big cities go, I liked it a lot."

"Is this your first visit to Charleston?" Rose asked.

"It is, and I've already discovered its considerable appeal." He smiled at Quinn. Rose did not recall seeing Quinn blush in the recent past. "This is my first foray into what is known, I guess, as the Deep South. There have been overnights for big games when I've briefly seen Charlotte, Atlanta, New Orleans, Tampa Bay and Miami. They almost sent me to Columbia once or twice after Spurrier went there to coach, but it didn't pan out."

Quinn had opened for dinner the bottle of red wine Rose suggested, and now Doss reached across to refill his glass and Quinn's. Rose had taken only a sip.

"So you approve of our little town?" Rose queried.

"Charleston has had many more illustrious accolades than mine, but this is a lovely and charming old city with a grand history. I'd love to see more. Coming here has most certainly been a greater adventure than I predicted when I left Dallas just a couple of days ago."

The shadow in Quinn's eyes appeared for the first time since she and Doss had come back in the afternoon. "I'm afraid I'm responsible for the most unpleasant part of that adventure. I'm so glad your eye is better. At least you won't have scars."

Doss looked squarely at Quinn as he lifted the wine to his lips and let the maroon liquid bathe his tongue before swallowing. "My mom always said that scars are a sign of character and a willingness to stick out one's neck. I would have done nothing differently in the past several days. Who knew chasing a sports story would allow me to enjoy the company I'm keeping this evening?"

Rose raised her glass, holding it out toward the center of the table. "To good company," she offered solemnly. Doss touched his glass to Rose's, and then to Quinn's as she joined the toast.

"Speaking of Reg," Doss continued, wishing to return to the positivity of earlier in the evening, "I'm eagerly awaiting his decision to take the job in Dallas. I think he and I could be good friends. That's not always true of the players I encounter, but I like Reg more every time we talk, and I appreciate the insights you ladies have kindly given me into his past. His is a great story."

Quinn sighed deeply, slowly, touching her napkin to her lips as though her appetite had left. "Think of the life that was waiting for him before he went to jail for what I did." She spoke quietly, looking down. "Think of the fame. The money. He'd have had the life he and his mother had worked for. There would have been applause and awards. He'd have gotten endorsements and been paid to advertise for big companies. And he'd have been paid all those millions that the best players make in sports. He'd have had it all."

Doss was thinking as fast he could, peering plaintively at Rose for assistance, not wanting the lighthearted timbre of the evening to turn and Quinn to be reclaimed by the quicksand of her own consternation. He had enjoyed her every sunny smile since the first he'd coaxed from her at the ice cream parlor.

Rose sat very still, her fork at a standstill between her plate and her mouth. She was looking at Quinn but spoke to Doss.

"Is that true, Mr. Kincaid," she inquired very seriously, "that Reg would have made not only his basketball earnings but that he'd have earned much more from doing ads on TV like Kobe Bryant?"

Puzzled, Doss answered. "It's almost certainly true."

Rose placed her fork back on the plate, bite not taken. "Would the two of you kindly excuse me for a few minutes," she asked, already using her hands to help her rise from her seat at the table. "I must make a quick telephone call."

129

Bubba Chastain's thoughts did not often stray, during his leisure time, to the cases over which he presided. The sway he held over the lives of those who came before him did not trouble or weigh upon him. He rarely mulled over a pending situation, and a disposition was usually apparent to him early in a case's presentation with utter and categorical clarity. People either managed their lives well or poorly, and he was called upon simply to apply the consequences of poor choices. He had made a few of those in his own life, and he understood the price.

The law, however, fascinated him, a study as fluid as language, less exacting than math. Every case presented the possibility of positing a precedent for scrutiny; each decision laid a building block for further refinement.

His father had been in jail, usually an overnight stay for public drunkenness or a few days for violation of the rules for selling liquor, making the judge's first impression of the law a cop who appeared to take his father away. They didn't necessarily come if his father drank heavily and swore at or hit his mother. They didn't come when mother or son was afraid, and his father could certainly make them afraid. They didn't come to keep the grungy liquor store from being robbed on more than a couple of occasions. Sometimes in the middle of a sunny afternoon they came with handcuffs and pieces of paper, and his father returned a day or two later none the better or worse. It appeared an arbitrary and mystifying system carried out by people with authority greater than that of his parents.

The judge reveled in the atypical action, either civil or criminal, that presented enough nuance to invite remotely rigorous rumination. He found it rare that the most convincing arguments by a duo of talented litigators left the scales of justice near balanced. Here on a

Thursday evening after a pleasant dinner which he'd cooked at home, Judge Chastain was slightly annoyed to find his concentration broken once again as his mind wandered waywardly forward to Friday morning's scheduled preliminary hearing for George Howe's son. He had thought himself engrossed in his reading, enjoying the intricate plot of a spy novel by one of his favorite authors, sipping a superb brandy. His favorite chair was comfortable. The background music was Mozart. A slight breeze bathed him as the ceiling fan turned overhead.

Laying the book open on the table beside him, he reached for the brandy.

130

Rose found her fingers trembling as she drew them down the page of the telephone book. She had climbed the stairs resolutely to her room, closing the door quietly behind her, uneasy about leaving Quinn and Doss so abruptly. She hoped the young man had read her expression and would take it upon himself to keep Quinn company until Rose returned. It should take her no more than a few minutes.

The telephone rang just as she placed her hand upon it, causing her to draw back with a start. Taking a deep breath to steady herself, she answered quickly.

"Mrs. Pinckney?" The woman's voice was not familiar.

"Yes."

"This is Joan Ellison, the night nurse at Roper Hospital. I don't mean to bother you, ma'am, but there is a note for me to call you if there should be any change in Mrs. Howe's condition."

"Oh, of course. I did leave those instructions." Rose's thoughts jumped to the subject at hand. "Is there some news about Mrs. Howe?"

"I'm so awfully sorry to tell you, ma'am, but Mrs. Howe has passed away. It happened less than an hour ago."

Rose was caught wordless for a few moments.

"Mrs. Pinckney? Again, I'm so sorry. Are you all right?"

"Oh, yes, yes. I'm all right. It's just such awful news."

"Yes, ma'am, it is. I wish I could have called with something better."

"Well, thank you, my dear. You've been very kind. I do appreciate your calling. Goodnight now."

131

"Shall we just finish our dinner as instructed?" Doss tried to sound amused. "Is your grandma always so spontaneous?"

Quinn was bewildered and slightly concerned by Rose's sudden departure. "Grams has a mind of her own. If she doesn't come back down pretty soon, I'll go up and check on her. I'm most surprised that she's forgotten the pie in the oven."

"Well, we can surely take care of that, can't we?" Doss grinned. "I know I don't want it to burn up after I saved space for it. Will a buzzer sound or something when it's done?"

"Oh yes, Quinn replied. "There will be a buzzer."

"Well then, let's let Miss Rose take care of her business while we anticipate the taste of that pie. Will it be as yummy as the smell?"

"There's no doubt about that. May I refill your tea? Maybe you can tell me more about the places you've been."

"I think I've been talking nonstop. I don't know anything about where you've been. Is it New York, Smith College and Charleston? No foreign exploits or visits to exotic places?"

"Grams wanted to take me all sorts of places during summers and Christmas breaks. She wanted me to see the places she'd seen. But Mama would never agree to let me go. By the time I started high school, Grams couldn't travel well because of her knees. Then she got me a laptop so we could look all around the world. I clicked, and we did virtual travel."

"She's been quite an influence in your life, hasn't she?"

"She's been everything."

132

Rose had composed herself and her thoughts, drying tears that came unbidden after the call from the hospital. She pictured Martha Howe sitting in her living room only a couple of days earlier, calling upon all her motherly instincts to protect her son. She recalled how Martha's confidence had come apart, shattering like fine crystal as, eye to eye with Quinn, she saw the scar and obviously remembered the broken window. Rose sensed that she had seen then and there the moment when Martha died. But she could not have predicted it would be so literal, so soon, and by Martha's own hand.

Her rush of thoughts prior to the call had been interrupted. A gust of hope and curiosity had propelled her up the stairs. Had she had a revelation, her prayers answered by an epiphany, or was her new notion a shot in the dark, a grasp at the last straw through which to suck back Quinn's life. Rose knew her city. She knew full well that the system of justice had this mess firmly in its teeth, its unforgiving jaws grinding. Time was running out. Lifting the receiver from its cradle, Rose Beauregard Pinckney recreated the essence of her question and renewed her resolve. Peering at the number she had found, she dialed carefully. There was one ring, then a second and a third.

"Hello." It was the deep bass of Judge Chastain.

"Your Honor, this is Rose Pinckney. I was hoping to impose upon your evening for just a bit of advice. If it's a bad time, we can talk at your convenience, though I must say that in this case, time is truly of the essence."

"It's always a pleasure to talk with you, Miss Rose. As a matter of fact, I was a little at loose ends here and having trouble keeping my mind on my reading."

"Well, Judge, that's good for me because I believe I'm in somewhat of a pickle. And time is not on my side."

"My curiosity is piqued. Plunge ahead."

"Okay, Wynfield Eldridge, are you sitting down?"

Judge Chastain's belly rippled with his deep chuckle. "Not only am I sitting down, but I'm bolstered if need be by a very good bottle of brandy sitting here on the table. And I know something is afoot if you're using my given name. I'm not sure anyone else even remembers it."

"I'll never forget your mother, God rest her soul, calling you by that name when she was ferociously upset. On those infrequent occasions when I visited the store, my real interest was always in seeing how you were faring. I marvel to this day at your success against those odds. It warms my heart."

"I know you didn't call to review my success, Miss Rose. And you needn't flatter me to butter me up."

"I'd like to run something by you."

The judge took another sip of the brandy. "I hope you've not hatched another plan to inflict me upon a new woman of your acquaintance. Have you not taken note by now that not everyone finds me charming?"

Rose smiled only slightly, reminded of her several unsuccessful matchmaking attempts involving The Honorable Wynfield Chastain. With this man, just in the prime of his life, each of her tries had been thoroughly thwarted by his blatant directness of manner or by the failure of the woman to merit his interest beyond a first meeting

"Don't fool yourself that I've conceded defeat, Wynfield Eldridge."

"Not for a moment."

"Well, Winfield, I try never to say things I wouldn't repeat publicly, but what I'm about to say next must remain between us. As you'll quickly see, I'm not trying to make news. I'd like you to listen with an open mind and not jump to conclusions or poke fun at my lack of legal expertise."

"My lips, as they say, are sealed."

"I must take that as your solemn word."

"You have my word, Miss Rose."

Assured her confidence would be kept, Rose proceeded. "You will be presiding over a case against the young MacArthur Howe tomorrow morning, and I..."

"Wait," came abruptly from the judge. "I had assumed this discussion would not involve any matter coming before me. If it does, then I'm afraid we cannot have this conversation. Could you discuss this with Marshall Stoney? You've known him a very long time, and you could ask him for objective advice."

"I considered it. Marshall is a good man and a fine friend, but I doubt he'd be surprised at my calling him a stick-in-the-mud. He'd not hear me out beyond a few words because his attitudes are as old and stuffy as his age, and his lack of adventurous spirit is tedious. I hope you'll pardon my saying so."

Bubba Chastain would like to be able to roll with laughter at the entertainment he found in Rose's candor, but his girth precluded any such behavior.

"Be assured that I thought it through very carefully, Your Honor, Rose continued, knowing full well that she had mentally searched her contact base with lightning speed in the moments it took to climb the stairs minutes earlier. "I'm convinced there's nowhere to turn but to you."

"There can be no further mention of any current legal matter unless you want to visit me in my chambers with an attorney of your choice. I know you understand my position."

Rose chose her words carefully, striving to coalesce for the judge the unlikely scenario that would serve her purpose. "My interest is not in the charge against either Mac Howe. I assume you are aware of the tragic automobile accident that injured the young basketball player Reginald Fallon and how it affects his future."

"I've been a fan of his, and one could hardly miss the story in the Post and Courier." The judge was puzzled at the turn in the discourse. "It's a real shame, but I'm not aware of litigation over it. I assume you're going to enlighten me."

"Indeed. Reg got his injuries while riding in a Charleston police vehicle. He was the first person arrested for the attack on MacArthur Howe, arrested only hours after it happened. He'd been at a party down the street, was quite tipsy and resting in the rain, as fate would have it, just beside the straight razor Quinn Ravenel used on the Howe boy and discarded as she ran away. She got that razor from my house."

Bubba Chastain sat up straighter, returning the brandy to its place on the table as though even that might distract the attention he now focused on Rose's story. "I think," he spoke slowly, "that you now have my undivided attention."

"You see that my focus is not on any case of yours. Someone I love is out on a ledge, and I'm trying to find a way--any way--to get her down."

"Okay, I'll bite. How can I help you with that?"

"I'd like to know if the young Reginald Fallon could file suit against Charleston for ruining his future."

"What!" the judge exclaimed, edging toward the front of his seat. How did Charleston ruin his future? This whole town has been cheering him on for years."

Rose continued. "He was taken to jail for something he did not do. He was just a young black male sitting in a garden minding his own business and ended up in a police cruiser. It changed everything for him. I'm told that athletes playing at a professional level make millions, not only in outrageous salaries but from endorsing products of big companies willing to pay more millions. Is that indeed the case?"

"It is," the judge answered. "But you're not planning to offer legal counsel to Reg Fallon after a little chat with me, are you? I've not heard any rumor of such a lawsuit on the courthouse grapevine, and I would hope, for the sake of Charleston itself, you aren't encouraging one."

"Don't fret about that, Your Honor. I have no intention of encouraging a lawsuit. First and foremost, I haven't time. I was thinking of an alternative course of action to all this legal chicanery, which is already upon us. I just needed to know from a learned confidante that if such a suit were brought, there is a realistic possibility of it being heard."

"Not only is there a realistic possibility, there's a decided likelihood. Without more details, I can't assess it definitively, but I'll tell you that any attorney worth his salt would sink his teeth into even the whiff of such a cause of action." The judge's mind raced ahead, putting together in mental outline just the way such a case would be made.

Rose continued, bringing the discussion full circle. "It would be an explosively negative story for this town, don't you imagine, Winfield Eldridge? The sensibilities of Charleston have been so recently assaulted. The Civil War is history, but the killing at Mother Emanuel and the police shooting of Walter Scott are not."

"Again, I must agree without hesitation."

Now the deep sigh came from Rose, expressing multiple emotions. She had the seed of a plan and reassurance that it was plausible. She had a glimmer of hope. She had so little time. And she was very, very tired.

"I must thank you, Wynfield Eldridge. I know it's late. You can't imagine how helpful you've been."

The judge was not prepared to be dismissed so abruptly. He had forgotten the book on the table. "That's it?" he asked.

"I said I wasn't going to meddle in affairs of the court. And you promised that this little conversation never happened. Please don't forget that. Goodnight then."

The line went dead on the judge's end as Rose hung up the telephone. He sat very still, carefully recapping the conversation. Reg Fallon had been arrested. His career-ending injuries, now nationally discussed in sports circles, could be blamed on a wrongful arrest. Now it seemed that Rose, no ardent basketball fan, was inquiring about a potential lawsuit on behalf of the Fallon boy for lost future earnings. That gnawing he had pushed away earlier about Friday morning's events now turned to a full-blown preoccupation.

FRIDAY

133

Julia was up, but she was startled by a ringing telephone at seven o'clock on Friday morning and especially surprised to hear the voice of Rose Pinckney.

"Is everything alright?" she asked, immediately concerned for Quinn in light of this morning's scheduled hearing. Julia recognized full well the dread Quinn was harboring, knowing that at some point in these next few hours she would see MacArthur Howe.

"Oh, we're just fine, my dear," Rose responded. "I wanted to share a piece of information with you before you left for the courthouse. And I wanted to ask if you'd help me with a little plan I'm formulating. I waited as long as I could; I hope I didn't wake you."

"You know I'd be more than happy to help with anything you need, Miss Rose. Would you like me to come for Quinn a little earlier than we'd planned so you can tell me about it?" Julia was perplexed, expecting Rose to be concerned only about getting Quinn through the day.

"Could you come later in the morning, as soon as you're free? I'll make us a nice lunch."

"You know," Julia reminded gently, "this hearing could be lengthy. It's likely to be well after lunchtime, and then we might need to put all our efforts into supporting Quinn. This is going to take a toll on her. Celia is planning to come home with you when the hearing is over."

"Well, dear, the hearing won't be taking long, and you don't have to come for Quinn. She is fine, but I'm calling with rather sad news. I know it won't please you any more than me. I'm afraid Martha Howe has passed away."

Julia was as unprepared for this revelation as she had been when Celia told her of Martha's hospitalization. "She's dead? Are you sure?"

"I'm sure. The hospital called me last night. I know it's upsetting, Julia, but I felt I should let you know first thing this morning.

You needn't come for Quinn because the hearing will most certainly be postponed."

"Do you think that likely?" Julia responded. "I've not had enough experience here to know the custom. In a serious matter like this, will a judge put things off because of the death of Mac's mother?"

"I've no doubt of it whatsoever," Rose answered with certainty. "Last night I was praying on my old knees for time. Since the hearing was today and disclosure of the whole mess would surely follow, I despaired that it was too late."

"Too late for what, Miss Rose?"

"Too late for me to carry out the plan I mentioned earlier. And I need your advice, Julia. Will you come by later in the morning? I can't tell you what a help it would be."

"I'll be there. Of course I'll be there. I'm not as certain about the hearing. Will you be sure that Quinn is ready as planned in case we need to go on with it?"

"I will. We'll be ready for whatever happens."

Julia heard the click on the line as Rose ended the conversation.

134

Bubba Chastain had slept in fits and starts, not a result of too much brandy, he thought, but due to lying awake puzzling over Rose Pinckney's telephone call. She hadn't asked him for anything, no action, not even substantive legal guidance. She was fishing, it seemed, into the likelihood of a successful lawsuit by Reg Fallon, an action she said she was not trying to promote.

Moreover, the judge was puzzled at the early-morning call from his old friend Mendel Comings, requesting that this morning's preliminary hearing be held in chambers and that Mendel be allowed to attend as a friend of the case. There would be no lengthy presentation from either side, Mendel had said, indicating that he did not wish to insert himself in Collie Rivers' case and was calling strictly off the record. That would be a gift of time, the judge conceded, because he had set aside three hours to hear testimony about whether this case should proceed to trial. An efficient resolution would allow him time to delve into other matters needing his attention and maybe even a leisurely lunch over at Anson where they knew to put shrimp and grits on a plate when the judge walked in.

As he made order of the files on his desk, The Honorable Bubba Chastain cleared his mind for the upcoming meeting. It was quite possible, he supposed, that both parties would simply present multiple motions for discovery, though it seemed Mendel would have said so, but the judge was not inclined to allow any unwarranted delay. He wanted this matter moved along in the most expedient manner.

The judge grasped the knot at his throat, making sure the silk tie was adequately lodged between the collar points of his Italian-designed shirt. He had foregone the black robe, pleased to do so at a simple proceeding in his own comfortable quarters. As he checked his reflection in the large bronze-framed mirror across the room, the buzzer called for his attention. "Judge Chastain?"

"At your beck and call, my dear," he pushed the button and responded, repressing the tinge of crankiness he felt from a night of insufficient rest.

"Mr. Rivers is here with Mr. Comings, Mr. Cantrell and Miss McKenzie, sir. Would you like me to send them in?"

Bubba frowned. "Is anyone else with them," he asked, further baffled that the principals were not at the courthouse.

"No, sir."

"I'm already a little testy this morning, Hannah Marie, so you might as well just usher the four of them in and we'll see what poppycock and horse feathers they've cobbled together for my entertainment today." He enunciated dryly for the benefit of the waiting lawyers.

When the door opened and the four filed into his office, the judge sensed a level of unease not expected at a hearing in chambers. Each of the four appeared tense, bringing into the room a palpable air of taut expectancy.

Judge Chastain motioned expansively, offering seats to the quartet as he resettled himself into the oversized high-backed chair behind his desk. "I'm a little stumped at your request, Mendel," he began without preamble. "I hope y'all aren't trying to muck up my calendar with a bushel of hogwash." Looking directly at Mendel, he waited for a response.

"No such intention, Your Honor," Mendel replied levelly. "We have an unusual situation. I have been to the hospital where the defendant's mother was taken by ambulance. I'm sorry to say that Martha Howe has passed away."

The judge pursed his lips, his expression turning appropriately serious. "Colonel Howe's wife is dead?" he asked.

"It was sudden and totally unexpected, Your Honor. And since only a matter of hours has passed, I took the liberty of preparing a consensus request by all parties and their attorneys for a brief continuance of this proceeding. Begging Your Honor's understanding, it was all but impossible to expect a coherent appearance by the defendant at this hour. He and his father are shocked and inconsolable. You'll find the parties and counsel are all of the same mind."

A frown appeared and deepened on the pudgy brow of Bubba Chastain. He looked around the room at each of the four faces, finding them intent upon his own.

"Alan?" he stated the prosecutor's name as a question, fishing for a sign of dissent.

"We regret Mrs. Howe's passing, Your Honor and agree that it would be most difficult for the defendant to participate in his own defense. The State will go along with whatever the Court decides."

The judge had no reluctance to postpone this morning's preliminary hearing. Though surprised at the report of Mrs. Howe's sudden death, he clearly saw it as more than sufficient reason to delay. Mendel Comings, he was certain, had accurately anticipated the judge's sympathies.

"Will the parties be prepared to proceed two weeks from today?" Looking from one to the other, His Honor awaited a response.

Once again, Mendel spoke for the other three. "That's more than generous, Your Honor. We thank you."

"Please convey my sympathy to the family. I'm sorry to hear about Martha Howe. She always seemed a lovely woman."

135

Julia arrived breathless at the top of the steps to Rose Pinckney's front door, hardly aware of the humidity and the building heat as part of the cause. She had been so prepared for this morning's ordeal that the actual event was anticlimax. Mendel's call right after she had spoken with Rose was affirmation that Martha Howe was dead and that the hearing would likely be postponed. Mendel had assured her that Charleston justice did not have so philistine a penchant as to continue with a proceeding in the face of such grief and misfortune. Mendel had known Bubba Chastain long enough, he assured her, to be sure of his reaction. Calls were being made and outcomes assumed before Julia had finished her first cup of coffee. She was not at all certain that dragging out this saga was in the best interest of anyone, least of all Quinn whose state of mind was increasingly fragile.

Before she rang the bell, Julia paused to collect her thoughts and take a couple of deep breaths. The early-morning call from Rose had left her utterly baffled, seeming to lack the usual coherence she expected from the elderly woman. She had a plan, she had said. She wanted Julia to help. No matter what the plan, Julia was sure, there would be no distracting Quinn from the angst and apprehension of the two long weeks to come. Julia concluded that time in this case was not a gift but a cruel turn of events from which no good could possibly ensue. It would simply prolong Quinn's distress.

Celia answered the door. Julia had not noticed her car on the street. Nevertheless, the sight of her relieved Julia to an extent she had not deemed possible.

"I thought you'd never get here," Celia began. Though her voice was calm, her eyes signaled a quiet excitement. "How did everything go at the courthouse?"

"Just as Rose predicted," Julia responded. "Judge Chastain continued the preliminary hearing for two weeks."

Celia took the briefcase from Julia's hand and started toward Rose's kitchen, from which there wafted the scent of something warm and sweet mixed with just-brewed coffee. Through the doorway, Julia saw Rose and Quinn sitting at the table. She was surprised to see Doss Kincaid, laptop open on the table in front of him, and delighted to see the smile on Quinn's face, subdued but genuine.

"Don't get up," Julia said, motioning for Rose to keep her seat. "Whatever I smell, you know I can get it myself."

Lowering herself back down into the seat, Rose looked at Julia with warmth and affection. "I know you can, my dear. I know you can. Just help yourself to the warm bread. I made potato salad for lunch, and Celia has been creating sandwiches, but I'll bet you could use a nice cinnamon bun after the morning you've had."

"It was much less stressful than the morning I expected," Julia replied, getting a saucer for the bread. "The judge gave a two-week continuation without qualms."

Doss Kincaid spoke up, his voice a honey tenor contrast in a kitchen filled with women. "I hope you're up for some midday coffee,

Miss McKenzie, because I'm the reason there's a whole new pot. Sadly, I had to admit I don't function properly without my constant drip."

"Nor do I, Mr. Kincaid. I didn't expect you'd still be in Charleston, though of course I'm happy to see you. You're looking notably better than when I saw you last."

"I'd be on a plane right now if Miss Rose hadn't called at midnight to stop me. I've found her to be a woman of considerable powers of persuasion, not unlike another of my new acquaintances here in Charleston." He grinned and raised an eyebrow, obviously not reluctant to remind Julia that she was instrumental in his acquiring the black eye just days earlier. "My editor is getting a little hot about my schedule. I'll have to go soon."

"Rose called you at midnight?" Celia's eyes widened.

Using her most proper voice, Rose interceded. "Now you know full well that young folks like Mr. Kincaid are not in bed at midnight. I felt I should give him plenty of time to change his travel plans in case he chose to stay and help us today."

"And here I am." Doss stated the obvious. "And you've arrived just in the nick of time, Miss McKenzie. I'm a good enough reporter, if I do say so myself, but I'm no lawyer."

Julia turned from the cinnamon roll she was putting on the small plate. "You need a lawyer?" she asked.

"I can write a story so plausible it will make the hair prickle on the back of your neck if you care about this town. But I don't know the legal terms I need to throw out there."

"Legal terms? What are you writing?" Julia asked, pouring coffee into a chunky coral-colored mug like the one Doss was using.

Rose held up her hand, signaling her wish to provide the explanation. "I haven't discussed this with Julia. She had enough on her mind this morning. But now, Julia dear, sit down and let us pick your brain."

"You're not going to believe what Rose is cooking up, Jules," Celia chimed in, looking up from the chicken salad mixture she was spreading on whole wheat bread. "If this came from anyone else, I'd be laughing all the way out the door of the padded cell in which I'd left her. I'm just going to watch your face as you take it in."

Celia held up both her hands, palms forward, a shield against Rose's frown of protest.

"Let's let Julia draw her own conclusions," she asserted firmly. "You'll hear me out with an open mind, won't you, my dear? Never mind Celia's witty reference to the padded cell."

"I'm well accustomed to Celia's witticisms," Julia smiled, taking a seat beside Quinn across the table from Rose and Doss Kincaid. "But you have my full attention except for the part that will be focused on this cinnamon roll." Julia pulled off a section of the bread and popped it in her mouth.

"I was thinking," Rose began, "of the impact it might have if Reg Fallon sued this City for what he'll miss because he can't play basketball. Mr. Kincaid tells me that there are millions of dollars paid to professional athletes over a career, and many millions more when advertisers pay them to speak on behalf of their products. This would have been Reg's future had he not been waylaid by his unfortunate arrest. Am I getting it right, Julia?" Rose focused her earnest gaze on Julia's face.

"He certainly had a lucrative future, Rose, There's little question about that." Julia's furrowed brow showed her perplexity. She chewed slowly, listening attentively.

"So," Rose continued, "wouldn't it be reasonable for Reg to sue this City for his loss? He was injured in a car belonging to the City and driven by a City employee. I'm thinking a multi-million-dollar lawsuit would be devastating for Charleston, to say nothing of the adverse publicity that would follow. This is a Southern city. Reg is a young black man. It seems to me a case could be made that a city with a racial history as precarious as ours should no longer be making stereotypical assumptions."

Everyone was quiet, searching the faces of Rose and Julia. "I'm not sure I understand where you're going," Julia responded slowly, swallowing first. "I didn't know Reg was thinking along these lines."

Doss was tapping his thumb rhythmically on the edge of the laptop. "He's not. I'm writing a mock story, Julia, pretending it would be the lead story in USA Today on a Monday morning a year from now detailing all the ruckus and scandal resulting from the trial of a case against the City of Charleston. What's the legal term for Reg being in jail when he didn't do anything?"

"Wrongful arrest?" Julia queried, following the logic.

"And what about the fact that he's black?" Doss continued.

"Well, there's racial profiling," Julia offered, sipping her coffee to wash down the last bite.

"And the future--both fame and wealth--no longer open to him because the cops hauled him off for a crime committed by a white woman--nothing personal," he added with a glance at Quinn. "What about that?"

"I see where you're going. Because of his arrest and the car accident, he's now lost all the possibilities of his future fame and fortune." Julia stated it, understanding in theory. "But, again, are you saying Reg wants to sue the City?" She thought reflexively of Sonny and the unwarranted guilt he already carried.

"No," Doss replied matter-of-factly. "I'm just writing a story as though he sued them. Miss Rose wants us to put it together this afternoon so she can put it in front of a few folks over the weekend. It's dated a year from now. We were hoping you'd help to be sure I'm not out of line with the terms of my fictitious lawsuit. She seems to think she might use such a story as leverage."

"Leverage?" Julia tried to associate this conversation with the morning's hearing or Quinn's dilemma in general.

Rose could now further describe her plan. "You've seen the efforts made to keep Mac's situation, as well as Quinn's, under wraps. We don't like scandal here. We're the Southern city extolled for our hospitality, our civility and our well-promoted Southern gentility. We would like even less the pointed accusation that Charleston is prone, after decades of effort to the contrary, to blatant racial bias. This is a tourist town, a place where we pride ourselves on our genuine Southern charm and infused with refinement and grace. Discretion here is a cardinal virtue. Do you believe anyone influential here would be pleased at the prospect of having Charleston recast as the villain, still the oppressor and engaged in blatant discrimination against a young man of color?" Rose's own color now heightened as her expression reflected her ardor. "I thought I could just lay Mr. Kincaid's piece of fiction in front of an influential eye or two. It might make some folks receptive to the dismissal of any number of scandal-producing charges. It might be an incentive for the only people who could do so to apply some pressure where we ordinary folks cannot. Or it could result in my going to jail on a charge of sheer impertinence." She smiled. "If you'll show Julia what you've done so far, Mr. Kincaid, I'll go upstairs and make an appointment to present our work. Even though poor Martha's death allowed us a reprieve, we haven't any time to waste."

Thoroughly puzzled now, Julia looked from one face to the next, turning last to fix a quizzical expression on Celia.

"I told you," Celia grinned, drying her hands on one of Rose's white cotton tea towels. "There isn't anything going on already that can't be complicated further by a little lunch at the Beauregard Pinckneys'."

136

Sonny had tried Julia at home, at her office and on the cell phone. After hearing the news of Martha Howe, he had inquired to find this morning's hearing for her son postponed. It was, of course, the expected course of action under the circumstances, but he assumed Julia would not be happy about two more weeks of anxiety for Quinn.

The weekend was upon them, and Sonny realized that he was assuming he could see Julia. They had made no plans. Her mind had been full of pleadings and oral arguments and the rapidly approaching moment when Quinn would be in the courtroom with MacArthur Howe.

Sonny would come up with a plan for the weekend before Julia returned his call. He missed her.

137

Reg Fallon would be, instead of a star in the NBA, a cog in the wheels that move and promote the game. It was a consolation prize, but he would be near the action if the doctors were wrong. He had just acknowledged as much to Weldon Scott on the telephone when he accepted the offer pending Julia's approval of a new contract. Doss Kincaid had offered to share his bachelor-friendly apartment until Reg found his own place. Dallas was a new world. His hand was still on the phone when Quinn opened his door,

"Hey, girl. What a great surprise."

Quinn smiled and walked to the bedside. It was easier now to give Reg a hug with fewer tubes and monitors in the way. "I love seeing you getting better," she trilled. "When are they letting you out of here?"

"They keep saying it's a matter of days, but no one will say yet just how many. There'll be crutches and braces and physical therapy, but I'm ready for all that. If I could walk now, I'd be down at the nurses' station pestering them until they wanted to get rid of me."

"They tell me, Mr. Pain-in-the-Neck, that you're a delightful patient, and they like having you around," Quinn responded with a teasing grin. "They'll probably want to keep you here until Christmas."

"By Christmas I'll be shooting three-pointers from behind my new desk in Dallas," Reg offered back. "But enough about me. What's going on with you out there in the real world?"

Quinn slid up gently into a spot on the foot of the hospital bed, crossing her legs and taking a yoga-like pose. "I'm going to tell you a story," she said. "This is all Grandma Rose's idea, and she's going to do it this very day or this very weekend unless you object."

"I can't imagine objecting to any idea of hers, but go ahead. Entertain me. Does it start with 'once upon a time'?"

"It starts," Quinn began, "with what happened to me four years ago. And it ends with you threatening to sue Charleston for arresting the wrong person."

"I'm doing what?"

"C'mon, Reg, you're a captive audience, so just let me finish the story. It's not about you. It's about me. Grandma Rose is trying to help me get out of this mess, but I need your permission."

"You've got it. So, tell me what I'm doing." Reg sat up straight.

138

Julia returned Sonny's call, but not until she was already at home on Sullivan's Island. It would be good to join him for a beer or two, she agreed, if he would come across the bridge. She was exhausted but could use a little good company for a nightcap by the sea. There was a little place just down the beach, the only pub within walking distance. A short walk would do her good, she assured him when he offered to pick her up. Sonny arrived first, happy that Julia made time to end this day in his company.

"That's the latest," she finished recapping. "I can't make this stuff up, and I'm going to try not to think about it for just tonight."

The clock struck ten, and the waitress looked toward them once more, checking to see if refills were needed. "You might as well come on down to my house for one more beer," Julia offered. "My brain is tired, and I really want my feet up."

Sonny studied Julia, weighing this option. "Your place?"

"My place doesn't rock with the waves like yours, but it's okay."

"Sure, why not." Sonny shook his head agreeably. He tossed dollar bills onto the table as he backed his chair. He stepped toward

Julia's chair, but she was up quickly, draping the strap of her bag over her shoulder and heading for the door. She pushed through ahead of him, holding it open casually behind her.

"I know your truck is here," Julia said, but I'm just a couple of blocks away. You want to get your toes in the sand?"

He started around the building, turning toward the beach side. "Let's go."

Sonny stopped to let Julia onto the narrow boardwalk across the dunes, following behind her. She seemed small in front of him, and he resisted putting his hand on her shoulder. Her dark hair glistened in the moonlight, her arms brown beside her. Her gait was smooth, her bearing nonchalant. He almost collided with her back as she stopped to take off her sandals.

"I've decided it's a sin to walk on the beach with shoes," she explained. Sonny leaned on the wooden railing and stooped to remove his as well. Julia smiled approvingly and waited.

The air was heavy with late summer, the day's receding heat still competing with the ocean breeze. There were clouds, the moon only partially visible, almost full. As they walked down from the dunes and into the surf, light from beach houses faded, peering here and there from behind the sea oats and beach grasses. The moon seemed to sail in and out among the clouds, making light and dark shapes on the gentle surf as it caressed their toes.

Julia broke the silence. "You don't think there's a grain of hope in Miss Rose's plan, do you?"

"I knew you couldn't let it go," he replied, "not even for a few hours. Whatever Rose has up her sleeve, I think it's a hard climb up a long hill, McKenzie. It's what they call in sports terms a 'Hail Mary'," Sonny continued. "You haven't read the finished product, and you don't know exactly what Rose is going to do with it?"

"Like I said, they were still pouring over it when I left. Doss Kincaid appears to be a good enough writer, and it was so good to watch Quinn caught up with him in this fiction they're creating. Rose was providing the bones, the history, the intent, and Doss, Quinn and Celia were adding the meat and the drama. I was just there to verify the legal language and eat cinnamon buns. I did learn a few more things about Charleston."

"Miss Rose knows this town, and I would hate to bet against her instincts." Sonny tried again to read this night. Was it just shop talk after all? "Are you glad for the extra time to prepare, or do you just want, for everyone's sake, to get it over? I know it's taking a toll."

Julia sighed deeply, pausing to consider. "I can always use more time," she acknowledged, "but I could also use several good lawyers from my old firm. I could name them right now."

Sonny glanced sideways at Julia, seeing her in shadow and profile against the moonlight playing on the tide. He was not accustomed to the indecision he was feeling, warding pins and needles from the back of his neck. Julia had invited him to her house. This was hot water, despite the cooling surf on his feet, and he was walking right along, one foot after the other, telling himself he would only wade in a little way.

"I've learned not to underestimate you, McKenzie. Maybe you should do a little of the same."

"Thanks," Julia grinned lamely. "And thanks for coming all the way over here. I know it's been a long day for you too. You don't need to feel obligated to come for another drink if you're tired," she added, giving him an out. "

"No," he spoke deliberately, softly, finding her hand with his, "I want to."

He hadn't changed his pace, hadn't missed a step. Her thoughts raced. She hadn't meant to do this kind of thing again, wasn't going to take this kind of risk. We can't make real people play a part we've written, she reminded herself. They write their own parts. In real life, it's all extemporaneous; you can hold out the script, but you can't make anyone read it.

They walked on quietly, each carrying shoes in one hand while the fingers of the others curled tentatively together. They could be two friends simply walking down the beach in casual conversation except for the current of chemistry now passing palpably between their fingers.

"Here," Julia turned. "This is my house."

"Got your key?" Sonny questioned.

"It's not locked," Julia said.

"Oh, now there's a piece of information. The lady doesn't even lock her doors when she's out," Sonny grimaced. "I'll try not to spread that around down at the station."

Sonny followed her across the sand and up the wide steps to her back deck. She dropped the sandals almost automatically just outside the glass door.

"Is this where we leave the shoes?" Sonny queried.

"I do." Sonny dropped his as well, and entered Julia's kitchen where the soft glow from a night lamp blended with moonlight. He pulled the screen door closed as Julia opened the refrigerator. "What'll it be, Detective?"

"Can I give that some thought?" Sonny spoke softly. Julia turned to look at him, still bent toward the shelf in the refrigerator door. His eyes held hers. Her heart began to pound. She closed the door, her hands empty, turning toward him as she tried to clear her mind.

Sonny had made the decision. Taking the few steps toward her, he put his hands on both of hers, holding them gently at her sides. He gave her a long moment, but there was no question in his eyes. Julia recognized the look, knowing now she had known it all along. Her breath came more rapidly as her chest tightened with excitement. It was both an old and a new feeling.

They were inches apart, and Sonny moved closer, raising her hands, turning her palms to his, backing her against the wall. Julia felt dizzy, sensing everything in slow motion, smelling the closeness of him as he pressed the backs of her hands against the wall, the length of him easily against her now. His intention was evident. His hold was firm; his eyes were gentle, his breath warm on Julia's face. She knew she could not speak. Something in her ached. He watched her eyes, pulled her hands together behind her head, testing for reluctance, feeling none. And then, finally, slowly, his lips were on hers. This was not to be a tentative beginning. Julia felt fire. His body pressed into hers, harder now, excitement building more rapidly than either of them had anticipated. He had not expected her reaction. Neither had she. She tugged her hands, but he did not release them, instinct taking control. Holding her hands, he pulled back, desire his entire expression. He looked down as Julia's chest moved, her breathing fast, her eyes on his. One of his hands held both of hers, the other moving to the buttons on her blouse. He unbuttoned each one slowly, looking as the cloth parted, then pushing it aside to reveal Julia's breasts. He touched them, each one in turn, stroking the nipples with his finger. They were erect even at first, growing firmer with his touch. Julia breathed, moving in no other way, watching Sonny's hands on her. He lowered his head, brushing her with his lips, touching her with his tongue.

His eyes returned to hers. "I can't wait, McKenzie," he said simply.

Julia's knees felt ready to buckle beneath her, but her arms locked hard around his neck. Their bodies came together as magnets, greedily, lips finding lips, Julia's wanting now as apparent as Sonny's. There were tears in her eyes, tears she could not understand. He kissed them, kissed her cheeks, kissed her neck. She could not get close enough. He slipped the blouse from Julia's arms, unzipped the skirt and dropped it to the floor, backing her onto the carpet a few feet away, kneeling with her as he pushed the panties from her waist and lay full length on top of her. He kissed her again as she undid the buttons of his shirt, trembling, trying to hurry. He watched her hands, helping her with his zipper, then standing above her to remove his clothes.

They could go more slowly now, knowing what was to come, feeling its certainty and enjoying the anticipation. Sonny parted Julia's legs and knelt between them, drawing a line with his finger between her breasts and down her stomach. "I want you, McKenzie."

"I'm so glad."

He lowered himself over her, resting on his hands, kissing her cheeks, chin, ears, eyes, letting his mouth find her breasts once again, tracing her nipples with his tongue. The warmth in her grew, multiplied as she felt him hard against her belly. Her hands found the hardness, touched and stroked him between their bodies until he moaned. And then he raised himself, put his hands under her, and she felt him hard against her softest places, looked at his face as he entered her, gently, easily at first, restraining his hunger, testing hers.

Julia pushed herself against him, recalling desire. His movement became quicker, deeper, and he let his body down full length against Julia's, their skins warm and moist together, their lips finding each other. Julia made small sounds, her fingers kneading Sonny's back as she moved with him, drawing lines in the dampness across his shoulders as she tried to pull him closer, closer. His movement was rhythmic, patient, and Julia knew he was aware of her, waiting for her. She pushed toward him, clasping her legs around him. His lips were on her neck, and she felt his breath in her ear.

"Easy, McKenzie," he whispered, and Julia warmed, felt, held her breath.

SATURDAY

139

As August sun streamed through the tall etched glass window of Judge Chastain's office, Rose tugged the shawl closer around her shoulders. The air conditioning was very effective, the courthouse duly quiet as only a few municipal employees were at work on a warm Saturday afternoon. Appropriately, their own lawns were being mowed, weekend chores attended, and many a refreshing drink accompanied avid golfers and sailing enthusiasts in full leisure mode around the Holy City.

Rose sat composed. She had pled the meeting's urgency by telephone the previous evening to each of the four men at the table, giving away nothing. Judge Chastain had offered his office. It was extraordinary to get such a request from Rose Beauregard Pinckney, a woman who had given much to the City. Sitting beside her, looking uncomfortable but resolute, was Willa Fallon.

Steaming cups of coffee sat in front of Judge Stoney and Mendel Comings. Joe Riley, apologizing and last to arrive, had brought an iced concoction from Starbucks. The Honorable Wynfield Chastain sipped something unknown. Marshall Stoney and Mendel Comings were discussing baseball when the Mayor took his seat. Now their attention turned to Rose.

"Thank you for taking this time. I won't need much of it. We've all grown up here. Each of you is familiar with the wretched mess involving Mac Howe and Quinn Ravenel, now both legal matters. I've been praying that this Pandora's box be closed, and I have come from these old knees to the four of you. No court can help any of us. MacArthur Howe cannot bring back his mother; Quinn Ravenel cannot reclaim her virginity; Reg Fallon's career cannot be restored. No legal proceeding, however thorough and fair, can mend what has been damaged or recover what has been lost

"Reg's mother is here with me, as moral support and to give her son's blessing." Rose glanced to her left and laid her hand on Willa's. "We just want precious lives to go on and our beloved Charleston to thrive. The story I'm leaving with you would bankrupt the City and tarnish its reputation. Must we air all this dirty laundry for the world to savor?"

Several printed pages lay face down before each of the men.

"Quinn Ravenel, very dear to me, is Reg Fallon's friend. Unless the legal matters involving Quinn and Mac Howe are dispensed with quietly and quickly, Reg will file a multi-million-dollar lawsuit against this City. The news story I've given you is currently fiction, dated a year from today. Don't allow it to become reality on the front pages of national newspapers and splashed across TV screens."

Heads snapped to attention around the table. Rose motioned to the papers, offering they be read, thinking with gratitude of what a good lawyer and a sports reporter had produced.

"Jury selection begins this morning in the matter of Reginald Fallon against the City of Charleston, South Carolina. A highly-charged crowd had gathered by seven o'clock in the morning, vying for position. Welcomed by a sweltering summer heat, the low overnight was eighty-four degrees. Vendors moved among admitted voyeurs, selling both hot and iced coffee and sweet tea. Streets were barricaded to automobile traffic, blocking off the entire several-square-block area between King and Church Streets and from Tradd to Queen.

"Flights over the weekend were packed with reporters, civil rights activists and the simply curious wanting a look at the young basketball star and his Los Angeles lawyer whose name has become a household word as this trial approached. All efforts to settle have apparently failed.

"Mr. Fallon alleges that a lucrative future was denied him by representatives of the City when he was falsely arrested late last summer. That arrest placed him in a police vehicle which was slammed head-on by a drunk driver. The young man's injuries have been diagnosed as career-ending just as he prepared to launch a signed stint with the Dallas Mavericks.

"The Reverends Al Sharpton and Jesse Jackson have spent considerable time in Charleston during the past month and are expected on the Courthouse steps this morning, accompanied by leaders of the ACLU. Sharpton's opinion editorial in yesterday's New York Times has incensed some and been applauded by others. The NAACP has bussed in activists from around the country, and civil rights advocates have been arriving singly and in groups until there are no hotel rooms to be found in Charleston or the surrounding area.

"The plaintiff's case, already argued eloquently in the media for the past six months by his attorney, accuses this City of his wrongful arrest for an unprovoked attack on a young military officer here at home on leave from Fort Bragg. The confessed attacker, a young Charleston woman, has since admitted the crime.

"Reg Fallon, a promising basketball talent, asserts that he was taken into police custody because he was a young black man sitting on a fateful rainy night near the scene of a violent crime. Fallon has no previous record, not even a parking ticket. After placing him in the police cruiser, any further search for a culprit was discontinued.

"Mr. Fallon is asking the City to replace his likely future earnings to the tune of millions of dollars, claiming he can only be made whole by a prudent estimate of the dollars routinely paid by team franchises and by corporate advertisers who engage prominent athletes to promote their products and services. When asked how much he thinks is reasonable, Cavaliers headliner LeBron James said only 'a lot'.

"Among those expected today on Broad Street, in addition to Jackson and Sharpton, are several mayors from the South, CNN's Anderson Cooper and Wolf Blitzer, NBC's nightly news anchor Lester Holt, veteran columnists Tom Friedman and Peggy Noonan, and Southern author John Grisham.

"Oprah Winfrey will be broadcasting a live daily special on location from here in Charleston beginning on Wednesday, and The Charleston Place Hotel, just blocks from the Courthouse, has confirmed that more than two floors of their posh accommodations were reserved well in advance by the news networks of CNN, NBC and CBS. FOX and ABC have secured similar space at The Mills House. Many of those reporters have gained permission to construct temporary but sturdy elevated structures for their cameramen at vantage points around the Courthouse, and a helicopter passed and hovered above the crowd, sending live feed of the ever-morphing crowd below.

"If the melee that erupted into violent clashes over the past weekend are any indication, the Mayor may have to take further action to control the growing numbers of onlookers, some behaving as congregations singing hymns and some carrying signs with words ranging from philosophy to obscenity. South Carolina's Governor has offered to activate the State's National Guard to assist law enforcement with crowd control.

"Though Charleston has curried the increasing favor of tourists and been named 'most charming' and 'most *hospitable' in recent years, its reputation seems in dire jeopardy as pundits harken back to the dark history of the Stono Rebellion in 1739, Denmark Vessey's slave rebellion in 1822, and the infamous first shot of the Civil War fired right here from Fort Sumter, where monuments still stand testimony to the South's epic battle for the right to keep their slaves."*

Rose unfolded herself from the chair slowly, reaching for her cane and her shawl. "I don't know why you should pay me any mind, but I am profoundly grateful for your time and your friendship. This is not a threat but a 'mayday'." Holding Willa's arm for support, they left the room without looking back, wondering if these influential leaders of prominence and character might use their clout and connections to deliver the leverage for which Rose ached to pry apart the jaws of justice.

None of the four men had spoken a word.

EPILOGUE

October is a splendid time in Charleston. While other parts of the country might be experiencing the first snowfall of the season, the Lowcountry basks in warmth as the sun moves back toward the equator, leaving less swelter and more ease. Marsh grasses begin to take on their winter color. Tidal creeks reflect a sky less brilliantly blue and more restful azure hosting lazy white wisps. Though some southern trees lose their leaves, the many magnolias and breathtaking liveoaks, open arms extended, remain green all year. The scent of someone starting his fireplace on a chilly evening added autumn ambience to the neighborhood.

Celia had just sent Pete to bring in a log, though they were likely to spend a good part of the evening on the back deck where Pete was cooking on the grill, giving his wife a respite from preparing dinner and displaying his own barbeque skills. Julia had arrived earlier, and Sonny was on his way. Quinn would be picking up Rose after changing out of the clothes a kindergarten teacher wore in the classroom.

Tonight was a celebration of sorts. Summer's end had brought such unexpected havoc for this small flock of friends and family, such a snarl of woe and suffering. Rose had not shared with anyone the source of the call bringing relief on that mid-week August afternoon. She had been home alone so that no one saw her tears shed in pure gratitude. She had been holding her breath for days on end. She had prayed. Finally, people she loved were granted absolution. People she had known for years had moved mountains. She would express her thanks one day at the gates of heaven for this one more blessing. It was remarkable, a gift of grace without parallel.

"Are you telling me that you think this whole story could really never come to light?" Julia asked again, sipping from her red wine.

"I think that's entirely possible," Celia replied.

"And you promise you don't know what Rose did with that story we just made up sitting there in her kitchen?"

"I promise."

"But people must know. Here and there, friends of friends of nurses and cops and even people close to those involved must have discussed what they know."

"Charleston is woven from a skein of sins, secrets and skeletons, Jules. Some say it's why the air is heavy, although that's commonly attributed to honeysuckle and crepe myrtle."

Julia continued to shake her head. "In D.C.--in fact in most places I can think of--this story would have been front page. There would be reporters on the lawns of everyone involved."

"Have you forgotten that this is the place where we refer to the Civil War as 'unpleasantness'?" Celia had to smile. "If you're one of us, it's not likely you'll be paraded before the world for your membership in the flawed human race. We keep our secrets to ourselves and our sins among friends. Judgments are made, of course, but quietly and unspoken. If you blow it irredeemably, it's like excommunication."

"Isn't that a religious term?"

"Well, Jules, would you rather be banned from Heaven or Charleston? Think about it."

"You have a point."

"You think it will never, ever come out?"

"Not aloud. Not in public. Not ever."

"That's astonishing.

"Don't you find an odd comfort in it?"

"If I could believe it, maybe. But it's still part of the real world, Cele, and the world isn't like that. In many ways, it's often a cold, cruel place. I can't help but wonder."

"I think if you still wonder, Jules, you're missing the whole point I've been trying to make."

"Which is?"

"It's Charleston."

Made in the USA
Columbia, SC
20 June 2017